THE YOUNGER WOMAN

MANDY BYATT

Published by AVON
A division of HarperCollins*Publishers* Ltd
1 London Bridge Street
London SE1 9GF

www.harpercollins.co.uk

HarperCollins*Publishers*
Macken House
39/40 Mayor Street Upper
Dublin 1
D01 C9W8
Ireland

A Paperback Original 2023
1
First published in Great Britain by HarperCollins*Publishers* 2023

A catalogue copy of this book is available from the British Library.

ISBN: 978-0-00-845994-9

Typeset in Sabon LT Std by Palimpsest Book Production Limited,
Falkirk, Stirlingshire

Printed and Bound in the UK using 100% Renewable Electricity
at CPI Group (UK) Ltd

For Rich – with love

CHAPTER 1

She'll tell him tonight.

Even though he isn't in the best of moods, a common occurrence lately, she'll tell him tonight.

Lottie stares through the rain-spattered windscreen into the greyness of the late afternoon. There's a storm approaching, pewter anvil clouds shrouding the hills on the horizon. Not that the weather will matter to them. They'll be snug and cosy in the cottage, just the two of them. She can't wait to see his face when she speaks those words that he probably thought would never come from her mouth. Over a plate of spaghetti bolognaise and a glass of white to celebrate their wedding anniversary, she'll tell him.

The car swings right and accelerates up the single-track lane, away from the main road, away from the storm ahead. Like the weather, the traffic all the way has been terrible, a stream of cars nose to tail along the M6, heading for the big lights switch-on at Blackpool. It's always the same, year after year, no matter what time they set off.

1

She's tried to distract Nick, telling him what went on at her theatre school's play last week, how the kids had been so excited, even the teenagers who pretended they weren't, but Nick – as usual lately – hasn't paid much attention. Instead, he's huffed and puffed all the way through the jam, ignoring her attempts to engage him in a game of eye-spy, blasting his horn when someone cut in front of him. He hadn't wanted to go to Fairview this year, had said he was too busy at work, but Lottie had insisted. After the past few months, heaven knows they both need it. A break away from the norm. And the not-so-norm.

She's flicked stations all the way there, trying to find a song he likes, finally settling on a local channel that plays Eighties music. But now, ten miles away from the motorway, the dual carriageway that hugs the peninsula behind them, the radio signal is lost as the car climbs higher and higher.

And then they're there, Nick indicating left – although they haven't seen a car for twenty minutes – heading along the lane, the grazing sheep on either side jerking up their heads at the intruders.

Lottie blinks. Blinks again. 'There's a light on. In our bedroom.' They call it their bedroom, even though it doesn't belong to them – it's just the room they always stay in when they visit Nick's parents' holiday cottage in the Lakes.

Nick sighs. 'Thought you'd checked they wouldn't be here? Told you we should have stayed at home.'

Lottie feels her shoulders ride up. Nick's parents are supposed to be arriving tomorrow, along with the rest of their friends, a surprise for Nick's birthday. She'll kill

2

his mother if she's come up a day early – it would be just like Gwen to want to spoil Lottie's carefully laid plans. 'Shall we just go back?' she says.

Nick reaches for her hand, gives it a squeeze. 'Sorry, I know I've been a grumpy old sod lately. Work, you know? It's hard to shake it off.'

'I'll shake it off you.' She gives him a wink, licks her lips in the silly way that always makes him laugh.

'Let's hope no one's decided to come here this weekend, then.'

She feels a drop in her stomach. He's saying the right words but does he mean them? Nothing in his face or his voice is telling her he wants to whisk her up the stairs and straight onto the bed. Her fingers find her wedding ring, twisting the platinum band round and round.

Fairview comes back into view. There isn't a light on in their bedroom. There isn't a light on anywhere. Lottie rubs at her eyes. She must have imagined it. Is this yet another example of her fertile imagination making something up? An image of Tasha, Nick's former PA, floats into her mind before she shakes it away. She won't let anything spoil tonight.

Pulling the car to a stop, Nick stares up at the bedroom window, where the thick brocade bedroom curtains are open, before casting a quick glance at the garage. 'Doesn't look like anyone's here.'

He gets out of the car and sprints through the driving rain to the front door. Lottie follows him, grappling with the hood of her jacket, fighting to get it over her head, but the wind whips it away.

The door is locked. Nick fiddles with his keys, finally finding the one he wants. 'Hello,' he calls as he steps into the large, open-plan room that covers most of the downstairs. 'Anyone home?'

Flicking on the light with one hand, Lottie unzips her coat with the other. While it's not warm in the cottage, it's definitely aired. Usually, when they first get there, it's warmer out than it is in, no matter what month it is. There's silence, apart from the loud tick of the grandfather clock in the corner of the room. 'Just us, then,' Nick says, before turning towards the open front door.

'Aren't you going to check upstairs?'

'Don't be daft, Lots. There's no one here. Just us.'

'Nick.'

He shakes his head and then bounds up the stairs before Lottie can remind him to take off his shoes. Gwen won't be impressed at the dirty marks on the carpet. Nick's footsteps thump on the narrow floorboards overhead. Fairview is three hundred years old, has been in Nick's family for ages, a former tithed cottage once bequeathed to a long-dead ancestor, a groundsman for the huge stately home a couple of miles away that is now a chichi hotel.

'All clear,' he says, bending down so as not to hit his head on the low doorframe as he comes back into the room. It's a big space width wise, Nick's grandfather having bought up the cottages either side and knocked them through, sometime in the 1950s, but the ceilings are low and the walls are crisscrossed by timber beams.

'Has someone been sleeping in our room?' Lottie says as they head out back into the dusk to fetch their bags.

The rain has eased slightly but there's a shroud of mist hanging over the hills in the distance. Hopefully it'll clear by tomorrow. The view, down over the valley, is stunning, something she'll never get tired of seeing. Rolling hills, deep forest framing them, a glimpse of the edge of Coniston Water far in the distance.

'So what if they have? It's not *our* room, is it?'

Lottie ignores him, pulls her jacket around her and picks up a couple of the carrier bags, leaving the heavy stuff for Nick. She hopes he's going to lighten up a bit. His mood has gone downhill over the past couple of months, hardly talking to her and then snapping when he does open his mouth. He's having problems at work but it's not her fault, is it? And she thought with *that woman* out of the way everything would be better between them. As he carries their bags upstairs, she sneaks a quick look at his phone that's lying on the kitchen island. It's got face recognition on it, but she knows his password, of course. There's no signal – not surprising as the mobile reception in the cottage is never great. But there are no new messages either. She lets out a long breath. Of course there won't be.

After checking his work emails for the tenth time, all the while grumbling about the Wi-Fi signal as it dips in and out, Nick gets a fire going, so that the open-plan room is cosy by the time she's finished knocking together the spag bol.

They sit at the large wooden kitchen table, Nick shovelling the spaghetti into his mouth while she picks at hers. He's telling her about the latest round of problems with the derelict hotel that four months ago his firm won the contract to redesign. He's worried the contractor is screwing him over. He's worried that everything that could go wrong with the build is going wrong.

'What does Kas think about it all?' she asks.

'Kas has his own projects.'

'Can't you put your heads together about it?' Lottie says, even though she already knows the answer. Nick isn't a collaborator – he likes to work on his own, always has done, not trusting other people to do things the way he likes them done. Whereas Kas is very much a people person – just like her, although in his case too much sometimes with the ladies. She loves working with other people, although she's loath to admit she's found her calling in running the theatre group. Just as well she has found her calling though, seeing as she's going to turn down the role that could have made her.

She checks her phone while Nick rambles on. There's one bar of signal. Ginger still hasn't come back to her. She wonders if the casting director has gone back to Los Angeles. But she would have still returned her call, wouldn't she? Maybe she knows what Lottie is going to say – that she can't take the job. Nick comes first. Family comes first.

Lottie takes the plates, scrapes the remains of her spag bol into the pedal bin, squirts washing-up liquid into the sink.

'Leave that,' Nick says, filling his glass and topping up hers. He hasn't noticed she hasn't touched it, that she's just lifted it to her lips and let the wine stain them.

'It won't take a minute.'

'Lots, come on. Leave it.' His hands are around her waist, guiding her back to the table where a small box sits on her placemat. It's wrapped in shiny paper, the corners folded neatly, ribbon and a bow on top.

'Happy anniversary,' he says.

Her hand flies to her mouth. She hasn't been expecting anything. They don't do presents for anniversaries – coming to Fairview, just the two of them, finding time for each other, is enough. Especially after the last few months. So why this year? She wonders if it's a gift given out of guilt, before telling herself to stop it, telling the voice inside her head to shut up.

'Aren't you going to open it?'

Tears prick at the corners of her eyes. 'We don't do gifts.'

'Well, it's a special one, isn't it? Ten years? I know it should be tin or aluminium but, well, even I know that's not very romantic.'

'We don't do gifts,' she says again.

Nick looks down at his hands and then back up at her. 'I haven't been very easy to live with these past few months, work and . . .' His Adam's apple bobs up and down as he swallows. 'And, well, I just wanted you to know I love you, Lots—'

She smiles at their joke. 'I love you more, Mr Moore.' And she does. She loves Nick more than anything, has loved him since the day she first clapped eyes on him.

'Who's that?' Lottie had whispered to Ruth as a tall guy with a floppy fringe waved at Ruth as he'd made his way to the changing rooms.

7

Ruth had stopped pedalling. 'Nick? I work with him.'

'Oh my God, he's gorgeous.'

'Cool it, sister, you're red enough as it is,' Ruth had said.

Lottie had wiped at her face with her gym towel. 'You didn't tell me you worked with such a hottie.'

Ruth had rolled her eyes. 'Doesn't float my boat.'

Nick pushes the box towards her now. 'Go on, then, open it.'

'We don't do gifts,' she says for the third time, even though she has got him something. It's tucked away in her bag, the best present she could ever give him.

'I'm not expecting a present,' he says, 'if that's what you're worrying about.' He reaches for her hand, draws it up to his lips. 'I just want you, Lots. Nothing more.'

She swallows, stares at his blue eyes, so blue that on their first date she had asked him – as people always do – if he was wearing coloured contact lenses. 'Nothing fake about me,' he'd said then, words that at times over the past few months she's clung on to.

'Just you,' he says again.

Lottie sniffs, trying to hold back the tears. These are the words she's wanted to hear, the words that would have pushed away that horrible, crawling suspicion of what her husband was up to, why he was working later and later, coming home stinking of whiskey.

Her nails slide under the Sellotape, discarding the wrapping paper to reveal a blue box with the words Tiffany & Co embossed on the top.

She opens the box and gasps. An eternity ring, diamonds circling a platinum band, lies on a bed of crushed satin. 'Oh, it's beautiful. Gorgeous.' With her hands on his face, she kisses his lips, breathing him in, her Nick, still her Nick.

'Put it on then. Here.'

He takes the ring, slides it onto her finger, just as he did with her engagement ring eleven years ago and her wedding ring a year after that. It's a perfect fit. Just like they are. How could she have ever doubted him? How could she have ever doubted her marriage? Nick wouldn't let anything come between them – deep down she knows that – wouldn't let anything or anyone come between them. And nor would Lottie.

He pulls her down to sit on his lap, his hands on her stomach.

'I did get you something,' she says. She can't keep it in any longer. She doesn't want to keep it in any longer.

'I told you, I don't want—'

She gets off his lap and reaches for her bag, takes out a long thin box.

'A pen,' he says, ripping at the paper, spotting the Montblanc name. 'Always wanted one of these. Very fancy.'

He opens the box, his fingers reaching inside and then stops. 'What? What?' he says again, before he takes out the pregnancy test stick and peers at it. 'I don't understand.' He turns it over, waves it at her. A pink cross stares back at them. 'Whose is it?'

'It's mine, you idiot. I'm pregnant.'

He shakes his head. Opens his mouth and then closes it again. She's said some mad things to him these past few months, she knows that now, and he's looking at her at this very moment as if this is just another of her inane utterings.

'I'm pregnant,' she says again.

'But how? You can't be.'

'I can be. I am. Emma said it might happen, didn't she? And that other consultant we saw before her. They both said sometimes it just does.'

He pulls her back towards him, resting his cheek on her stomach. 'I promise I'll look after you, both of you. I'll never let anyone or anything hurt you,' he says, softly, as if he's speaking to the cluster of cells inside her. 'It's a miracle.'

It is a miracle, a miracle they've finally done it, finally made a part of them. And it's a miracle they've done it in the worst few months of their marriage. They've hardly touched each other, only making love a handful of times.

And then he cries, and they're both crying, and he's ushering her to the sofa and putting a cushion behind her, and shaking his head, tears rolling down his face.

'We need champagne. We need to celebrate.'

'We'll get some tomorrow.' She'd been meaning to bring a bottle but had forgotten, left it in the fridge.

Nick goes over to the wine rack in the kitchen. 'There's bound to be one here.' He pulls out a silver-foil-capped bottle before shoving it back in the rack. 'Prosecco? No, got to be champagne.'

'Prosecco will do, darling.'

'We are toasting our baby's head with champagne. I bet there's some in the cellar,' he says, moving over to the white-painted door at the far end of the kitchen. 'It's locked. Where's the key? It's always in the lock.' He darts to the front door, picking up the two keys from the keyholder, trying them in the lock of the cellar door, but with no luck.

'Never mind, I'll go down to the village.' He tugs on his boots.

'You've been drinking.'

'I'll walk across the fields. It'll take me half an hour, there and back.'

'Nick, it's throwing it down.' Just as she says the words there's the boom of thunder in the distance. 'Honestly, darling, stay here. They'll charge you a fortune for champagne in the village shop.' She knows that won't stop him. Nick's business is doing well, more than well. They have one of the biggest practices in the area and employ over seventy people.

'You, my darling, are worth it,' he says, coming over to her and kissing the tip of her nose.

'I bet the shop's closed now.' She grabs hold of his hand, tries to pull him down onto the sofa with her. 'And I'm not drinking anyway.'

'But I am! Me, a daddy, at long last.' He shakes his head as a grin spreads across his face. 'I can't believe it.'

Smiling, she squeezes his hand. She wants to tell him to go easy, there are still many months ahead of them, that everything isn't cut and dried yet, but she doesn't want to dampen his spirits, wants them to enjoy this night, to let it fill them with hope and love, so they'll always have it, even if something does go wrong. And

11

it won't, anyway. Nothing's going to go wrong from now on.

'Don't be long, then.' Lottie doesn't want to be here on her own. It's so remote and the woods surrounding it are dense and dark. Anyone could be out there. Anyone could be in the cottage. She thinks of the light she thought she saw upstairs. And the heating had definitely been on recently – the house had felt warm and it never did, not even in the height of summer. Maybe Nick's folks had been up in the week – perhaps his stepfather, Felix, wanted to get to the bottom of the rat problem in the cellar before the big party this weekend.

'Take the torch and be careful,' she says as Nick shrugs on his coat and grabs his phone.

'I'm always careful.'

'I mean it, Nick. It's pitch-black out there.' There's the flash of lightning in the distance and then another clap of thunder. Lottie gets the torch out of the cupboard and hands it to him before he heads through the door. 'For God's sake, don't get struck by lightning.'

'You worry too much.' He kisses her on the cheek and disappears into the howling night.

'Be careful!' she shouts, but he's already gone, the torch lighting both his way and the rain as it splinters through the filthy night.

Lottie switches on some lamps, casting a glance up the dark stairwell before shutting the door to the first floor with a firm push so it catches on the latch. And then she washes the dishes, switching on the radio to fill the silence in the cottage. Some teenage pop star she's never heard of is performing a concert with the London Philharmonic. At least she knows some of the songs. She hums along and, with the washing up done, makes a start on dusting the living room, smiling at the photos dotted around the place: Nick when he was younger, his mother's arm around his shoulders, a photo of Gwen and Felix in a frame on their wedding day, Nick shirking at the side, a sullen thirteen-year-old.

She makes herself a weak tea and sits down, switching on the TV, flicking through the channels to see if there's anything that might catch her attention. The grandfather clock booms nine. What time did Nick leave? It must be at least forty minutes ago. She gets up and goes to the window, peering through the curtains. It's inky out there. The rain is still hammering down, the wind howling like an injured animal. Hopefully it's blown the storm away. There's no moon and no light from Nick's torch. She'll ring him – if she can get a signal. She roots in her handbag, pulling out her phone. There's one bar. Before it disappears she calls him, frowning when his answer-phone kicks in.

The phone connected to the landline is sitting on a small table next to the grandfather clock. When she puts the receiver to her ear, there's nothing. The storm must have brought down the telephone line.

Settling back onto the sofa, she stretches out, laying her head on a cushion. There's a drama on the TV, the usual stuff about a married couple and a bunny boiler. She yawns and puts another cushion under her head.

Bone-tired – that's the only way she can describe how she feels. Her eyelids grow heavy as she tries to concentrate on the programme.

A bang and a small yelp – just like the one Gwen's miniature poodle, Scampi, used to make – fill the silence. She opens her eyes as she realises the yelp has come out of her own mouth. All the lights are off, the TV too, and she's there alone in the silence, alone in the dark, the only light coming from the open fire. 'It's just the electricity,' she says out loud, to make some noise, to convince herself she's not scared. The electricity is forever going off in the cottage. You can't have the washing machine on at the same time as the kettle or else everything trips. Felix keeps promising to get it sorted but his head is in the clouds, practical things not his bent. Or maybe everyone's electricity is out? Maybe the storm has damaged a pylon. Only one way to find out.

She levers herself up, feeling for her phone on the coffee table. It's half past nine. Nick left an hour ago. What's taking him so long? She'd try him again but there's no signal at all now on her mobile. She presses the screen to switch on the torch. She hasn't much battery left and her charger is in her overnight bag upstairs. Still, there's enough time to go down into the cellar and trip the switch back on. She knows where the fuse box is – it's to the right on the wall, not far from the bottom of the stairs.

She glances at the door. She doesn't want to go down into the cellar. Has Felix got rid of the rats? Vermin

14

definitely aren't her thing, especially rats with their knowing eyes and thin tails. She'll wait for Nick to come back. He won't be long.

She turns off the torch on her phone. Five slow minutes pass. She imagines her eyes might become accustomed to the dark but, after another five minutes, everything in front of and around her is still pitch-black.

She's being silly. There's nothing in the cellar that can harm her. The rats will probably be more scared of her than she is of them.

She switches the torch back on, is halfway to the door when she remembers it's locked. That's that, then. Nothing she can do. And, anyway, Nick's sure to be back soon.

Five more minutes pass. Ten.

In the kitchen, her hands search the shelves, the mugs where Felix keeps old screws and the like. The key must be somewhere. And then the torch picks out Nick's keyring. He always used to have a key to the cellar on there. But he hadn't mentioned it earlier. Maybe he'd forgotten?

The fifth key on the ring fits the lock perfectly.

The doorknob is stiff, always has been. She gives the door a shove and it flies open. An icy blast makes her shiver. It's always cold in the cellar, even when it's thirty degrees outside. She peers down into the darkness. She should just wait for Nick to come back. He'll surely be here any minute. He wouldn't want her going down the cellar steps. They're stone, cold, uneven. Gwen slipped on them only last year and broke her ankle.

She puts her hand on the wooden banister. She's being ridiculous. She's just over one month pregnant, and she's forty-five, not seventy-five. And she's not scared of the dark. Peering into the gloom, she angles her phone so the light from its torch shines on the steps. Twelve down to the bottom. With a last glimpse at the front door to check Nick isn't about to come barrelling through it, she pulls the cord for the strip light so that it will come on as soon as she flicks the trip switch.

God, it's cold. She wishes she'd put on her jacket. And there's an unpleasant smell, damp mixed with something fetid, something off. Are the rats still here? When she reaches the bottom step, faced with a blank stone wall in front of her, she turns to her right and points the torch at the cellar floor. She hates rats. Slimy creatures, wet fur, those whip-sharp tails and pinprick eyes. Can they jump? Might they be attracted to the light from her phone and lunge at her? Taking a deep breath and telling herself to get a grip, she shines the phone torch at the fuse box. Just as she thought, one of the switches has tripped. She flips up the plastic casing and pushes up the switch. The strip light springs into life, garish, blinding her. She blinks. And then laughs when she spots a bottle of champagne standing proud on a shelf on the opposite side of the room. Of course Gwen would have a bottle of champagne down here. Gwen only drinks champagne. Nick will kick himself when he realises there was a bottle in the house, and that the key to the cellar was on his keyring all along.

Moving towards the shelf where the champagne is, Lottie watches where she's putting her feet, on the lookout

16

for anything scurrying across the floor. But there's nothing. Just a silence. And that awful smell. Rats. Felix needs to get a man in – it's obvious his trips over the summer up to Fairview have been in vain.

Lottie stretches for the champagne bottle but the shelf it's sitting on is too high for her to reach. There must be something she can stand on. A large cardboard box filled with old paperback books is stacked against one wall. It should carry her weight but the books might shift inside the box when she stands on it. She definitely doesn't want to fall. And then, stuffed into the corner of the room, behind some piled-up paint pots, she spies the gleam of a metal stepladder. That will do.

She can reach the stepladder but hasn't got the strength to lift it from behind the cans of paint. With a grumble, she starts to unstack the pots, looking around for an empty shelf to put them on. There's one on the other side of the room. She lifts two pots and carries them over, sighing when she finds she can't reach the shelf because there's something on the floor in front of it, a mound with a green tarpaulin covering it.

She swears under her breath. What is she doing? Nick will be back soon. He'll have champagne with him.

Her mind made up, she turns quickly, her fingers losing their grip on one of the tins of paint. It crashes to the floor, its lid flying off. She jumps back as red paint splashes onto the tarpaulin. 'Shit!'

She picks up the paint pot, ramming the lid back onto it. The tarpaulin looks new. Damn. She'll have to buy Felix a replacement. Perhaps she can wash it though? Or

17

at least scrub at the paint before it dries? There aren't too many splashes on it. A bit of Vanish might do the trick.

Lifting the corner of the tarpaulin, she pulls at it. It won't shift. It's caught on something at the other end.

With a sigh, she lifts up the tarpaulin to investigate what's trapping it.

And then she stops.

She closes her eyes and then opens them again.

She takes a deep breath in, holds it for a count of four, and then breathes slowly out.

She blinks again.

There's a foot, at a strange angle. A woman's foot, clad in a high heel, the stiletto broken.

Lottie's breath catches in her lungs, wanting to escape in a scream. With shaking hands she shoves the tarpaulin to the side. And yet she has no need to uncover what's there, not really, for she suddenly knows what she'll find, what's lying in the dark corner of the cellar.

There's a woman on her side, naked except for the high heels, green-tinged skin, long, red hair spilling down her back, her face shoved up against the wall.

A face Lottie doesn't have to see, for she knows, without a doubt, that it belongs to *that woman*, Tasha, Nick's former PA.

THEN

CHAPTER 2

Lottie picked up her phone and unlocked it. Just to check. Just to check the mobile signal hadn't disappeared, as it did every now and again. Just to check the clinic hadn't rung and she'd somehow missed the call.

She clicked onto her recent calls list. Hannah had phoned this morning, wishing her luck and telling Lottie she'd read her tarot cards for her and all would be well. Jasper, her agent, was next on the call list, a brief conversation, four minutes and thirty-six seconds, one in which he'd sighed and told her things were still quiet and he would certainly call her as soon as he heard of any, as he put it, *interesting possibilities*. But there was nothing from the clinic.

What was taking them so long? Her consultant, Emma, had promised she'd be in touch this afternoon as soon as the lab had confirmed how many eggs had been fertilised. It was now ten past five. Did Emma work normal office hours? Would she be clocking off at half past, picking up her bag and rushing home to her family, or

21

was she there late into the night, her loved ones abandoned as she helped desperate couples to become families? She had a daughter – Lottie had noticed the photo of a chubby-faced girl dressed in pink in a silver frame on her desk. Emma might have already left, picking her up from school, cooking her fish fingers or chicken goujons or whatever it was primary school children ate.

But Emma worked for a private clinic, not the NHS. A clinic that, according to its website, 'put families first'. So maybe she would work as long as she needed to in order to ensure the clinic kept its promise. Lottie and Nick had chosen it because it had a high success rate. Why not throw everything at it, they'd agreed, knowing that it was probably the last throw of the dice for them.

Lottie scrolled through her contacts until she found the number for the clinic. She should call Emma. Put herself out of her misery. She put her hand to her stomach. She'd felt a little tender there for the past four days but then she always did after the operation to retrieve her eggs. Her finger hovered over the green call button. It was nearly quarter past. She would ring them.

'Hey,' Nick said as he came through the door, making her jump.

He threw down his laptop bag and planted a kiss on her cheek. She wanted to grab him, snuggle into his embrace, have him hold her and tell her everything was going to be okay. But he strode to the fridge, grabbing a bottle of Peroni off the top shelf. 'What's new?' he said as he rummaged through the cutlery drawer, searching for the bottle opener. Poor Nick. Lottie knew what he wanted to ask, could tell by the way his eyes flitted to everything in the room, everything except her. But saying the actual words, asking if the clinic had called, was too much for him. Nick was the sort of person who preferred not to hear bad news, would rather have another week of waiting – no news is good news and all that – whereas Lottie was itching to know how many eggs had taken.

'Not much.'

He squeezed her shoulder and then hopped onto a stool next to her, helping himself to a handful of peanuts from a bowl. 'Uh-oh.' He nodded at the notepad Lottie had open in front of her. 'The list lunatic strikes again.'

'If I don't write it down, it'll never get done. Curtain's up in seven weeks and now it seems I might not have a leading man. Connor's mum called earlier,' she said, in answer to Nick's raised eyebrow. 'A football tackle. Nasty. Apparently he's at the hospital, getting it X-rayed. And all the costumes still need to be sorted and—' She ran her finger down the list she'd started two hours ago. Under the title of the play, *Time-Slip*, she'd written ten items. Ten items and a lot of doodles. Of flowers, love hearts. Of baby names. She quickly turned over the page and then realising what was on the page facing her, turned that page over too, in case Nick clocked what she'd written there.

'I thought Hannah was going to give you a hand?' Nick threw a nut into the air and caught it in his mouth.

'She has. Been a great help. But she's got her own work.'

'Work? In my book, work is when you have to get your backside out of bed before midday, pay tax and—'

Lottie slapped his hand away from the nuts. 'It's not easy being freelance, you know. She does work hard.'

'Yeah, right. Sitting around meditating, or doing that Recky stuff—'

'Reiki.'

'Whatever. Call that hard work? I could massage people's feet all day. Now that would be the life.' He leant to the side and made a grab for her foot.

'That's reflexology,' Lottie laughed as she kicked his hand away.

'On second thoughts. Not everyone's got your gorgeous feet. Urgh. Think of all that hard skin, yellow toenails and—'

'Okay, I get the picture,' Lottie said, putting her hand over his mouth and giggling when he licked her palm. 'What time is the restaurant booked for?' She glanced at the oversized clock on the kitchen wall. 'I could have met you there.' She was touched he'd come home to see if the clinic had made contact, had probably been sitting at his desk all afternoon, waiting for her to call, worrying that she was lying in a heap on the floor, all cried out because it was bad news. Grasping his hand, she lifted it to her lips and kissed his fingers. This was just as hard for him as it was for her, perhaps even harder. She wanted a baby, of course she did, but mainly because she knew he wanted to be a father.

'Seven for drinks. Pascale's is booked for eight. We're meeting in The Tavern first.' The evening had been arranged for a while, a meal to celebrate Nick's company winning a six-figure contract to design a new hotel

24

complex. The timing was unfortunate. Tomorrow or the day after, God willing, they'd be dashing down to the clinic in London for the embryo transfer. He'd offered to change the date of the company do but Lottie had reassured him it would be fine, had said a night out – as long as it wasn't too late a night – would do them good. 'We don't have to go,' Nick said, 'if—'

Lottie put her hands over her ears before Nick moved them gently away. 'Sorry.'

'We said we'd be positive. You know how important Hannah says our mind-set is.' Tears clogged Lottie's throat. It would be fine. It had to be. During their last attempt three eggs had been fertilised although only one embryo had been viable. Panic formed a tight knot in her stomach. The numbers were decreasing each time. She tried to put the thought out of her mind. The IVF would work. It had to. Seven failed rounds were enough for anyone. Especially someone who was fast approaching forty-six.

Nick picked up his phone. 'I'll book an Uber.'

'I'll drive.'

'I'll book an Uber.'

She swallowed. So, Nick presumed it would be bad news, thought she would definitely be needing a drink.

'Done,' he said, slipping his phone into his trouser pocket.

'I'll just finish this list and—'

Nick grabbed at her pad, holding it aloft with one hand, flicking through it with the other, while she stretched to reach it.

'Nick! Give it back.'

'Hang on. I thought this was a list about the play. What's this? Mrs Moore, I hope you aren't . . . You *are*, aren't you? Balloons? Food? Lots, you promised. It's not a big birthday, after all.'

'You're only forty-three once.' She grabbed the notepad off him, hugging it to her.

'Seriously, darling. Let's just celebrate on our own, just me and you. That's what we always do.' He put his arms around her and started to nuzzle at her neck. 'What do you say? I'm going to be busy with the new hotel complex these next few months. It'll be nice to have something to look forward to. Eh, Lots? What do you say?'

'All right,' she said, the lie easily falling from her mouth, as she pulled away from him. 'Just me and you at the cottage. Same as always.'

'Deal?' He held out his hand.

'Deal,' she said, shaking it, crossing the fingers of her other hand behind her back. 'Now let me just finish my list and then I'll go and get changed. Mustn't forget to book the cattery,' she said as Belle, their Russian Blue, jumped off his seat on the sofa and came towards them.

'You're a freak, you know that, right? A listical luna-ticical freak.' He kissed the tip of her nose before picking up Belle and whispering to him, 'But I do love you.'

'Are you talking to me or the cat?' Lottie threw a nut at him. 'It's all right for you, Mr Boss Man, you don't have to do your own organising. You're lucky, you have me to do that for you here and good old Pauline at work.'

Nick put Belle down and filled his dish with biscuits. 'Pauline's divorcing me.'

'What?'

'She's handed in her notice. She leaves at the end of August.'

'No! Has she finally done it? Is she going to Scotland? She's always said she'd move nearer to her daughter when she retired.' She didn't wait for Nick to reply. 'Good for her. You'll miss her though.'

'Couldn't have happened at a worse time. But what can I do?' Nick shrugged, snatching up another handful of nuts. 'And, anyway, Ruth has found me the perfect replacement.'

'Oh?'

He chewed and then took a swig of his lager. 'Someone who's been working as a temp for us. She's very good. Ruth rates her. I haven't spoken to her much.'

'The big boss can't be wasting his time with the underlings, eh?'

'Precisely. And, anyway, that's what I pay Ruth for. Hiring and firing.'

'Well, if she's half as good as Pauline, you'll be okay. What's her name?'

Nick threw his empty bottle in the recycling bin and helped himself to another from the fridge, opening it and taking a swig before he answered. 'Natasha, I think.'

'You think? Nick, she's going to be your right arm. It would help to know her name.'

'Natasha, yes. It's Natasha. Everyone calls her Tasha though, but it would be Natasha, right? I'll call her Natasha. Tasha seems a bit too familiar.' He cracked his knuckles. 'I am the boss, after all.'

'Where's she come from again?' Lottie asked, checking her phone to see if she still had a signal. Three bars.

'Oh, it's an internal promotion. She was doing some temping in the accounts department and was keen to get something permanent. Ruth says she's great. Enthusiastic and young and—'

'How young are we talking?' Lottie put down her phone. 'Does she have enough experience? Pauline's been your PA forever. There's nothing she doesn't know about what goes on in your office. And that can only come with years of learning on the job.'

'I don't know – early twenties, maybe? I didn't ask. You can't ask anything in the interviews these days, can you?' Nick wiped his mouth with the back of his hand. 'Or else you'll have the heavy brigade down on you.'

'And rightly so.' Lottie picked up her pad and studied the list she'd made. There was so much to do before opening night. This year's play had to be a success. Another theatre school had opened in the centre of Manchester, owned by some up-and-coming actor who'd had a small role in a James Bond film. Some of the pushier mums had already moved their kids there. 'Do you think you'll get on? Does Pauline like her? Is she nice?'

'Pauline's very nice, you know that. Nicer than my own mother.'

'I can't argue with you there.' She pointed her pen at him. 'Anyway, are you avoiding the question? Is she some supermodel type with the brains of Stephen Hawking?'

'Pauline?'

'Very funny. This Natasha or Tasha, or whatever her name is.'

Nick started to pinch at her waist, trying to tickle her. 'Is wifey jealous?'

Giggling, she slapped his hands away. 'I'm not sure a twenty-something would be interested in an old crock like you, darling.'

'Hey, I'm not forty-three yet.' He laughed. 'You're probably right though. She's just a kid. Talking of which . . . has the clinic called?' And there it was, out there, what Lottie had been waiting to hear as soon as Nick arrived home: the question stuck in his throat, the question he'd been dancing around.

'No.' As soon as the word left her mouth, her mobile started to buzz. They both peered at the screen, knew it was the clinic, knew the number off by heart.

She pressed the answer key, put the phone on loudspeaker. Nick clutched her hand, his thumb rubbing hers.

'Mrs Moore?'

'Hi, Emma.'

'Hi, Lottie. How are you doing?'

I'm annoyed you're exchanging pleasantries with me when all I want you to do is to tell me if any of the eggs have fertilised, she wanted to say, but didn't. 'Fine, thanks,' she said instead. 'You?'

'Yes, well, thanks.' Emma paused. Just a brief pause, a millisecond probably, but it was enough to tell Lottie that it wasn't good news. 'Is Nick there with you?'

'I'm here.' Nick put his arm around Lottie, drawing her in so tightly she felt as if he might break her shoulder bones. And yet, it felt comforting, the citrusy, fresh scent of his aftershave, the smell of him, and the weight of his chest, his arm around her, something solid to hold on to when everything else was slipping away.

A tear made its way from Lottie's eye all the way down her cheek, dropping from her chin, landing onto her notepad. She wanted to end the call, turn the phone off, throw the bloody thing at the wall so it would smash into pieces, anything to stop the words she knew Emma was going to say.

Lottie lay in the bath, a glass of wine at her side, nearly empty. Belle sat on the closed toilet seat lid, as he always did when Lottie was in the bath.

Nick wiped his face with a towel. 'Are you sure you don't mind? I can stay here. It's no problem; people will understand.'

'You haven't told anyone? Nick?' She'd kill him. They'd said they'd keep this attempt to themselves, were tired of people constantly asking them how 'the baby thing' was going, were tired of their commiserations when they said *badly*. She hadn't even told Ruth. Hannah knew, of course she did – there wasn't much that got past her best friend.

'No one knows.' Nick bent down, pecking her on the lips. 'It will happen, Lots. We will have a child of our own one day. We should try again.'

'I can't think about that now.'

'I know, darling.' He patted some aftershave onto his neck. 'You'll be okay?'

'I'll be fine. Top my glass up before you go, will you?'

'Drinking's not going to help, Lots.'

She pursed her lips, trying to hold in the words she wanted to scream: that right at that moment drinking was the only thing that would help.

A minute later and he was back, putting the glass on the side of the bath. 'You will be careful, won't you, darling?'

'Don't worry, I won't be doing a Whitney on you.'

He frowned.

'She drowned in the bath? Although I think drugs were her downfall, not the drink.'

Nick's Adam's apple bobbed as a shadow passed across his face. She wanted to stuff the words back into her mouth. 'I'm sorry. What a bloody stupid thing to say.'

He ran his hand through his hair. 'I'm not going.'

God, she really was a prize idiot. Nick didn't like to talk about Louise, his first wife. And he certainly didn't like to talk about the fact that she'd taken her own life. 'I'm sorry,' she said again. 'Come here.'

She kissed him, hard, trying to convey in her kiss that she would never leave him, like Louise had done.

'Are you sure you'll be all right?' he asked.

'I've told you, I'll be fine.'

'I won't be late.' He gave her a last kiss before he checked his reflection in the mirror, pushing his fringe out of his eyes.

'Have a good time,' she said as he shut the bathroom door behind him.

She waited until the front door slammed before she let the tears fall. Huge, hiccupping sobs filled the bathroom.

31

Belle lifted his head and meowed at her. She took a swig of wine, and then another, trying to calm herself, telling herself it would be okay, she would get through this – they would get through this. But no matter how loud the positive angel on her shoulder spoke up, the devil on her other shoulder drowned it out. She was useless, hopeless. She'd failed at becoming a mother. Hannah said children were souls, just waiting for the right parents to be born to. Lottie had snorted but it had been comforting, in a way, what she'd said, the belief that her child, their child, was out there, waiting somewhere for her. Only now, it wasn't comforting any longer – it seemed no child wanted her as a mother.

She really was useless. It wasn't even as if she could call herself a career woman – she'd failed at that too. The acting parts had dried up over the years, forcing her to do the one thing she'd always said she'd never do – start a theatre group. And even that wasn't going well. It limped along, children forced there by parents who believed their child was the next big thing, only one or two of the kids with any natural ability. And even those, once they reached adolescence, found experimenting with sex and booze much more tempting than pretending to be someone else in a dusty community centre.

She should give it up – it wasn't like they needed the money. But then what would she do? The only castings Jasper got her these days were for training company videos and she couldn't even manage to land them. No one wanted a washed-out, over-the-hill, forty-five-year-old. Everything was starting to drop – her skin, her bottom, the bags around her eyes – the camera wasn't kind to her anymore. And with HD – she shuddered – she couldn't even go there. It wasn't that there weren't parts for the more mature woman, there were, but they seemed to be dominated by a handful of actresses who'd served their time in soaps and who graced the gossip pages of the tabloids.

She reached for one of Nick's T-shirts that was hanging out of the dirty laundry basket next to the bath. Wiping her face with it, she breathed in the scent of him, that earthiness of his sweat that she'd be able to pick out anywhere, mixed with the citrusy smell of the Acqua di Parma aftershave he always wore. Thank God for Nick. At least she had him. He'd been a rock throughout her fertility issues, never once making her feel that their inability to conceive was all down to her. When, of course, it was.

She took another swig of her wine as she remembered their very first appointment with a gynaecologist. The briskness with which he'd summed up her infertility, the tears afterwards as she told Nick she wanted a divorce, begging him to go and find someone who could give him the child he longed for. She hadn't meant it, of course she hadn't. She was just looking for the reassurance that Nick wouldn't cast her aside, wouldn't find someone else to build a family with. And he had reassured her. Why wouldn't he? He loved her.

She sank back into the bath. Okay, so she didn't have a baby, or a career, but she had Nick. She had a husband who loved her.

She picked up her phone and opened up the gallery, flicking through the photos of him, pausing at the one taken in the bedroom of their ski chalet in St Moritz earlier in the year. She'd caught him deep in thought, a side view of his face, that jaw, his sexy stubble, the brown floppy hair. Her stomach still did that flip thing it did whenever she saw him. She googled him, as she often did, wanting to see his successes on the page in front of her. Nick Moore. Renowned architect. He'd been long-listed for a prestigious prize a few years ago, or rather the building he'd worked on had. She scrolled through the images of him, clicking on her favourite one, the one on the team page on his company website.

She scrolled further down the page. Everyone who worked at the company was on the website. 'We're a team,' Ruth always said, 'so why should it just be the directors on the website?' Her finger stopped at Pauline, lovely Pauline who'd sent her some flowers when the last IVF attempt had failed. She'd miss her when she moved to Scotland.

And then her finger stopped. Natasha Grant. Lottie downed the last of her wine, tipping back the glass to get the last drops into her mouth. That had to be her, Pauline's replacement. She scrolled through the rest of the employees. No, no other women called Natasha. There was no photo, just a shadow cut-out with *awaiting photo* written over the top of it. Her profile didn't say much, just that she graduated from Nottingham University with a business degree last year, which, according to Lottie's calculations probably put her at twenty-two. Her hobbies were listed as Pilates, going to gigs, and shopping. Sporty, young and well turned out then. And with a business degree, brainy too. Good. Nick needed someone he could rely on – common sense, as well as brains.

But she was only young. Twenty-two. Twenty-three years younger than Lottie. She probably didn't even know how to work the photocopier. Had she had other jobs? Work experience perhaps? LinkedIn offered up nothing, so she opened up Facebook and typed *Natasha Grant* into the search box. She was the fourth one down. A Nottingham graduate. That had to be her. She hadn't posted anything for months. Lottie flicked through the few photos on her profile. The pictures weren't clear and she couldn't be entirely sure she was picking out the right girl from the group of sozzled-looking students but, if she was right – and for some reason, she was sure she was – this Natasha had long red hair, just like Lottie used to have before she'd had hers cut into a shoulder-length bob.

Lottie picked up her wine glass and, realising it was empty, put it back down. She hoped Ruth had done the right thing in hiring this Natasha. Nick was going to be busy with the new hotel complex project – he needed someone he could rely on, not someone he would have to babysit.

She jumped as Belle's head appeared over the side of the bath. 'Okay, I'm coming. Two more minutes.' Searching for Natasha on Google, she found her Instagram page, and swiped quickly through the hundreds of photos she'd posted, trying to see if there was anything that might indicate she at least had a little bit of work experience. But there was nothing, just random photos – the cathedral in Palma; Gaudí's Basilica in Barcelona; 'The Kiss' – the Rodin statue in Paris; a pair of red high heels – Louboutins – or maybe a cheap knock-off pair; a girl, a black sunhat covering most of her face, ruby-red lips pouting at the camera.

And a photo of a sunset with the words *Decide What You Want And Go After It With Everything You've Got!* in script over the top of it.

Lottie rolled her eyes as she placed her phone on the top of the laundry basket. She took a breath and slipped back in the bath, putting her head under the water. The innocence of the young, believing that everything they wanted was within their grasp, that all they had to do was want something and it would be theirs. Poor Natasha. It seemed that the kid hadn't yet worked out that life didn't always hand everything to you on a plate, that it didn't matter how much you wanted something, there were no guarantees – no guarantees at all – that you would ever get it.

CHAPTER 3

I was late. On purpose. Always good to make an entrance, isn't it? To open the door and let everyone turn and stare as you strut through it. To have the women look you up and down, their nostrils flaring at the slinky top they think is too low-cut or the skirt that only just skims your crotch. To have the men lick their lips and think if only, if only they were a bit younger, if only they had the courage to talk to me. If only they'd left their wives at home.

Nick hadn't made that mistake, of course he hadn't. Wifey was nowhere to be seen. I knew what she looked like, had studied photos of her on the internet and in Nick's office. Her hair was red, like mine. Hopefully redheads were Nick's thing. Young redheads, that is. Wifey was plain as anything, a bland face no one would be able to pick out in a line-up. And old. No effing surprise he'd left her at home.

I pushed through the crowd, making my way to the bar, my eyes darting this way and that, searching for Nick.

He was sitting at a table, laughing at something someone in the group huddled around him had said. Despite the mass of bodies in the place, it was cold, the doors to the outside courtyard wide open, letting in the cool-for-July air. Summer? It was a bloody wash-out. I should have worn a jacket, but that would have covered up the skimpy top I had on, a gold sheath of material, low at the back, low at the front, the thin strings over my shoulders the only things making sure it didn't fall down.

The pimply teenager behind the bar made a beeline for me, ignoring the other customers. 'What can I get you?'

I shot a quick glance at Nick, trying to see what he was drinking. 'Red wine.'

'Merlot, Cabernet, Shiraz?'

I shrugged. 'Cheapest you have.'

'Are you with that lot?' He flicked his gaze in the direction of the gang from work. 'There's a tab behind the bar.'

'Make it your most expensive one, then,' I said. 'Large.'

He gave me a thumbs up and went off to get my drink.

I pulled my lip gloss out of my bag, rubbing it over my lips, pressing them together, trying to get a glimpse of myself in the mirror behind the bar. As soon as I'd got off the bus, it had started to piss it down. Not heavy, drenching rain, just a fine drizzle. I put my hand to my hair, hoping the hour I'd spent drying and straightening it so that it hung like a curtain down my back hadn't gone to waste. Pushing myself up onto my tiptoes, I stared into the mirror. Perfect – I was worrying for nothing.

The barman put my glass down on a napkin, winking at me before he moved off to serve someone else.

'What is that? Do you mind?' Nick stood to my left, so close that if I'd leant forward six inches, I could have kissed him.

Lifting my glass to his lips, he took a drink. He had the bluest eyes I'd ever seen. Like I imagined the colour of the sea to be in some faraway place. 'Better than the Shiraz. Same for me,' he shouted over to the barman, before taking another sip of my wine. 'Sorry,' he said, handing the glass back to me.

'No worries.' Our fingers touched as I grabbed the glass, sending a shot of electricity through my hand so strong I thought I might faint.

'Great you made it.'

'Cool idea, getting everyone together.' It wasn't. I couldn't imagine anything worse than spending time with my workmates outside of the office – I spent enough time with them during the nine to five. Why would I want to spend my free time with them as well, when I wasn't getting paid for it? I was only here for Nick. 'Congrats on the new contract,' I said, raising my glass. 'And thanks for inviting me tonight.'

'Thank Ruth,' he said. 'She reckons social events are essential for team building.'

'Glad she didn't choose bungee jumping.'

'Don't speak too soon. I wouldn't put anything past her.'

The barman put down Nick's drink. As Nick picked it up, I jolted forward, pretending the guy behind me had jostled me, the wine shooting out of my glass, splashing the front of Nick's shirt. 'Oh, fuck, what am I like? Here let me.' I whipped a tissue out of my clutch bag, and patted at his chest where the red stain blushed against his pale blue shirt. His body was firm, as I knew it would be.

'It's okay. Honestly,' he said, a pinkness to his cheeks as he stepped back from me. 'Though my wife will kill me. She bought me this shirt for my birthday.'

'Sorry,' I said, handing him another tissue. 'I'll buy you another one. She won't even know. Our secret.'

He shook his head, smiled. 'She'll find out,' he said. 'Nothing gets past my wife.'

I will, I wanted to say, but he was already moving away from me, heading in the direction of the gents', rubbing at his shirt with my tissue.

It was only a ten-minute walk to the restaurant but, thanks to the five-inch heels I had on, I lagged behind the others. When I finally made it through the door and to the area that had been reserved for us, the only seat left was on the table furthest away from Nick. At least I could see him from where I was sitting.

A girl from Accounts, Mary or Marie or something like that, tried to make small talk with me, some boring jabber about a late-night reality TV programme she was into. To my left sat Kas, who had ignored me all night – a sure sign he definitely had the hots for me. He wasn't a bad-looking bloke, Kas, but he was a bit too smooth for my liking, with his gelled-back hair and whiter than white teeth. And he was no match for Nick. I'd stared at him all night, willing him to look at me. He never did. Not once. Not that it mattered. I was going to play the long game. What was it Dad always said when he'd lost on the horses yet again? *Slowly, slowly catchee monkey.*

There was a sudden hush as someone clinked a knife against a glass. 'If I could have everyone's attention,' Ruth said. Even from where I was sitting, I could tell she was pissed. Her eyes were red, the words rolling around her mouth before she managed to get them out. I sighed. I had a feeling a long and boring speech was coming our way. 'We hope you've enjoyed the tapas. The prawns were my favourite. Scrummy! Anyway, for the desserts, we're all going to swap sweets . . . seats.' There were more than one or two groans, but I was already shoving my feet back into my high heels and grabbing my clutch bag from under the table. Now was my chance to get near – if not next to – Nick.

Ruth clapped her hands. 'Come on then. Chop, chop.'

I stood up, along with everyone else.

'Sit next to someone you haven't spoken to yet this evening,' Ruth shouted.

Moving between people, I kept my eyes on Nick. He seemed to be staying where he was. That made it easier. I just had to get over to his table and—

'Join us.' Ruth grabbed my hand, pulling me down next to her.

Kas sat down opposite us.

'I've been sitting with Kas all night.' I tried to stand up, but Ruth still had hold of my hand.

'Kas, bugger off,' Ruth said.

I wrenched my hand out of her grasp. 'No, it's okay, I'll—'

'You're fine. Kas,' Ruth said, pointing her spoon at the table where Nick sat, 'there's a free seat over there.'

Kas sighed, before picking up his glass of wine and heading over to Nick's table.

Ruth leant towards me. Her perfume was overwhelming. Heady, thick. *Poison*, if I wasn't mistaken. And mixed with it, the boozy dryness of red wine. It was an evil concoction that made me cough. 'Has he been pawing you?'

'Pawing me?'

'He fancies himself as a bit of a ladies' man.'

'Don't worry, I can handle him.'

'I'm sure you can,' she said, topping up my glass as she beamed at me. Her teeth were stained red from the wine.

'Ruth, are you ready?' Behind us stood a woman, petite with a blonde elfin crop, and a scowl etched onto her forehead. I doubted even Botox could help her out with those furrows. She held out a coat to Ruth. 'The taxi's here.'

'What? But it's not eleven yet. We haven't had our desserts.' Ruth put her arm around my shoulders. 'And I need to get to know the latest recruit. It's in my job description,' she slurred.

'Ruth,' the woman said again. 'The taxi.'

'I love your hair,' Ruth said to me. 'I can never do a thing with mine.' She patted at her dark mop of curls. 'You're like one of those women in the paintings.'

What the hell was she on about?

'You know, who is it, Claire?' She turned to the woman behind her. 'Rossini?'

'Rossetti.' Claire shoved the coat at Ruth. 'The meter's ticking.'

'I'm going myself now,' I said, eager to get rid of the pair of them. Kas hadn't joined Nick's table, after all, so there was still an empty seat there.

'Come with us. Share a taxi. That's okay, isn't it, babe?'

'Ruth.' Claire scowled.

'It's okay. My dad's picking me up,' I lied.

'Ring him. Tell him we can drop you. You don't want him coming out on a night like this, do you?' Ruth waved her arm at the window – it was still lashing it down.

'Ruth,' Claire said. 'Come on. Her father's picking her up.'

I looked at my watch. 'Yes, he'll have set off by now.'

'Oh, fair enough.' Ruth pushed herself up, falling to the side so I had to grab her. Claire caught her other arm, pulling Ruth towards her as she shot me a filthy look. They were out of the door before Ruth could say another word.

Nick glanced at the door, shaking his head as they left. And then, before I could reach his table, he was calling the waiter, handing over his credit card and punching his number into the machine.

'Spoilsport,' someone said. 'Stay, Nick,' said someone else.

He took some notes out of his wallet and threw them down onto the table. 'I have to get home.'

'Or else he'll be getting it in the neck from his wife,' Kas said.

'At least he's got a wife,' someone shouted.

'Touché.' Kas raised his glass.

Nick patted Kas on the shoulder and made his way out of the restaurant.

I counted to ten and then followed him into the wet night.

If I'd counted to twenty, it would have been too late – the taxi pulling up to the kerbside would have already whisked him away.

'Want to share?' I had to shout, the rain thundering down around us.

Nick opened the taxi door. 'Here, take it.'

'We can share. Where you heading?'

'It's okay,' he said, smiling. I could tell he was doing everything he possibly could to stop his gaze drifting to my chest where, thanks to the lashing rain, my nipples were visible through my sheer top.

'You'll think I'm a right wuss, but I'm always a bit scared of getting a taxi on my own.'

He chewed his lip. 'Which way are you going?'

'South.'

'Oh, that's the opposite end of the city from me,' he said.

It wasn't. He was lying. I knew where he lived. Had found his address online. He obviously didn't trust himself to be in the back of a cab with me. Which meant he liked me. Which meant that little devil of temptation was already whispering in his ear.

'She'll be all right with me, mate.'

Nick and I both peered into the taxi, at the old bloke who was sitting in the front.

44

'You'll be fine.' Nick put his hand on my back. Through the skimpy material of my top I could feel the warmth of his palm.

I hesitated. One last push. 'It'll be your fault if I end up dead,' I whispered.

And then another taxi was pulling up and Kenny, a boy from the estate who I'd gone to St Joseph's with – before he'd got kicked out of the high school in the first year – was hanging out of the window, beckoning me over. 'Hey, heard you were back, angel. Oi! Over here. Come on. Jump in.'

Nick moved his hand from my back to my shoulder. 'Do you know him?'

'Come on, the bloody meter's running,' Kenny shouted.

'It's fine,' I said, before Kenny could show me up any more. 'He lives near me.'

Nick smiled. 'Problem solved.'

'Cheers for tonight,' I said. 'And sorry about your shirt.'

'Don't worry.'

'Are you coming, or what?' Kenny shouted.

I wanted to kiss Nick. I wanted to reach up and kiss him but I didn't; I walked over to where Kenny's taxi was waiting.

'Hey, angel, looking good.' Kenny leant towards me as I climbed into the taxi, his lips trying to reach mine. He stunk of beer. And weed. I moved my head so he missed my mouth and ended up slobbering over my ear. 'Like that, is it? Halves it'll be then, angel.' He sniffed. 'Stroke of luck, wasn't it though, me seeing you? Thought it wouldn't be long before we caught up.' He gave me a wink and reached in his pocket for his roll-ups.

I didn't bother to reply. I stared out of the window, ignoring his mindless jabbering, the stench of beer coming from him, turning my head to give Nick a last smile before the taxi, and Kenny, whisked me away from him.

CHAPTER 4

'Sorry, sorry.' Hannah bustled in, smothering Daisy with a big hug and kissing Lottie's cheek. 'What have I missed?'

'Kyle throwing up because he was stuffing himself with Haribo, Megan sneezing over everyone and Connor's mum ringing to say he's broken his leg so he's out of the play. Apart from that, nothing much.' Lottie shoved the last of the beanbags into the wings, while Daisy got a broom and started brushing the stage.

'But Connor's playing the lead?' Hannah said. 'Isn't he?'

'Connor *was* playing the lead. I was hoping it was just a sprained ankle. Mind you, wouldn't surprise me if that's all it was.'

'What are you on about?'

'I get the impression Connor's mum believes her son is bound for greater things than this.' Lottie waved her hand at the stage. 'Wouldn't surprise me if she hadn't already signed him up for that new theatre group.'

'You're being paranoid. You can't fake a broken leg. He's not that good an actor, is he?'

Lottie smiled. 'No, you're right. He isn't. But he's the best of a bad bunch.'

'Oh, Lots,' Hannah said. 'Just what you need. On top of everything else.'

Lottie swallowed. She couldn't face her friend being sympathetic. Again. She'd had to end the call when Hannah had phoned last night, had pretended she'd lost her mobile signal, texting her later, reassuring her she was fine, and that, no, she didn't need her to come round. She was getting an early night, Lottie had said, a lie, because an early night was the last thing on her mind – sinking another bottle of wine was. She'd woken up on the sofa when Nick had arrived home, somewhere around midnight, his kisses reeking of garlic and red wine, a stain on his shirt directly over his heart as if someone had stabbed him there.

The door of the community centre opened.

Daisy's face lit up as her boyfriend appeared. 'Right, Mum, I'm off.'

Hannah frowned. 'But I thought I was giving you a lift to this party you're going to?'

'You said half past and now it's nearly seven,' Daisy said, picking up her rucksack. 'I called Trey.'

'Hey.' Hannah waved at Trey. 'Sorry, I got waylaid.'

'No worries.'

'Can he act?' Lottie asked Daisy. 'Can you act?' she called over to Trey. 'Fancy it?' She jerked her thumb at the stage.

'Me? No way.' He shook his head.

'Don't be late,' Hannah said as she gave her daughter a smacker on her cheek. 'You'll see her home, Trey?'

He gave her a thumbs up before slinging his arm around Daisy's shoulders and dragging her out into the night.

Lottie picked up a refuse bag, filling it with the rubbish the kids had left piled up by the bin – bottles of pop, crisp packets, Megan's soggy tissues.

'You okay?' Hannah said, following her.

'Fine.'

'Really?'

'Yes.' Lottie tried her best to summon a convincing smile. 'I don't want to talk about it. Or think about it.'

'We won't mention it then. Fancy a brew? Or something stronger?' Hannah patted the oversized jute bag she was carrying.

Lottie grimaced. After last night she wouldn't be drinking again for a while.

'Like that, is it? Tea it'll be then.'

Lottie glanced at her watch. 'I need to get going. It's my turn to cook.'

'Grab a takeaway on your way back.'

'I've got some pork chops defrosting in the fridge.'

'They'll keep. Nick can stick them in a risotto tomorrow.'

Lottie giggled. Nick's culinary skills only extended as far as rustling up a risotto. 'You're not going to take "no" for an answer, are you?'

'I need a favour.'

Was there ever a time when Hannah didn't need a favour? There again, it would be nice to be distracted by her friend's disasters – those she could cope with; it was her own she couldn't face. A quick cup of tea and then she'd get off home and see if Jamie Oliver had any good suggestions about how to make something exciting out of two pork chops.

'Back in a jiffy,' Hannah said, heading to the small kitchen at the back of the hall.

'So, what's this favour?' Lottie asked as Hannah handed her a steaming mug of black tea. 'No milk?'

'Only if you like it thick and rancid.' Hannah sat down on one of the orange plastic chairs that Lottie had fetched from the side of the stage.

Lottie grimaced as she lifted the mug to her mouth. Still, at least it was hot. The community centre was freezing, the heating on the blink again. Nobody would guess it was the height of summer – or supposed to be – it had rained non-stop for four months. She should really move the theatre group to another building. Nick was always pointing out properties to her, had even suggested buying a place. But Lottie had resisted. The centre wasn't far from where they lived and it captured kids from the suburbs south of Manchester and the outlying villages. 'So, this favour?'

'Daisy is trying to find a little summer job, to save up for university, you know? She was offered a job in the bar Trey works in. I don't reckon the manager realised she wasn't yet seventeen.'

'I'll ask Nick tonight. I'm sure he can find her some work.'

Hannah's nostrils widened as if she'd smelt something not to her liking.

'What?'

'I wasn't thinking about Nick's place. She's doing a bit of cleaning for our next-door neighbours and I was wondering if she could do yours. Just a couple of hours a week. She's a good worker.'

'Wouldn't she rather sit in an air-conditioned office than scrub my toilets?'

Hannah sniffed. 'I'm not sure it'd be her thing. She's a bit like me. God, I'd die if I had to sit in an office nine to five, week in, week out for the rest of my life.'

'You and me both.' Lottie took another swig of her tea. 'But it's only for a month, isn't it?'

'I think she's wanting more cash in hand. Nothing official like. That's why she's doing the cleaning work.'

'I'm sure Nick could sort something out. Not put it through the books.'

Hannah pursed her lips. 'No, it's okay. I wouldn't want him to get into trouble.'

'I bet you wouldn't.' Lottie grinned. 'Honestly, Hannah, it won't be a problem.'

'I don't want him thinking I'm hitting him up for favours.'

A sigh escaped from Lottie's lips. 'I'll ask Ruth then, if you prefer. I'm sure she can find Daisy something to do. Is she still set on doing biomedical science at uni?'

'Yep.'

'It's a shame she doesn't want to carry on with her acting. She could apply to the Old Vic, you know. I could give her a reference. They'd definitely take her. She's a natural and she's so gorgeous. Not that that should matter, but, you know, it helps. Casting directors will be falling over themselves to get her in their productions.'

'The casting couch?' Horror was written all over Hannah's face. 'Now she's definitely not going to drama school. And, anyway, she's got her heart set on being a pathologist. I blame myself for making her watch all those episodes of *Silent Witness* with me when she was little.' She gulped at her tea. 'Okay. Ask Ruth. It's only a month, isn't it?'

'Right. I'm sure they could do with an extra pair of hands. Pauline's leaving—'

Hannah's mug was halfway to her mouth. 'She's not! Pauline? She's been there for ages. What'll Nick do?'

'It's all sorted. He's got some new girl starting.'

'Girl?'

'Some temp who wants a permanent job.'

'How young are we talking?' Hannah narrowed her eyes at Lottie over the rim of her cup.

Lottie shrugged. 'Early twenties.'

'You'd have thought Nick would have taken on someone with a bit of experience.'

'That's what I thought but apparently she's great.'

Hannah snorted. 'According to who? Nick?'

'Ruth.'

'Hmm,' Hannah said before slurping at her tea.

'What?'

'Nothing.'

'Hannah?'

'Nothing.' Hannah plucked at a strand of her hair and started examining her split ends. 'It's just Pauline's a safe pair of hands. You know where you are with Pauline. Who knows what this new girl will be like?'

'Nothing much gets past Ruth. She wouldn't have hired her for the job if she wasn't any good, would she?'

'Hmm,' Hannah said again. 'I wasn't thinking of her secretarial skills. Look at my dad.'

Lottie rolled her eyes. Hannah's dad, a meek man with a walrus moustache and a bald head – not a lothario in anyone's book – had left Hannah's mum after thirty years of marriage for his much younger secretary. 'Nick's not your dad, Hannah.'

'He'd better not be or I'll kill him.'

Lottie laughed. 'Bit strong, even for you.'

'Okay, I'll start with his bollocks first. Chop them off. And then take it from there.'

Lottie laughed again. Hannah could always cheer her up. Even if she was dissing her husband, conjuring up ways to torture him. Lottie had never understood why Hannah didn't like Nick. Over the years she'd tried asking her about it, why she could always find an excuse not to come around to the house when he was there, why she'd never agree to go out for a drink with them and her latest fling. She'd often wondered whether Hannah was jealous. It had been just the two of them after all, sharing a flat after they'd returned from their three years of backpacking around the world. Just the two of them in a new city, hardly knowing anyone, except Ruth of course, and then Daisy had arrived eight months after they landed back in the UK. The two of them caring for Daisy, a little family, until Lottie had fallen for Nick eighteen months after

53

they'd settled in Manchester. Thank God Hannah had agreed to move there, rather than going home to Norwich. And thank God Ruth had persuaded Lottie to go to the gym that day – she wouldn't have met Nick otherwise.

Hannah peered at Lottie from behind her mug. 'Things okay between you two? Have you decided what you're going to do about—'

'I thought we weren't going to mention it?'

'Sorry,' Hannah said. 'You know what you need? A good night out.'

'Oh no.' Lottie shook her head. 'It takes me a week to get over a night out with you.'

'Not with me. With Nick. When was the last time you went out, just the two of you? A mad night out followed by a mad night in?' Hannah winked. 'Know what I mean? Sex. Swinging from the chandeliers and all that?'

Lottie felt the heat rise up her chest. She couldn't remember the last time they'd had sex. Nick was usually up for it, but she could always find an excuse. It wasn't as if she didn't fancy him, of course she did, she fancied him more than anything; it was just that every time they made love she thought of how she'd let him down, how she hadn't been able to give him the baby he wanted. It was easier to feign a headache.

Hannah reached over and rubbed her arm. 'It's his birthday soon, isn't it? Why don't you whisk him away to Paris, somewhere romantic?'

'We're going up to Fairview.'

'Bloody hell, Lots. Never heard the phrase "a change is as good as a rest"?'

54

'We like it at the cottage and, anyway, I'm planning a surprise party for him. On the Saturday. We'll go up Friday night to celebrate our anniversary and then everyone can join us on the Saturday. It won't be anything grand. Just his parents, Ruth and Claire, you and Daisy. Trey too if that's okay with you. Bring Jon. He's more than welcome.'

'Jon? Who's Jon?'

'The guy you were seeing? The one with the tattoos on his . . . ahem.' Lottie coughed, and widened her eyes.

'Oh, that Jon. He's last month's news. It's Craig now. His tattoos are just on his arms. But he does have the most enormous . . .' she paused for dramatic effect '. . . motorbike.'

Lottie giggled. 'I'm sure he does. Where did you find him?'

'He's Trey's dad. Known him for ages.'

'Blimey. What does Daisy think about that? I bet she's horrified you're sleeping with her boyfriend's dad.'

Hannah put down her mug, a wicked look in her eye. 'Who says we're sleeping together?'

'Yeah, right.' Lottie grinned as a blush crept across her friend's cheeks. 'So, you'll come to Nick's party?'

'I'm washing my hair that weekend.' Hannah raked her hand through her curly mop.

'You'll need more than a weekend for that.'

'Hey! You're supposed to be my friend.'

'Exactly, so you can't let me down.'

'Oh, all right.' Hannah gave a theatrical sigh. 'But I'm not buying Nick a present. I mean, come on, what do you get for the man who's got everything?'

55

Lottie's phone buzzed. She scrabbled in her bag, found her mobile and read the message. She wouldn't need to cook after all – Nick was still in the office, would be another couple of hours, had to finish something off.

'Do you fancy grabbing a bite to eat? My treat.' She held her hand out to Hannah and pulled her out of her chair. 'What do you say? We could go to the Thai?'

Hannah rubbed Lottie's arm. 'I've got a date. Why don't you come along? I'm meeting Craig at the rock bar in the city centre. Come on. It'll do you good.'

'No, you're fine. Go off and enjoy yourself. I think I'll surprise my husband in the office.'

'Sure?'

'Sure. I'd never stand in the way of a hot date.'

Hannah winked at her. 'You just remember what I said. About the s-e-x. But watch out for the carpet burns. Those office tiles are very scratchy.'

'And how would you know?' Lottie said, winking back.

Lottie came out of the Siam Orchid with two brown paper bags – Penang Chicken for her and Pad Thai for Nick. His office wasn't much out of her way and he'd be starving, all thoughts of food forgotten, his head stuck into the designs for the new hotel complex.

She couldn't be bothered to drive down into the basement garage, where there'd be a space at this time of night. Instead, she pulled up on a single yellow line, down the street from the building where Nick's office had the whole of the top floor. She could never remember whether you were allowed to park on single yellows or not, but she was only going to be ten minutes – she'd just drop off the food and leave him to it. She flipped down the sun visor and peered at herself in the mirror. What a state! Big black rings under her eyes where her mascara had run. And her nose was red and shiny as usual. There'd definitely be no carpet burns tonight, even if she wanted to have sex with her husband – which she didn't.

She was reaching for her bag when she saw Nick's metallic red Mercedes Coupé swing out of the basement car park. Great – he'd finished earlier than he'd been expecting to. She'd follow him home. He'd be happy she'd grabbed a takeaway – Thai was his favourite.

She put her keys into the ignition, determined to tail his car so she could surprise him by beeping her horn at him. The traffic lights at the end of the street turned to red. She glanced over her shoulder to check the street was clear. It was. When she turned back, she was surprised to see Nick's car had stopped outside his office. Perhaps he'd forgotten something? She was just about to pull out, to drive up beside his car, open her window and shout and wave, when someone came out of Nick's building. Someone tall, slim. Someone with long red hair and high heels. Someone who Nick had jumped out of the car for. He held the passenger door open for the woman, his hand on the small of her back, guiding her in, before he bolted back around to the driver's side, hopped in, and – with a roar of the engine – sped away through the traffic lights.

Bang went sharing their takeaway at home. The woman was probably a client. Something to do with the new hotel.

Lottie frowned. She'd put his Pad Thai in the fridge. He'd have to heat it up when he got home – whatever time that would be. And then Lottie remembered where she'd seen that red hair before. She ran her hand through her own short bob. Of course, the woman wasn't a client. The woman had to be Tasha, his new PA. But where were they going at this time of night? It was gone half seven. Perhaps they had a late meeting in another part of town? Or maybe there was a drinks thing? Nick was always having to schmooze clients – it came with the job. He usually asked her to go with him. People always found it fascinating talking to an actress, even one that hadn't had a proper job for some years. Still, he knew she'd got the rehearsal for the play tonight. He must have asked Tasha to stand in for her. God, she hoped the girl wouldn't show him up. At least Lottie had an understanding of how Nick liked to handle his projects – and his clients. This temp couldn't know any of that yet.

A piercing horn sounded behind Lottie's car, so loud that she yelped, her heart hammering. A black four-by-four was idling in the road, waiting for Lottie to move out.

'Sorry, sorry,' she mouthed, pushing the car into first gear as the woman driver sounded the horn again. 'Keep your hair on!' Lottie pulled out into the road, pressing her foot to the floor, shooting through the traffic lights as they turned red, her eyes searching for Nick's car.

Perhaps she could join them. But then she remembered her red nose and her Panda eyes. Maybe not.

Not that she had a choice, anyway, for the car, Nick, and the woman were nowhere to be seen.

CHAPTER 5

I'd never been in a Mercedes before. I'd never been in a new car before. Dad had always driven second-hand cars, old bangers at that. I'd never breathed in that artificial smell of newness I knew you could buy in an air freshener. Kenny had had one once – the air freshener, not the car. It hung in his bedroom, trying to block out the stench of sweat and weed.

I rubbed my hand over the soft cream leather of the seat. 'Nice car.'

'Not bad.' Nick tapped his fingers on the steering wheel. 'Treated myself. Early birthday present.'

'How early?'

'Only a couple of months. My birthday's in September. The tenth.'

'Are you a Libra?'

He shrugged.

'He's a Virgo,' Ruth piped up from the back seat. 'A moody bugger.'

For a second, I'd forgotten she was there, sitting in the

60

back seat like a bloody huge gooseberry, the third spoke in the wheel that we – well, certainly I – didn't want.

'I'm the least moody person, I know,' he said, winking at me.

Ruth let out a 'ha'. 'Tell that to my sister.'

I turned around as best I could in my seat. 'Your sister? Was that her? Claire, wasn't it? In the restaurant with you last night? You don't look like sisters.' They didn't. Claire was petite and blonde with a resting bitch face. Ruth had olive skin, dark, jet black – obviously dyed – curly hair, and was large, at least a size fourteen by my reckoning, although she hid it well under the old-fashioned power suits she always wore.

Nick laughed. 'Claire is Ruth's partner. How is the hangover, by the way?' he said, over his shoulder.

Ruth let out a huge yawn. 'What hangover?'

I felt my cheeks redden. I wasn't usually so slow on the uptake. I remembered the filthy look Claire had shot in my direction last night, how she'd pulled Ruth away from me. Was Claire jealous? Had Ruth been coming on to me?

'Ruth is my sister-in-law,' he said. 'My wife's sister.'

His wife's sister? That could make things awkward for me.

'I introduced them. She's blamed me ever since.' Ruth punched Nick lightly on the arm.

She was joking. She had to be – Nick was surely the best thing that had ever happened to her sister. Didn't she know that? Ungrateful cow. He was the best thing that had ever happened to me. The moment I saw him on my first day in the office, I knew the dreary old life I'd returned to was suddenly about to get a whole lot brighter. I used to sneer at people who said they knew they'd met their soulmate within three seconds of speaking to them. Until it happened to me.

I'd have to watch out for Ruth though. Was she suspicious of me already? Was that why she was here? Or had Claire's jealousy last night been spot on? Did Ruth have the hots for me?

Ruth leant forward and touched the arm of my jacket. 'I love this on you. It's such a good colour. Where did you get it?'

A giggle rose in my chest. I knew my charms could work on men. But I'd never had a woman come on to me before. 'I forget,' I said, 'but thanks.' Maybe it wouldn't be a bad thing if she did want to jump me. Maybe I could use her interest to my advantage, pump her for information about Nick and his wife, find out if her sister's marriage was on solid ground, find out if there were any chinks in it I should know about, chinks I could work on to make them huge, gaping holes.

'What star sign are you?' I said, over my shoulder.

'Aquarius. You?'

'Libra. I reckon that makes us a match. Air signs together.'

Nick tutted. 'Don't let Claire hear you say that.'

'Not everyone's got your dirty mind,' Ruth said. 'It just means we get along well.'

Nick laughed. 'It's a load of bollocks.'

'Bil, language!'

'Bill?'

62

'Sorry.' Ruth's face appeared in the gap between the seats. 'It's what I call Nick. Bil. B, I, L, Bil, short for brother-in-law. He hates it, don't you?'

'Nope.'

'Liar.'

Nick pressed a button on the dashboard. 'I think we'll have some music on. To drown you out.'

A song I'd never heard before filled the car.

'Oh, I love this,' Ruth shouted over the music. 'Reminds me of my dad.'

Ruth leant forward, so close to me I could smell the mint of her chewing gum. 'He died five years ago. Cancer.'

'Oh my God, I'm so sorry.' And I was too.

Ruth shrugged. 'Just got to get on with things, haven't you?'

She was all right, Ruth. Annoying, but all right. I sensed she was like me. A fighter. I'd lost my mum years ago. Not that she was dead. Just dead to me. It made you tougher. It made you want to grab life with both hands. To go for what you wanted. To not take any shit from anyone.

The rain lashed at the windscreen as the song ended and another track came on. We'd left the city centre, travelling down the dual carriageway, north of the city, whizzing through suburbs.

'Where is it we're heading again?'

'The other side of Manchester. You don't have to be home for anything, do you?'

'No.' I'd called Dad before we left, said I would be late back. He'd moaned. 'What'll I do for my tea?' he'd said.

'There's a ready meal in the freezer. A cottage pie. Stick it in the microwave.'

'You know I can't work that bloody thing. I'll wait for you.'

'Don't wait,' I said, but he'd already hung up.

Nick changed gear. 'I'll drop you home after. Where do you live?'

'There's no need.' There was no way I wanted him to see where we lived. It was the same suburb of Manchester he lived in, but on the rough side of town. The part of town he'd probably never visited in his life.

'It's no bother,' Nick said.

'I'm meeting up with some friends later.' I crossed one leg over the other. It sounded good, that. Sounded like I had friends. I didn't want Nick knowing that, since I'd come back, no one spoke to me – no one except Kenny that is. He'd tried to kiss me again when we'd got out of the taxi last night, lunging for me. But he hadn't counted on me being too quick for him and the beer slowing him down. 'Can't blame a bloke for trying,' he'd slurred as I'd slammed my front door in his face.

'Anywhere nice?' Ruth said from the back of the car.

'Just for a few drinks. Come along if you like.'

'Me? But I'm not dressed for a night out.'

'You're fine.'

'Okay then. That would be lovely. I'll have to let Claire know.'

'Out two nights on the trot, Ruth?' Nick said.

She patted his shoulder. 'Are you saying I'm too old, Bil? I can't keep up with these young bucks?'

64

'That's exactly what I'm saying. You and Claire are usually in your pyjamas by seven, slippers on, pipes at the ready.'

'Shut up and put something a bit more upbeat on.'

He shook his head and pressed a button on the stereo. The Pussycat Dolls filled the car, screeching about how much hotter they were than some bloke's girlfriend. Funny. But not a good tune. I was more of a Seventies rock sort of girl. Give me AC/DC or Led Zep any day. I blamed Maggie, my mother's sister, who sometimes used to pop round to check I was all right. She'd bring one of her boyfriends with her, her LPs on loud as they made out in the lounge while I sat in my bedroom.

Staring out of the window, as the city sped by, I wondered if Maggie was still in Manchester or if she was somewhere far away. I hadn't heard from her in years. Had she kept in touch with my mother? I leant my cheek against the cold window. What did I care if she had or not? I didn't give a damn about that stupid old cow. She had made her dirty bed. Let her fucking lie in it.

'Enjoying it, the work?' Nick said as we turned off the dual carriageway.

'Great.' I smiled. It was boring as fuck to be honest. The only good thing about it was seeing Nick every day.

'Well, Ruth is very pleased with you. Says you're a great worker. Don't you, Ruth?'

From the back of the car came a soft snore.

Nick laughed and shook his head.

'There's a lot to learn,' I said, hoping he might offer to spend some time with me.

'Don't worry, Pauline will show you the ropes. There's nothing she doesn't know.'

'I'm not sure she likes me.'

Nick's head swivelled towards me. 'What? Don't be daft. Pauline likes everyone. If she didn't like you, you'd know about it.'

Pauline didn't like me. I could tell that. It was the way she tutted at my short skirt, shook her head if I filed something in the wrong place, sighed if I asked her to explain once again how the appointments diary worked. Stupid bitch. Who did she think she was? Not that I was worried. Her days were numbered, weren't they? I would soon have her job.

I crossed one leg over the other, very slowly, and then unwound the scarf from around my neck, squeezing my arms into my sides, so my breasts strained at the thin white fabric that was covering them.

'Hot?' he said.

'Very.'

There was the sheen of sweat on his upper lip. 'Yes, it is a bit,' he said, pressing the air-conditioning button. Cool air blasted out towards us.

'I'm bloody freezing,' Ruth moaned from the back.

'We're here now,' he said, pulling the car up in front of a run-down mansion that had definitely seen better days.

I wanted to be on my own with him. I wanted to wander around this old knacker of a building with him, join him in his excitement at how he was going to bring it back from the dead, talk about how I could help him do that.

66

But Ruth tagged along with us, moaning the whole time about being cold. I didn't see how she could be – she had a good layer of fat to keep her warm. She was right though, the abandoned building was freezing, but at least the electrics still worked.

'What do you think, then?' he said to me and Ruth, spreading out the plans he'd brought with him on a deep windowsill. 'The whole ground floor will be a mixture of restaurants and the upper floor a spa.'

Ruth crossed her arms. 'Er, aren't you missing the obvious? Where will people sleep?'

'This building will be surrounded by courtyards. New builds, but you won't be able to tell. And there'll be a penthouse, just the one, at the top of this building.'

'It's going to be amazing,' I said.

'It is, Bil.' Ruth winked at Nick. 'We'd better get a discount when it opens. We could come for a spa day,' she said to me.

'Too right.' I had no intention of coming here with her – I'd be coming here with Nick. I could imagine us sipping a cocktail at the piano bar, eating in the fancy restaurant, and then him taking me up to the penthouse suite and making love to me slowly, oh so slowly, on the huge bed.

'Where are the loos, Nick?' Ruth asked.

'Downstairs. To the left of the entrance. If they work, that is.'

'You want to go, before we head back?' she said to me. 'I need to do my face if we're going for drinks.'

Just then her mobile started to ring.

'Hi,' she said, answering it.

Claire, Nick mouthed at me.

'Yes, just out at the new hotel project. With Nick.' She peered at her watch. 'Not sure. We might go for a drink after—'

She paused, her foot tapping away. 'Oh, okay then. Yes.' She put her phone down by her side. 'Will we be long, Nick?'

'Five minutes.'

'I'll be home in half an hour,' she said, her phone back to her ear. 'Bye. Bye. Yes, love you too.' She frowned at me. 'I'll have to do drinks another night. Claire's cooked.'

Nick grinned. 'Not her famous Devil's Chicken? You can't miss that.'

'Funny,' Ruth said.

'Not a problem.' I gave her a thumbs up as she made her way out of the room. Finally, finally I would have him to myself – for five minutes at least. And hopefully, when he'd dropped Ruth off, I'd get to spend some more time with him. Maybe we could go for a drink. Just the two of us.

'So,' Nick said when she'd left the room, 'what do you really think?'

'You're amazing,' I said.

Heat flashed across his cheeks. 'My wife thinks so.'

My hand flew to my mouth as I realised what I'd said. 'I meant all this is amazing.'

He pretended to study the plans.

'What does your wife make of the place?'

'She hasn't seen it yet.'

'Right.' I felt a glow inside me. Nick was obviously obsessed with this project, and he'd chosen to share that obsession with me, rather than with wifey. I bit my lip, walked over to a ladder propped against the edge of a gaping hole in the ceiling.

'What's up there?'

Nick looked up. 'That's the ballroom. The stairs have rotted. That's the only way up at the moment.'

'Can I go up?'

'No, best leave it. It's not safe.'

'Are you afraid of heights?' I said, folding my arms.

'Who me? No.'

'After you, then.' I held out my arm. 'Age before beauty.'

'Cheeky.' He came over to the ladder and put one hand on it. 'After you. I insist. I'd take those off though.' He looked down at my shoes. He was right. The stiletto heels were far too high to be going up ladders in. And, anyway, I couldn't trust them not to break – they were a cheap pair of fakes I'd picked up from Counterfeit Street on Bury New Road.

I slipped them off and stood at the bottom of the ladder, thankful I'd painted my toenails. 'You'll hold it.' It wasn't a question.

'I'll hold it,' he said. 'I won't let you fall.'

I climbed slowly, as slowly as I could, aware he was at the bottom of the ladder, looking up, right up my skirt. I reached the top, uttered a few 'wows'. I didn't care what it was like – it was an old building, only fit for knocking down, if you asked me. 'It's amazing,' I shouted down to him.

'I told you it was. Come on down now.'

'Are you still holding it?' I said as I made my way down the ladder, as slowly as I'd gone up it.

'Yes. I've got you.'

If only he had, I thought as I neared the bottom, springing from the third rung up, landing heavily so that I bumped into him and he had to catch me.

His hands steadied me. His breathing was heavy. I held my breath. Our faces were close. So close.

'Are you two coming?' Ruth shouted from downstairs, breaking the spell. 'I need to get going.'

'On our way,' Nick shouted back, moving away from me, whipping the plans off the windowsill, folding them rather than rolling them, avoiding my eye.

I tried to keep the grin from my face as he held the plans in front of him. Was that his desire for me he was covering?

'Ready?' he said, staring at a spot six inches to the left of my face.

Ready? He had no idea just how ready I was.

CHAPTER 6

Through a small gap in the curtains, the beam of head-lights lit up the bedroom. The slam of a car door and the crunch of gravel was followed by the rattle of keys in the front door lock and then Nick shouting her name.

Lottie pulled the duvet up over her face, causing Belle who was lying next to her to let out a grumble. Ignoring him, she closed her eyes.

'Lots?' Nick came around to her side of the bed, sitting down next to her, the weight of his body causing her to rock towards him, and Belle to jump off the bed with a meow. And yet Lottie still kept her eyes closed.

'Lots?' He put his hand to her head. 'Are you not well?'

She opened her eyes, blinking as he put on the bedside lamp. 'Thanks for waking me,' she said, pulling the duvet back up around her.

'What's the matter? It's not yet ten.'

'Period.'

'Ah, Lots, shall I fetch you a hot water bottle? Have you taken some tablets?'

Not waiting for an answer, he pushed himself off the bed and left the room. She could hear him rummaging in the bathroom cabinet, searching for the blister pack of ibuprofen that was hiding in plain sight on the kitchen counter top. The combi boiler boomed as it fired up.

He came back into the room, slipping under the duvet next to her, even though he was fully clothed, leaning over her and pressing the hot water bottle to her stomach. 'Here you go. Careful, it's hot. I can't find the ibuprofen. Will paracetamol do? Lots?'

'I want to sleep.'

She moved away from him, curling up into a foetal ball.

The bed shifted as he struggled out of his clothes, flinging them onto the bedroom floor. And then his body was next to hers, refusing to let her go. His heat seeped into her, warming that spot above her right hip where it felt like someone was gouging out her insides with a teaspoon. He knew her. Knew where she was hurting. Knew what to do to soothe the pain.

After a couple of minutes, he moved away from her. 'I'm going to grab something to eat.'

'There's takeaway in the fridge.'

He got out of bed, letting cold air rush in as he lifted up the duvet. Lottie tutted and threw the duvet over her head, before pulling it down so she could watch him. He padded over to their walk-in wardrobe, taking a pair of pyjama bottoms and a T-shirt off a shelf. She'd bought him those for his birthday a few years ago, his face a picture when he'd opened them. 'What do I need pyjamas for?' He'd grabbed her, showering her with kisses, peeling her clothes off as he pushed her back onto the sofa.

She bit her lip. Those days of passion were long gone, muffled by endless rounds of IVF. Their lovemaking had dwindled away. The only thoughts occupying their heads were her cycle, which clinic to try next, and just how long it would take them to have a baby. Conceiving hadn't given them one single sleepless night when they were first married – they'd assumed it would happen when the time was right. But when Lottie hit forty, doubts had crept in. Her acting jobs had dried up, while Nick's practice had got busier. She was fed up and bored. He was stressed. They'd – stupidly – waited another year and then they'd gone to see a fertility specialist.

She closed her eyes but sleep wouldn't come. And she needed those ibuprofen. When the microwave pinged, she got out of bed.

'Hey.' Nick jumped off his stool as she walked into the kitchen. 'Shall I get you a plate?'

She shook her head.

He held the pack of tablets aloft. 'Found them,' he said, pouring her a glass of tap water. 'You look like shit.'

'Thanks.' She swallowed the tablets gratefully, finishing the water and then refilling the glass before joining him at the breakfast bar.

'I'd have rushed back if I'd known you were going to the Siam Orchid,' he said, pointing at the bowl of Pad Thai in front of him. 'I've died and gone to heaven.' He placed his hand on top of hers. 'Shall we go out tomorrow night if you're feeling up to it? We could even stop over somewhere? What do you say? How about that little place in the Peaks?' He winked at her.

A Friday night away? Not like him – he was usually fit for nothing at the end of the week. 'Sounds lovely but aren't you busy with the hotel project?'

His face clouded over. 'You're right. No rest for the wicked, eh?'

'It's not long till our weekend at Fairview. Just over eight weeks and counting.'

'Can't wait to have you all to myself,' he said, sucking on a long noodle until it disappeared between his lips.

'Pig.' Lottie smiled and shook her head. 'How was the meeting?'

'Meeting?'

A pain jabbed next to her right hip. She rubbed at the spot.

'I called round to the office. Thought you might be hungry.'

His fork hovered in front of his mouth. 'Oh, darling. Sorry. You should have let me know. I took a drive out to the hotel. I took Ruth—'

'Ruth? That wasn't Ruth I saw getting into your car.' Confusion swept across his face.

'I was parked up just down the road. I stopped off to give you that.' She jerked her head at his plate.

'Oh, right. You just missed us, then. That's a shame. You could have come too. I'd love to show you the place. It's amazing.' He speared a large piece of chicken and stuffed it into his mouth.

'I'd love to see it.' Lottie hopped onto a stool. Nick

74

usually took her to all the sites he was working on. 'So, who was that? Your new PA?'

'Who?'

'Doh. The woman getting into your car? The redhead?'

'Oh, right. Yes. That was Tasha.'

'Tasha? What happened to keeping things formal?'

'Sorry, Natasha.' He twirled some noodles around his fork.

'Has she started then? Pauline's not leaving until the end of August, is she?' She ran her finger along the sharp edge of the blister pack, accidentally slicing her skin.

'Tasha – Natasha – is shadowing Pauline at the moment. Just trying to make her feel part of the team. She'll be handling all the day-to-day stuff once Pauline's gone. Questions from contractors and the like.'

'And you need to get to know her. She'll be your right-hand woman.'

'Exactly.'

'Exactly.' Lottie rubbed at her side where the pain was the worst.

Nick put down his fork. 'Sorry, sweetheart. I will take you to have a look at the new site. You've been so busy with the play.'

'I know. It's fine.' Lottie pinched a piece of chicken off his plate. 'Did she like it then?'

'Seemed to. Not sure Ruth was much for it though.'

'Ruth? I didn't see Ruth in your car.'

'She was in the back. We'd gone down to the basement car park together. Tasha, needed the loo before we left so I picked her up at the front of the building.' He gave Lottie a puzzled look.

'Right.'

He picked up his fork and stabbed at a piece of chicken, a grin on his face. 'Darling, everything okay?' He suddenly let out a bark of a laugh. 'Are you jealous?'

'Me? Don't be ridiculous.' Lottie hopped off her stool and busied herself with sucking at the cut on her thumb. As she turned on the tap and stuck her thumb under the cool flow of water, she felt a flush creep up her neck. Jealous? She'd never been jealous in her life – okay, perhaps when Ruth got a First and she only got a two-one – and she certainly wasn't jealous of some slip of a girl.

Nick came over to her, putting his arms around her waist and his head on her shoulder. 'You've cut yourself,' he said, noticing the blood oozing out of the soft pad of her thumb. 'Let me see that.' He unwrapped himself from around her, took her thumb, studied it for a second and then placed it between his lips.

Lottie pulled her thumb out of his mouth. 'You call that blood?'

'Oh, sweetheart. Is the pain really bad?' He wrapped her in his arms. 'I'll take you out to visit the complex at the weekend. I promise. Now, go on, sit down,' he said as he spooned the Penang Chicken out of the foil carton and into a dish before putting it in the microwave.

'I should come into the office and meet her, this Tasha.'

'You should. You'd like her. Everyone does. Kas is already trying to poach her from me.'

'Fancy his chances, does he?'

'You know what he's like. A sucker for a pretty girl.'

'So, she's pretty then?' What was wrong with her? What did it matter if she was pretty or not?

'You are bloody jealous.'

'I'm not!' But even as the words came out of her mouth, she worried that they were a lie – was she jealous? It was so unlike her. She trusted Nick implicitly. He'd never looked at another woman and never would do – she knew that. Was it Tasha's youth? Was that her issue? Probably. She sighed – her own youth seemed like a distant dream.

He shook his head and reached for her hand, kissing her knuckles. 'She is pretty, if you like that sort of thing. But very young.'

Lottie snorted.

'Which means, darling, she'd never go for an old fart like me.'

'Exactly.'

'And, anyway,' he said, 'you're the only one for me. Got that?'

She leant over to kiss him. 'Don't you forget it. So, Kas is interested in her? What about the gorgeous Sienna?'

'Seems like things might be cooling between them.'

'No! Poor Kas. Well, maybe this Tasha will help him take his mind off things.'

'Unless Ruth gets in there first.' Nick winked at her.

'Ruth? Is Tasha gay then?'

Nick grinned. 'How should I know? That wasn't one of the interview questions. I don't think you're allowed to ask about people's sexual orientation these days. All I know is Ruth blushes every time she speaks to Tasha.'

'She does?'

'That's cheered you up.'

Lottie did suddenly feel a whole lot brighter. And it wasn't just to do with the fact that the pain in her side had eased. She'd been trying to convince Ruth to cut her losses with Claire for years. Claire was a moody old thing who Ruth pandered to and always had done. Maybe this Tasha would be just the incitement Ruth needed to finally make the break.

The microwave pinged. Lottie hoped so. Ruth would be far better off without Claire. Far better to be on her own, she was always telling her, than in a relationship that just wasn't working.

CHAPTER 7

A hand, Jaffa-orange nails, waved in front of my face, making me yelp and my heart bang in my chest.

'Sorry, didn't mean to scare you,' Ruth said as I popped out my earphones and slowed my pedalling.

'Trying to finish me off, or what?' Grabbing my towel from the front of the exercise bike, I grinned as I wiped at my forehead and my chest, before taking a swig from my water bottle. 'I didn't know you came to this gym,' I said, once my heart rate had slowed.

She had already hopped onto the bike next to me. 'Why do you think I sorted out the staff discount for this place? It's on my way home.'

'Ah, and I thought you only had the employees' best interests at heart.' I winked at her. 'Isn't that new gym and spa in the city centre more up your street?' It was in some top-dollar hotel owned by an ex-Man-United player. Way out of my price range. But not Ruth's. She was a director of the firm, drove a BMW, wore fancy designer clothes. It was sure to be much more her thing than this chain gym on a grubby industrial estate. But on the way back from the site of the new hotel complex last Thursday, I'd mentioned that I'd taken advantage of the staff perk and joined GymSpot.

So it was an odds-on bet, as my old man would say, that she'd roll into the place one day. A week to the day later and here she was.

'Thought I'd give this a go first. Don't mind me joining you, do you?'

'Course not,' I said. 'Nice to have some company.'

She grinned and took a sip of water. 'I usually stick to the treadmill. Just walking though. Dodgy knees.'

No surprise there. She was carrying a bit of extra weight. 'I love your gym gear, by the way. Sweaty Betty? Orange is your colour.' It wasn't. The clothes she had on were a perfect match for her spray tan. She looked like a giant prawn.

'There's no getting away from what Lycra shows up though, is there?' she said, pointing at the couple of inches of fat bulging out of the top of her leggings.

'Get away with you. There's nothing to you.'

Rolling her eyes, she stabbed her orange-tipped finger at some buttons on the bike and started to pedal. Slowly. I'm surprised the speedometer on the bike didn't show she was going backwards.

'On your own?' It would be useful to know if her misery of a girlfriend was about to turn up and see me off. She reminded me of something, that Claire – what was it now? – ah, that was it: a little yapping Chihuahua.

Ruth stopped pedalling. Obviously, movement and talking was too much for her, and she preferred the latter.

'My sister was supposed to come with me. She cried off at the last minute though.'

'Nick's wife?' I said, just to check she hadn't got another sister.

'Yep. The very one. There's only me and her. Thank God. One sibling is enough, isn't it? What about you?'

'A brother. Danny.'

'You're lucky,' she said. 'No flawless sister to be compared to.'

'You don't get on?'

'Oh, don't get me wrong – we get on brilliantly. She's Miss Perfect though. Know what I mean? She's done everything right. Found the perfect man. Got the perfect marriage. Can never do any wrong in my mother's eyes. Whereas me? I am the—' she took her hands off the handlebars and folded her arms '—the child who must not be mentioned. Not very liberal views my mother. Big into religion. Very big.'

'When did you come out to your parents?'

'I didn't. I never will. I tried to tell my mother when I was about fourteen but she just ignored me, pretended she hadn't heard. I should have told Dad before he died, been honest with him.' She chewed on her fluorescent thumbnail as she started pedalling again. 'So, you can see how it is. My sister is the golden child and I'm not even a mucky shade of bronze.'

'No one's perfect. And people's marriages can appear perfect from the outside but usually they're not.'

'Thanks,' she said, 'for trying to make me feel better. I appreciate that. But she is perfect. The perfect marriage. And a perfect husband.'

I felt heat rising in my chest. Perfect? Nick was like a god to me – gorgeous, kind, funny. He was more than perfect. 'There must be one thing less than perfect about her,' I said, grabbing my towel and wiping my face with it.

She glanced at me and I worried I was pushing it too far, too quickly. 'Well, there's been no patter of tiny feet yet. And it's something they both want. A lot. My mother isn't exactly pleased about that. She's already bought a cot. However she's going to get that over from Portugal, I'll never know. She retired out there a couple of years back,' she said.

I started to pedal more furiously. I'd found it. The chink in their marriage. Nick and his wife wanted a child, yearned for one, and it hadn't happened for them. I decided there and then I would put my chisel into that chink and yank away at it, forcing it wider and wider until it split into two.

'Here you go.' Ruth handed me a coffee. I would have preferred a smoothie, or a milkshake, but I knew how important it was to mirror people, to pretend you liked what they liked, that you were on their wavelength. You could win them over that way.

'Claire doesn't do the gym, then?' I said as we found a seat in the café overlooking the squash courts. Two men were banging a ball back and forth, their trainers squeaking each time they moved.

She shook her head. 'The only time she sets foot in here is when she comes to pick me up.' She glanced at her phone. 'Talking of which, I can't be too long.' She took a sip of her coffee. 'She's a runner. Hates running machines though. Likes to be out in the open. The wind in her face and all that. I used to go with her but she got fed up with me trailing behind.'

No effing surprise that Claire was a runner. She had that pinched, drawn look about her that runners often have. 'Been together long?' I took a mouthful of my drink and immediately wished I hadn't. Coffee wasn't my thing. I could handle a weak cup of Mellow Bird's, but this was like brown sludge.

'We met just after uni.'

'Wow, a while then.'

'Yes.' She stared off into the distance and then back at me. 'What about you? Is there anyone?'

I hesitated. What to say? If I told her there was someone, someone I was in love with, that might put her off, but if I lied, and said there was no one, she might be put off by that too, think I was undesirable. 'I've got my eye on someone.'

She glanced at me, but I looked away, pretending to watch the guys in the squash court.

'Shame your sister couldn't make it.' I put down my coffee cup. 'I would have liked to meet her.'

'She pops into the office sometimes. I'm sure she'd love to meet you too. I bet old Bil's told her all about you.'

I was sure Nick's wife wouldn't like to meet me, especially if he had told her about me climbing the ladder in my short skirt at the new hotel last week. He hadn't been able to look me in the eye at work since. We'd had conversations, of course we had, but he'd always looked off to the side, or at a point six feet behind me, his Adam's apple bobbing as he swallowed to work some saliva into that gorgeous mouth of his.

No, I thought, as Ruth and I said our goodbyes – if Nick's wife had even the tiniest of inklings of the plans I had for her husband, I was sure she wouldn't want to meet me at all. Unless it was to tell me to stay the hell away from him.

CHAPTER 8

'Lots!' Ruth enveloped Lottie in a perfume-filled hug. 'Feeling better, hon?'

'Much better, thanks,' Lottie said as she studied Ruth's face. She hoped Nick hadn't said anything about their failed IVF attempt. It's not that she minded Ruth knowing, of course she didn't, it was just she couldn't face the sympathy and the pitying looks – she'd had enough of those from Hannah. And, anyway, talking about it wouldn't change anything. She just wanted to forget about it for now, put it behind her until she was ready to talk to Nick about what they'd do next. He wanted to give the IVF one last go, she knew that, but she wasn't sure she could cope with the disappointment again. 'Just a summer cold,' she lied to cover why she'd been laying low for the past week and had cried off from going to the gym last night. She sat down in a chair opposite Ruth. 'You okay?'

'Me?' Ruth went over to the fancy coffee machine in the corner of her office. 'Never been better. What'll it be? Americano, cappuccino, espresso?'

'Builder's tea?'

Ruth held up a jar filled with different wrapped teabags. 'At least have a herbal tea – someone's got to drink the damn stuff.'

'I'll stick to builder's.'

'One day you'll get out of your comfort zone.'

'Look who's talking.'

Ruth ignored her, plopping a tea bag into a cup and pressing the button for hot water. She opened the small fridge that was hidden behind a cupboard door. 'Normal milk, soya, oat or almond?'

Lottie pulled a face.

'I don't even know why I'm asking.' Ruth popped two sweeteners into her own cup, before spooning a heap of sugar into Lottie's.

'Claire okay?' Lottie asked. 'Haven't seen you two for ages. Fancy coming round this weekend? I'll ask Nick to whip up his risotto.'

'Can we get a takeaway?'

Lottie laughed.

'Don't tell Bil I said his cooking was crap, will you?'

'I won't tell him you called him Bil either.' It annoyed Nick when Ruth called him that – and, obviously, that was why Ruth continued to do it. 'Do you call him that here, at work?'

'Of course I do.' Ruth grinned.

'Claire okay?' Lottie asked again. 'How's the novel coming along?'

Ruth handed her the mug. 'Yes, great. Nearly finished.'

'You've been saying that for the past ten years.'

Lottie sipped at her tea. 'Did she go for that teaching assistant job?'

Ruth pulled a face as she carried her coffee back to her desk. 'She went, but she didn't take to the head teacher who interviewed her. Something about their differing opinions as to how English Lit is taught in schools.'

'She didn't get it then?'

'Oh, she got it.'

'That's great.'

Ruth sighed.

'Isn't it?'

'She didn't accept it. Couldn't compromise her views, apparently.' Ruth shrugged.

'What have I told you, Ru? You're too soft on her. Put your foot down. I can't remember the last time she had a job.'

Ruth blew on her drink. 'I don't mind helping her out. She'll finish her novel soon and then I'm sure she'll get it published. It'll be on the shelves in Waterstones before we know it. And then she'll be able to keep me.'

'It's been years.' Lottie picked at a loose thread on her skirt.

'It takes ages to write a novel. You can't just bang it out, you know.' Ruth put down her cup. 'She'll get there one day.'

'Only if she finishes the damn thing.'

'I've told you, Lots, she's nearly finished it. She's had to do a lot of research. Don't go on about it. It is what it is.'

Lottie took a slurp of her tea, trying to figure out what to say, knowing she had to tread carefully. Ruth's temper didn't blow very often but, when it did, it was spectacular.

'Isn't there something here she could do? You keep saying you're all run off your feet.'

Ruth flinched. 'No, no way. We see each other enough at home, thank you very much.' She picked up her pen and started twirling it between her fingers. 'Come on, I mean, could you work with Bil?'

Lottie shook her head. She loved Nick to bits but she didn't want to spend every waking hour with him.

Ruth pointed her pen at Lottie. 'I rest my case.'

'Everything's okay, isn't it, between you two?'

Ruth's gaze flicked to her laptop screen. 'What?'

'Ru?'

'Yes, of course. Sorry, just let me reply to this email.'

Ruth tapped on her keyboard as Lottie looked around the room, taking in the low-slung couch in the corner, the glass coffee table, the pot plants everywhere. They'd only been in the building for six months, having moved from crappy offices on the other side of the city, but Ruth had certainly put her stamp on things. Lottie knew she worked long hours, guessed she probably preferred sitting in the office than sitting at home with misery-guts Claire.

'Everything's fine, is it, then?'

'What?' Ruth said.

'Between you and Claire?'

Ruth sighed. 'You don't have to worry about me all the time, you know?'

'That's my job, to look out for you.' And it was – she'd always looked out for Ruth. She'd lost count of the number of scrapes she'd got her out of over the years.

'I don't need looking out for, hon. Everything's fine. Honestly. We're like an old married couple, aren't we, Claire and me?'

'But without the certificate.'

'Don't *you* be going on about that as well.' Ruth shook her head. 'What's a certificate prove? Nothing. If you love each other, why do you need a piece of paper? A piece of paper won't stop a relationship falling apart. It's not superglue.'

'Is your relationship falling apart?'

'Lots! For God's sake!'

'Okay, cool it, sister.' Lottie held up her hands in a gesture of resignation.

Ruth scowled before breaking out into a grin. 'Anyway, you haven't just called to give me a grilling, have you? To what do I owe this pleasure?'

Lottie felt her cheeks redden. Ruth could always suss her out, especially when she wanted a favour.

'Ah, and I thought you were here to see me,' Ruth said. 'Can't keep away from each other you two, can you? Mr and Mrs Perfect.'

Lottie stuck out her tongue. 'If you say so. Anyway, I'm not here to see Nick. It's a favour I'm after. From you.'

'Intriguing.'

'Not really. Hannah's asked if you'd have any work for Daisy, just during the holidays.'

'Little Daisy?'

'She's nearly seventeen. Off to uni next year. She needs the money.'

'I'm sure we can find her something to do. Like you said, we're not short of work.'

'Great.'

'And?' Ruth chewed the end of her pen. 'Out with it. What else is going on? You look like you're about to pop.'

'I've got a casting later!'

'Woohoo.' Leaning over her desk, Ruth held out her hand for a high five. 'That's brilliant news, hon.'

'I know, right? It's all last minute. Jasper called me up this morning. It's for some new American drama. The producer and casting director are over here on a recce. They're after a Brit to play one of the lead parts.'

'OMG, that's amazing. Bil's going to be chuffed to bits for you.'

'God, I really hope I get it, Ru.'

'You will, of course you will. You're a brilliant actor!' Ruth jumped up out of her chair and held out her hand. 'Come on, let's go and tell that husband of yours.'

'I don't want to interrupt them,' Lottie said as she and Ruth looked over at the glass-walled meeting room where Nick and Tasha were sitting at a table, three suited and booted men opposite them.

'Those are the owners of the new hotel development. The Dolos Resort they're calling it.' Ruth sniffed. 'Sounds a bit Greek to me.'

'Ha ha, very funny,' Lottie said, slapping Ruth on the shoulder. 'Is that her then, the new PA?'

Ruth's face lit up. 'Nick's really pleased with her. Says she's got some great ideas.'

'Wasn't she just a temp? She's not an architect, is she? I thought her degree was in business?' Lottie felt herself blush. How mortifying if she had to admit that she'd googled Tasha. But she'd only been checking that she was up to the job – for Nick's sake.

Ruth didn't seem to have picked up on what Lottie had said. 'She's talking about retraining. She started off temping, just to get her foot in the door.'

'And now her foot is firmly in the door.'

'Oh, she's great,' Ruth said. 'You haven't met her yet, have you? You'll love her.'

Lottie stared at her husband and his new PA. Lottie couldn't see her face but Nick was nodding and smiling at something Tasha was saying.

'She's so nice,' Ruth continued. 'Just moved back to the area. I don't think she's got many friends, poor thing. I'm taking her into town for a drink next week.'

'Who are you taking out for a drink?' Kas appeared behind them, making them both jump.

'Hey,' he said, kissing Lottie on the cheek. 'How's my favourite woman in the whole world?'

'Hey, Kas.' Lottie gave him a hug. 'Long time, no see. How is your favourite woman in the whole world? How is Sienna doing?'

He wagged his finger at her. 'Now you know I was on about you.'

'Not sure Sienna would be impressed.'

Behind his back, Ruth was shaking her head, her eyes wide. Lottie suddenly remembered that Nick had told her things were waning between the pair.

Kas rocked back and forth on his heels. 'Sienna's gone back to Oz.'

'Oh, right. Sorry. I've put my foot in it.'

'You can put your foot in it any time you like.'

Lottie rubbed at his arm. 'Is it really over then?'

'Lots, honestly. Could she get any further away?'

'You'll soon meet someone new,' Lottie said.

He gave a mock sigh. 'All the nice girls are taken.'

She shook her head and laughed. 'I'm sure you'll find someone soon. You're still going to come to the cottage for Nick's birthday?'

'I'll be a right Billy No-Mates.'

'It's seven weeks away, the tenth of September. You're bound to have hooked up with someone by then.'

He grinned. 'That's what I love about you, Lots. Your utter belief in me.' He turned to Ruth. 'When are you taking out Tantalising Tasha? Mind if I tag along?'

'Put your tongue back in, Kas.' Ruth shook her head.

'Ooh, I've got some competition.'

'Don't be stupid.' Ruth folded her arms and stared at him. 'Haven't you got work to do?'

'Can't blame a guy for trying, eh, Lottie?' He moved off, giving Lottie a wink.

'It wouldn't have hurt to invite him,' Lottie said to Ruth. 'He's probably lonely.'

'It's a girls' night out. Hey, why don't you come along?'

Lottie sighed. 'I'm too busy with the play. Thanks, though.'

'Shame. You'd really like Tasha.'

She was sure she would. Everyone seemed to.

Ruth glanced at her watch. 'Anyway, I've got a meeting in five I need to prepare for.' She pulled Lottie towards her and kissed her cheek. 'Good luck with the audition, hon. You'll smash it. Let me know how you go on. And if it turns out you're playing opposite Lily James, you will invite me to the set, won't you?'

Lottie gave Ruth a thumbs up, before looking over at the office where Nick and Tasha and the visitors were, keeping her fingers crossed her husband would spot her and invite her in. Why shouldn't he introduce his wife to his most important clients? But he didn't see her; he was leaning towards Tasha, so close he would only have to move a couple of inches to kiss her. Lottie swallowed. And then sighed. She really needed to get a grip on her overactive imagination.

She walked slowly past the office, trying to get a good view of Tasha. But it was no use – Nick's PA had her back to her. Lottie couldn't see her face. But she could see enough. She could tell from her slender neck and the way her hair was piled up on her head that the girl was beautiful. Beautiful and young. She lifted her chin and sucked in her stomach as she made her way to the lift.

'Charlotte Moore?'

The young male assistant shouted Lottie's name, tutted while Lottie scrambled to her feet and then slammed the door after her as she entered the audition room.

At the far end of the large hotel conference room, a man and a woman sat behind a desk, various snacks and drinks spread out before them.

'Take a seat,' the man said to her, without looking up.

Lottie perched on the chair in the middle of the room.

'Hey, I'm Nuala Rogers,' the woman said with a smile. 'But everyone calls me Ginger. And this is Brad Fallon.' The man carried on flicking through some pages in front of him.

'Thanks for coming in today.' The woman had a British accent, something Lottie couldn't place but it definitely had the hint of a Mancunian twang to it. A brightly coloured scarf – pinks and yellows to match her dress – was wrapped around her head in a sort of turban, pinned so tightly it looked like she might not have any hair. A similar scarf, though a different pattern, was wrapped around her neck. Lottie couldn't stop staring at her. She was like a gorgeous exotic bird.

'You got the script?' Ginger said. 'Sorry we haven't given you a lot of time to prepare.'

'We've been struggling to find anyone.' Brad rubbed his hand across his forehead, but still didn't look up.

Lottie felt her stomach drop. Great. She was probably one of the last in a long line of people they'd seen. Still, if they were struggling to find someone, surely that meant her chances were pretty good?

There had only been two other women waiting in the hallway. Lottie recognised one of them – a soap actor who, according to the tabloids, had been sacked because she was a bit too fond of the drink. The other woman had four kids and had recently separated from her husband who had cheated on her with her younger sister. Lottie knew this because the woman had told her the whole story while they waited. 'A right fucking bitch' she'd called her sister, adding that she'd warned her to watch her back. 'No one would blame a wife for getting her revenge, would they?' she'd said to Lottie as she made a slicing motion across her neck. Thankfully, the young assistant had then called Lottie's name, saving her from answering.

'We won't take just anyone,' Brad said. 'The person has to be right for the role.'

A bead of sweat trickled between Lottie's breasts. She took off her jacket, wishing she'd put on a blouse with sleeves, aware her arms were starting to go. She hadn't quite got bingo wings – not yet – but they wouldn't be far off.

Ginger tapped her pen against her impossibly white teeth. 'How about you tell us a bit about yourself?'

'Well, I studied at the Bristol Old Vic. I've been in a couple of independent films, done a lot of radio work over the years, a few bit parts here and there, and a couple of theatre tours. I've done some voice-over work too. Adverts, audiobooks, that sort of thing.'

Brad whispered in Ginger's ear.

She scribbled something on her pad. 'Can you do an RP accent? You know Americans.' She rolled her eyes. 'They struggle to understand anyone who doesn't sound like the Queen.'

Brad shot her a scowl.

Lottie put on her poshest accent. 'Oh, golly, I can certainly do upper class. I once played a second cousin – or was it third – to the dowager countess in *Downton Abbey*. Maggie

Smith was the countess.' She didn't add that she'd only had two lines – and that those had been cut.

Ginger laughed. Brad continued to scowl.

'You want to read for us then?' Ginger said. 'You have a copy of the extract with you?'

Lottie blushed. The script was sitting on the console table at home. It had been the only thing she'd had to remember to bring with her. 'I've learnt it,' she said, hoping that this time her memory didn't fail her.

'Impressive,' Ginger said. 'You only got it this morning, didn't you?'

'I'm a quick learner.'

Brad finally looked up, pulling his glasses from his head and putting them on. 'Is there anything that might stop you getting a work visa for the States? Any criminal convictions, drug offences, anything like that?'

'Nothing I've been caught for. Yet, anyway.'

Ginger smiled. Brad didn't.

'You read the brief then?' Ginger asked. 'The part we're casting for is a woman in her late forties, someone with a bit of sass but who's no schmuck. The series starts with the woman finding out her husband has cheated on her.'

Lottie thought of the woman sitting outside – she would certainly be able to play the part convincingly.

'We're looking for a crazy bitch,' Brad said, his nostrils flaring. 'Do you think you can do "crazy bitch"?'

'It's my middle name.' Alongside liar, she thought – she didn't often have call to be crazy. Still if Brad wanted crazy, that's what she'd give him.

Brad put his hands behind his head. 'Great. And you're—' he glanced down at his notes '—forty-five, but I can see you can do late forties no problem.'

'Brad!' Ginger said. 'Ignore him. This British weather makes him grouchy.'

Lottie swallowed, aware her face was aflame. Brad was going to get the full crazy bitch from her in a minute if he wasn't careful.

'You're free to travel?' Brad said, leaning back in his chair. 'We'll be shooting both series back-to-back so it would mean a six-month commitment. No problem with your husband or kids?'

Lottie took a deep breath. Would he ask a male actor the same question? Brad was doing a good job at riling her. Maybe that was part of his plan. She crossed her arms. 'I don't have children.'

'Cool.'

She plastered a smile onto her face. Did she want this job? Could she stand to work with someone like him?

'So no barriers to spending a good chunk of time in LA?' Ginger asked. 'Your husband okay with that?'

'Yes, of course.' Nick would be made up. And so would she. Six months away from the UK. Six months away from Nick's office. Six months away from normal lives. From all the stress of the fertility treatment. It was just what they needed. New surroundings, a fresh start away from all that had gone on. And Nick loved the US. He would jump at the chance. He could work from wherever he needed to.

Ginger poured a glass of water and took it over to Lottie, her dress – a diaphanous material – flapping around her as if she were about to take off. She had on gorgeous high heels, vertiginous emerald spikes that Lottie was amazed she could walk in.

'In your own time,' Ginger said. 'Break a leg.'

Lottie took a deep breath and began. She hadn't had time to practise much but she gave it her all, striding across the room, crying at one point when the script called for it – that wasn't a stretch, she only had to think of the call from the clinic last Wednesday – and shouting with rage the next. She thanked her overactive imagination for planting a picture of Tasha in Nick's car in her head, her hand resting on his leg as he drove along, holding on to the image even though she knew it was nonsense. Brad wanted crazy? She could do crazy.

By the time she'd finished, she was shaking. She wiped at her top lip, at the damp she could feel there.

Ginger clapped. 'Bravo!'

Brad scowled at Ginger and then at Lottie.

'Ask the next person in on your way out,' Brad said, with a flick of his hand.

'Thanks for coming,' Ginger said. 'Great to meet you. I'll be in touch. Very soon.'

'Thanks for letting me audition.' Lottie grabbed her bag and pushed back her shoulders. Despite not getting any of the castings she'd been to in the past year, she had a good feeling about this one. She'd obviously impressed Ginger, even if Brad seemed to have taken an instant dislike to her.

Lottie stopped at the door and turned to give Ginger a smile, knowing that this woman had the power to change her life. *Pick me, pick me,* she wanted to shout. *I can be the crazy bitch you're looking for.*

CHAPTER 9

'What's this shite?'

Before I could duck my old man picked up his plate and flung it across the kitchen. It smashed against a cupboard, red shards of crockery flying everywhere. The spaghetti bolognaise clung to the plastic door, slowly slithering down in one large lump, until it dropped with a huge splat onto the brown lino.

With a shake of his head, he snatched up his *Sun* newspaper and stomped out of the room, slamming the kitchen door behind him. The TV went on, the noise nearly deafening me. It wouldn't be long before the old bag next door started hammering, firstly on the adjoining wall and then on the front window.

I took the cloth out of the full washing-up bowl and started to wipe at the cupboard door and the floor, before getting out the dustpan and brush and trying to sweep up the broken plate. My arms worked furiously. How dare he. How bloody dare he? Did he think I'd be here if I had a choice, if he hadn't blackmailed me with his cock-and-bull sob story into staying?

Chronic fatigue syndrome, that's what he'd been diagnosed with. I hadn't believed him, had insisted I went to the doc's with him, just to make sure he wasn't having me on, that his inability to get out of bed some days wasn't just down to him being a lazy arse. And despite the doctor confirming his diagnosis, I still didn't believe him – my dad was adept at pulling the wool over most people's eyes – he was surely doing it just to get the social. He had no trouble going to the pub most nights, or walking down to the bookie's. It was doing a job, or even thinking about doing one, that would have him lying in bed.

'You're lucky you have your daughter to take care of you,' Dr Baxter had said to Dad. 'You couldn't manage on your own.'

I'd smiled, the dutiful daughter, and asked the question I'd been wanting to know the answer to since the doc had confirmed the diagnosis: 'How long will it take him to recover?'

Dr Baxter had taken off his glasses and rubbed at the bridge of his nose. 'Well, it's difficult to say with something like this. Some days he might be quite well and others . . . well, others he'll struggle to get out of bed. The thing to do is to not overexert himself. Just doing the washing-up could set him back for some time.'

I had to stop myself from laughing out loud. Washing up? When I got back there was a mountain of crockery all over the house. It was as if he hadn't washed up for the three years I was away. 'Okay, I get that,' I said in answer to the doc, 'but when will he be over it? How long will it take him to be back to normal?'

Dr Baxter's fingers fidgeted with the corner of a piece of paper on his desk. 'It's hard to say. Some people do get over it, in time; whereas others . . .'

I'd wanted to cry. Right there in the surgery. Bawl my bloody eyes out. Was it some sort of joke, something they'd cooked up between them? Would they collapse into fits of giggles at any moment and shout, *Fell for that one, didn't you?*

But no, it seemed they wouldn't. So I left with a prescription for the chemist in one hand, my other hand supporting the old man under his elbow, him clinging on to me, dragging me down. The old fucker. I would catch him out. I hadn't been back long but one day I would catch him out. He needn't think I'd stay around, just 'cos he was having everyone on. And, anyway, I had things to do. People to love, to live with. Nick.

The TV blared on. Some crap he watched on some obscure channel. I tipped the remains of his spag bol into the bin. I should have known it was a mistake to serve him something he considered 'foreign'. But I'd wanted to practise. I'd never been much good at cooking and while I preferred a takeaway, I was guessing Nick would want a woman who could rustle up something more exotic than beans or cheese on toast.

Taking a beef roast ready meal out of the freezer, I banged it in the microwave and looked at my watch. The old git was off to the pub tonight, would announce himself well enough to take the car, and wouldn't be back until well past last orders, minus the car. Funny how his illness never showed itself at night-time. And funny how he always took the car. He did it just to spite me, knowing I'd take his keys and use it if he wasn't around.

Sod him. What did I care? With him out of the house, I was free to do what I wanted. I'd have plenty of time to spruce myself up, jump on my bike and cycle past Nick's house. It wasn't far. Half an hour if I took the short cut through the estate, forty minutes if I cycled around it. It all depended on who was about. If Kenny was hanging around, swigging from a can of Diamond White, I'd be done for. Honestly, how old was he? This estate, being back here with Dad, it was as if time had stood still. Kenny had always been a bum, a loser, and always would be. First, he'd take the piss out of me for riding a pushbike instead of a proper bike – which was a joke as my hair-dryer had more power than the scooter thing he drove – and second, he'd start on at me, as he always did: 'Fancy a drink? No? Reckon you're better than me, do you? Just 'cos you work in some fancy office. You didn't mind when we were kids. Couldn't get enough of me then.'

It didn't matter if I ignored him or shouted at him to leave me alone, that he should get over it, get over me – a few fumblings in the first year at high school, before he got kicked out, and he thought we were soulmates. It was my own fault for getting in the taxi with him last week. I should have pretended I didn't know him, should have jumped in the other taxi. Made Nick get in with me.

The microwave pinged. It'd better be bloody worth it.

Wifey had better be out. Round at Ruth's having a sisterly chinwag or on a Friday night out with the girls. I didn't care, as long as she wasn't there.

I imagined the surprise on Nick's face. Surprise and then delight. I didn't know what excuse I'd give him for knocking on his door, but I would work that out when I got there. Something would come to me. It always did. And maybe, just maybe, I wouldn't need an excuse. If the look on his face the other night at the hotel when I'd jumped off the ladder was anything to go by, I wouldn't need any excuse at all.

She wasn't out. Wifey.

I stood in the dark, grateful they lived on the way out of town, on a country lane, grateful there were no street-lamps to light me. I had a torch with me, of course – it was bloody dark out there, but I'd switched it off before I wheeled my bike anywhere near to their house.

They weren't overlooked by any neighbours. Which might explain why none of their curtains were drawn. Who was around to gawp through the windows? A passing farmer on a tractor? A smelly sheep in the field over the road?

So I stood there, in the pitch-black, about twenty feet away from their window, in the shadow of their boundary wall, staring at them as they sat at their kitchen island, eating. I couldn't make out what was on their plates but I was guessing it wasn't a ready meal ping dinner. They were sharing a bottle of wine, Nick drinking more than her, topping up his glass every five minutes. She was jabbering away, gesturing with her hands as if she were telling the most interesting story ever, while Nick shovelled the food into his mouth, and – from what it looked like to me – nodded in all the right places.

God, was he bored or what? Did she ever shut up? Did she ever let him get a word in edgeways? It wasn't a conversation they were having, just a one-sided splurge from her.

Perhaps he was used to it though. Perhaps he'd learnt to shut out her droning on. I remembered what Ruth had said about them wanting to have a baby and not being able to. Perhaps wifey was boring him to death about her ovulation cycle, telling him when they'd have to get down to it. She looked like the type who'd have a chart pinned to the wall somewhere. Poor Nick. No wonder he'd seemed to get excited when I'd fallen into his arms. I imagined sex for him and his dried-up witch of a wife was just in and out. Routine. Very boring.

He yawned. It was as if he'd picked up on my thoughts. Or maybe I'd picked up on his. He topped up his glass again. Obviously drinking to get through the evening with her. How many times had he wished he'd chosen someone else, someone like me? Someone young and exciting? Someone who could give him kids, unlike his useless wife?

And then they were getting up, Nick stacking the dishwasher, wifey slapping him away and rearranging the pans. He bent down, out of sight behind the island, appearing a few seconds later, another bottle of wine in his hand. She shook her head but he opened it anyway, filling her glass despite her trying to move it away from him.

I would drink with him. I would drink with him all night if that's what he wanted. I bet she was one of those prissy women, the sort who totalled up each week how many glasses of wine she'd had, who never went over the recommended amount, both for her health and her waistline. I wasn't surprised. She wasn't a slim Jim, by anyone's imagination. She'd done that thing I'd seen some of the girls I'd lived with while I was away do once they got comfortable in a relationship – she'd let herself go. Her hair was piled up on her head, not in a chic way, like you see in a magazine, just plonked on her head in a scrunchie. No surprise there – she seemed like the sort of woman who didn't like to let her hair down. Not what Nick needed. Or deserved.

They moved into the living room and I followed them, leaving my bike by the outside wall and, careful not to make any noise on the gravel, moving around to the other side of the house.

Nick chose a single chair, pointing the remote at the TV, while she settled onto the sofa. But then she was patting the seat next to her, beckoning him over.

Don't. Don't. I said the words in my head like a mantra.

But he got up and went over to the sofa, putting his arm around her and pulling her into him.

I felt tears prick at my eyes. What was he doing? He was mine. It was me who should be sitting there with him, breathing in the spice of his aftershave, my hand on his chest, his belt buckle, my fingers working away to free him.

There was a sound and it took me a few seconds to realise that I was making it. I was crying.

Nick looked up, towards the window. Did he know I

was here? Would he leave her, come running out to me, wanting to know what was wrong? Would he put his arms around me? Hold me?

But his gaze moved back to the TV and then to her face as she reached up and kissed him.

I bit so hard on my bottom lip I could taste blood in my mouth. I wanted to kill her. In that moment, I wanted to kill her.

She got up suddenly, peering out into the night, as if she could see me, a frown on her face, before she drew the curtains, shutting me out.

Perhaps she knew then I wouldn't let her stand in my way. Perhaps she knew then I was after her husband, that I wanted to take him away from her. Perhaps she knew then she would kill me before she would let me do that.

CHAPTER 10

'What are you doing here?' Lottie whispered.

'Nice way to greet your husband.' He kissed her cheek. 'Managed to get away from work early for a change. Came to see how things were going. And thought I'd take you for a drink afterwards to make up for having to work for most of the weekend.' He put his arm around her waist. 'Will you be long?'

'What do you think?' Lottie nodded towards the stage where gangly fourteen-year-old Dylan stood, one hand on his hip, words – though not necessarily the right ones – tumbling from his mouth. What he lacked in recall, he made up for in cockiness.

'Is that your new leading man?' Nick snorted. 'I've got more acting ability in my little finger.'

'The part's yours,' Lottie said, giving him a little push. 'Go on.'

She giggled at his horrified expression. 'Go and sit out the front. Your folks are there.'

Nick peeped around the edge of the stage curtain. 'What are they doing here?'

'Don't you recognise it? The throne Daisy is sitting on?'

'Oh, God. The tip is the only place for that old thing. Hang on, that's not Daisy, is it?' he whispered. 'Last time I saw her she was a spotty adolescent. You ought to be doing *The Ugly Duckling*. She's certainly blossomed.'

'I know, I've said to Hannah she should go to drama school. She's got a natural talent and with looks like that she—'

'Shush!' Dylan glared over at them.

'Sorry, sorry!' Lottie said.

Dylan stuck out his bottom lip. 'I've lost my line now.'

Lottie flicked over the page in the script she was holding. Where was it now? Ah, there it was. '"And do you think you might have told me you were leaving me?"'

'I've done that one.' Shaking his head, he let out a long, theatrical sigh.

'"It's lies, all lies,"' Daisy said.

This time Dylan stamped his foot. 'I'm not lying.'

'It's your next line, idiot. "It's lies, all lies."'

Nick snorted. Lottie, trying not to do the same, shooed him away.

'Are you sure you don't want to come to the pub with us?' Lottie said, when she'd finally ushered the last of the kids out of the door.

Nick's parents were shrugging on their jackets.

'The chair will be okay here, won't it?' Zipping up his maroon blouson, Felix frowned.

109

'Nick'll move it into the storeroom, won't you, darling? It'll be quite safe.'

'Don't worry, Felix,' Gwen said. 'It's only a fusty old chair.'

Felix pushed his glasses up onto the bridge of his nose. 'It's been in my family for years that has. I'd hate to see it ruined.'

'It's been in the cellar at Fairview for years.' Gwen sniffed.

'And that's why I took it out of there.' He looked around him before lowering his voice. 'I found some droppings there.'

'Mice?' Lottie shuddered. She hated mice, anything with a tail.

Behind the lenses of his glasses, Felix's eyes narrowed. 'A bit larger than that.'

'Urgh! Rats? No.'

'Don't be a silly girl now,' Gwen said, tutting. 'A rat won't hurt you. Imagine how a rat would feel if it saw you towering over it.'

Lottie clamped her lips shut to stop herself from biting back at Gwen. One of these days she would give Nick's mother what for, would tell her where to shove her snide comments.

Felix put his hand on Lottie's arm. 'It's quite all right. I've put down some poison. That'll soon get rid of them.'

'We're going to pop up there every week or so and check what's happening with them. Make sure they're gone for . . . you know.' Gwen widened her eyes at Lottie.

Lottie stifled a groan. Trust Gwen to try to ruin Nick's surprise. But it was fine. He hadn't heard what his mother was saying – he was engrossed in his phone, tapping away on it.

'Anyway, you won't allow the children to eat or drink when they're sitting on it, will you? Or stick chewing gum under the seat. I know very well what kids are like.'

'Felix.' Gwen's voice took on an even higher pitch than normal. 'Things have changed a bit since you stood at the front of the classroom and, anyway, Louise has everything in hand, I'm sure.'

'Mum!' Nick's head whipped up from his phone.

'What? What did I say?' Gwen had a smirk on her face. 'Oh, heavens, did I call you Louise? Sorry, Lottie. What can I say? It's my age.'

'Don't worry about it,' Lottie said, turning to stack the chairs. 'Honestly, it's not a problem.' Lottie meant it. It wasn't the first time Gwen had called her by Nick's first wife's name. It didn't matter to her, even if Gwen was hoping it would. Louise had been dead for seventeen years, but had been a part of Nick's life for twelve years before that, his childhood sweetheart from the age of fourteen. Lottie remembered when she'd first met Gwen, how Gwen had gasped, had said, 'Oh, but you're *very* like Louise. She had such an angelic face though.' Lottie had laughed it off. Let Gwen dig at her all she liked. It hadn't mattered to Lottie then that Nick had been married before – and that, in his mother's eyes, no one could ever take Louise's place – and it didn't matter now. Louise wasn't a threat.

And yet Gwen had been right: she and Nick's first wife were very similar. Lottie had found their wedding album in a box in the attic, not long after she had moved into Nick's house, and had flicked through it guiltily – both she and Louise had long red hair and pale, freckled skin. An image of Tasha and her Titian locks came into her head. She put her hand to her hair, suddenly wishing that she had kept it long, like Nick had wanted her to.

'I am sorry, Lottie,' Gwen said, emphasising *Lottie* long and slowly, the smirk a thin red line on her powdered face.

Felix coughed. 'Anyway, you'll take care of the chair?'

Lottie squeezed Felix's arm. 'It'll be fine. I swear on my life,' she said, and immediately wished she hadn't.

'Oh no, dear, don't do that. It's not that much of a treasure. Whereas you,' he said, kissing her on the cheek, 'most definitely are.'

Nick rolled his eyes and chewed at his lip.

Lottie returned Gwen's glare with a smile. Felix always made a fuss of her. He was a former English Lit teacher and then a research associate in the literature department at the uni, and they could chat for hours about books they liked.

'If I could have my wife back, please.' Nick grabbed hold of Lottie's hand.

'He takes after me – Nicky. He never did like to share,' Gwen said as she picked up her bag. 'I remember when he gave – now what was his name? – Alec, that's it, the little boy who lived across the road, a right pasting.'

'A pasting? Over what?' Lottie looked at Nick. She

112

couldn't imagine him giving anyone a pasting – he wasn't the violent type.

'Something to do with a toy car, wasn't it, Nicky? Or was it a toy train?'

Nick scowled as he cracked his knuckles. 'I pushed him over, that was all. We were seven.'

Felix peered at Nick over his glasses. 'It was a bit more than that if I remember rightly. Didn't the poor lad's parents come round?'

'We'd better be getting back,' Gwen said, grabbing Felix by the elbow.

'Thanks for dropping off the chair,' Lottie said, ushering them to the door. Nick was about to blow.

'Yes, that's right,' Felix said. 'They ended up calling the local bobby to have a word with him.'

'How would you know? You weren't there.' Nick stood with his feet planted far apart, his arms crossed. 'Wasn't that before your time?'

'Don't be rude, Nicky.' Gwen turned to Felix. 'You didn't mean anything by it, did you now, darling?'

'Or maybe you were there, hey, Felix? The friendly next-door neighbour, sniffing around my mother even before my parents split up. Maybe that's why they split up.'

Felix shook his head. 'You know that's not why, Nick.'

'Do I?'

'Come on, Felix.' Gwen plucked at the arm of Felix's jacket.

Felix shrugged her off. 'I think Nick should apologise.'

'Or what? You'll send me to my room? I'm not a child anymore, you know,' Nick hissed.

'Then don't act like one,' Felix said.

Nick snorted, opened his mouth, closed it again, and then pushed past them, banging the hall door behind him as he left.

Lottie sighed. Gwen and Felix had been married for thirty years and Nick still couldn't accept it. Which was strange as it wasn't as if Nick had anything to do with his real dad – he never even talked about him. Never. Lottie had tried to get him to open up over the years, counting on a bottle of red wine to loosen his tongue, but he refused to be drawn. Lottie didn't even know his real father's name. Whatever had happened had cut him deeply. Poor Nick. He hadn't had it easy. First his father leaving him, and then Louise.

'Ignore him. He's got a lot on at work,' Lottie said, kissing Felix on the cheek. Whatever had happened back then, she was certain that gentle, lovely Felix was not to blame at all.

Gwen sniffed. 'Maybe it would be for the best if we didn't come up to the cottage for his birthday weekend.'

'Don't be silly,' Lottie said, despite the fact that she would much prefer it if Gwen and her barbed comments weren't there for what was supposed to be a couple of days of celebration and fun. 'He'll have forgotten about it in an hour.'

'He does fly off the handle at the silliest little things. Anyway,' she said, making a 'mwah' sound as she kissed the air a couple of inches from Lottie's left and then right cheek, 'lovely to see you, darling. I'm sure you'll knock the play into shape. I don't know why you chose

114

such a complicated one – all that trickery with moving back and forth through time, and there are so many characters. You can't go wrong with something nice and simple like *Jack and the Beanstalk*.'

Felix rolled his eyes at Lottie. 'How many weeks till opening night?'

'Just over five. The week before Nick's birthday.'

'Lovely.' Gwen sniffed. 'Plenty of time to turn it around then.'

Lottie's stomach dropped. Was the play a mess or was Gwen just being her usual bitchy self? At the start of the rehearsal Lottie had gone over to say hello to a group of the mums. As soon as she got near to them they'd stopped talking. Were they discussing how best to extricate their kids from the theatre group so they could enrol them in the new one? It wouldn't surprise her. She just hoped they wouldn't do that before the play opened.

From somewhere a mobile started to ring.

'That'll be Nick,' Lottie said. 'He's probably down the road in the Queen's Head.'

She waved them off and scooted over to her bag.

But it wasn't Nick. It was a number she didn't recognise.

'Hello?' Hello?' Damn it, had she missed the call?

She peered at the screen and then put the phone back to her ear.

'Hello?' she said again.

'Is that Charlotte?'

'Yes, speaking.'

'Hey, Charlotte. Ginger here.'

For a second, she couldn't place the voice or the name. But then she realised who it was: the casting director from America. The Brit in the peacock dress. 'Oh, hello.'

'Not caught you at a bad time? Sorry to call out of working hours.'

'No. It's not a problem. None at all.'

Lottie held her breath. Why was Ginger calling her at this time of night? It couldn't be, could it? She, Charlotte Moore, the washed-out, old has-been actress hadn't gone and got the part, had she?

Lottie walked over to the table where Nick sat glued to his phone.

'Grab this,' she said, her arm nearly dropping off thanks to the weight of the ice bucket she was carrying.

Nick slipped his phone into his jacket pocket.

'Sorry, work?' Lottie said.

'Never mind that. What's all this?' He nodded at the bottle of Moët nestling in the wine bucket. 'What are we celebrating? You haven't done old fart Felix in, have you?'

'Don't be mean.'

'Sorry.' He grabbed her hand and kissed her knuckles. 'I'm apologising to you. Not to him.'

'Well, you should do. You were bloody rude.' She slipped off her jacket. 'Really, Nick, you need to get over it. Your mother's happy. Doesn't that mean anything to you?'

'Of course it does,' he said, taking her jacket from her and placing it on the large windowsill behind them. 'I just wish she was happy with someone else.'

116

'You're jealous. Felix is lovely.' She was goading him, as she'd done in the past. He always looked like he wanted to say something about his stepfather but that whatever he did want to say was somehow stuck inside him. As it was now.

'I just don't like the bloke.'

With a sigh, she leant forward and kissed him. That was all she was going to get out of him today.

'Enough about him,' he said, holding her hand and rubbing his thumb across her palm. 'What's with the champagne?'

'I got it!'

His face was blank.

And then she realised she hadn't told him about the audition, had convinced herself in the five days since she'd gone to the casting that she wouldn't get it, that they were probably after someone younger, prettier, slimmer than her. So she hadn't told Nick anything about going for the part, hadn't wanted him to get excited when she knew there was no hope at all.

Only there was now, wasn't there? No need for hope, though. She'd got it!

'How do you fancy six months in the US?' she said, unable to stop the grin spreading across her face.

'The States?'

'Los Angeles.'

'What are you on about, Lots?'

'I went for an audition last Friday.'

'And?'

'I only got it!'

117

'What? Oh my God, darling. That's brilliant.' He pulled her towards him, feathering kisses all over her face until she moved away. 'But you never said! You didn't say, did you? Have I not been listening again? This Dolos Resort job, it's—'

'I didn't tell you because I didn't think I'd get it. And after the audition, I definitely didn't think I would.'

'Oh?'

'Some arsehole of a bloke there.'

'But you did get it.'

'Yes!'

'That's brilliant. Just brilliant.'

'I know, I can't believe it.' She took the bottle of Moët out of the ice bucket and handed it to Nick. 'Are you going to open that, or what? Let's leave the car. Get a taxi back.'

Nick removed the foil and twisted the wire, turning the bottle until the cork popped out with a gentle hiss. He filled their glasses and handed one to her. 'To my gorgeous, talented wife!'

As they clinked glasses he reached over again and kissed her.

'Tell me all about it then.'

'It's a new US show. A miniseries. In LA. Six months. All that sun.'

'Oh, Lots, I'm so pleased for you. I'm jealous though. Will you let your poor little husband visit?'

'What?' Lottie took a sip of her champagne. 'You're coming with me. We can rent a house. On the beach maybe. Malibu? Isn't that where the stars live? Who knows, J.Lo and Ben Affleck might be our neighbours.' Lottie laughed and topped up her glass.

'How much are they paying you?' Nick said. 'Sounds heavenly, sweetheart, it really does, but I can't go to the States just like that, can I? I've got the business to run. The new hotel development. It's turning into a much bigger project than I imagined.'

'So you keep telling me. You promised to take me to see it at the weekend.'

'Sorry, darling. I'll take you there soon.' He ran his hand through his hair. 'And much as I'd love to come to LA with you, I just can't get away at the moment.'

Lottie took a large swig of her drink, coughing when the bubbles went up her nose – Nick always looked at the downside of things before he looked at the positives. 'You can work from anywhere, can't you? You came with me before when I did that show down in London.'

'But that was London. And I commuted up and down. Cost me a fortune on the train. You're talking about LA. It's the other side of the world.'

'There's Zoom. You do work from home sometimes now.'

'I have to be here, darling. The hotel project is massive. I—'

'What about Kas?' she said, cutting him off.

'I'm sure he'd love to go with you.'

Lottie swiped at his arm. 'I meant . . . can't he help you out with the hotel job?'

'Dolos is more than a job, Lots. And, anyway, Kas has got his own projects. You know we're really busy.'

119

'But it's only six months.'

'Exactly. Six months. It'll go by like that,' he said as he clicked his fingers. 'You go. I'll come out for a couple of weeks when I can get away. It'll fly by.'

Lottie put down her glass. 'I'm not going without you.'

'Don't be daft. Of course you are. This is a great opportunity for you. You can't let it pass you by, just because of my job.'

Lottie shook her head. 'There'll be others.'

'A US TV show? It's something you've always dreamed about. You have to go.'

She crossed her arms. 'I'll miss you.'

'And I'll miss you, darling. But it's the job of a lifetime. What's Jasper said?'

She'd called her agent on the way to the pub. He knew, of course, had been dying to call her, but Ginger had apparently insisted on being the bearer of the good news. 'He'll be fine about it. I haven't signed a contract. I'm not going.'

'Lots, you—'

She grabbed hold of Nick's hand. 'I don't like leaving you home alone.'

'I'm a very big boy, now. I can take care of myself.' He took a swig of his champagne. 'Though I can't promise I won't be calling in at the Siam Orchid most nights for a takeaway.'

'There'll be other parts.'

'Darling, you have to take it. It'll be good for you. After, well,' he said, taking a deep breath, 'after the IVF. It'll give you a break. Let you clear your head. Give you some time to think about whether we should give it one last go.'

She squeezed his hand. 'I will think about it, I promise. I know it's what you want. But I wanted us to go to LA together.'

'I'll come and visit you when I can and—'

'No.' Why was he pushing her like this? Did he want rid of her for six months? And if so, why? An image of Tasha came into her mind, of her flaming red hair, Nick's hand on the small of her back, their heads together, within kissing distance, in the meeting room. She swallowed.

'What, you won't let me visit you? Oh right, you'll be having it away with all those movie stars over there, is that it?' He pinched at her waist but she smacked away his hand.

'You can trust *me*.' The words – or rather the emphasis she placed on the 'me' – shocked her as much as they seemed to have shocked Nick.

His brow furrowed. 'And you can trust me, darling – you know that.'

She picked up her glass. Of course she trusted him. This was Nick. 'Sorry,' she said, reaching for his hand again, rubbing her fingers over his palm. 'I don't know why I said that. Of course I trust you.'

What had got into her? Was it Gwen bringing up his ex-wife – his gorgeous ex-wife – that had got to her? She downed her drink. Bloody Louise. Bloody Miss Perfect. If Louise had lived, would she have been able to give Nick the child he wanted? No doubt she would have, a whole bloody gaggle of kids.

121

She topped up their glasses. 'Come on, let's celebrate.'

'Here's to you,' he said, holding his glass out to her. 'My brilliant wife. To your new job. And to six months in Los Angeles. You lucky thing.'

Lottie raised her glass. She was lucky. She had a part that most actors would die for. And a husband who loved her. She put the glass to her lips. She really did have it all.

CHAPTER 11

'Bloody hell, you nearly gave me a coronary,' I said, my hand flying to my heart. 'I didn't think anyone would still be here.'

Nick yawned as he walked across the office towards me. 'Big meeting tomorrow about the hotel project.'

'You work too hard,' I said. 'Can't Kas help you out?'

He rolled his eyes. 'You sound like my wife.'

If only, I thought, as Nick leant past me and switched on my desk light.

'You've not come to rob the place, have you? Not sure you'd find much. A few packets of biscuits. Hobnobs, if you're lucky.'

I giggled. He looked good, better than ever. His shirtsleeves were rolled up, he had a six o'clock shadow on his face, and his hair was sticking up as if he'd been running his fingers through it. 'I've lost my purse.'

'Is it in your bag?'

It's a good thing the lighting was low – he couldn't see the blush spreading up my neck. I hugged my bag to me. 'No. I've had it inside out.'

'That's what my wife always says. And guess what? It's usually in there somewhere.'

'Well, I'm not your wife, am I?' The words were sharper than I wanted them to be. I smiled to soften them. 'It definitely isn't in there.'

Nick cocked his head to the side. 'Do you want me to have a look?'

'It's not in there.' I opened my desk drawers, my eyes and fingers searching through them.

'Any luck?' Nick asked.

'Nope.'

He got down on his hands and knees, pulled out my chair and started searching under the desk. His back strained at his blue shirt. I wanted to reach down and touch him, to take off his shirt, rip off my top and lay my skin against his. 'Nothing under here.'

'Watch your head,' I said, but it was too late – he gave it a right wallop on the corner of the desk. 'Oh, shit, are you all right?'

He pushed himself up, shaking his head back and forth and then rubbing at the spot where he'd cracked it. 'I'll live.'

'Let me look.'

'I'm fine.'

'Sit.'

He sat down in my chair, swivelling it so he had his back to me. I stood as close as I could to the chair without touching him and yet I could still feel his body, like a magnet, pulling me towards him.

'Anything there?' he said.

I touched his dark hair, smoothing it down, wanting to cover it in kisses. 'It's bleeding.'

He patted at the spot, pulling his fingers away to reveal blood on them. 'It's just a graze – it'll be fine.'

'It looks a bit more than a graze. I'll get the first aid box.'

'I'm fine. Honestly.' He got up and made his way back to his office.

'Where are you going?' I said, following him. 'Maybe you should go to A&E. Get it checked out?'

He reached in his jacket pocket and got out his wallet. 'Here,' he said, holding out two twenty-pound notes. 'Take it. And cancel your bank cards.'

I shook my head. 'It's probably on the kitchen table at home.'

'Take it,' he said just as a trickle of blood made its way down his forehead. He touched his fingers to it and then looked at the blood on them.

'Stay there.'

I hurried over to Pauline's desk where the first aid box was kept. This was going better than I'd expected. I'd imagined a bit of flirting, followed by a suggestion, from him, of course, that we could grab a drink somewhere. I didn't imagine I'd get to touch him, to play nurse, to be so close I could breathe him in.

'Give it here,' he said as I strode back into his office. 'I can do it.' He held out his hand but I ignored him.

'You're not a very good patient, are you?' I laid the box on his desk, opened it and found some antiseptic wipes and a roll of plaster. 'Have you got any scissors?'

'Somewhere.' He scrabbled about in his top drawer, before opening the larger drawer underneath. There was a bottle of Jack Daniel's in there, two crystal tumblers.

'Good for shock – whiskey.'

'I'm not sure I'm in shock.'

'I am.'

His mobile suddenly started to ring. We both glanced at the caller display. His wife.

'Don't mind me,' I said.

He reached over as if he was going to answer it, but then he touched the screen and the ringing stopped.

'Are you going to do the honours?' I said, nodding at the bottle.

'Go on then. But just a small one. I have to get going.' He tapped his fingers on his phone.

'Sure. We're not planning an all-nighter, are we? I have places to be myself.'

'Oh? Who's the lucky man?' He blushed when he realised what he'd said.

'Woman.'

His face went even redder. 'Oh, sorry, I didn't realise.'

'A friend,' I said. 'Just a friend.'

'I should just pour the drinks, shouldn't I?' He lifted the tumblers and the bottle out of the drawer. 'Ah, here they are.' He handed me a pair of scissors.

I cut the plaster while he poured the drinks.

'What shall we drink to?' I said as he passed me my glass.

'How about to you finding your purse?'

For a second, he nearly caught me out, but my brain

caught up with my face and I smiled, clinking my tumbler against his and taking a swig of the whiskey. It was fiery in my mouth, down my throat. Another sip and I could feel the alcohol rushing to my head. I put down my glass. 'Let's sort you out.'

I took an antibacterial wipe out of a pack in the box and stood behind him, dabbing at the cut on his head. 'Ever thought of being a nurse?' he said. 'You've got a very light touch.'

'My mother was a nurse.'

'Was? What does she do now?'

'She doesn't do anything.'

'Oh God, sorry. When did you lose her?'

I dabbed at the cut again. 'Oh, it was a long time ago. I was very young.'

'That must have been hard.'

I swallowed. 'It was.' It wasn't. I don't think I even cried. She'd never shown me any affection when she was there, so when she left, I didn't miss her at all. I'd never felt any love for her, just as she'd never felt any love for me. But hate? I hated her all right. But alongside that there was an emptiness too, a dirty fucking hollow where that mother-daughter bond should have sat.

'Anyway, I didn't get my nursing skills from my mother. I'm forever patching up my brother Danny's boys. Those two can't go anywhere without falling over and scraping their knees.'

'How old?'

'Five. Twins.'

'Ah, that must be nice.'

'I love them to bits.' I dabbed at his head. 'You got kids?'

'No. Haven't been blessed with them. Yet. Ouch,' he said as I sprayed some antibacterial onto the cut.

'Does it hurt?'

'Well, you start to think you might never have them . . . oh, sorry.' He coughed. 'You meant the cut.'

I put the plaster on his head and swivelled him towards me. 'You'll have them one day,' I said.

'Hope so.'

'I can't wait. I want to be a young mum.'

'I'm sure you'll make a great mum.' He took a swig of his drink, before pointing to his head. 'Will I live, then?'

'Just about.' I threw the wipe into the bin. 'It might be worth getting checked out by a professional though.'

'Oh, I think you're the only professional I need.' He coughed again when he realised what he'd said. 'What, with your mum being a nurse. You must have inherited some of her genes.'

Jesus, I hoped I hadn't. She didn't give a shit about anyone. I took a swig of my drink and eyed him over the rim of my glass.

He poured himself another slug, holding out the bottle towards me.

'Better not. It's gone to my head.'

'Is this a private party or can anyone join in?' Claire stood in the doorway, one hand on her hip.

'I've lost my purse,' I said as Nick said, 'I hit my head.'

She stared at the bottle of whiskey on the desk. 'Right. Where's Ruth?' She looked around Nick's office as if her

128

girlfriend might be hiding under the desk. 'She said she had a late meeting. I was in town so thought I'd get a lift back.' She lifted her chin. 'I've been at the central library, doing some research. On how they garrotted people in mediaeval times.' A smirk spread across her face. 'Don't worry, I'm writing a novel.'

'Great,' I said, although it wasn't and I hadn't a clue what garrotting meant. 'I've always fancied writing a novel myself.' I hadn't but I wanted to keep her on the subject of her book and away from thinking about what Nick and I were doing, sitting in his office, after work, knocking back a bottle of JD.

'Lots of people fancy writing a novel,' she said, sniffing, 'but not a lot of them can actually be arsed to do it. It's not simple, you know. It takes years and years of hard graft and—'

'Ruth left on time, I think,' Nick said. He'd obviously heard her droning on about her book a thousand times before.

'Yes, she said she was going to do some late-night shopping,' I added.

Claire narrowed her eyes at us. 'But she said she had a late meeting. Something about having to help you out with this hotel job, Nick.'

'Isn't it your birthday coming up, Claire?' Nick winked at her as he put the cap back on the whiskey bottle. 'She's probably out trying to find something special for you. A little white lie to throw you off the scent?'

'Oh, right. Yes.'

Silly cow. Ruth wasn't in some jeweller's in the Arndale, picking out a nice bracelet for her or a dangly pair of earrings – she was sitting in The Tavern, waiting for me to turn up. She obviously hadn't told Claire she'd offered to take me out for a drink.

'Well, thanks for—' Nick turned to me and pointed to his head. 'See you tomorrow. And I hope you find your purse.'

Claire gave me a tight smile as I passed her. I returned it with one of my own.

'Can I give you a lift home, Claire?' I heard Nick say as I collected my bag from my desk.

'No. It's fine. I'll text Ruth.'

I hurried to the lift, looking at my watch. I was only twenty minutes late. Would Ruth still be there? And even if she was, would she scuttle off as soon as she saw Claire's text? I slowed down, took a breath. I didn't think she would. Ruth had a little crush on me – I knew that and that was good, as I needed to keep her in my corner. I crossed my fingers that Claire wouldn't go sticking her oar in, tittle-tattling to Ruth about what she'd seen tonight.

Because Ruth might tell her sister and, if I were Nick's wife, I would come out fighting, guns a-bloody-blazing if I thought anyone was after my husband.

CHAPTER 12

Lottie banged shut the oven door with her knee and put the casserole dish onto the stove. She glanced at her phone again, willing it to ring or to beep. Where was Nick? Had there been another problem at work? It seemed that the new hotel project was jinxed – anything that could go wrong, had done.

'Smells delicious,' Hannah said, jumping off her stool. 'What can I do?'

'Pour us all another drink?' Lottie turned to Craig. 'I'm sorry about this. Nick's got a lot on at work at the moment.'

'He's probably got more important things to do than have dinner with us,' Hannah said.

Lottie winced. It had taken a while to persuade her friend to bring over her new boyfriend, but Lottie had persisted, believing it was for the best if they got to know Hannah's fella before Nick's birthday weekend. It had been a mistake. She could see that now. Nick wasn't Hannah's biggest fan, which might be another explanation, besides work, for why he was late. She took the lid off the casserole and stirred the beef bourguignon, scraping at the bottom of the dish where it had caught. And she couldn't imagine Nick being a big fan of Craig. 'I'm sure he won't be long.'

'No bother.' Craig took the wine bottle off Hannah and topped up their glasses until they were nearly overflowing. 'Don't suppose you have a cider, do you?'

'God, sorry,' Lottie said, wiping her hands on her apron. She opened the fridge door and peered inside the fridge. 'No cider, but there's Peroni and Stella.'

'Stella it is then.'

Lottie handed him a bottle. She searched through the cutlery drawer for the bottle opener but, by the time she'd found it, Craig had already banged off the top using the heel of his boot and was guzzling the lager as if he hadn't drunk for a week.

Hannah laughed. 'What are you like?'

Yes, what *was* he like? Hannah's boyfriend was the sort she usually went for – alternative, no proper job, slightly on the grubby side – but there was something about this one, with his tattoos and his long biker beard, that made Lottie uneasy. In a million years she wouldn't have marked him down as Trey's dad. Trey was a bit of a cool nerd, all drainpipe trousers that finished three inches above his ankles, a goatee beard – nothing like Craig's ZZ Top one – and a pair of oversized, dark-rimmed specs. This man in front of her looked like he'd be at home in a heavy metal band.

Still, best not to worry. Knowing Hannah it would all be over in a couple of weeks and she'd be moving on to someone else – hopefully. And, if she didn't, Lottie would have to think of a way to politely un-invite Craig to Nick's weekend bash. She didn't fancy him turning up there, cracking open bottles of Stella on his boots. She couldn't imagine what Gwen and Felix's faces would be like. Ruth would probably love him, think he was hilarious, while Claire would scowl at him from a corner – and scowl at Ruth too, for laughing. Kas would no doubt reckon Craig was a bit of a geezer, with his love of motorbikes and Man City, and would have a great time trying to match him drink for drink.

'How are the rehearsals for the play going, Lots?'

'Has someone said something?' She knew that some of the theatre group mums went to the same yoga class that Hannah did.

'No, why would they? This one,' she said, turning to Craig, 'could get a degree in paranoia.'

Lottie was about to reply that she wasn't being para-noid, that another of the kids had dropped out of the play, when there was a crunch of gravel on the driveway, followed by the slam of the front door closing.

'Whose is that motor—'

'Nick. You made it,' Lottie said as her husband came into the kitchen.

Nick threw down his laptop bag. 'God, sorry, I forgot you were coming.' He went up to Hannah and gave her a smacker on the cheek. She didn't return it but instead wiped at the spot where his lips had touched her.

'Pleased to meet you, mate.' Craig raised his bottle as Nick held out his hand.

'Likewise,' Nick said. 'Looks like you've made the right choice there—'

'Craig,' Lottie said quickly, knowing Nick had probably forgotten Hannah's boyfriend's name.

'I knew that,' Nick said, winking at Hannah.

Hannah scowled and rubbed at Craig's arm.

Craig raised his bottle again. 'Cheers, mate. Have we met before? Your face seems familiar.'

Nick shrugged. 'Don't think so.'

'You've probably seen a picture of him in the *Manchester Evening News*,' Hannah said. 'Nick's a very important person, aren't you, Nick?'

'Only to you, Hannah,' Nick said, with a grin.

Hannah snorted and took a slug of her drink.

Lottie put the tenderstem broccoli and Chantenay carrots into a serving dish as Nick reached into the fridge. 'Where were you?' She didn't know why she was asking. She could smell the whiskey on him.

'Sorry.' He lifted the lid of the casserole dish. 'Smells gorgeous. Almost as gorgeous as you.'

'Get a room,' Hannah said, making a face at Craig. 'Anyway, Nick, shouldn't we be drinking champagne? Aren't we here to celebrate Lottie's big news?'

Nick opened the fridge again. 'For once, Hannah, you're right.' He pulled out a bottle of Veuve Clicquot and popped the cork with a flourish while Hannah got the champagne saucers from the dresser.

'I've never met an actress before,' Craig said, downing the champagne in his glass before they'd done a toast.

'You have to call them actors,' Nick said, filling the glasses.

'Eh?'

'Women's equality and all that.' Nick grinned.

Hannah's face turned pink.

Lottie put her hand on her friend's arm. 'He's trying to wind you up. Ignore him.'

'Who, moi?' Nick held his glass aloft. 'Here's to my brilliant wife!'

They all clinked glasses.

Lottie took a long drag of the champagne, the bubbles going straight to her head. She felt herself growing calmer. This was her time. She'd waited so long for this. She'd called Ginger earlier. Had accepted the role. Ginger had been delighted, had promised to call the lawyers straight away about the contract.

'Are you excited?' Hannah said.

'I can't believe it.' Lottie held out her glass to Nick so he could top it up. And she couldn't. How could she have thought of turning down the part? It was a role she'd only ever dreamed of getting. And Nick was over the moon for her. He was already looking at flights so he could join her in LA for the first couple of weeks. She felt a bubble of happiness, something she hadn't felt for a long time, not since they'd started on their roller-coaster of an IVF journey five years ago. Six months away. It would do her good. It would give her – as Nick had said – space to think about what she wanted to do next, whether to go for one last IVF attempt or not. Anyway, she didn't need to think about that now. She took a swig of her drink. She had so much to be thankful for – Nick and now this role. 'I really can't believe it,' she said again.

'Well, I can.' Hannah beamed at her.

Nick put his arm around her shoulders. 'And so can I.'

'Right, you two,' Lottie said to Hannah and Craig when they'd finished off the bottle of champagne. 'Go and sit at the table.'

'What can I do?' Hannah said as Craig pushed a sleeping Belle off a chair, before sneezing three times in a row.

'You okay?' Hannah shouted over to him.

Lottie's hand flew to her mouth. 'Oh, God. Is he allergic to cats?'

'Not that I know of. But they say it runs in families, don't they? Daisy says Trey can't even look at a picture of a cat without his nose running.'

'And I bet she wipes it for him. Young love, eh? Talking of which. Go and sit down. Check he's all right. I have my helper here. It's the least he can do, seeing as though I've done all the cooking.'

'Sorry,' Nick said as he cleared the glasses and chose a bottle of Malbec from the wine rack.

Lottie stirred the casserole. 'Can you put the mash in a dish when you've opened that.'

Nick uncorked the red and then grabbed the pan.

'Where were you? You don't want to be doing too much.' This was the second evening this week he'd come home late. She knew what he was like. He'd stay working

136

at the office all night, if he needed to. He was a perfectionist. She knew he kept a bottle of JD in his desk drawer. Had shared a glass with him on one or two occasions in the early days. 'Is it the hotel project?'

Nick busied himself with scraping the mash out of the pan. 'I went for a beer with Kas. He's been a bit down since Sienna went to Oz.'

Lottie's stomach flipped. The casserole dish tipped in her hands, its contents nearly ending up on the floor.

'Careful, darling,' Nick said.

'Bloody hell, thought that was our tea done for then,' Craig shouted over to them.

'Here, let me. It's heavy.' Nick tried to take the dish off her.

She pushed him away. 'I can do it, thank you.'

With shaking hands, Lottie carried the dish over to the huge oak table that sat between the kitchen and the living room, placing it onto a mat. She stared at it. Nick was lying. He hadn't been out with Kas. She'd called Kas earlier, just before Hannah and Craig had arrived, asking him if he could drop Nick's birthday present – there was no way she could hide the hard paddleboard in the back of their car – in at Fairview on his way past. She knew Kas was going up to Keswick to visit his parents at the weekend. She'd invited him around for dinner but he'd declined, said he wouldn't want to disappoint the lucky lady he was taking out tonight.

Nick plonked down the bowl of mash and then pulled out a chair, sitting opposite Craig, engaging him in some conversation about football and whether City would do the treble this season.

'You okay, Lots?' Hannah said, getting up and following Lottie back to the kitchen. 'Here, let me.' She took the tea towel off Lottie and got the red-hot plates out of the oven.

'Fine. Fine. Just annoyed. You know.' She nodded towards Nick. 'It's just bloody rude. He knew you were coming around.'

'Don't worry about it. I'd rather he had stayed in the pub with Kas.' She squeezed Lottie's arm. 'Grab the veg then.'

Lottie did as she was told and followed her friend back to the table. She placed the dish in the centre and handed the serving spoon to Craig.

'Cheers, love. Smells fucking fantastic.'

Hannah laughed. 'Language.'

'Blimey, we're all adults, aren't we? Hey, Lottie?'

Lottie gave him a brief smile as she helped herself to a spoonful of carrots. She doubted she'd be able to eat anything. She looked across at Nick who was smirking as Craig piled up his plate. Nick had lied to her. Nick never lied to her.

'So, how did you two meet?' Nick said, once everyone had filled their plates.

Hannah speared a piece of broccoli. 'He's Trey's dad.'

'Trey?' Nick asked.

'Daisy's boyfriend.' Hannah piled some more mash onto her plate. 'You remember. My daughter? Your wife's goddaughter?'

138

'Right. Is she old enough to have a boyfriend?'

Lottie sighed. 'She's nearly seventeen, Nick. I told you at the rehearsal. You saw her there.'

'Blimey. Time flies.'

'She's going to do a month in the office over the summer.' Lottie took a sip of her wine. 'Ruth sorted it out,' she said in answer to Nick's blank look.

'I didn't know he was Trey's dad when we met,' Hannah said, after taking a slug of her wine. 'He was doing some odd jobs at the Reiki centre.'

'What is it you do, mate?' Craig said to Nick. 'Must be something fancy if you can afford all this.'

'I'm an architect. I design buildings. Mostly hotel complexes.'

'Neat. If you ever need an odd-job man.'

'I don't really get involved in that side of things.'

'You don't like to get your hands dirty, do you, Nick?' Hannah raised her glass towards him, a smirk on her face.

'No, unlike you,' Nick shot back. 'Are you still doing those mud massage things?' He turned to Craig. 'Lottie came back looking like she'd had a fight with a hippo.'

Craig cracked up, the chunk of beef he was chewing visible in his wide mouth.

'It was clay,' Lottie and Hannah both said at the same time.

Nick shook his head. 'What will these women fall for next? Clay . . . has the power to turn back the clock.'

'Shut up, Nick.' Lottie put down her fork.

He reached for her hand but she pulled it away. 'Hey, I was only joking. We like a bit of banter, don't we, Hannah?'

'Banter's supposed to be clever, I think?' Hannah said to Craig.

'Women don't do banter, mate,' Craig said. 'Got another Stella?'

Lottie jumped up. 'I'll get it.'

She opened the fridge door and bent down, enjoying the cool air on her face. She wanted them to go. It had been a mistake. Nick and Hannah would never get on. And this Craig? What did her friend see in him?

But it wasn't just Craig. She wanted them to go so she could ask Nick where he'd really been this evening.

'Lots! Craig's dying of thirst here.'

Returning to the table, she scowled at Nick as she banged down the bottle on to the mat in front of Craig.

'Can we come out to LA for our holidays, then?' Craig asked as a phone started to buzz, causing them all to look around.

'Sorry, that's me.' Nick pushed back his chair, going to his laptop bag and upending it until he found his ringing phone. 'Won't be a min,' he said, before leaving the room and closing the door behind him.

'Busy man, your fella.'

Lottie studied Craig's face to see if he was being sarcastic or implying something. It was hard to tell as he was concentrating on shovelling the casserole into his mouth. She leant back in her chair, straining her ears to try to make out Nick's conversation.

'Is Nick going over there with you?' Craig asked.

Lottie shook her head. 'Too busy with work.'

Hannah snorted. 'Has he not heard of Zoom?'

'Zoom?' Craig said. 'What's that?'

Hannah ignored him. 'You'll be okay on your own in LA?'

Lottie lifted her chin. 'Of course I will. The casting director, Ginger, is really nice. And it's only for six months.'

'Ginger?' Hannah frowned at her.

'Her real name's Nuala. Her surname is Rogers.'

'Cute.' Hannah rolled her eyes.

'I went to school with a girl called Nuala,' Craig said as he shovelled more food into his mouth. 'It's Irish, isn't it? Lots of Irish girls at my school. Catholic, it was. Niamh, Aisling, Siobhan.'

'I didn't have you down as a Catholic,' Hannah said.

'Nah, I'm not. It was the closest school to us. Not that it mattered – I didn't exactly spend much time there.'

Lottie tried to catch Hannah's eye, but her friend was busy piling more beef bourguignon onto Craig's plate.

'Sorry about that,' Nick said as he came back into the room, a too-bright smile plastered onto his face.

Lottie stared at him. 'Work?'

'Isn't it always?' he said, not looking at her as he sat down and picked up his fork.

By the time Hannah and Craig had left, picked up by Trey and a very giggly Daisy on their way home from a party, Craig promising to pick up his motorbike first thing, Lottie had a pounding headache.

141

She let Nick stack the dishwasher and clear up as she got ready for bed and took off her make-up. With a sigh, she put the toilet roll back onto the holder and picked up the bottle of handwash from the floor. Both Daisy and Trey had been dying for the loo when they'd arrived and Daisy had gone bounding up to the family bathroom. As she straightened the white towel on the handrail she noticed a dirty yellow stain smeared on the corner of it.

God, how drunk had Daisy been? She'd seen the look Hannah had given her when she'd finally come back downstairs. Lottie threw the towel into the laundry basket and peered into the toilet. There were definitely signs someone had thrown up in there. She cleaned the toilet and squirted some bleach around the rim. Like mother, like daughter. Hannah always threw up if she got drunk. There'd been many a night, especially when they were in Oz together, when Lottie had sat with her, holding her hair back as she chucked up her guts into the toilet bowl.

Lottie switched on her bedside lamp. She got under the cold sheets and lay there, wondering if Nick would come to bed before she fell asleep.

Her eyelids were beginning to flutter when he came into the bedroom. She watched from under her eyelashes as he slipped off his clothes – throwing them onto the dressing table chair as he usually did – before he edged into bed next to her.

'How's Kas?' she said as he plumped up his pillow.

'He'll live.'

He gave her a quick peck and then turned away from her. 'Seems an all-right sort of guy, that Craig.'

'Hmm.' She couldn't be bothered to argue with him. Not about that anyway. 'Where did you go? With Kas?'

He shifted slightly and then let out a snore. And then another.

She waited ten minutes to check he really was asleep and then slipped out of bed, tiptoeing over to the dressing table, keeping an eye on him as she searched his trouser pockets for his phone. Nothing.

The kitchen floor was cold, the underfloor heating off for the night, as she rifled through the pockets of Nick's jacket. Where was his phone? It had to be somewhere.

In the living room, she checked every surface: behind cushions, down the side of the sofas. And then she spotted it, lying next to the TV.

She picked it up. Did she really want to do this? She wasn't the sort of woman who snooped through her husband's phone. She should just ask him in the morning where he'd been – there was probably a perfectly simple explanation as to why he'd lied to her. Perhaps Kas's date had been cancelled?

She looked towards the stairs. Listened. She looked at Nick's phone. And then she tapped in his passcode. He'd told it to her, knowing his memory was awful: 230611, the day they got married.

The phone sprang to life. She scrolled through his call log. The last number was from a contractor, Jimmy Parkinson, a man she'd met on a few occasions at work functions. She opened up Nick's messages, just as the phone beeped.

Thank you for tonight x

It was from someone called Nigel. Who was Nigel? She'd never heard Nick mention a Nigel before. Nigel? No, she didn't know a Nigel. She stared at the text. It wasn't from a man, it couldn't be. A man didn't put a kiss. Nigel. No, she'd never heard him mention someone with that name before – she was sure of it. And then it came to her. N for Nigel. N for Natasha. No, it couldn't be, could it?

Lottie felt a burning pain just below her ribs. Was Nigel just a cover? Had her husband lied to her because he couldn't admit the truth? That he'd spent the evening drinking whiskey with his PA when he should have been at home with her, entertaining their guests?

CHAPTER 13

I checked my pocket for the tenth time as I rode along. It was still there – the nail I'd found in the cutlery drawer. There was all sorts of crap in there, so much that it was sometimes hard to find a knife or fork. Dad was out at the pub again – a trip to the bookies on a Saturday, followed by a lunchtime session, was a lifelong routine. I'd wheeled my bike from the side passage and jumped on it, taking the path around the outside of the estate, avoiding the small bit of scrubland in the centre of the houses, where there was a sorry bit of a play area for the kids, in case Kenny was hanging out there. He really needed to grow up. I'd been quite sweet on him in the first year at St Joseph's, for about a month anyway, but that was before he'd turned into a version of his old man, running errands for him, errands that involved selling pot and ecstasy, errands that had got him expelled from school.

In the three years I'd been away, he'd changed even more. I had no doubt he was into some very dodgy things, dodgy things I had no intention of going near. There was no way he was dragging me down with him. I might have once settled for someone like Kenny, got knocked up, married him, put our name down for a house, a brood of kids. Settled. But not anymore. I'd been away. Seen what life could offer. And I wanted it for myself.

The weather was on my side. It had pissed it down for ages but the sun had finally come out yesterday, drying everything. I slowed the bike as I reached the end of Nick's lane. I would only stop if wifey's car wasn't there. Obviously. I hoped he was at home. If he wasn't I'd go into the office, although turning up there again, for the second day in a row, might take some explaining. I giggled to myself – would it take more explaining than happening to be riding past his house when I got a puncture? My old man always said I'd got a brass neck, but so what? You had to go for what you wanted in life. No one was going to hand it to you on a plate. The text message I'd sent him last night had perhaps been a bit too much though. He hadn't replied but I wasn't going to let that put me off.

I stopped and checked my face in my compact mirror. Still gorgeous. The ride here had put a bit of colour in my cheeks. I looked good. Young. Alive. Totally opposite to wifey.

I jumped back on my bike and cycled towards Nick's house. Bingo. Her car wasn't there. But Nick's was. Perfect.

Hopping off the bike again, I fished in the pocket of my cut-off jeans and found the nail. I stabbed it once, twice, three times into the bike's tyre, pressing on the rubber until the tyre was completely flat before pushing the nail all the way in. I then wheeled my bike, as best I could, towards Nick's house.

Just as I reached his driveway, Nick came from around the side of the house, pushing a lawnmower, the cord draped over his shoulder.

'Hey,' I said. 'I didn't know you lived here.'

He came over to me. 'Nice day for a bike ride.'

'If you haven't got a puncture.'

He crouched down and examined my tyre. 'You've got a nail stuck in it.'

'No shit, Sherlock.'

He smiled up at me. 'Cheeky.'

'How's the head?'

'From the bump or from the whiskey?'

'We only had the one. At least I did. Let me look. Is it still sore?'

He jumped up before I could put my fingers on his scalp. 'It's fine. Thanks for sorting me out.'

'Any time.'

'Find your purse, did you?'

'You're not going to believe it,' I said, 'but it was in my bag all along.'

He shook his head. 'Have you got a puncture repair kit?'

'What do you think?'

'Always be prepared,' he said.

I gave him a wink.

'Come on, I've got one in the garage.' He picked up my bike and I followed him around to the side of the

147

house. There was a smaller barn there, huge oak double doors on the front of it that he pushed wide open.

'Wow, neat,' I said. 'This is nicer than my house.' It was too – everything was on shelves or hanging from pegs. The floor was clean. There were rafters and beams. It smelt of wood. Fresh.

'Here we are,' Nick said, pulling a box out of a drawer. He turned the bike upside down, asking me to hold it as he kneeled in front of the wheel. I stared at the top of his head, trying to make out the cut under his hair. He smelt delicious. A mixture of sweat, freshly mown grass and the spicy aftershave he always wore.

I was aware his eyes were in line with my legs. I'd chosen to wear cut-off shorts on purpose. They were Daisy Dukes, just about covering my arse cheeks. And I'd spent the morning lathering myself in fake tan.

'There you go,' he said, after five minutes. 'All sorted.' He righted the bike and felt at the tyre again.

'I owe you one. It's a long walk back. And, me, being the idiot I am, have left my water bottle at home.'

'Do you want a drink before you go?'

'No, you're all right. I'll survive.'

He pushed my bike out of the garage and leant it on the side of the house. 'Come on, can't have you dying of dehydration on the way home.'

He went through a side door and I followed him into a smart utility room. It had a coatrack on the wall, homemade bags hanging from it – one for pegs, one for carrier bags. There was a boot holder and a couple of bowls with cat biscuits in them.

He took me through into the kitchen. I'd seen it from the outside, of course, but being in there I could truly appreciate what a gorgeous house it was. There were wooden cupboards and a huge wooden island. The walls were painted a soft green and there were cutesy things hanging about, love hearts and nice pictures. It was like something out of a magazine.

'Water or juice?'

'Juice is fine.'

He went over to a contraption on the side, picked three large oranges from a bowl and started to cut them up.

'Oh, don't go to any trouble. I thought you meant out of a carton.'

'You can't beat fresh juice. My wife won't drink anything else.'

Of course she wouldn't. Stuck-up cow. What was wrong with a carton of cheap orange juice from Tesco?

He filled a glass and one for himself and handed mine to me. He took a huge gulp of his and then started to clear away the mess he'd made.

'Here, let me do that – the least I can do.'

I picked up a cloth and started to wipe at the sides.

'No, you don't have to do that.'

'I don't mind.'

'Give me the cloth.'

I stuck my hand on my hip and dangled the cloth in front of him.

'I am the boss.'

'Does that mean I always have to do what you tell me?' I flung the cloth at him.

'Of course it does.' He grinned. 'At work, at least.'

'Anything I can do to help with the hotel project? I don't mind working tomorrow?'

'On a Sunday? That's sweet of you. Thank you. But no. Just be bright and early Monday morning. We've got a lot to do.'

'Yes, sir,' I said, saluting him.

He laughed. 'Anyway, I'd better be getting back to my lawn.' He put his glass in the dishwasher and held out his hand for mine. I drank the juice as slowly as I could. I didn't want to leave. I never wanted to leave. I wanted to stay in this house with him forever. I wanted him to make fresh orange juice for me every day.

He headed towards the utility room door.

'Do you mind if I use the toilet?' I said, wiggling on the spot. 'It'll save going behind a hedge on the way back.'

'Sure. Second door on your left,' he said before disappearing outside.

With him gone, I had a good chance to have a nosy at the living room. It was a large open-plan space; comfy, squishy sofas with rose patterns; candles everywhere; cushions. I made my way into the hallway, pushing open the door in front of me. It was a study. A huge dark wood desk, books lining the walls. The second door was the downstairs toilet.

I looked up the stairs. There were photos all the way up. I glanced towards the window. Nick was out there, mowing the lawn. I'd be quick. He'd never know I'd been snooping around his house.

I headed up the stairs, one at a time, taking in the

150

photos. They were of Nick and wifey. All of them. The pair of them on their wedding day, on holiday, at a party. I wanted to throw up. The happy couple. So in love.

I reached the landing at the top. There were four doors. The first led into a guest bedroom. The second was a family bathroom. The third was an empty room with a rowing machine in it. And the fourth was their bedroom.

I pushed open the door and went inside. It was the sort of bedroom I would kill for. There was a huge bed, a brass bedstead, an expensive throw covering a hideous quilt cover, all pink flowers and butterflies. There were low windows, with a window seat. And a dressing table with potions and pots on it. Of course, she'd need those. I picked one up, a night cream: La Mer. It probably cost more than I earnt in a week. There was a lipstick, Dior, lying on its side. I picked it up and opened it, slicking it across my lips, smacking them together in the mirror. It was a disgusting colour. A coral pink. I wiped the back of my hand over my mouth and fished in my pocket for my lip gloss, rolling it back and forth, tasting the strawberry flavour, pouting at myself in the mirror.

My stomach flew into my mouth as something behind me moved. My heart thumped as I turned around. It was only a cat, stretching on the bed. I went over and sat down next to it, putting my hand out to stroke it. It purred and then suddenly it swiped at my hand, drawing blood. 'You little bastard,' I said, bouncing up and down a couple of times on the bed. It meowed and then jumped off. Served it bloody right. It wouldn't be coming into the bedroom when I lived here. There would only be me and Nick in this bed.

There were books by her side of the bed. Trashy novels. If Nick was my husband there'd be no time for reading.

And there was a wedding photo too. She was laughing at something he was saying. I put my hand over her face. Soon I would be opposite him in a photo like this.

I was about to open her bedside cabinet when I realised it had gone quiet. I glanced out of the window. Nick had stopped mowing. I dashed from the room, running down the stairs, taking them two at a time, rushing through the kitchen and out into the open air.

I got my bike and wheeled it around the side of the house to where Nick stood.

'All okay?'

I smiled. Part of me felt like crying. Why should she have it all? Why should she have that perfect life with my Nick? But the other part of me felt a rush of excitement, of hope. I could have what she had. I could. I could have this house. This life.

And, more importantly, I could have Nick.

CHAPTER 14

'This is going to be a bundle of laughs.' Nick headed towards the bar, leaving Lottie standing in the foyer, looking for a place to leave her drenched umbrella. It was about the only thing he'd said to her since they'd left the house – he hadn't been impressed at all that she'd accepted Ruth's invitation to Claire's writers' event on his behalf – had tried to get out of it – but she'd insisted he went with her.

Nick was right though – it was hardly going to be a wild evening. The average age of the people there was about seventy.

Ruth was in a far corner of the room, waving her over.

Lottie pushed past people, a *sorry* here, an *excuse me* there, until she reached Ruth.

'Thought you weren't going to make it,' Ruth said, as she went to pull Lottie into a hug before thinking better of it. 'You're soaking, hon.'

'Sorry, the traffic is terrible.' Lottie pushed her hair behind her ear. God knows what she looked like. 'It's a monsoon out there.'

'What do you expect? It's August. School holidays. Doesn't it always rain? The good weather at the weekend was just a blip. Here,' she said, handing Lottie a glass. 'Sorry, they don't have any flutes. The Prosecco-drinking crowd has bagged them all.'

Lottie took a sip. 'Champagne?'

'To celebrate you getting the US TV thing. I knew you'd do it, you star. Cheers.'

'Cheers.' Lottie clinked her glass against Ruth's.

Ruth grilled her about the part, while Lottie scanned the crowd, trying to catch sight of Nick. 'Have we missed anything?' she said, turning back to Ruth.

'Only the talk from the Agatha Christie nut and a very boring discussion on serial killers. Claire's on the panel after the break. It's about research.'

Lottie winked. 'Well, she's certainly an expert on that. She'd have written that book by now if she—'

'She needs to get it right, Lots. You know what people are like. Someone's bound to pick her up on it if she doesn't. And there's a lot to learn about mediaeval torture practices.' She looked at her watch. 'Hopefully we can escape straight after her panel.'

'Did you book that new Indian?' Lottie said as she lifted her glass to her lips. 'The one near the art gallery?'

'They were full. I booked Angelo's instead.'

Lottie narrowed her eyes. 'Hmm. Nothing to do with Claire preferring Italian to Indian, I suppose?'

'The new place was booked out. It's just opened,' Ruth said again. 'And Bil will be up for the Italian too, won't he?'

154

Lottie shrugged. He'd been quiet since Friday night, when Craig and Hannah had been for dinner. But, then again, so had she. She wanted nothing more than to ask him who he had been drinking whiskey with that evening and why he'd lied to her. And just who this *Nigel* was. In the past five days, she'd opened her mouth many times to ask him where he'd been – but the fear of having to admit that she'd looked at his phone had stopped her. He wouldn't be happy – at all – that she'd done that.

Lottie peered into the large ballroom where about two hundred chairs had been laid out. 'God, I didn't think there'd be this many people. Is she nervous?'

Ruth downed her drink before answering. 'You know Claire. It's hard to tell.'

'How are things?'

'Fine.'

'Fine as in good or fine as in don't ask?'

Ruth studied her empty glass.

'Oh, Ru, I don't know why you bother. You should just end it.'

Ruth's eyes suddenly flashed in anger. 'How can I? Sorry.' She swallowed. 'It's not that easy, is it?'

'These things never are but—'

'No, Lots. You don't get it. She . . . she said she can't live without me.'

'People say that all the time. They don't mean it. She'd get over it.'

'You think so?'

'Yes. Of course she would. She'd meet someone new. Within six months she'd be saying it was the best thing that had ever happened to her.' Lottie wanted to laugh at the words coming out of her mouth. She was a fine one to talk. She caught sight of Nick weaving his way across the room, a drink in each hand. She wouldn't get over Nick if she lost him. She took a deep breath. But she wasn't going to lose him, was she? She was making a mountain out of a molehill. There was probably a simple explanation as to why he'd lied to her the other night. There had to be. She just had to ask him.

'How did your drink with Tasha go?' she said quickly before Nick reached them.

Ruth's glum face lit up. 'Really well. She's so nice.'

Lottie elbowed her. 'Tell all.'

'There's nothing to tell. We met for a drink.'

'Oh, yes?'

'Honestly, your dirty mind. I was just being friendly. She's only recently back in the area. All her mates are scattered around the country.'

'You like her, don't you?' Lottie rubbed at Ruth's arm as the heat rose in Ruth's face.

'I've told you, she's very nice.'

'And does she think you're very nice?'

'Lots!' Ruth cast a nervous glance in Claire's direction. 'Shut up!'

'Sorry,' Lottie said. And she was sorry. She was pushing Ruth simply because she wanted to try to find out if Tasha was gay. Because, if Tasha *was* gay, she wouldn't be making a play for her husband, would she? She could rule her out as the 'Nigel' that was sending Nick messages.

'You okay?' Ruth said, giving her a funny look.

'Fine.'

Nick joined them, giving Ruth a perfunctory kiss on the cheek and frowning at the glass in Lottie's hand. She put down her empty glass and took the G and T off him. She'd asked for a Sauvignon. He was obviously miles away. Elsewhere.

Ninety boring minutes later and Lottie was shrugging on her coat.

'Will she be long?' Nick said to Ruth.

Claire was standing at the far side of the room, talking to the people she'd been on the panel with.

'Go, if you like.' Ruth cast a glance in her girlfriend's direction. 'We can get a taxi to the restaurant. No point you two hanging around. You sure you don't fancy the Italian?' she asked Nick again.

'I need to go through the project budget when we get home,' Nick said, fishing in his jacket pockets and finding his car keys.

'We'll wait,' Lottie said. 'We can at least give them a lift, can't we, darling?' She turned back to Ruth. 'You'll never get a taxi with all this lot here.'

Ruth put down her glass. 'All ready for next week, Bil?'

Lottie looked from one to the other of them. 'Next week?'

'The exhibition in Birmingham? You've forgotten.' Nick sighed.

'I didn't forget. You never told me.'

'I've been going there for the past twenty years, Lots. Second week of August.'

157

'Right.' She had forgotten – it was the big exhibition they attended every year. But Nick usually mentioned it. Usually asked her if she wanted to go with him. But not this time. She fiddled with the paper straw in her gin glass. It was soggy. And so was she slightly – she was on her fourth gin. 'Who's going?'

'Just me and him,' Ruth said. 'We haven't got a big stand this year. We can hardly cope with the work we've got. We need to focus on recruitment. We're struggling to fill some roles.'

'You're focusing on recruitment,' Nick said. 'I've got some meetings lined up about the Dolos project.'

Lottie sucked at the straw. Nothing came through it. 'I could come and give you a hand.'

'What about the play?' Ruth turned to Nick. 'Didn't you say Lottie couldn't help out because of the rehearsals?'

Lottie frowned at her husband.

'What? You are stressed about the damn thing. She's got it in her head that the parents are moaning about her,' he said to Ruth.

'I'm sure they're not.' Ruth nibbled at her thumbnail.

'Exactly,' Nick said, pointing at his head.

Lottie glared at him. The parents had been moaning about her – she was sure of it. And they were probably right to. She hadn't been able to knock Dylan into shape yet. She doubted he'd ever get his lines right. There was so much to do before opening night.

'Lottie's right though, Bil. It might be a bit much for just the two of us. I could always ask Tasha, see if she fancies helping out,' Ruth said.

Nick frowned. 'I don't think that's such a good idea.'

'Oh?' Lottie and Ruth both said at the same time.

Nick stole a quick glance at the other side of the room, to check Claire wasn't on her way over to them. 'One, I need Tasha to handle things while I'm not in the office and two, I reckon you have ulterior motives.' He crossed his arms and sniffed.

Ruth's cheeks flamed. 'What do you mean?'

'Come on, Ruth. You fancy her, don't you? It's a bit unprofessional.'

'Don't be bloody ridiculous!' Ruth cast a worried look in Claire's direction.

Nick cocked his head to the side. 'Am I being ridiculous?'

'You . . . you. Honestly. You've got some nerve, Nick, you really have.' With that, Ruth stalked over to Claire.

Lottie stared at her husband. 'What did Ruth mean by that?'

He shrugged. 'Touchy or what? You coming?' he said, without waiting for an answer.

'For God's sake, Nick,' Lottie said as she caught up with him. 'Did you have to go in with your hobnail boots?'

'I was only winding her up. Truth hurts, eh?'

They reached the revolving door. 'Certainly does.' She put her hand on the door to stop it rotating so they were both trapped in the glass compartment. 'Who's this Nigel then?'

He stared at her. 'Nigel?'

'You heard me: Nigel.'

'Nigel who?'

'You tell me. I'll give you a clue. The "thank you for last night", kiss Nigel. That one.' She crossed her own arms to mirror his stance.

'Have you been looking at my phone?'

'I . . .'

He took a step back as if she'd slapped him, before shaking his head. 'Why would you look at my phone, Lots? Don't you trust me?' He swiped away her hand and pushed on the door, tumbling out into the night. Lottie ran after him, not caring she was getting soaked, not caring she'd left her umbrella propped up in the foyer.

By the time she got to the car, Nick was revving the engine.

Flinging open the door, she jumped into the warm interior, the air vents blasting out hot air, the windscreen misted up. Nick wiped at the glass furiously with a piece of tissue before throwing the soggy bit of paper into the door-well and wrenching at his seatbelt.

'You lied to me. You said you were out with Kas on Friday night, when Hannah and Craig came over, and I know you weren't because I'd called him and asked him to come over and join us. What's going on, Nick? Where were you?'

Nick ran his hand through his wet hair. 'I can't believe you, Lottie. Really, I can't. I'm stacked out with this hotel project and here you are having a go at me.'

'For God's sake, Nick, just tell me! Who's Nigel?'

Nick stared straight ahead. His chest rose as he took a deep breath. 'Nigel is my . . . what do people call it

160

these days? My birth father. That's all, Lottie. That's all. I met up with him.'

'Your dad?' She tried to grab his hand but he wrenched it away. 'But I thought you weren't in contact with him?'

'I'm not.'

'But he got in touch? That's lovely – really, Nick. After all these years. Why didn't you say anything?'

'There's nothing to say.'

'You haven't seen him for, what, over thirty years and there's nothing to say about it?'

'Exactly.' He pulled at his seatbelt again. 'I met him to put him straight. To tell him to leave me alone.'

'But he's your dad.'

'He was,' he said, putting the car into drive and heading out of the car park.

'But don't you think—'

The car lurched forward as Nick slammed his foot on the brake.

'For God's sake, Lottie.' A gob of spittle flew out of his mouth and landed on her cheek. 'Can't you understand I don't want to talk about it? The past is the past. You can't change it. Even if you want to. One wrong decision and everything goes to shit.' He slammed his hand on the steering wheel. Silence filled the car until he took a large breath. 'Listen, he's trouble, my father.'

'What do you mean?'

'He's been inside.'

'Prison?'

Nick ran his hand over the steering wheel. 'Mum divorced him as soon as he got out.'

Lottie tried to take in what Nick was telling her. 'I didn't know. What was he in for?'

'Let's just say he can't ever walk away from a fight.'

'But maybe he's changed.'

Nick turned to her. 'Do people change, Lots? I'm not sure they can.'

'But thirty-odd years – it's a long time.'

'Exactly. Too late now. Can we just forget about it? Please?'

Lottie reached for his hand and this time he let her take it. 'I'm sorry, darling. Of course we can.'

He gave her a tight smile before snatching his hand away. 'And don't ever look at my phone again, Lottie. It makes me think you don't trust me. And I don't like that. I don't like that at all.'

Lottie squirmed. What an idiot she'd been. Putting two and two together and making five.

A gnawing sense of shame made her stomach flip – she'd never been the sort of woman who went snooping through her husband's things and she didn't want to be.

She really needed to get a grip of herself. Nick wouldn't cheat on her. How could she ever believe that he would?

CHAPTER 15

I stood in the toilet cubicle, checking my make-up was spot on and re-curling my hair with the travel irons I'd shoved in my bag before I left the house. August and it was like bloody April. I'd got a taxi from the station, not caring it cost nearly thirty quid – the bus would've taken ages. I slicked some more lip gloss across my lips and blew myself a kiss as someone banged on the door for the third time.

'Where's the fire?' I said to the old biddy in the wheel-chair who was waiting outside for me.

'That's a disabled toilet,' she rasped at me. 'Can't you read?'

'How do you know I'm not disabled?' I said, giving her a scowl before walking off. Some people were so bloody rude. I'd been diagnosed with ADHD when I was little. Or was it asthma? I forget what the old man had said. Whatever it was, I'm sure he claimed extra social because of it. Surely that classed me as disabled?

I'd registered for the exhibition in advance so all I had to do was find my name badge. It was on a bright green lanyard, the name of the main sponsor in large letters all over it. Green. Who had chosen slime green? It clashed with the baby pink blouse I had on. I flashed it at the security guard and then stuffed it into my pocket.

The map of the halls was in the guide I'd picked up. Scanning through I found Moore and Perera. I didn't know much about exhibitions but even I could tell their booth was in a crap position – on a back wall in a row full of small booths. It might suit me though – the fewer people that walked past, the more time I'd have to talk to Nick.

My mouth was dry. And yet my palms were sweaty. I longed to take off the stiff suit jacket I'd bought at the weekend but I hadn't ironed the back of my blouse so that was a no-no. Up ahead was a sign for refreshments. I wound my way along the rows until I reached a large fenced-off café area. It was buzzing, people chatting, mobiles ringing, the clink of crockery, the hiss of the coffee machine. I helped myself to a glass of water, downing it in one go.

What would Nick say when he saw me? What would Ruth say? Would they be mad I'd turned up uninvited, or would they be pleased at my enthusiasm for the job? I'd booked a few days off so it wasn't as if I was skiving. And I had a story all planned out, had set it up last week in the office, in fact – I'd been visiting my gran in Birmingham, a break from looking after my dad, and thought I'd stop in at the exhibition on my way back to Manchester. Nick and Ruth weren't to know I'd been at Piccadilly Station at six to make sure I caught a cheap train before the rush hour prices kicked in. Anyway, apart from not being able to afford the later tickets, it was better to leave early. I didn't want the old man asking any questions.

'Hey! It is you.' Ruth tapped me on the shoulder. 'What are you doing here?'

'You don't mind, do you? I've never been to an exhibition and I wasn't doing anything. Reckoned you might need a bit of help. I know how busy you both are.'

Ruth beamed at me. 'But I thought you were having a few days off?'

I shrugged. 'Am I being a bit of a swot?'

'No, of course not! It's lovely to see you. It's very quiet where we are and,' she said, leaning in close to me, so close I could smell her *Poison* perfume, 'to be honest, I've run out of things to talk about with Bil. And the exhibition has only been open half an hour.' She looked down at my empty glass. 'I was just going to grab a couple of coffees and some pastries. Fancy the same?'

'Sure. I'm booked in for a spin class at the gym tomorrow.'

'Are you still going to GymSpot? I haven't seen you in there lately.'

'I changed my days.' I hadn't. I'd only gone to the gym to get in with Ruth and now it seemed I was more than in with her. There was no way I was working up a sweat for no reason. Gyms were for mugs. Plus, I didn't want to bump into Nick's wife. I didn't want to hear her talk about him, about how wonderful her life was with him. I'd give myself away. Yeah, I was a good actress, but not that good.

'You've no need to go to the gym, anyway. There's nothing to you. I wish I had your figure,' Ruth said.

'You're just being nice.'

She hooked her arm through mine. 'I'm not. One thing you'll learn about me is I find it hard to lie.'

'I bet that gets you into trouble sometimes.'

'Too right. More often than I can count. Now, what do you fancy? A cinnamon swirl or an apple turnover?'

After loading up with a mixture of coffees and pastries she led the way to the booth. I was glad I'd bumped into her before seeing Nick – she'd swallowed my lie, that I'd just turned up to give them a hand, so hopefully Nick would too. Did it matter if he didn't though? Didn't I want him to know I was here just for him?

My stomach rolled as I saw him. He was scribbling in a notebook, his head bowed.

'Look who I found,' Ruth said.

He lifted his head, delight flashing across his face quickly followed by confusion. 'What are you doing here? Aren't you supposed to be visiting your gran?'

A warm feeling filled me – he was obviously keeping track of me, paying attention to where I was.

'Thought I'd call in on my way home.'

Ruth plopped a coffee and an apple turnover in front of him. 'She's come to give us a hand. Employee of the month, or what, Bil?'

Nick took the lid off his cup. 'Of the year, I'd say.' He winked at me as Ruth fiddled with her pastry.

'Nice,' I said, indicating the exhibition stand that lined

the back wall. There were pictures of some of the hotels I guessed the firm had worked on since he and Kas set up the practice.

'We usually have a much bigger space but we can't keep up with the work we've already got coming in. Especially with the new hotel project.' Nick blew on his coffee. 'We definitely don't want any more.'

'Just more people to do the work,' Ruth said, taking a bite of her cherry turnover. A thick mush of glistening fruit oozed out of the other end of it and splattered down her white blouse. 'Oh bugger.' She cast about for somewhere to put down her coffee and pastry.

'Here, let me.' I whipped a tissue out of my bag and went over to her. 'You are a mucky pup,' I said as I wiped at her blouse. As I did so, my hand brushed against her boob and I could feel her nipple harden.

'Okay?' I asked. Her face turned bright red. Nearly as red as the cherry mark on her blouse.

'You should probably go and wet it in the loos. Otherwise it'll stain.'

She handed me her coffee and threw the remnants of her slice into the bin. 'Back in a jiffy,' she said, picking up her bag and heading off.

'You shouldn't do that,' Nick said as I perched on the stool next to his.

'I know. I've probably made it worse, rubbing it in like that.'

'Flirt with her, I meant.'

'Who said I was flirting?'

'Weren't you?'

'Nope. Women don't do it for me.' I pushed my hair behind my ear. 'I'm a man's woman. Through and through.'

He coughed and fiddled with the cardboard casing around his cup. 'How's your bike? No more punctures?'

'No. All fine. Thanks so much for fixing it.'

'That was a long nail. Surprised you didn't go over the handlebars when that went in.' He took a long swig of his coffee and stared at me.

I stared back until he spoke: 'Why are you here?'

'To find out about the exhibition. To find out more about the company. To help out. Give you a hand.' I held out my hand to demonstrate, palm up.

He glanced about him quickly and then, with his index finger, traced along the lines of my hand, slowly, softly.

My breath caught at the back of my throat. My stomach did a flip. And then another. It was the most erotic thing anyone had ever done to me.

'You shouldn't play around with people.'

'Who says I'm playing, Nick?'

'Aren't you?' he said, snatching his hand away from mine, just as Ruth came back into view at the far end of the walkway.

CHAPTER 16

'Love you,' Lottie said, before Nick hung up the phone. In the flurry of goodbyes between them, she couldn't make out whether he'd said it back to her.

He'd been quiet since the night of Claire's writers' event. She'd apologised to him, more than once over the past week, reassuring him that she did trust him and telling him, in as gentle a way as she could, that if he'd just opened up to her, then none of this misunderstanding would have happened. 'There was no misunderstanding on my part,' he'd said. And he'd been adamant there was nothing to open up about regarding his father – as far as Nick was concerned, Nigel meant nothing to him and he didn't want to talk about him.

Perhaps the two days he was away at the exhibition would do them good. It wasn't as if she hadn't loads to do anyway, what with the play and the arrangements for his birthday weekend at Fairview. The list in front of her wasn't getting any shorter. Kas hadn't been up to his parents' yet, thanks to his mum having a nasty summer cold, but he would definitely be going before the party and he'd promised to drop off the paddleboard on his way there.

She gazed out of the window. The weather had turned again – instead of the rain they'd had during most of the summer, there was now a mini heatwave. Time to dig out a pair of shorts. The forecasters were saying it would only last three days at most. She wanted to check over the scenery for the play later – she didn't want anyone saying it looked like the kids had made it themselves from cardboard. There would be a lot of humping and shifting stuff – hot and heavy work.

Her shorts were in a plastic box under their bed, along with the rest of her holiday clothes. She hadn't had cause to go in there yet this year – Nick had been so busy at work they hadn't had time to book the two weeks in Greece they usually did. And the crap weather had meant shorts were definitely out. She'd need her summer clothes for Los Angeles though – according to her research the average temperatures for the autumn and winter never dipped below twenty degrees in the day.

'Urgh,' she said as she got on her hands and knees and peered underneath the bed. There was a lot of dust. And Belle had been sick right under the middle of the bed. With a sigh, she got back up and went down to the kitchen, to arm herself with rubber gloves, plenty of kitchen roll, a cloth and carpet cleaner.

Lying flat on her stomach, she scraped at the now stuck-down sick, trying not to retch as she pulled it towards her. If Nick were here, she could have asked him to help her move the frame – it was really heavy, definitely a two-man job. With all the gunge removed, she shook the carpet cleaner, tipped it upside down, gave it a squeeze and, with her arm stretched out under the bed, moved the brush back and forth across the carpet.

Sweat was dripping down her back by the time she'd straightened up. 'Right,' she said, pulling out the plastic box containing her summer clothes. As she tugged the container, something moved, just out of her peripheral vision. She yelped, scared it might be a mouse – Belle was forever bringing her presents, but he usually left them in the utility room. She peered under the bed, letting out a sigh of relief. It was only a lipstick. Her fingers reached for it, drawing it to her. It wasn't a lipstick; it was a lip gloss.

Lottie never used lip gloss, hadn't since she was a teenager. And she'd never heard of the brand. She favoured Clarins or Dior. This was cheap, lurid-coloured packaging with sunflowers on. Something someone young would use. She felt herself go hot and then cold. Her stomach was doing a dance. This wasn't hers. What was another woman's lip gloss doing in her bedroom? She opened it up, took out the wand, smelt it. A strong synthetic scent of strawberry hit her nose. She ran the wand across the back of her hand, grimacing at the bright red, sparkly trail it left behind. It was tacky. Flashy. Something that someone would wear to make a statement or to seduce. Who did it belong to?

Tears stung at the back of her throat as she recalled the photo of Tasha she'd seen on Instagram. The girl's face hidden coquettishly under a hat, just her mouth showing, a mouth that was a streak of red. Did this gloss belong to her? She swallowed. Of course it didn't. Here she was again, putting two and two together and making five. She had to stop jumping to conclusions.

She stared out of the window. It was a good day for washing. She put the lip gloss on the bedside cabinet and then started stripping the bed, throwing the quilt onto the floor, pretending to herself that she wasn't examining the bottom sheet as she pulled it off the bed. There was a jolt in her stomach – there was a red hair on the underside of Nick's pillow. She held it up to the light streaming through the window. Was it hers? She held it up to her head. It was the same length as her own hair. She placed it carefully on the bedside cabinet, next to the lip gloss. And then she tugged at the sheet, took off the pillowcases and ripped the white jacquard cover off the duvet.

She pushed the box of clothes back under the bed. Shorts wouldn't do. Not today. Picking out some white cropped trousers and a green linen blouse that matched the colour of her eyes, she topped it off with the heavy gold chain Nick had bought her for Christmas, and some Kurt Geiger sandals that made her three inches taller. After carefully applying her make-up, she teased and curled her hair. 'Beautiful,' she said to her reflection in the mirror.

Time to meet this Tasha. And the perfect time too, with Nick away at the exhibition. Time to reassure herself that the lip gloss didn't belong to this slip of a girl. She

172

thought again of the text message, of Nick's lie that he'd been out with Kas. She was being silly – he'd explained why he'd lied, that the message had been from his father. Still it wouldn't hurt to meet this Tasha, to size her up once and for all.

Lottie picked up the wedding photo that stood on her dressing table. She took a deep breath in slowly to the count of four, held it for a count of four, and then breathed out slowly, as Hannah had taught her to do when she got herself into a state. Over the last few years, Hannah had been great at reminding her that the paranoid thoughts that often threatened to overwhelm her were just that – thoughts. And thoughts that she had conjured out of nowhere. She breathed in deeply again. The lip gloss didn't belong to Tasha. She'd probably bought it herself years ago and forgotten about it. She picked up the strand of hair again, and held it against her own hair. She was being silly – it was a perfect match.

Lottie strode into the practice, past Ruth's, Nick's and Kas's empty offices, heading for the main open-plan area where everyone else sat. In the glass-walled meeting room, Kas stood in front of a screen, nodding as a couple of suited blokes talked at him.

Lottie scanned the room, searching for Tasha's flaming red hair.

'Lottie,' Pauline said, standing up and taking off her glasses, leaving them hanging on a chain around her neck. 'What a lovely surprise. Sorry I missed you the other week.'

173

'Hi, Pauline.' Now that she was here, Lottie felt her confidence slipping. On the way across town she'd thought of an excuse for turning up at the office out of the blue – to say goodbye to Pauline. What she hadn't fathomed out though was what she would say to Tasha when she met her. 'Just thought I'd pop by to wish you well. When do you leave again?'

Pauline beamed. 'That's nice of you. I go in three weeks. The end of August.'

'Nick will miss you.'

'Oh, I doubt that. Tasha seems to have everything in hand.'

Lottie swallowed as she studied Pauline's face. Was there a hidden meaning behind her words? Before she could ask exactly what Tasha had in hand, Kas's voice boomed across the room. 'Pauline, would you mind making some more coffee?'

The secretary rolled her eyes at Lottie. 'Don't men know how to switch on a coffee machine? Back in a jiffy.' She shook her head and bustled away.

Lottie looked around the room again. Where was Tasha? In the loo perhaps?

'Lottie!' Daisy appeared from a side door, her hair sticking up, a smudge of dirt on her cheek.

'What have you been up to?' Lottie said. 'Come here.' She took a tissue out of a box on Pauline's desk and wiped at the mark on Daisy's face.

Daisy reared away from her. 'You're worse than Mum.'

Lottie felt her stomach twinge as Daisy laughed.

'I'm filthy though, aren't I?' Daisy said. 'I've been

174

filing in the archive room.' She lowered her voice. 'It's sooo boring.'

'Are you getting on okay, apart from that?'

Daisy blew a huge pink bubble gum bubble, letting it pop before she answered. She scrunched her nose up in exactly the same way that Hannah did when she was lying. 'It's not bad.'

'Nick's not being a slave driver?'

Daisy scratched at her arm. Lottie suddenly felt sorry for the girl. Hannah's dislike of Nick had obviously rubbed off on her daughter, and Daisy was too polite to say so.

'It's mostly Kas I work for.' Daisy sniffed and pulled a face.

'What's with the face? Everything okay?'

Daisy tucked her hair behind her ear. 'Nothing. I'll just be glad when the month is up.'

'He's a bit of a joker, isn't he, Kas?'

'Likes to think he is.'

'And a bit of a ladies' man too. Sometimes he thinks his banter is funny when it's not.'

Daisy's face turned crimson. 'He's fine, Auntie Lottie. I can handle him.' She crossed her arms.

'I'm sure you can.'

'Too right. He's too busy trying to impress Tasha anyway than to bother with me.'

'Is he now?' Lottie said. 'Where is she, by the way?'

Daisy shrugged. 'Haven't seen her today. Maybe she's gone down to the exhibition in Birmingham with them? I'm sure I heard Ruth asking her about it.'

Lottie felt the heat rising up her neck. Ruth had said it would just be her and Nick. In fact, Nick had been adamant that she shouldn't ask Tasha to help them out at the exhibition. How come the plans had suddenly changed?

Daisy must have picked up on Lottie's face because she suddenly said: 'Or she might be off. I overheard Pauline in the break room yesterday. Apparently she has a lot of time off. A sick father. Or maybe it's her mother. I'm not sure. I don't pay much attention. Too busy filing.'

Lottie kissed her cheek. 'Don't worry about it. I just wanted to meet her. Say hello. You get back to your work.'

'Thanks. Sooo looking forward to it.' Daisy sloped off, as Pauline came back to her desk.

'Tasha around?' Lottie asked. 'I was hoping to say hello to her.'

A frown creased Pauline's forehead. 'Ruth rang to say Tasha wouldn't be in today. Not sure why.' She let out a long sigh. 'I'm just keeping my head down and concentrating on getting to the end of the month.' She held up her hands in a gesture of resignation. 'Whatever happens after that, they'll all just have to get on with it.'

'Don't blame you,' Lottie said. Her mind was whirring. What did Pauline mean? Get on with what? 'Remind me which hotel Nick is staying at in Birmingham, Pauline?'

'Give me a minute. He booked it himself.' The secretary sat down and tapped away at her computer. 'The Crowne Plaza. Going to surprise him?'

'I most certainly am,' Lottie said, giving Pauline a wave and striding across the room.

* * *

176

When Lottie reached Ruth's office, she snuck a quick look along the corridor before slipping inside the room and closing the door behind her. To the left of Ruth's desk was a row of filing cabinets, labelled alphabetically. She opened the one marked 'E-H' and flipped through the files searching for Natasha Grant. There it was. With a quick glance to make sure that no one was walking past, she pulled a brown manila folder out of the drawer. She flipped open the folder, looking for the one thing she wanted: Tasha's address.

'Lottie?'

Lottie dropped the file as she turned to find Kas staring at her. She picked up the folder and stuffed it back into the filing cabinet, slamming the heavy drawer shut.

'What are you doing?'

'Oh, God, you nearly gave me a heart attack.' Lottie grabbed her bag and made her way towards the door.

'Can I help you with something?'

'I was after Pauline's home address,' Lottie said, trying to usher him out of the door.

He crossed his arms, refusing to budge.

'But you know where she lives. We've been there many a time for dinner.'

'Doh,' Lottie said. 'I know where it is, of course I do. But I don't know the address.'

'Why do you want her address?'

'I want to send her some flowers. She's been very good to me these past ten years. Do you remember when she made me that cake when I broke my wrist and—'

'You could just send them to the office?' Kas said, a

puzzled look on his face. 'She's not leaving for another few weeks.'

Lottie sighed. 'I know that, Kas, but I wanted to drop round with them, take her a cake and a bottle of bubbly. She'll be going home to that empty house. She'll feel like she's lost a family. I thought it'd be nice to be there for her.'

'But why do you need her address, then?'

Lottie shook her head and smiled. 'I'm going to get a present sent to her, as well.'

Kas frowned. 'Right.'

'You men. You just don't get it, do you?'

Kas shrugged. 'Obviously we don't.'

'I've got to dash, Kas. Is your mum better yet? Have you decided when you're going up to visit your parents?'

'Not sure. I'll drop Nick's present at the cottage though. No problem.' He shook his head. 'Can't understand why you didn't get him an inflatable paddleboard rather than a hard one. Lucky I've got a roof rack.'

'You know Nick. Only the best for him.' She kissed him on the cheek.

'I'm looking forward to the weekend,' he said.

She gave him a hug, peeling away from him when he held on a bit too long. 'We're looking forward to having you. Bet you've been feeling it, with Sienna . . .' she hesitated, trying to find the right word '. . . leaving.'

'It has been a bit strange,' he said, 'but, you know me, I've got other irons in the fire.'

'Yes, you said. Date go all right the other Friday?'

'Of course.'

'Good for you. She's a lucky girl, whoever she is.'

He winked at her. 'Could have been you. You should have married this partner.'

'I'm very happy with Nick,' she said, aware her voice was sharp.

'Hey, I was only joking.' He winked at her.

Lottie sighed. 'Sorry, one of those days. I really have got to dash. Let me know when you're going up to the Lakes,' she shouted over her shoulder as she headed towards the lift.

Once inside, she finally let herself breathe out. Had Kas believed her? Was he going to the filing cabinet right now? He'd surely clock which folder she'd stuffed back in there. She didn't even know if she'd put it in the right place.

So what? She didn't care if Kas realised what she was doing. She was doing what she had to do – putting her mind at rest. Because if Tasha was at home, then she wouldn't be in Birmingham – with Nick.

Lottie parked at the end of Tasha's street and got out. She didn't really want to leave her car – it wasn't the nicest part of town by any stretch of the imagination – but she didn't want to park outside Tasha's house. She didn't want to be too obvious. If there was a sick parent there, she didn't want to cause them any grief.

She strode off down the street, avoiding the dog poo that seemed to mark every other metre, the bits of rubbish, McDonald's wrappers, bottles of Coke pushed into hedges. She counted the numbers of the houses as she passed. Sixteen, eighteen, twenty, twenty-two. She looked across the road. Twenty-three, that was it. Tatty lace curtains hung in the front room; the low privet hedge that separated the small scrap of front garden from its neighbour was overgrown; the door, a dirty shade of red, had peeling paint on it. She wondered if Nick knew this was where Tasha lived. She gazed up at the window on the first floor. Was that her bedroom?

Lottie's heart hammered in her chest as she crossed the road. She wanted Tasha to be at home but what would she say if she was? All the way there she'd tried to think of an excuse as to why she'd come to see her. The best she'd been able to come up with was that she was just passing and had heard that Tasha's father wasn't very well, and wondered if there was anything she could do to help. But then Tasha would surely wonder how Lottie had got her address. Weren't personal details supposed to be confidential? Some law the EU had brought in? Or maybe that didn't apply now that the UK had come out of Europe?

When she reached the door, she almost turned round. But a flick of the curtains in the house next door, the scrunched-up face of an old woman peering through the grimy glass, stopped her.

After taking a deep breath, she rapped at the door, once, twice. She stood back. Waited. No one answered. She leant towards the door and listened. Nothing. Where was Tasha? Suddenly, more than anything, Lottie wanted her to be here and not in Birmingham with her husband.

Moving to the front window, she bent down, peering under the curtains where there was a couple-of-inches gap between them and the sill. The room was empty. She could make out a brown settee, a worn-down chair and a large TV. Nothing else.

'They ain't in.' An old woman with a walking stick was peering over the hedge of the house to Lottie's left.

'When will they be back?'

The woman narrowed her eyes at Lottie. 'Who's asking?'

'I'm a work colleague of Tasha's.'

'Hmm.' The woman squinted at her. 'You have the look of the social about you. Checking up on them, are you?'

'I'm after Tasha.'

'Well, they ain't in.'

'I can see that. Do you have any idea where they are?'

'How should I know?' The woman crossed her arms. 'I'm not their bloody keeper, am I?'

The nosey next-door neighbour was still standing on her front step as Lottie strode back to her car. As she pulled off from the kerb, her phone rang.

She stopped the car, earning herself a loud beep and the finger from a man in the car behind her. She ignored him and pulled her phone out of her bag. Ginger.

'Hey, Charlotte. How's it going?'

'Great, thanks. How are you?'

'Couldn't be better. Listen, d'you fancy getting together for dinner tonight? I have a late meeting but could do eight thirty? We need to talk through the role, if you're up for it.'

Lottie hesitated. The last thing she felt like doing was being sociable.

'Brad's busy tonight, so I thought it'd be the ideal time for us girls to catch up.'

'Of course, I'd love to,' Lottie said. How could she say no?

'I've booked the Sydney Grill.'

'Lovely. See you then.'

Lottie hung up. Ginger's invite had put paid to the idea that had been forming in her head – that she'd drive down to Birmingham, surprise Nick at the exhibition.

Then again, she'd be finished with Ginger by ten thirty, eleven at the latest. And Birmingham wasn't far, was it? An hour? An hour and a half maybe? If she drove like the clappers she'd make it for midnight.

Her hands were sweating as she switched on the ignition. Why shouldn't she go down there? Why shouldn't she surprise her husband? Nick would be made up. Wouldn't he?

CHAPTER 17

'You've been a great help today, hasn't she, Bil?' Ruth said as she topped up my wine glass.

Nick raised his glass towards me. After a round of cocktails to start, we were well on our way down a second bottle of Chianti, although Ruth had drunk the majority of it. I wondered if she always sunk a load every night – and who wouldn't, living with a misery guts like that Claire? – or if she was using the drink to bolster her nerves because I was there.

'I'm learning loads,' I said. 'And I've really enjoyed it.' I was learning a lot. Not about the business. About Nick. About the way he ran his hand through his floppy fringe when he was nervous or tired, how he liked apple turnovers but not cinnamon rolls, how great he was at talking to the people who came on the stand, how stressed he was about the new hotel project. I was also learning that Ruth had the serious hots for me – even if she hadn't admitted it to herself yet.

Ruth hiccupped. 'Sorry,' she said, hiccupping again, as

she touched my arm. 'We've enjoyed having you with us, haven't we, Bil?' She pointed at my plate of cannelloni. 'Aren't you much for that? Here, swap if you like.'

'I'm fine. Not that hungry.'

'Here.' She held out her fork. 'This carbonara is delish. Go on, try some. She'll be wasting away, won't she, Nick? There's nothing to her.'

There wasn't anything to me, compared to Ruth, but, although I was slim, I still had the curves that men loved. 'You've got a great pair, angel,' Kenny said, every time he saw me, adding a wink in case I didn't get quite how much he wanted to do me.

'Come on, just a teeny-weeny bite.' Ruth waved the fork in front of my face. A sudden flash of my mother doing the same when I was three or four came back to me. Her eyes were brown, like chocolate milk buttons. Sad. Lined by kohl. I'd forgotten that.

Nick pushed away his empty plate. 'Leave her, Ruth. She said she's not hungry.'

'Who made you the boss?' Ruth scowled at him, threw her fork onto her plate and hiccupped again. 'Let's stick to the drink, then.' After seeing that there were only dregs left in the wine bottle, she flagged down a passing waitress. 'Tequila shots, please. Three each.'

'Ruth!' Nick shook his head. 'Don't forget the exhibition's still on tomorrow.'

'You met with the owners of the hotel project today, didn't you? Thought you said you'd got an easier day tomorrow.' Ruth leant towards me, her voice low. 'He is such an old fuddy-duddy.'

184

Nick pushed his fingers through his hair. 'An easier day than I've had today, hopefully.' He glanced at his watch and I followed his gaze, down to his tanned arm, brown hairs covering it. I had the sudden desire to lean forward and lick him. His phone buzzed. He glanced at it, before turning to me. 'What time's your train again?'

'Nine.' We'd taken a taxi into the city centre so I could catch the last train home after we'd eaten.

Ruth hiccupped again. 'Bil, come on. The night's still young.'

He laughed. 'Just because you've been let off the leash.'

Ruth scowled. 'I'm not a bloody dog.' She picked up her phone and switched it off. 'There.'

I reached under the table, searching for my bag, my hand, accidentally on purpose, brushing Nick's knee. His leg didn't move. He didn't spring away from my touch, he just stared at me, a questioning look on his face.

'I should be going,' I said, picking up my bag. 'I don't want to miss the train.'

Ruth clapped her hands together, like a child that's had too much sugar. 'Why don't you stay at the hotel? It'll be fine. Help us out again tomorrow. And then I can give you a lift back. Save you the train fare.'

'I don't know,' my mouth said while inside I was screaming: 'yes, yes'.

'Ruth.' Nick sighed. 'She has to get back.'

'Oh, go on,' she said to me. 'Don't you be a spoilsport. Like him.' She flicked a stray peppercorn at Nick. 'Go on. It's not often I get a night away from . . . from home. Please. I need a drinking buddy.'

I deliberately didn't look at Nick. 'If you're sure?'

'Don't you have things to do tomorrow?' he said.

I shrugged. 'Nothing I can't put off.' Dad would go ballistic. I'd already had an earful when I'd called him to say I'd be back late. He'd wanted to know what he'd do for his tea, moaning when I reeled off the list of ready meals in the freezer he could choose from. He wasn't the least bit interested in where I was, whether I was safe. No surprise there. It had never crossed his mind to worry about me before, so why would he start now? In the three years I'd been away, he hadn't called me once. Not once. Yes, he would go ballistic when he realised I wasn't back in the morning. He liked his breakfast in bed, whether I had to go to work or not. A bacon sarnie, lashings of butter, topped off with brown sauce. And a mug of tea, so strong you could stand your spoon up in it.

Ruth clapped. 'That's settled then. Ah, here we go,' she said as the waitress appeared with a tray full of tequila shots, salt and lime.

Ruth grabbed the tray off her and handed me and Nick three each. 'One after the other. Okay? No wussing out.'

'You know I can't do tequila, Ruth.' Nick crossed his arms.

'All the more for us, then, hey?' She winked at me.

'Go on, you're the boss. You have to join in. For team morale.' I pushed a glass towards him. He'd only had a couple of glasses of wine with the meal and had sipped at the cocktail Ruth had ordered for him.

186

He shook his head and waved his still-white napkin in the air. 'Okay, I surrender.'

'On three,' Ruth said. We all sprinkled salt onto the side of our hands and then tipped our heads back. I'd forgotten quite how fiery tequila was. I'd only had it once before. At a party when I was at school. Kenny had brought a bottle of it with him, had passed it around, making sure I got an extra-large shot.

'Oh, God,' Ruth said, the piece of lime halfway to her mouth as I coughed and spluttered. 'Have you never had tequila before?'

'Of course I have. Just went down the wrong way, that's all.'

Nick chewed on his lip, a smile on his face.

I pointed at his empty glass. 'I thought you didn't do tequila.'

He picked up another shot. 'If you can't beat 'em, join 'em.'

An hour later and we were in the hotel bar, another bottle of wine and a few shots down.

'I need to go to bed.' Nick tipped the last of his whiskey into his mouth. He was knackered, poor thing. Knackered but hot.

It was half eleven. 'Me too.'

'We need to get you a room.' He picked up his jacket.

'Come on, you,' he said to Ruth, holding out his hand. Her eyes were rolling ever so slightly in her head.

'One more.' She slammed her hand down onto the table so that our glasses jumped.

'Ruth.'

She let out a big sigh. 'You are such a spoilsport, Bil. For the life of me, I don't know what my sister sees in you.' She turned to me. 'Do you?'

'No,' I said, narrowing my eyes at Nick, 'she can't be with him for his drinking ability, anyway.'

Ruth hiccupped. 'Well, he must have something about him.' She widened her eyes and started to giggle before her face turned serious. 'Urgh, yuck. I never, never, never, never, ever want to find out.'

Nick stood up. Even in the dim-lit bar I could tell the blood was rushing to his face. 'Come on, you, let's get you to bed.'

Ruth tried to get up before falling in a heap back into her chair. 'You shouldn't be trying to take your sister-in-law to bed.'

Shaking his head, he bent down and caught her under one arm, pulling her up.

I grabbed her bag and we headed for the reception desk, Ruth between us, her arms linking ours.

'I'm sorry, we're fully booked,' the bright-eyed receptionist said, after we'd enquired about a room for me.

'S'no problem. You can stay in my room.' She leant towards the receptionist, and whispered, 'I've got twin beds. I'm not meaning anything by it. I have a partner so don't you be inplying . . . imferring . . . saying I'm up to something.' She pointed her finger over the desk. ''Cos I'm not.'

'That's fine. The charge is per room.' The receptionist smiled at me. 'If I could just have your name for security purposes.'

I gave her my name and the three of us made our way to the lift.

'I look bloody awful,' Ruth said, once we'd persuaded her to get into the lift and not return to the bar for another drink. She peered into the mirror, poking her tongue out. 'My tongue is bleeding!'

'That's red wine, you idiot.' Nick rolled his eyes at me over the top of her head and I giggled.

At the tenth floor we all got out.

I fished in Ruth's bag for her door key, found it and pushed it into the entry lock, relieved when it flashed green and not red.

'You'll be all right?' Nick said from the corridor as I steered Ruth into the room.

'Bugger off,' Ruth shouted over her shoulder, 'we'll be fine. We don't need you and your . . . your . . .' She collapsed into hysterics.

'I'm just next door. Knock if you need me.' His eyes met mine briefly before he pulled the door shut.

I gave Ruth a little push.

She fell onto the bed nearest the window, landing on her front, her head squashed into the pillow. 'I've been drugged.' She lifted her head from the pillow for a second before collapsing back into it.

'With tequila and red wine. Here, let's get you out of your clothes.'

'Naughty,' she said, turning over and trying to sit up. 'Claire wouldn't like it. Oh no, no she wouldn't. Not at all. She'd be very, very, very mad. She gets very jealous, yes, she does. Very, very, very jealous. She would—' she

189

made a slicing motion across her neck with her finger '—if you were here. You first and then me. She said she would and I believe her. I really, really do. And we don't want to get on the wrong side of her,' she said, through her hiccups, 'because she knows how to torture people.' She started cackling madly like a crazed hyena. 'Research for her novel,' she finally got out.

'Best not to tell Claire then,' I said, unzipping Ruth's trousers and, grasping the ends of the legs, pulling them off her in one smooth movement. I'd had plenty of practice with my old man over the years. First with the drink and now, since I'd come back, with this fatigue thing he was saying he'd got. He was definitely swinging the lead – he was as right as rain, except for when the social called or he had to go to the job centre or the doctor's.

Giggling, Ruth tried to pull me towards her. 'You are very, very, very lovely.' She fixed what I'm sure she thought was an alluring pout onto her face.

'I know.'

She tugged me so hard I fell forward, my face only a couple of inches from hers. She lunged at me, her red tongue pushed out towards my mouth.

I levered myself up. 'You're drunk.'

'I am,' she said and laughed manically, before suddenly bursting into tears.

I offered her a tissue from a box on the bedside cabinet, but she refused to take it, burying her face in her pillow.

'It's the drink,' I said. 'I'll get you a glass of water.'

After locking myself in the bathroom, I brushed my teeth with the toothbrush I had in my bag and helped

190

myself to her toothpaste. I touched up my make-up, reapplying my lip gloss so that my lips plumped up, sweeping a hint of blusher onto my cheekbones. When I went back into the bedroom, a toothbrush mug filled with water in my hand, she was on her back, snoring loudly.

I lay down on the other bed, watching the minutes tick by on my phone. When twenty minutes had passed, I got up and stood over her. She was out for the count. I tiptoed out of the room, taking the key with me.

I stood outside Nick's door and took a breath, before tapping on it lightly.

He must have been standing behind it because within three seconds the door was open and there he was, a shy smile on his face.

'You said to knock if I needed you,' I said, taking a step towards him.

CHAPTER 18

'Hey, you sure you won't have another glass? This is supposed to be a celebration.' Ginger lifted the bottle of Dom Pérignon out of the ice bucket. She'd certainly pushed the boat out.

Lottie hesitated. She would have liked nothing more than to celebrate with Ginger – after all, it wasn't every day she got to go to the Sydney Grill, and talk to a casting director about a part, *her* part, in a major new US series – but at that moment all she could think about was driving down to Birmingham, and what would be waiting for her when she got there. Nick had sent her a very short text on her way to the restaurant, saying he was out with clients, would be late back and would call her tomorrow.

'Just a little glass?' Ginger said.

'No, I'm fine, honestly. One's enough for me. Sorry, I should have mentioned it. I'm off to Birmingham later.'

'Birmingham? Tonight? What's happening in Birmingham?'

Lottie felt the knot in her stomach tighten. 'My husband's down there. At an exhibition. Said I'd join him.'

Ginger raised her glass. 'To love's young dream. Can't bear to be apart? Can you manage six months without him?'

'Oh, God, yes.' Lottie didn't want Ginger to think she'd be mooning around like a lovesick teenager all the time. 'Nick's thrilled for me.' She swallowed and sipped at her sparkling mineral water. It was true. Nick was thrilled for her. Was that because he was pleased she'd landed such a big role, or because he wanted her out of the way? She stared at Ginger's champagne. Right at this moment, she'd kill for a glass.

Ginger sniffed. 'Some guys can be jealous. Especially if they're not in the biz. Great he's so supportive.'

Ginger was smiling but Lottie thought it was through gritted teeth. If she was reading the situation correctly, it seemed Ginger's partner might not be so supportive of her career. She glanced at Ginger's left hand. There was a faint white line on her ring finger.

Ginger caught her glance. 'Divorced.' She raised her glass again, and took a large gulp. 'Three months ago.'

'Sorry to hear that.'

'Jeez, don't be sorry. Best thing ever. Given me a new lease of life. I can now just dance to my own tune. Anyway, he was a complete waste of time. Should never have married him in the first place.'

'Oh?'

'On the rebound.'

Lottie bit her lip. When she and Nick had first got together, she'd wondered if he'd been on the rebound, if it was too soon for him to be considering a serious

193

relationship, let alone marriage. His wife had only been dead five years. Five years was nothing when you'd lost someone you'd spent most of your teenage and adult years with. And he hadn't dated anyone else in that time. He'd only had two girlfriends in his whole life he'd told Lottie – her and Louise – had never, as he'd put it, *felt the need to sow his wild oats.*

Ginger brushed a crumb from the arm of her dress. Again, she was dressed like some exotic bird, this time all greens and oranges, on her dress, her long scarf and the turban she had on. 'What do they say? Marry in haste, repent at leisure. My first love was the guy for me. Always will be.'

Lottie took a sip of water. Nick was her first love. She'd had relationships before him, of course she had – she'd been thirty-four when they'd met – but she'd never been in love with any of the men she'd dated. Nick was different. As soon as she'd clapped eyes on him in the gym that day with Ruth, she'd known. It was as if a firework had gone off inside her, every cell fizzing and buzzing. 'Childhood sweetheart?' Lottie said.

'Something like that.'

'What happened to him?'

Ginger's eyes misted over. She shrugged. 'Crap got in the way and we ended up splitting. Nine months later I met Frankie, my husband.'

'Were you married a long time?'

'Too freaking long. Seventeen years. Met him almost as soon as I stepped off the plane in California. We got hitched the moment I was legally allowed to do so. Would

194

have married him sooner but my mum wouldn't give us her permission.' She ran the tip of her knife over the white tablecloth. 'She was very clingy.'

'Oh?'

'My old fella had died. Unexpectedly.' Ginger took a long swig of her champagne.

'Oh, I'm sorry to hear that.'

Ginger shrugged again. 'Don't be. He was a bastard. Anyway, America was supposed to be a new start for me and Mum. Just us girls, you know? And then I met Frankie. And that shattered all her dreams. Jeez, I was one selfish bitch.'

Lottie speared a piece of asparagus. 'No, you weren't. Sometimes love just whirls you up and you've got to go with it. I was the same when I met Nick.'

'Been married long?'

'Ten years. We were married a year to the day after we first met.'

'You held out for the right man.'

'Yes.' Lottie dabbed at her mouth with her napkin. 'And I had to. Sort of. Nick was married before.'

Ginger's eyes widened. 'Way to go, girl! You were the other woman? That'll stand you in good stead. Chrissie, the role you're playing, is the other woman.'

The other woman? Lottie swallowed. She could never imagine being that sort of woman. 'Oh, no. Nothing like that. I didn't know I was waiting for him.' Lottie put down her fork. 'I'm not making much sense, am I? Nick was a widower. His wife was his childhood sweetheart. They married young. But then she died.' Why was she giving this woman she hardly knew her life history? She had that kind of face, the sort that made you want to spill everything you were thinking and feeling.

'Oh Gawd. That's even worse.'

Lottie frowned at her.

'You can never match up to a dead wife, can you?' Ginger patted Lottie's hand. 'Ignore me! I always get like this when I've had a drink. Can't stop my big mouth.'

Lottie smiled. 'It doesn't matter.' And it didn't. She couldn't be worrying about dead women. It was the ones who were alive she had to watch out for.

'Anyway,' Lottie said. 'Back to the part. I thought it was Chrissie's husband who's having the affair?'

'He is. But Chrissie is too. She's one mad bitch. Tries to kill her husband's mistress.'

Lottie swallowed. 'Blimey. Complicated.'

'That's life. Full of complications and secrets. I should know.'

'Oh?'

'Turns out I didn't know everything about my Frankie. The bastard cheated on me throughout our marriage. From the off. And I never had a damn clue. Isn't that always the way? Wifey is the last to know?'

Lottie's stomach flipped. She put down her fork. 'You never had an inkling?'

'Not a one.' She pronounced each word slowly. 'What a dumb bitch, hey? Guys. They can be so cunning, can't they?'

Lottie's mouth was dry. Ginger was right. Men could be cunning. Women too. Sometimes they'd go to any

196

length to get what they wanted. Was the trouble Nick was having with the hotel project all lies? Was he using that as a cover to meet up with Tasha? Did Nick want Tasha? Had he stopped wanting Lottie? Was that why he'd been so quiet lately? 'Sorry,' she said, aware Ginger had been asking her a question while her mind had been running away with her.

'What happened to your husband's first wife, then? She died? The big C, was it?'

'No.' Lottie hesitated. 'Suicide.'

'Oh, fuck, how awful. Why did she kill herself?'

Lottie gulped at the woman's forthrightness. Still, she'd been in America nearly half her life – was it any wonder she said it like it was?

'Sorry,' Ginger said. 'Tell me to mind my own.'

'It's fine. I don't mind you asking. I'm not entirely sure I know the answer though. I think she'd been depressed.'

'You've never asked your husband? Jeez, I grilled my ex on the first night I met him. There wasn't a thing I didn't know about him and his family after that.' She snorted. 'Apart from the shagging around he did, of course. He forgot to mention that.' She took a swig of her champagne. 'Can't believe you haven't asked him, though.'

Lottie shook her head. Nick had given her scant details about his first wife's death and she hadn't wanted to push him. If he'd wanted to tell her, he would have. It was something he'd always live with, but nothing that affected their relationship; he'd assured her of that. The one thing she did know about his first wife was that she'd been very clingy – that was something he'd let slip once. By clingy did he mean Louise hadn't trusted him? Had he given her reason not to? It was something that had never crossed her mind – until now. 'The past is the past, isn't it?' Lottie said.

'Sometimes the past rears its ugly head, girl.'

'How did you find out about your husband? That he was cheating on you?'

'Caught him in bed with his latest fling. Our bed,' Ginger said, shaking her head. 'Dumb fuck, as we say in the US. Guessing it was her idea. She wanted me to find out.' She raised her champagne flute. 'Good luck to her. She'll need it. Some guys can't keep it in their pants, can they?'

Tears clogged the back of Lottie's throat. She took a large mouthful of mineral water, trying to wash them away.

'You okay?'

'Fine.' She plastered on a smile. 'Tell me more about the role. I can't wait to see the scripts.'

'You not got them yet?'

Lottie shook her head. 'Nor the contract.'

Ginger rolled her eyes. 'Brad. He's useless. I'll get onto him in the morning.'

'Shame he couldn't make it tonight.' She hesitated. 'He's happy that I got the part?'

'Sure is. Thinks you're perfect. Tonight's nothing personal. He's just a busy guy.' She winked at Lottie. 'Or at least he likes to imagine he is.'

As Ginger talked about the role and the series in general, Lottie tried to concentrate on what she was saying, hoping she was nodding in all the right places. She had to make her escape. She had to get to Birmingham to find out if Tasha was there or not.

They were finishing their coffees when Lottie spotted Gwen, Felix and Claire, hurrying along the street outside. They'd probably been to the theatre – *Evita* was on at the Palace. Gwen was an avid musicals fan, Claire too. The pair of them had bonded at Gwen's Abba-themed sixtieth birthday party over their love of *Mamma Mia!* and they usually went to see every show that came to Manchester.

Felix had no doubt come to collect them. He was good like that. She waved as they passed the window but got nothing in return. Funny, she was sure Felix had seen her. Claire too. Was Claire annoyed with her? Lottie had been surprised when she'd called the previous evening, suggesting they meet up while Nick and Ruth were in Birmingham. Claire wasn't one to propose things off her own bat. She usually tagged along with a bored look on her face whenever there was any sort of social gathering, the sort where you had to converse with each other. Probably why she liked musicals – all the music left no chance to talk to the person you'd gone with.

Lottie unwrapped a chocolate mint. Perhaps Claire had realised her headache was just an excuse. Claire had seen her; she was sure of it. Sod her. The sooner Ruth's patience with Claire ran out, the better.

* * *

It was gone eleven by the time they'd finished chatting. For the whole of the previous hour, Lottie had kept looking at her watch, wishing Ginger would get the hint, but the casting director didn't seem intent on going anywhere.

They hugged outside the restaurant. Ginger was such a nice woman. Lottie was relieved. Brad might not have taken to her, nor she to him, but at least she could rely on Ginger when she got to Los Angeles. She'd warmed to her immediately – she was her sort of woman – earthy and liked a laugh. And it helped she was British. They were on the same wavelength.

She headed for the motorway. She'd been tempted to tell Ginger the real reason she was going to Birmingham. But the woman might think she was mad, travelling seventy-five miles on a whim. Or would she? Ginger didn't trust men – that much was clear – and she had every good reason not to. Hearing what had happened to Ginger had convinced Lottie that going to Birmingham to find out for herself if anything was going on was the only thing she could do.

CHAPTER 19

'Have you got any paracetamol?' I whispered as Nick opened the door. 'Sorry, have I woken you?'

He ran his hand over his face and then through his hair. With the other, he pulled down his T-shirt but not before I got a glimpse of golden skin, taut abs. He had on tight black underwear, his legs muscly and shapely beneath them.

'Headache?' he asked.

'Not me. But when Ruth wakes up, she's going to have a hell of a hangover.'

'You'd better come in,' Nick said, stepping back to let me into his room.

As I walked past him, I could smell the rich spiciness of his aftershave and a hint of the whiskey he'd been drinking in the bar, mixed with the mint of toothpaste.

His room was neat, no clothes strewn around, no bits and bobs on the sides, no wet towels, empty cups, loose change. Everything was in its place.

'Ruth okay?'

'Snoring her head off.' I sat down in one of the chairs next to a small table near the window, crossing my legs. My mother had been tall too – I could tell from the wedding photos I'd once found in a box in the airing cupboard. I wondered if there was anything else I'd inherited from her, besides long legs and a complete and utter loathing for my old man.

Nick opened his briefcase and searched through it. 'She got a bit giddy, didn't she? She doesn't usually drink that much. At least I don't think she does.'

I shrugged. 'We all need to let our hair down every now and then, don't we? And I'd turn to drink if that Claire was my other half. Talk about resting bitch face.'

'She's not that bad.' He grinned. 'Just a bit intense, you know. They've been together a long time.'

'Does your wife approve of Claire? Or does she reckon her sister could do better?'

His head shot up from his briefcase. 'My wife?' He coughed, his face turning pink. 'She thinks Ruth could be happier. But me, I can't work out if Claire is the problem or Ruth.' He held up a blister pack of tablets. 'Here we go. Thought I had some somewhere.'

He threw them at me and I caught them with one hand.

'Good catch.'

I winked. 'That's what all the boys say.'

'I'm going to have to watch you, aren't I?'

'Hope so.'

Leaning forward, I opened a cupboard door to reveal the mini bar. 'Fancy one?' I reached inside and picked out a couple of miniature bottles of whiskey.

He shook his head and took them from me, emptying the contents into two tumblers that stood on a tray next to the TV.

'Cheers,' he said, handing me the glass. 'Thanks for helping us out. And thanks for looking after Ruth.'

'My pleasure.' I sipped at the whiskey. It was like fire in my throat. 'She likes a drink, all right, does our Ruth. Is your wife the same? Two peas in a pod?'

'God, no.' He downed the contents of his glass in one mouthful. 'My wife doesn't drink much.'

'She's not a teetotaller, is she? Boring.'

'You don't mince your words, do you?' He lifted the glass to his mouth, even though it was empty. 'We're trying for a baby. She wants to be as healthy as she can be.'

Ah, the elusive baby. 'Well, my mother drank every day when she was pregnant with me. Did me no harm, did it?'

He eyed me over the rim of his glass. 'No, I can see that.'

'You'll make a great dad.'

'You think so?'

I sipped at my drink. 'Definitely. How lovely. A baby. I can't wait to have kids. I love them.'

'Oh, yes, you told me about your nephews. Twins.'

'They're brilliant. Love 'em to bits. I spend a lot of time with them.'

'They're lucky.'

Was he flirting with me? 'Not like having your own though, is it? I just need to meet the right man and then—' I knocked back the whiskey in one and put my glass on the table. 'I should be going. It's late.'

He cleared his throat. 'Yes.'

I stood up.

He did the same.

And then he was on me, pushing me back against the wall, his hands all over my body, his whiskey-laced tongue push, push, pushing between my lips.

CHAPTER 20

Lottie strode into the hotel reception. Roadworks on a large part of the M6 meant that it was nearly one in the morning and yet there was still a bunch of drinkers in the bar, laughing loudly and ordering another round. She cast her eye over them, but neither Nick, nor Ruth, was with them. Nor was there any sign of a redhead in high heels.

She made her way to the lift, ignoring the look the woman behind the reception desk shot her. The hotel was huge – nearly three hundred rooms, she guessed. There'd be no way of knowing if she was a guest or not. And she didn't have to ask which room Nick was in – and risk the receptionist calling up to his room to check whether he was expecting a visitor. A quick call to Pauline earlier – after she'd been to Tasha's house and found she wasn't there – had given her that.

Lottie stepped into the lift and checked her reflection in the mirror on the wall facing her.

There was a deep line of worry etched on her forehead.

She rubbed at it with her finger, before turning her attention to the rest of her face, quickly applying some lipstick and a brush of powder to try to tame her rosy cheeks. Her hand shook as she slicked the lipstick across her lips. Coming to Birmingham had seemed a good idea earlier but now she was here . . . what would she do if her suspicions were right? And what would she do if they were wrong? What if Tasha wasn't here, in Birmingham? What if Nick cottoned on to why she'd turned up and accused her again of not trusting him?

But she had to know if that woman was here or not. She'd risk Nick's anger if she was wrong. She had to know.

The lift doors slid open. Lottie stepped out, squinting at the metal plaque on the wall. Nick's room was to the right. She followed the corridor around, through a fire door, taking a left turn before heading along another corridor. Her legs were shaking. Everything was shaking.

Finally she reached room 1047. She plastered a smile on her face and tapped on the door. There was no answer. Her stomach flipped. Was he not in his room? Was he in Tasha's? Lottie peered along the corridor. She should have asked the woman on reception if Natasha Grant had a room booked – though perhaps she wouldn't have been able to give her that information. Or maybe Tasha and Nick had played it safe? Maybe Tasha was booked into another hotel and they'd waited until Ruth was asleep before Nick went to join her?

She put her ear to Nick's door and listened. Was that voices she could hear? Or was she imagining things?

Perhaps he had the TV on? Or maybe the sounds were coming from the next room? Even though it was deathly quiet in the corridor, it was difficult to tell.

Her heart felt as if it was going to burst out of her chest. She lifted a shaking hand to the door and knocked again, this time more loudly.

And then the door was being pulled back and there Nick was, completely starkers in front of her, blinking at her as if he'd seen a ghost.

'Lottie? What? Has something happened? What are you doing here? What time is it?'

'It's ten past one.'

'Why are you here?' He rubbed at his face.

'Surprise!'

He made no sign of moving.

'Are you going to let me in, or what?'

She didn't wait for him to say yes. She pushed past him and headed into the room. Her heart was hammering so loudly she thought she might faint.

The room was empty. Apart from his suitcase. Everything was typical Nick, everything in its place. And there was no naked woman lying in his bed. Her shoulders dropped down from under her ears as she let out a long breath. Tasha wasn't here.

Nick slipped back under the covers. 'What are you doing here, Lots? Is everything okay?'

'I missed you, that's all,' she said as she stripped off her clothes. 'It's all right if I miss you, isn't it?'

'Of course it is. I just wasn't expecting you. And not at this time of night.'

207

'I was out with Ginger.'

'Ginger?'

'The casting director. Not a problem, is it, me showing up?'

He held the covers open and she slipped between them, finding his whiskey-tasting mouth with hers, kissing him hungrily to stop herself from crying out with relief.

'Late night?' she said, when he pulled away and yawned.

'You know what Ruth's like when she has a taste of freedom. I had to drag her upstairs.'

'Don't blame her. She was probably high on having a break from Claire.'

He turned over and she snuggled into his back, wrapping her right arm around him, her palm flat on his chest. Tasha wasn't here. Not in this room. But it didn't mean that Nick's PA wasn't in Birmingham.

'I could give you a hand tomorrow if you like.'

Was it her imagination or had his body suddenly stiffened?

'I'm going back in the morning. I need to get over to the hotel complex. There's a problem with the roof. And anyway, day two is always quiet. Ruth can cope on her own.' He turned back towards her. 'And now I have my very own chauffeur. Thank God. You take your life into your own hands when you get into a car with Ruth.'

Lottie tutted at his comment but her mind was whirring. Did he not want her at the exhibition? Was that because Tasha *was* there? Lottie suddenly felt exhausted by it all, by the constant worry going around her head.

'I love you, Lots.'

208

'I love you more, Mr Moore.' She found his mouth again. He was hungry for her in a way he hadn't been for ages.

Afterwards, Lottie lay in the dark, eyes wide, as Nick snored softly beside her. She felt like a fool. She'd come all the way to Birmingham in the early hours of the morning to try to catch her husband out. And all because she'd found a lip gloss under her bed – one that, the more she thought about it, she'd probably bought herself. Ginger hadn't helped either, with her stories of her husband who couldn't keep it in his pants. She'd throw away the lip gloss tomorrow – forget all about it.

Along with her unfounded suspicions. Didn't her lack of trust say more about her, about just how insecure she was, than about Nick? She'd never doubted him in the past. Why did she now? Had the hormones she'd been pumping into her body over the past five years finally caught up with her? Were they making her irrational, paranoid? Or was her insecurity down to the fact that she couldn't give him the one thing he wanted – a baby – and that, deep down, she feared he would find someone who could?

She closed her eyes. Maybe counselling would help. Maybe she could look into it in LA. Didn't everyone have therapy over there? A therapist might help her to see that it was her overactive imagination that was hurting her, rather than her husband.

Might help her to see that Nick wasn't the guilty party here at all – she was.

CHAPTER 21

'Morning.' I shielded my eyes at the bright light streaming in through the window. 'Thought you might need this,' Ruth said.

I blinked. Ruth. For a second, I'd forgotten I was there, in the hotel, had thought I was back in my childhood bed, the thin sheets shrouding me, had thought the images rushing into my head, of Nick holding me, loving me, had been part of a dream.

But they weren't. They were real. Memories. The start of many more to come.

'Extra strong. Caffeine is great for hangovers.'

I pushed myself up and took the cup and saucer she was holding out to me. 'You were the one who was out cold.'

'Yeah, sorry about that.' She sat down on the bed opposite mine, picking up her phone so she didn't have to make eye contact with me. 'I didn't embarrass myself, did I?'

'No, you fell straight to sleep,' I lied. I'd keep the fact she'd tried to kiss me to myself – for the time being at least. Who knew when information like that could come in handy? I tried to make out whether she knew anyway, whether she was just fishing to see if I'd say anything, but her dark curls were hanging in front of her face so I couldn't tell what was going through that head of hers.

While she fiddled about with her phone, I took a sip of the dark liquid, wincing at the strength of it. Water, that's what I needed, not coffee. My mouth was parched. Not from the drink but from kissing Nick, from licking him, sucking him. I'd slunk back to Ruth's room just before one, relieved to find she was still snoring her head off. She'd get to know about us soon, I was sure of that – hell, the whole world would know soon – but I had to let Nick tell wifey first before everyone else found out.

Ruth turned her phone to face me so I could see the time on it. 'I would have let you sleep on, but we need to get going.'

I was surprised I'd slept. After returning to the room, I'd lain there, listening to Ruth's snores, my hand on the wall behind me, the wall that separated me from Nick, going over what we'd done, what he'd done. He'd been hungry for me, couldn't get enough of me, turning me this way and that before holding me in his arms. I would have liked to have fallen asleep, to wake up next to him, but there was Ruth to consider.

Ruth's phone buzzed into life. 'Hey,' she said, answering it. 'Sorry, sorry, we were out. With clients—' she cast me a guilty look '—well, I'm speaking to you now, aren't I? Of course I want to talk to you, Claire. Don't be like that, babe. I put my phone on mute and forgot to switch

211

it back on.' She mouthed *breakfast* at me and pointed at the floor before leaving the room.

Although I didn't want to wash Nick's scent off me, I showered and put on the clothes I'd been wearing yesterday, spraying myself liberally with perfume before I left the room. With Ruth out of the way at breakfast, there was time, more than enough time, to have a rerun of last night. I pushed my chest out and knocked on his door with a shaking hand. What was wrong with me? I couldn't be nervous, could I? I put my ear to the door, listening. I could hear voices. The TV? Funny, I didn't have Nick down as a breakfast TV watcher. I rapped on the door and took a step back. I waited. Nothing. Perhaps he'd already gone down and had left the TV on?

Breakfast was in the restaurant on the ground floor. I helped myself to a small glass of cranberry juice and then another, before taking a hot plate and filling it with sausages, bacon, scrambled egg, fried bread, beans, mushrooms, black pudding – the works. I was suddenly ravenous.

Ruth was sitting at the far end of the room, on a table for two, next to the window. Had I already missed Nick? I wandered over to her. Maybe it was for the best he wasn't there though. I wanted to speak to him on his own without his sister-in-law sitting next to us. We had plans to make – and the first one was when I was going to see him again. The exhibition was over today – and I couldn't stand the thought of him going home to wifey.

'Not surprised you're hungry after last night.'

'What?' I said, knocking my glass so that cranberry juice splashed onto the white tablecloth, leaving a streak of red. I dabbed at it with my napkin. Had she heard us? Had she heard me coming back into the room?

'You hardly touched your cannelloni.'

I let out a breath. 'Yes, it's caught up with me. I'm bloody starving.'

There was an unappetising bowl of muesli, a black coffee and a glass of water in front of her.

'You need something more than that to soak up the alcohol you sank last night.'

She gave me a weak smile. The whites of her eyes were bloodshot. I'm sure they hadn't been this morning. Puffy, yes. But bloodshot? No.

'Everything all right?' I helped myself to the tomato ketchup, spooning the entire contents of the little bowl onto my plate.

She picked up a sachet of sugar and started twisting it between her fingers. 'Fine.'

'Well, you don't look fine,' I said, shovelling some beans into my mouth. 'There's no need to feel embarrassed. I've been drunk a thousand times before. Don't worry about it.'

She carried on fiddling with the sachet. 'It's not that.'

'Go on.'

She took a deep breath. 'Claire's pissed off. She was trying to get hold of me all last night and I didn't ring her back.'

'What's her problem? She knew you were at the exhibition, right?'

'We're not often apart. And when we are, we always make sure we say goodnight to each other, no matter how late it is. She was worried about me.'

213

I took a slurp of my juice. I wondered what it felt like to have someone worry about you. No one worried about me. Ever. My old man only worried if I wasn't there to run around after him. And my mum? She hadn't given me a backwards glance when she left. I thought about Nick, about what we'd shared last night. I felt a rush of something, deep in my stomach. This was it – I'd finally found someone who would care enough about me to worry when I didn't answer my phone.

'You should give her the push.'

'What?' She blushed. 'What? Why?'

I speared a sausage. 'Shit, sorry. Our Danny always says I'm far too blunt. I just get the impression you're not very happy. Why stick around if you're not? Life's too short.' I was one to talk. I wasn't happy at Dad's, more than not happy, but I was still there, fetching and carrying for him. Still, once Nick had given wifey the old heave-o, I would be out of Dad's and moving in with him. I could imagine myself in his house, chatting and drinking with him in his kitchen while he cooked, cosying up in front of a film in his living room, making love to him in that gorgeous bedroom – although those disgusting floral pink bedclothes would have to go – a photo of us on our wedding day on the bedside cabinet.

'She loves me.'

'There you have it,' I said, pointing my knife at her. 'She loves you. But do you love her?'

She ripped at the top of the sugar sachet, its contents spilling onto the table. 'I've been with her a long time.'

'All the more reason not to waste any more time.' I took my piece of fried bread and wiped it around my plate.

'I couldn't. It would kill her.'

I drained the last of my cranberry juice. 'So? What's more important? You being happy or Claire being hurt?'

'Your brother's right. You're very straightforward,' she said. 'I like that.'

'What's the use of covering everything up with lies?'

She ran her finger through the spilt sugar. 'I'm not used to being on my own.'

I wanted to reach across the table and slap her. She was staying with someone because she didn't want to be on her own. When I first met her, I thought she was like me – a fighter. But she wasn't; she was weak. So weak. I'd spent all my life on my own. It hurt, being alone. Not having someone to share things with, not having someone to worry about you. But it was better than being with the wrong person. I could have easily stopped being on my own. I could have married Kenny – I was in no doubt he'd have jumped at the chance, still would – and ended up hating myself and him for my weakness. My mum came into my head again. Was I more her daughter than I realised? Had she known my dad was the wrong man and walked away? Fair play to her. I wouldn't have stuck around with him. But she'd left me too. I could never forgive her for that.

'You probably think I'm a right wuss, don't you?' Ruth said. 'Me, Miss Capable at work. And here I am, worried about being on my own.'

I rubbed the napkin across my lips. 'I doubt you'd be single for very long.'

Her cheeks flushed pink as she reached over and grabbed my free hand. 'That's nice of you to say.'

I squeezed her hand back before snatching mine away.

'I wonder where Bil is?' she said, glancing at her watch. 'I banged on his door earlier but there was no answer.'

'Perhaps he went to the gym?' For a second, I was back in the room with him, running my hands over his firm chest, his biceps. 'He looks like the sort of guy who takes care of himself.'

Ruth snorted. 'Are you joking? Old Bil wouldn't go near a gym. My sister says he's a right lazy arse.'

'I doubt that,' I said, feeling the need to defend him.

Her brow furrowed. 'Well, she would know. She's married to him. She knows what he hides under his designer suits. And I'm guessing it's a lot of lard.'

I felt the heat flame my cheeks.

'No, you haven't, have you?'

'What?'

She narrowed her eyes. 'You haven't got a crush on him, have you?'

'What?' I lifted my glass. 'Don't be stupid.'

She gave me a knowing look as she brushed the sugar off the table. 'I was wondering why you turned up out of the blue yesterday.'

I put down my fork. 'I came to help you out. And to learn more about the business. What do you take me for, Ruth? I don't go around stealing people's partners.

Whether they're men or women, for that matter. I only date single people.'

'Oh, God, I'm sorry. I didn't mean to—'

'Forget it. You're tired. And you're upset.'

Tears welled in her eyes. She blotted them with the paper serviette lying next to her bowl.

'Think about what you're going to do about Claire, Ruth. Only you can make yourself happy.'

'You're right,' she said as her phone buzzed. She clicked on it. 'It's Bil. I don't believe it. He's had to go back to the office. Something to do with the hotel project.'

'Why?' My stomach gave a jolt. Was Nick avoiding me? Couldn't he stand to see me after what had gone on last night? No, that wouldn't be it. There had to be a genuine reason why he'd had to go back up to Manchester. Was it something to do with the hotel project? I knew he'd been having loads of problems with it. Or maybe he'd gone to tell wifey their marriage was over. That must be it. I imagined her face when he said the words, the tears and then the anger that would rip through her. She might come gunning for me. I wouldn't blame her if she did. If I was married to Nick, I'd finish off any woman who tried to take him off me.

'Hasn't said. Just that he's sure we can handle things between us. We will, won't we?'

'Of course we will,' I said, winking at Ruth. 'We'll kill it.'

CHAPTER 22

'Champagne?' Felix held a bottle of Bollinger aloft.

Lottie nodded. She could get used to drinking champagne. Twice in one week. And she hadn't had to pay for any of it. Ginger had picked up the bill on Wednesday night.

'Darling,' Gwen said as she swept into the kitchen. 'I was saving that bottle for a special occasion. There's a bottle of Prosecco in the pantry. I'm sure Lottie would prefer that. It's what everyone's drinking nowadays, isn't it?'

Before Lottie could speak, Felix was peeling the foil off the cork, unwinding the wire and twisting the bottle. 'Nonsense! We're celebrating. It's not every week our daughter-in-law lands a part in a US TV show.'

The cork popped with a bang, making Nick – who was peering at his phone, his head bent – jump and swear. Loudly.

'Felix!' Gwen shook her head as Felix filled the glasses too quickly so that they overflowed. 'You nearly gave

218

Nicky a heart attack.' Gwen rubbed at Nick's arm. 'Work busy, darling?' she said.

Nick shoved his phone in the back pocket of his jeans. 'Got a beer, Mum?'

'Of course.' She disappeared off to the pantry, returning with a Peroni. She uncapped the bottle and handed it to him.

'You won't join us in a glass, Nick?' Felix said. 'To celebrate your wife's success?'

Nick held his bottle in the air. 'Fine with this.'

Felix raised his glass. 'Gwen.'

She sniffed and picked up a glass.

'Here's to you, Lottie,' Felix said. 'Congratulations.'

'I've only done a cheeseboard.' Gwen put down her glass. 'We're round at Audrey and Julian's for a bite in half an hour.'

Despite the gnawing emptiness in her stomach, Lottie smiled. 'That's fine. We have plans anyway.' They hadn't, but they could pick up a takeaway on the way home. 'Where's Scampi?' The poodle was always about, yapping at their ankles, or stuffed under Gwen's arm.

Felix put his arm around Gwen's shoulders. 'We had to have her put down. Her kidneys.'

'Oh, sorry, I didn't know.'

Felix kissed his wife's cheek. 'Gwen's been very upset about it, haven't you?'

Gwen blew her nose. 'She had a good life.'

'She did that all right,' Nick said, widening his eyes at Lottie over the top of his mum's head.

'Anyway, enough of that. We're here to celebrate. Tell

219

us all about it, then, Lottie,' Felix said as Gwen said, 'How did the exhibition go, darling?'

Nick helped himself to some Stilton, cutting off a big wedge and throwing it into his mouth, before giving his mother a thumbs up.

'You work too hard.' She sighed.

Lottie could agree with Gwen on that score. They'd left the hotel by six thirty yesterday morning, Nick wanting to meet the contractors on site at nine. He'd said again how delighted he was she'd come to see him – it had saved him getting the early train back. She blushed at the thought of how jealous – and stupid – she'd been. Fancy turning up at the hotel like that, trying to catch him out.

'Tell us all about your new show, then,' Felix said, topping up Lottie's glass. 'Can we tell people yet? Audrey and Julian's daughter has just made rear admiral in the navy. We need to have something to boast about.'

Gwen put her arm around Nick's waist. 'I think having a son who's one of the top architects in the country is enough to boast about, don't you?'

Lottie took a sip of her drink, the bubbles tickling her nose. She would never be good enough for Gwen, she knew that. She wondered if Nick's first wife had felt the same. Probably not. Gwen still had a wedding photograph of Nick and Louise in her bedroom. Lottie had seen it once when Gwen had asked her to fetch her slippers when she'd broken her ankle. 'They're by my bedside cabinet,' she'd said – the same bedside cabinet the silver photo frame stood on. It was a lovely moment the photographer had captured, an intimate moment: Louise with her head thrown back, laughing at something Nick had said. Nick looked like a different person. So young, he still had the puppy fat on his face, no sign of the frown lines that he now had.

'Lottie?' Felix pushed up his glasses onto the bridge of his nose.

'Sorry, I was miles away. I'll be playing one of the lead roles, Chrissie, a woman out for revenge on her cheating husband.' She glanced at Nick but he'd taken his phone out of his pocket and was busy tapping away on it.

'It's so exciting.' Felix beamed at her. 'And you'll be based in Los Angeles?'

'Yes, for six months. You'll have to come out and visit,' she said, directing the invite to Felix. Felix would love LA. It was so far from anything he'd ever known.

'We will, won't we, Gwen?'

Gwen sniffed. 'I'm not sure I can get the time off.'

Gwen was a volunteer at the local charity shop. From what Lottie had seen – and heard – she thought she was queen bee, a captain of industry, when really all she did was sort through bags of clothes and books people brought in. And boss around the women who volunteered with her, of course.

'You could always come on your own, Felix,' Lottie said.

Gwen spluttered, bubbles from the champagne shooting out of her nose.

'Mum, are you all right?' Nick lifted his gaze from his phone and clapped her on the back.

Lottie did her best to hide a smile but when Felix widened his eyes at her, a giggle escaped her lips. She coughed, trying to hide it.

Felix poured a glass of tap water and handed it to Gwen. 'Here.'

'It went down the wrong way,' Gwen said, taking a sip of water, before fishing out a handkerchief from the sleeve of her cardigan and wiping her nose with it.

'Nick's coming out to visit, aren't you?' Lottie said, smiling at the back of her husband's head as he busied himself at the cheeseboard.

'If I can get away from work.'

'What?' Lottie put down her glass. 'You said—'

'We'll visit her, won't we, Gwen?' Felix shot Nick a look.

Nick shot him one back. 'Are you allowed in the States, Felix?' Nick said, before stuffing the cheese-topped cracker into his mouth.

Gwen blanched. Felix took a slow swig of his champagne.

'You haven't been done for smoking a bit of weed, have you, Felix?' Lottie said, with a smile.

Nick smirked. 'Ooh, a bit more than that, Lots.'

'We really need to get going.' Gwen lifted the cheeseboard off the table.

'It was a misunderstanding, that's all,' Felix said.

Nick crossed his arms. 'Right.'

A shadow passed across Felix's face. 'We could all sit down and discuss exactly what went on back then, if you'd like, Nick? I'm sure Lottie would want to know.'

Gwen screamed as her champagne flute slipped from her fingers and smashed on the immaculately clean kitchen floor tiles.

They all stood staring at the glass before Felix sprang into action, retrieving the dustpan and brush from under the sink and, on his hands and knees, sweeping up the shards of glass.

'We'll be off, then. Thanks, Mum,' Nick said, giving Gwen a peck on the cheek.

Lottie felt his hand on her elbow, steering her away and out of the door. 'Thanks,' she shouted over her shoulder as they headed into the dark night.

'What on earth was all that about?' Lottie said once they were in the car and safely out of earshot.

'I'm starving.' Right on cue, Nick's stomach rumbled. 'Didn't you say they'd asked us for dinner?'

'That's what Felix said when he invited us.'

Nick shrugged. 'He obviously got it wrong. Thai? Indian? What do you fancy?'

'I fancy knowing what all that was about. Why can't Felix get into the States?' Lottie had an inkling it was drugs. Weren't all academics fond of a bit of the wacky baccy? They were eternal students, weren't they?

'It was something and nothing.' Nick honked his horn at a driver who had failed to notice the lights had turned green.

'So it was drugs?'

'Thai?' Nick said, indicating left.

'Nick? Was it drugs?'

He pressed a button on the dashboard, and the car reverse-parked itself into a tight space on the side of the road.

Lottie waited as he turned off the ignition. 'Nick?'

He took his hands off the steering wheel and cracked his knuckles. 'He was accused of – what shall we say – being a little too friendly towards a girl at the school where he taught.'

'No.' Lottie shook her head. Not Felix. She couldn't believe it. 'What happened?'

'He wasn't charged. It was her word against his. Felix said she wanted to get her revenge because he'd given her a bad mark for an essay.'

'He lost his job?'

'I'm not sure. He made out that he jumped, rather than being pushed. Said teaching wasn't for him. He'd only been there a year, so it seemed a plausible excuse. Went back to doing research at the uni.'

Tears stung the back of Lottie's throat. Poor Felix. 'Who was it, the girl?'

'Some random. I forget her name. I was away at uni at the time. Didn't find out until a few years later what had gone on.' Nick shrugged. 'Sorry, I shouldn't have said anything.' He leant over to kiss her but she moved her face away from his lips.

'It's Felix you should be apologising to. Why did you say that about him not being able to get into America? You knew he hadn't been charged.'

He tried to grab her hand but she snatched it away. 'Sorry.'

224

'That was a mean thing to do, Nick.'

Nick shrugged. 'He's such an arse. And he's always all over you. Hey, come on, I was only winding him up.'

He got out of the car, sticking his head back in. 'Pad Thai and Penang Chicken? Sticky rice?' He slammed the car door and dashed through the rain to the restaurant.

Lottie let out a long sigh. Nick hated Felix, blaming him for splitting up his parents' marriage. And yet how could Felix be responsible for breaking up Gwen and Nigel? It seemed that Nigel had done that all by himself – Gwen wasn't the sort of woman who'd stand by her man, not one who had spent time inside. She sighed. It had all happened such a long time ago. Nick had been a child. Wouldn't it be better if he met his dad and talked it all through with him? But Nick was adamant that he didn't want to talk to Nigel. What exactly had his dad done to make Nick want to have nothing to do with him?

Lottie's stomach grumbled. She peered through the windscreen. She was starving too. She needed something stodgy – spring rolls. Fishing in her bag, she found her phone and pressed Nick's number, shaking her head when his phone started to ring. He'd left it in the well by the gear stick. She glanced at the restaurant. Nick was sitting at the bar, nursing a beer, reading a paper as he waited. There was no way she was getting out of the car – it was lashing it down. She wanted a spring roll, but not that much.

She threw her phone into her bag and picked up Nick's phone. No, she mustn't. She looked at the restaurant and then back at the phone. Hadn't she told herself she wouldn't snoop? But maybe, if she knew what was going on with his dad, she could find a way of bringing the two of them together. And, anyway, it wouldn't be snooping, it would be helping.

She glanced at Nick again. And then she got his phone out and tapped in the passcode, scrolling through, up and down, until she found Nigel's name. Holding her breath, she tapped the screen. There was a string of messages. *Where are you? Are you avoiding me? I have to see you.* And the last one. The worst one of all. The one that made Lottie's stomach twist under her ribs so hard she thought she might throw up: *I'll tell your wife if you don't get in touch.*

CHAPTER 23

'Have you been avoiding me?' I strode into Nick's office on the Tuesday morning, banging the door behind me. He'd spent Friday and yesterday working from home. I'd lost count of the number of times I'd called and texted him. But he hadn't replied. Not once.

He put down his pen and ran his hand through his hair. 'Sorry. I've been busy. This new project's driving me mad.'

'It doesn't matter. You're here now. I'm here now.' I moved around to his side of the desk but he jumped up as if I were infected with something. 'No one will be in for ages.'

'Listen,' he said, glancing at the door. 'You're a really nice person. Really, you are. And gorgeous. But. I can't do this. I'm married. The night when we . . . the night at the exhibition . . . that was a mistake.'

He looked so scared I wanted to put my arms around him. 'It'll be okay,' I said.

'It will?'

227

He let me go to him then. I grabbed his hand, touching the thick gold band on his wedding finger. 'You're a good person too. Like me. You don't want to hurt your wife. I get that. But she'll live. She'll get over it.'

I thought of my dad. He'd never got over my mother leaving him. Had never been with another woman since. Had tarred us all with the same brush. Thought we were disgusting. Tarts. Slags. The lot of us. I know because he told me so. Nearly every day.

'No.' He shook his head. 'I don't want her to get over it.'

'Hey, I'm not sharing you.'

He snatched his hand away from me. 'It was a mistake. I love my wife. I—'

'You didn't love her the other night when you were fucking me.'

The words hung there in the air between us before he spoke. 'I'd had too much to drink.'

'Not that much.'

'It was a mistake. I love my wife. I'm happy with her.'

I wanted to put my hands over my ears. Why did he keep saying that? Why? He loved me. We were going to be together. 'I can make you happy.'

'God, I'm sorry. I really am.' He reached in his pocket and drew out a folded piece of paper, handing it to me.

It was a cheque. For five thousand pounds.

'What's this?'

'I think it's best if we let you go.'

'You're trying to pay me off? You want your grubby little secret out of the way?'

'It would be best for everyone. You're young. I can give you a good reference. I can—'

'I'll tell your wife.'

He caught hold of my arm, his fingers squeezing into my flesh, his face close to mine, the bitter tinge of coffee on his breath. 'You keep away from my wife. Do you hear me?' He shook my arm. 'Do you hear me?'

'You're hurting me.' I tried to push him away but his grip was too strong. 'I won't tell her, Nick. I was joking.'

'Promise me.'

'I promise, all right?'

He let go of my arm.

I rubbed at the bruise that I was certain would soon appear there.

I picked up the cheque I'd dropped. Stupid. So stupid. Now I had proof he was trying to buy me off. I breathed deeply, trying to calm myself. 'I'm sorry,' I said. 'Can we part as friends?' I held out my hand.

He took it. 'I'm sorry too. I should never have done it. No hard feelings?'

Shaking my head, I plastered a smile on to my face. 'None at all. I have been seeing someone else, anyway.'

'Oh?'

Was that jealousy or relief flitting across his face? I hoped it was the former. I wanted to hurt him. Just like he'd hurt me.

'Hand your notice in to Ruth,' he said, his attention moving in a flash away from me and back to his computer screen.

* * *

I trudged across the scrap of wasteland that counted for the only bit of greenery on our estate.

'Hey, angel, you skiving?' Kenny winked at me. 'You'll get the sack.'

'What do I care? I'm packing it in.' I grabbed the can of Diamond White he was swigging from and glugged it down in one. 'Got any more?'

'Back at mine.'

His mates sneered and whispered as we walked off. Fuck them. I needed to forget what had happened. Nick didn't mean it. He was scared, that was all. Scared of how he felt about me.

I flopped down on Kenny's threadbare sofa as he chucked me a can. He sat down next to me, too close for my liking. I edged away.

'Fancy a bit?' he said, taking a spliff from behind his ear and lighting it before handing it over.

As I inhaled deeply, I tried to let everything that had happened in the office with Nick wash over me, fade away.

Kenny switched on the TV and shoved a CD into an old player underneath it. *Pretty Woman*. What was he like?

'Thought you'd dig this,' he said in response to my grimace.

'Right.'

But I smiled and laughed in all the right places, drinking so many cans of Diamond White I lost count, sucking greedily at the spliff until I was away in another world.

I'd nearly blown it this morning with Nick. I hadn't meant it as a threat, telling his wife. I'd meant it as a way out for him – that he didn't need to tell her; I could do that. He was panicking. He didn't want to hurt her, that was all. He wanted me. It was there, in those blue eyes of his, even when his fingers were pinching my arm. He wanted to kiss me. Be with me. Do those things to me he'd done that night. I'd give him time. That was all he needed. Time.

I'd ring Ruth tomorrow, tell her I was going to take a couple of weeks off, make up some excuse about my dad. Two weeks. Nick would miss me. Deffo. And then he'd forget about me handing in my notice. Would want me back in the office. But two weeks? Could I do it? I missed him already. I missed him so much, his arms around me, his mouth on mine.

So, when Kenny moved his face towards mine, my body didn't resist. I closed my eyes and pretended it was Nick who was shoving his tongue down my throat.

CHAPTER 24

'Are you joking? You haven't asked him? Lottie. Come on. You have to ask him.' Hannah shook her head.

Hannah was right. Hannah was always right. Lottie had to ask Nick what the text messages had meant. And who had sent them. Were they from Nigel? Or was Nick using his real dad's name as a front, as she'd originally thought? Were they from Tasha? Just because she hadn't been in Birmingham with him didn't mean that nothing was going on. And what did the texts mean? *I'll tell your wife.* What was it that they were going to tell her? Lottie could only imagine the worst. She hadn't asked Nick because she couldn't bear the row that would come, never mind his answers to her questions. He'd know she'd been looking at his phone again. He would say she didn't trust him. He'd be furious, like last time.

And yet she needed to know. If it was Tasha and if it was the thing Lottie was dreading, then it was better to know, wasn't it? Or was it better not to know? If they were having an affair, was it better to hope the whole thing would just blow over? What if she confronted Nick and he admitted he was seeing Tasha? What would that do to their marriage? And even if he said it'd been a dreadful mistake, a one-off maybe, could she forgive him, or would it always be there between them? The same thoughts had been going round and round her head for the past five days. And she always said it was Nick who stuck his head in the sand . . .

Hannah folded her arms. 'If you don't, I will.'

'No! Are you joking? He'll go nuts. I'll ask him. Honestly, Hannah. I will.' Lottie suddenly wished she hadn't confided in her friend. The last thing she wanted was Hannah sticking her oar in, even if she did have her best interests at heart.

'As soon as he gets in?'

Lottie got the casserole out of the oven. 'As soon as my guests have gone. I'll ask him then.'

'I swear,' Hannah said, 'if he's been cheating on you—'

'I know. You'll chop his bollocks off.'

Hannah made a slicing movement across her neck. 'And the bloody rest.'

'I'm probably making something out of nothing. Putting two and two together and getting five. They probably are from Nigel. Something did go on in the past with his dad that Nick just won't open up about.'

'Hmm. Never trust a man who has secrets.'

Lottie laughed, even though she felt like crying. 'Doesn't everyone have something they hold on to, just for themselves? I bet your Craig has a fair few secrets to tell.'

Hannah picked up her bag. 'One, he's not my Craig, and two, I've only just met him. He might have secrets but, so what? He needs to maintain that air of mystery, at least for a bit longer, or else I'll be bored to death by him before you know it.'

'So, you're not bored of him yet, then?' Lottie asked, pleased to steer the conversation away from Nick and the texts.

Was she mistaken or was Hannah blushing? Hannah never blushed.

'I like him,' she said, fiddling with the strap on her bag.

'Oh my God, you've fallen for him.'

'I have not!' Hannah's face grew even redder.

'Good in bed, is he?'

'Charlotte Moore! Don't be filthy. And nosy.'

Lottie smiled to herself. Hannah must really like him – she usually wasn't backwards in coming forwards about her sex life.

'He's not bad,' Hannah said, before blushing again. 'The cards said I'd meet a Scorpio. What do you think of him? Do you like him?'

'Who am I to go against the cards?'

'Funny. Seriously, Lots. Do you like him?'

Lottie bent down to stack the dishwasher, giving herself a few seconds to formulate a response. 'He's not my type,' she said.

Hannah let out a belly laugh. 'He's not posh enough for you.'

'That's not what I said. And, anyway, I don't have to like him, do I? I mean, you're not the biggest fan of

Nick.' She shut the dishwasher and leant against it. 'You never have told me what you don't like about him.'

Hannah stuck out her tongue. 'He's not my type, is he? And you can't trust a man who has secrets.' She sighed. 'I've got to go. Taking Daisy to Durham Uni tomorrow to have a look around. Got an early start.'

'Got the day off work tomorrow, then, has she? She'll be glad to get away from that filing.'

'Exactly.' Hannah pulled a strand of hair in front of her face and examined her split ends.

'Did you ask Daisy if she and Trey were coming up to Fairview for Nick's birthday?'

'It's a no. I reckon she sees quite enough of Nick and Kas at work, without spending the weekend with them.'

'And she'd much rather spend it alone with Trey.'

'Can't blame her.' Hannah enveloped Lottie in a bear hug. 'Ask Nick tonight. And ring me when you've spoken to him. Doesn't matter what time it is. I want to know.'

'Sure you can't stay? You'll like Ginger. She's lovely.' Lottie wished she hadn't invited Ginger and Brad for dinner, even if she was lovely. How could she go to America if her marriage was in trouble? She wouldn't be going anywhere – she would stay and fight.

'Thanks for the invite but this woman needs an early night,' Hannah said as she made her way to the door.

Lottie glanced at the clock on the wall. She'd kill him. She really would. He knew Ginger and Brad were coming for dinner. Or had he not been paying attention when she'd told him? It wouldn't surprise her. His initial excitement at her landing the part had petered out. And whenever she'd chatted to him about the role, he'd been distracted by his phone or his laptop, nodding and saying *yes* when he thought she'd asked a question. Whatever she'd told him had probably gone in one ear and out the other.

Ginger was studying the photos that lined the walls. 'Cute pictures,' she said and then sneezed. 'This English weather, sunny one minute, cold the next.'

'Shall we start? I don't know where he's got to. We might as well eat in here if that's okay with you.'

'Sure.' Ginger looked at her watch. 'Likewise with Brad. He said he'd definitely be here tonight.'

Lottie got the casserole out of the oven. Maybe she should have made contact with Brad herself. Got his number off Ginger and not relied on her to ask him. Maybe he thought she was being rude by not extending the invite herself. Or maybe he just didn't like her. 'Can I ask you a question?'

'Sure.'

'Did Brad want me for the role? I know I asked you that at the restaurant and you said he did, but I get the feeling he isn't that keen on me.'

'Take no notice of him. We call him "Brad the Bad" behind his back. That's just how he rolls. He thinks you're perfect for the part.'

Lottie felt a blush of pride before remembering Brad had said they wanted someone crazy. Perhaps it was that and that alone that had swung it for her. Perhaps he'd recognised something in her, something psycho, something unhinged.

'Can I help out?' Ginger asked.

'No. Honestly. It's just something simple. I'm putting on a kids play in a couple of weeks. *Time-Slip* – have you heard of it?'

Ginger shook her head.

'I've been there all day sorting out scenery.'

'Are there still tickets?'

'There are some left for the final performance – a matinee on the Friday.'

'On a Friday? Won't the kids still be in school?'

'It's the school holidays. And we always finish with an early afternoon show. The kids have little brothers and sisters – and grandparents – they want to bring,' Lottie said. 'And we're having a bit of party for them afterwards. Jelly and ice cream and all that. Still want to come?'

Ginger started to reach for her bag. 'Sure. How much are the tickets?'

'Don't be daft. I'll reserve you a seat. The kids will be made up. Who knows, you might spot some talent?' Lottie thought of Daisy. Imagine if Ginger fell in love with her, had a great part that would suit her down to the ground. Maybe even one in the show Lottie was going to be in. Wouldn't that be wonderful? She loved Daisy – spending time with her in America would be fantastic. And then she remembered Daisy was all set on studying biomedical science at university. And that there might be a chance she herself wouldn't be going to LA anyway.

'Come on, let's start,' Lottie said, taking the lid off the casserole dish.

237

Ginger helped herself to three huge spoonfuls. 'Often work late, does he, your fella? Must be a bit lonely for you.'

Lottie shrugged. 'I'm used to it. He's married as much to his business as he is to me.'

'Better to be obsessed with work than with another woman – or women – like my ex.'

Lottie swallowed. Ginger had no idea how close to the truth she might be. Was that where Nick was now? Out with Tasha?

'Jeez, this is freaking awesome.' Ginger reached for her napkin but it slipped from her lap. As she bent down to retrieve it, the scarf around her neck slithered to the floor, revealing a nasty, jagged scar covering her throat.

Ginger clocked Lottie staring and snatched at the scarf, wrapping it back around her neck. 'Told you my ex was a bad one.'

'God, I'm sorry. I didn't realise.'

Ginger shrugged. 'It was only the once. I let my guard down. Never happened again.' She picked up her fork. 'This really is awesome. You miss good old British food when you live in LA.'

God, how awful for her. Poor Ginger. That wasn't just a nick on her throat. She'd said her ex had been a philanderer – she hadn't said he'd been an abuser too. Lottie smiled at her. She was as keen to change the subject as Ginger was. 'Isn't there a pub that does British food? In Santa Monica?'

Lottie had been in it once when she and Hannah had done their round-the-world trip.

'Yep, the Britannia. Not like the original though.'

There was the sound of a car pulling up, headlights sweeping through the window.

'Ah,' Lottie said. 'The wanderer returns.'

Lottie went into the hall to meet Nick. As soon as she saw him, she could tell he'd been drinking. He wasn't tipsy, far from it, but he'd had one or two. And whiskey again. She turned her face when he tried to kiss her so that he caught her ear instead of her lips.

'You promised, Nick. You promised.'

'I'm sorry, Lots, all right? Something came up.'

Lottie lowered her voice. 'What? What was so important you had to miss this evening? You know I wanted you to meet the US TV people. This is important to me. You're not the only one with a career, you know.'

'Don't nag, Lots. There's a problem with the existing walls. We were told they were structurally sound, but it seems they could fall over with one gust of wind.' He pushed his hand through his hair. 'It could ruin the whole project.'

'And you've only just found out?'

He grimaced, as if he had a bad taste in his mouth. 'Apparently, the contractor rang last week. But the message didn't get to me.'

'Oh?' Had the wonderful Tasha cocked up? Lottie hoped so.

'I just need to make—'

'Nick!'

239

'All right, for God's sake, let me use the loo, at least.'
'Two minutes,' she hissed.

'He's just freshening up,' Lottie said as she made her way back into the kitchen.

Ginger was flicking through one of Nick's architecture magazines.

'Thought I'd get up to speed before I meet him.'

'Oh, he won't want to talk about that,' Lottie said, knowing full well he probably would. 'I've got apple crumble and custard for pudding.'

Ginger beamed. 'More good old British food. Just like Grandma used to make.'

'Well, it's what Mr Waitrose makes so I'm sure it won't be half as nice as your grandma's.' Lottie took the pie from the fridge and put it into the already-hot oven. It wouldn't take long. There was the flush of the downstairs toilet. 'Top-up?' Lottie said.

Ginger held out her glass. 'Why not? Might as well make the most of not driving.'

'Don't you like driving on the left anymore?'

'Oh, I've got a hire car. A big four-by-four thing. Much too big for me though. And I fancied a drink tonight. I was counting on Brad dropping me back to the hotel. No worries. I'll take a taxi back.'

Lottie looked at the clock. Manchester United were playing tonight – getting a taxi could take a while. 'I'll ask Nick to run you.' It would serve him right for being late.

'Oh, Gawd, no. It's not a problem.'

'Nick won't mind.'

'Nick won't mind what?' he said, coming into the kitchen. 'What?' he said again, staring at Ginger.

Lottie took a deep breath. He was gawping at Ginger as if she had another head – as if, between Lottie reprimanding him in the hallway and him getting to the kitchen, he'd completely forgotten the casting director was here.

Lottie was just about to introduce Ginger when she jumped off her stool and enveloped Nick in a hug, kissing first one cheek and then the other. 'We meet at last!'

'Ye-es.' Nick peeled away from her. 'I didn't realise . . .'

'I told you Ginger was a Brit.' Lottie shook her head. 'Men. Do they ever listen?' she asked Ginger.

'Haven't met a guy yet who listened to me,' Ginger said, hopping back onto her stool. 'What do you say, Nick? Not been ignoring your wife, have you?' She wagged her finger at him.

Nick turned a bright shade of red. Lottie's stomach suddenly tightened. Oh God, he didn't fancy Ginger, did he? The woman in front of them was beautiful – there was no denying that. And today she was dressed in a long peacock-blue silk tunic, with matching silk pants and scarf, all topped off with another gorgeous matching turban. She was like an exotic model, with her pale skin and deep amber eyes.

Nick helped himself to a glass of wine. Lottie let him. She suddenly didn't want her husband giving this woman a lift home.

'Lottie tells me you're an architect,' Ginger said, resting her elbow on the kitchen island and her chin on her cupped hand. 'What are you working on at the moment?'

241

Nick took a huge swig of his drink before answering. 'Oh, it's incredibly boring.'

Lottie got the custard out of the fridge. Blimey. Maybe he wasn't going to go on about his bloody hotel project. Maybe, just for once, he was going to take an interest in her job, her career.

Ginger tried again. 'You'll be coming with Lottie to LA? We'll fix you up with a neat house. Maybe in Santa Monica? You can get to the beach then. Fancy a dip in the ocean every day?'

Nick drained his glass. 'Oh, I'm staying here. Work. You know how it is.'

'Will you cope, home alone?'

'I'll cope.'

He was smiling, but Lottie could tell his heart wasn't in it. It wasn't like Nick not to be friendly – she only hoped he was distracted by work and not anything or anyone else.

He ran his hand through his hair and stood up. 'Do you mind if I leave you two ladies to it?'

Lottie tried to catch his eye, but he was already halfway out of the room, a wine bottle in his hand.

Lottie stirred the custard. 'I'm sorry. He's got a lot on his mind at the moment.'

'Oh?'

Lottie liked Ginger, really she did, but she didn't want to talk to her about Nick's worries over the hotel complex and his worries over his father. And she certainly wasn't going to mention her suspicions about him and Tasha. 'Just work.'

'Isn't it always?' Ginger looked towards the oven. 'The crumble isn't burning, is it?'

There was a rapping on the door. Lottie glanced out of the window. A taxi sat on the driveway. Lottie hadn't heard it arrive. Had the driver sounded his horn and they'd been oblivious to it? Despite herself, Lottie had been in fits of laughter. Her cheeks ached. Ginger had been telling her about some of the goings-on during the last series she'd produced.

'It's your taxi,' she said to Ginger.

Ginger gathered up her bag. 'I'll just use the bathroom.'

'Second door on your left. I'll tell him you're coming.'

Lottie opened the front door. Craig stood on the step, grinning from ear to ear.

'Surprise!'

'Craig! What are you doing here?'

'Working for Uber, aren't I?' He sniffed and ran the back of his hand under his nose. 'Where is it you're heading again? Bit late, innit?'

'Oh, it's not me,' Lottie said as she beckoned him into the house.

'Where's Nick. Not back yet?'

She frowned. What did he mean?

'Oops. Ignore me. It probably wasn't him. Thought I saw him at that new place in the city centre. You know the one with the windows and that long bar? I was waiting outside for a fare. Probably wasn't though. My eyesight's not brilliant. Probably should wear glasses but they don't go with this beard.' He tugged at his long, straggly beard.

'Nick's at home.'

'Ah, see. I told you my eyes were bad.' He rubbed his hands together. 'Have I got the wrong address, then?' He got out his phone and scrolled through his messages. 'No, Chalfont Lane. That's this one, isn't it? I didn't know it was yours till I pulled in the driveway.'

'It's for . . . ah, here she is,' Lottie said as Ginger swept into the room.

'Your carriage awaits, my lady.' Craig held his arm out towards the door. 'Hang on. It isn't, is it?' The smile disappeared from his face. 'Nah, it can't be.' He rubbed his hand across his eyes. 'Tell me I'm seeing things? Nuala?'

Ginger stood there, a puzzled look on her face. 'Sorry, I don't think—'

'It is.' Craig shook his head. 'Fuck me. I never thought I'd see you again.'

A frown etched itself onto Ginger's usually wrinkle-free forehead.

Lottie shuffled from foot to foot. How embarrassing was this? 'This is Craig.'

'Craig Dalglish!' Ginger coughed. 'Small world.'

'What are you doing here?' Craig said, at the same time as Ginger turned to Lottie and said: 'We go way back.'

'You do?'

Before Lottie could ask any more, Ginger had given her a kiss, thanked her for the evening and was linking arms with Craig and jumping in the taxi.

Lottie closed the door. Well, what a small world it was. Mind you, Ginger did have a slight Mancunian twang to her accent. But, then again, Manchester was a big place. What was the likelihood of Ginger bumping into someone she knew? Probably quite small. What did they say though? There was only six degrees of separation between everyone on the planet?

Lottie had tried to stay awake but her eyelids were fluttering when Nick finally came to bed. He'd been in his study all evening. From what Lottie could make out the couple of times she'd been in there, he wasn't doing much, just huddling over the plans on his desk. She'd opened her mouth a dozen times to ask him who had sent the text messages, and what they'd meant by them but, despite having had at least a bottle of wine to herself, her courage had deserted her. So she'd lain awake, waiting for him, telling herself she would ask him when he got into bed, when his head wasn't full of work.

She had to ask him. She'd promised Hannah she would. Hannah had texted her while she was taking off her make-up, wanting to know what had gone on. And she had to ask him before the thoughts going round in her head drove her crazy.

Nick snuggled up behind her, pulling her in close to him, his arm around her, their legs entwined, his breath hot on her ear. 'I'm sorry, Lots,' he said. 'Do you still love me?'

She turned over so that their faces were only inches apart. 'Of course I do.' She kissed the tip of his nose. 'You work too hard though, darling. I'm going to worry about you when I go to the States. Who's going to take care of you?' She stared into his eyes, challenging him.

He put his hand to her face and kissed her softly. 'I'll miss you.'

Would he miss her? Or would he be glad to see the back of her? Glad to get her out of the way so he could carry on whatever he was up to? 'I'll miss you too,' she said.

Nick pulled away from her to lie on his back.

She shuffled over and laid her head on his shoulder, her arm wrapped around his waist.

'Maybe you were right, Lots. Maybe you shouldn't go.'

Lottie sprang away from him and propped herself up on her elbow. 'But you were the one who said I should. You said I couldn't let this opportunity pass me by. That six months would just fly by. You said I'd be an idiot not to go.'

'I know. It's just . . . I'll miss you.'

'Then come with me. Take six months off from the business. Give this project to Kas. It'll do you good. They'll cope. No one's indispensable, Nick.'

'Thanks, that makes me feel a whole lot better. Are you saying you might ditch me? Shack up with some bronzed Jason Momoa lookalike with a six-pack?' He pouted and she laughed.

'What's brought this on?' And then suddenly she realised what it was. Tomorrow was 18th August. The day Louise had killed herself. Not that Nick had ever told her that was the date. She'd been to the churchyard herself. Had seen the small urn that stood there.

'I will never leave you. Not even if Jason Momoa knocked on the door now.'

246

'You promise?'

'I promise.'

She snuggled back up to him. Where had Nick's about-turn come from? Had whatever been going on ended? Was his clinginess now down to guilt, down to a fear of losing her perhaps? She needed to know. She needed to know who had sent the texts and what they meant. She would count to ten and then she would ask him. She had to.

'There's something I need to tell you, Lots.'

Her stomach cramped. And suddenly, she didn't want to hear it, didn't want to hear whatever he was going to say. She just wanted to lie with him like this, pretend she'd never snooped through his phone, hadn't seen the messages, pretend he wasn't coming home late nearly every night, pretend she hadn't seen the way he'd looked at Tasha that time she'd gone into the office. 'Tell me tomorrow.' She let out a false yawn and he yawned too.

She felt his chest rise as he took a breath, felt his arm tighten around her shoulders. 'No, I need to tell you. I just don't know where to start.'

Whatever he'd done, he was sorry, she could hear it in his voice. 'Go on,' she said.

He took another shuddering breath, as if he were about to start crying. He never cried. Never.

'Is it . . . is it about the text messages?' Her voice was a whisper. 'From your dad? I know I shouldn't have looked. I'm sorry. Is he pestering you again?' It was what she wanted to believe, that this was all to do with his dad and nothing to do with Tasha.

247

Nick sat bolt upright, pushing her away from him, flinging back the duvet. 'I can't *believe* you! I can't believe you went through my phone again. After all I said.' He shook his head.

She put her hand on his back but he moved away from her.

'I was worried about you.'

'You were worried about you, more like.' He turned towards her, his face screwed up with pain. 'You still think I'm cheating on you.'

'*I'll tell your wife*. What do you imagine most women would think when they read that?'

'You don't trust me.'

'Is it Tasha? Has she sent those messages? Nick, tell me what's going on. Just tell me.'

'Tasha? What the hell are you on about?' He grabbed his pillow and headed for the door.

'Nick!'

'Nothing's going on. I keep telling you that, but you don't believe me. You just believe what you want to, the stupid stuff going round in your head.'

'I've seen that Tasha. I've seen the way you look at her.'

'For God's sake, she's with someone! And it's not me.'

'Ruth?'

'I don't know, Lottie. And I don't care. Can't you understand that?'

'Then what is it, Nick? Are the texts from your dad?'

Nick reached the bedroom door. 'Yes, Lottie. Yes, they're from my dad.' He suddenly burst into loud, angry sobs.

She jumped out of bed and went to him, pulling him towards her, holding him while he sobbed.

When the tears finally stopped, he lifted his face to hers. 'I'm sorry, Lots. He won't accept that I don't want him in my life. He's been threatening me—'

'Threatening you? Is that what the text was about? He said he was going to tell me what you'd done.'

Nick took a huge shuddering breath.

'Nick?'

'I shopped him to the police. He hit someone. Killed them.'

'Killed them? My God! Who?'

'Does it matter? I was the only witness. He went to prison. It was my fault.'

Lottie pulled him to her as he started to cry again. 'Shush. Shush. It wasn't your fault. It wasn't.' She waited until he was silent. 'Did all this happen when you were a child? You told me he'd gone to prison. That your mum divorced him because of that.' She hugged him to her. How bloody awful.

'No. This happened when I was married to Louise.'

'Married to Louise? But I thought you hadn't seen him for over thirty years? Since your mum divorced him?'

He wiped at his face with his T-shirt. 'I saw him on and off over the years. He went to prison for the first time when I was eleven. GBH. He was a hothead. Two years he got. And when he got out, Mum divorced him, said she'd had enough of him and his temper, married Felix. So Nigel moved to Spain. He used to come back, once or twice a year to visit me. And then—' he started to cry again '—he killed this man and got five years. And I had to testify against him in court. I was twenty-six. I hadn't seen him since that day. And now he's turned up, wanting to pick up where we left off.'

Lottie held him, kissed the top of his head. God, what a thing to have gone through. Poor Nick. He needed her. How could she not have noticed how down he was? It was no surprise. The devastation at the failed IVF attempt, all the hassle he was having with work. And now his father turning up out of the blue. Turning up and giving him grief. It must have awoken feelings in Nick he'd long buried. Feelings of guilt, of abandonment, too. First his dad leaving him and then Louise. Lottie bit her lip. And now here she was, about to do the same thing – swan off to America and leave him.

She swallowed. She would call Ginger tomorrow. Tell her she wouldn't take the part. There would be other parts, other opportunities. But there wouldn't be another husband. Not for her. She was certain of that. Nick needed her.

There was no way she was going to leave him on his own. No way at all.

CHAPTER 25

I lay on my bed, ignoring the shouts coming from my old man's bedroom. Let him get his own bloody tea and bacon sarnie. And while he was at it, he could make me one. Nothing better for a hangover than salty bacon, the stodge of white bread with lashings of brown sauce. My tongue was glued to the roof of my mouth. My stomach hurt. A low deep pain that was on and off. Maybe I'd got food poisoning? I'd ended up in the kebab shop at two in the morning. I'd been out with Kenny and his lot – again.

A night off for me tonight, that's what I needed. I was young but even so my body couldn't take nearly every night for a week on the booze. We usually ended up in The Plough, sitting in the back room, me and Kenny and a few of his mates. Like me, they'd been away. Unlike me, they'd had an easy time of it – free board and lodgings at Her Majesty's Pleasure. There'd been a lock-in in the pub last night, instigated by Kenny's dad, who was in there every night. He was so much of a regular he had his own beer tankard – with his name on it.

I swallowed. I needed a glass of Coke. Not that there'd be any in the kitchen. I'd neck down a couple of paracetamol and then a trip to Maccy D's it would be.

My eyes closed, I opened my bedside cabinet, fumbling inside for the box of tablets I knew was in there. My fingers lighted on another box. Tampons. My stomach pain worsened. I brought my knees up to my chest. What a stupid cow I was. It'd be period pain. It was always worse on the first day. I felt between my legs. Nothing. No dampness there. But my period was due, wasn't it? This week. Or was it last? I was as regular as clockwork, always had been. It was definitely this week.

I'd been on the day I'd accidentally on purpose bumped into Ruth in the gym, and that was four weeks ago, wasn't it? I counted back in my head. No. Five? It couldn't be. I opened my eyes as my fingers scrabbled for my phone, searching for the calendar. It wasn't five – it couldn't be. I'd got it wrong, wasn't thinking straight. I was probably still drunk. Twenty-four, twenty-five, twenty-six – my finger stabbed at the dates on the screen until I hit today's date. Thirty-four days since I'd had my last period.

Within five minutes, I was dressed and out of the door, ignoring Dad's shouts as I flew through the front gate.

My hangover was gone. Completely gone. My head was clear. My eyes were clear.

I didn't give McDonald's a second glance as I headed down the high street to Boots. I knew exactly where the boxes were – at the back of the store, next to the condoms.

'Ten ninety-nine,' the assistant, a snotty cow with a sneer on her face, said. 'Got a points card?'

'What? No.' I fumbled in my purse, thinking I might not have enough money. I had a tenner. I reached into my jeans pocket and there – thank you, God – a pound coin nestled in the folds of denim.

I waited for the one pence change. I didn't want to wait. I wanted to run. Run as fast as I could back home, lock myself in the bathroom, pee on the stick and wait to see if those two little pink lines would appear. But I waited. I held out my hand, keeping it firm and straight as the assistant dropped the penny onto my palm from a great height, obviously not wanting to touch me, not wanting to be contaminated by anything I might be carrying.

'I got you a glass of red,' I said, pushing it across the table towards him as Nick flung his laptop bag onto the seat.

He shook his head and scowled. 'I can't stay long. What do you want?'

'You've got time for a drink.'

'This isn't a date.'

What was he on about? This was a date. We'd arranged to meet in a bar in the city centre, not far from the office. I had on my gold, slinky top – the one I'd worn in the restaurant, the first night I reckon he'd really noticed me. He hadn't changed out of his office suit, but I hadn't been expecting him to. And he seemed tired, worn out even, a hint of stubble on his chin, and no sign of the spicy aftershave he always wore. But it was still a date. It was a nice place, all faux-leather seats and fancy lighting, crowded with after-work drinkers, men with loosened ties and girls who'd hitched up their skirts and slapped on a bit more make-up as soon as they'd escaped from their desks.

'I wanted to see you.' I reached for his hand but he snatched it away before my fingers could find his. 'I did what you wanted me to do,' I said. 'I handed in my notice.'

'You took your time. Ruth said you only called her this morning.'

'I wanted to be sure you wouldn't change your mind.'

He shook his head and reached into his laptop bag, drawing out an envelope. 'The reference you need. And here.' He pulled out a few pieces of paper and passed them to me. 'I printed off some jobs you might want to go for. The money I gave you—' he coughed '—will tide you over, until you get something.'

I'd forgotten about the cheque. Five thousand pounds. My pay-off. I'd keep it, even when he begged me to go back to him, which would be any second now.

'Are we done then?'

He wanted to get away from me, I could see that – I wasn't stupid – but I knew it was because he still fancied me, still wanted me. It was in the way he couldn't look me straight in the eye, how his gaze kept shifting to my boobs, which were neatly on display. His heart wanted me, but his head, that part that worried about what other people thought of him, was telling him not to give in to his desires.

'I think we're meant to be together.' He knew it. I knew it. 'Your wife will get over it.'

He blinked slowly. 'There's nothing to get over. Listen,' he said, taking my hand, 'you're a very nice girl.'

'Nice as in hot?'

'Don't.' He smiled, a flash of sorrow in his eyes. He wanted me. He did. He just didn't want to hurt wifey. He took a deep breath and squeezed my hand. 'You'll find someone new, someone your own age.'

'I won't.'

'You will. You'll find someone else.'

'I don't want anyone else. I just want you, Nick.'

'No.' He shook his head and let go of my hand.

'You want me, too. I can tell.'

'No. Please. It's over.'

This time I grabbed his hand, putting it to my stomach, holding it there. 'No, Nick. It's only just beginning. Can't you see that? It's only just beginning.'

CHAPTER 26

'Thanks so much!' Lottie shouted as the last of the parents left the community centre. Those who could, the ones who worked from home or had been good enough to take the morning off, had really come through when she'd put out a cry to help set up for the play's opening night. And when those mums she thought had been gossiping about her had turned up to lend a hand, she had to admit that maybe Hannah had been right, maybe they hadn't been bitching about her after all.

Hannah. She hadn't spoken to her much over the past couple of weeks, not since she'd told her what Nick had said about the text messages. She hadn't said as much but Lottie got the feeling her best friend wasn't entirely convinced the messages were from Nick's dad. Lottie had ended the call quite quickly. She refused to be suspicious and paranoid anymore. And Hannah didn't like Nick, she knew that – she would always choose not to believe him if she could.

Putting Hannah out of her mind, Lottie collapsed into one of the hundred and fifty chairs they'd laid out. She'd been there since seven, mopping the floor, painting the last bit of scenery, hauling in the refreshments from her car. The ticket price included a glass of wine or a glass of orange juice, Tesco's cheapest – she didn't have the energy to juice oranges. Lottie thanked God she hadn't included nibbles too. Two nights and a matinee on the Friday. She didn't know how she was going to get through it – she felt bloody exhausted.

The stage looked magical though, even if she had to say so herself. And Felix's throne topped it off. Would he mind she'd painted it gold? She'd been meaning to ring him but had then forgotten. Or maybe she hadn't forgotten. Maybe what Nick had said about the goings-on Felix had found himself caught up in all those years ago had left a bad taste in her mouth. Even though there was probably nothing to it. Felix hadn't been charged, had he? It was probably all a load of stuff and nonsense. And Felix had been nothing but kind to her – she should give him the benefit of the doubt. But there was also the business with how much Felix had been involved in Nick's parents splitting up. Was Nick right? Had Felix been messing about with Gwen while she was still married to Nigel? She sighed. She should forget it. It had all happened a long time ago.

The clock on the wall said quarter past twelve. She didn't have time for pondering – half an hour to get to the restaurant. Did she have time to try Ginger again? No, she'd do it later. She'd been calling her for the past two weeks to no avail. All she'd got back was a text message, saying she was really busy and that she'd be in touch soon. *No problem,* Lottie had replied, keeping her fingers crossed that they'd changed their minds about offering her the role. Maybe Brad had put his foot down and said that Lottie would get the part over his dead body. After all, despite the many promises from Ginger, the contract still hadn't arrived.

Jasper would go mad when he found out that she didn't want to take the role. He might even drop her. Lottie shrugged. It didn't matter what he said – she'd made her mind up. She was staying at home with Nick – he needed her and she needed him.

She stood up, catching the back of the chair to steady herself as she did so. She'd done too much. The last couple of weeks had been non-stop. She'd pulled out everything to make sure the play was a success. She put her hand to her forehead. It felt like she was burning up. Maybe she should give Pauline's leaving lunch a miss? After all, she had to be back at the community centre by four thirty at the latest. She'd told the kids to get there for five. She had some exercises, one or two fun games she wanted them to do, to get rid of all that nervous energy before they went on stage. And to sweeten them up. She'd been snappy with them over the past few weeks, tutting when they got their lines wrong, shouting when they wouldn't pay attention. Good job she hadn't managed to get pregnant – she'd probably make a terrible mother.

She made her way to the room at the back of the stage, going over to the rail where she'd hung her dress.

It was beautiful. A Vivienne Westwood, something she'd treated herself to, thinking it would be perfect for the parties she was bound to be invited to in LA. She supposed she could take it back to the shop. With a sigh she took the dress off the hanger. She couldn't let Pauline down. She'd done a lot for her over the years. She was sure the flowers Nick came home with, on her birthday and from time to time, were down to Pauline, as were the surprise nights away he sometimes booked. And, anyway, she needed to be there to represent Nick.

He'd come home last night looking absolutely terrible. The hotel was in a worse condition than anyone had thought. He couldn't make the lunch – he'd be onsite all day, trying to sort out the problem with the roof. Lottie had commiserated, had told him it was only another nine days and then they'd be up at the cottage, having the rest he needed. He'd pulled a face, said maybe they should give it a miss this year, that he didn't know if he could spare the time with work how it was. Lottie had shaken her head, had told him in no uncertain terms that he was having that weekend off – even if she had to drag him there.

Lottie slipped the dress over her head. It had cost a fortune. It was probably way too over the top for a lunch party, but she wanted to look good when she finally met Tasha. She knew her suspicions about the PA and Nick were nonsense, but she also knew that women took to her husband, found him attractive, would flutter their eyelashes at him and wish he was theirs. She'd be friendly to Tasha, of course – now she knew it was Nigel and not her who had sent the threatening messages to Nick – but if Tasha portrayed any hint she was interested in Nick, any hint at all, she'd put her firmly straight.

'Lottie!' Pauline said as Lottie weaved her way through the restaurant to the alcove where at least twenty people sat.

Lottie planted a kiss on Pauline's cheek, while checking out the other women at the table. 'Wouldn't miss it for the world.'

Pauline's eyes glistened. 'It's a shame Nick couldn't make it. How's he feeling?'

'Feeling?' she said before she remembered Nick had said he hadn't told anyone in the office, not even Kas, about the problems with the new complex.

'I don't want to worry them,' he'd said. Lottie had sighed. That was the trouble with Nick – he took too much on his shoulders, bore everything, not letting people help when he should.

'Was it something he ate?'

'He's fine. He'll live,' Lottie said in reply to Pauline's worried face.

Ruth waved at Lottie from the far end of the table.

'I thought you'd gone missing,' Ruth said as Lottie sat down next to her. 'Haven't seen you for ages. It must be three weeks. More maybe.'

'Sorry, sorry, I've been busy with the play.' Lottie planted a kiss on Ruth's cheek, before she leant over the table to give Kas a kiss.

'I'll call round for the paddleboard on Friday,' he said as he held out a bottle of wine to Lottie.

'Not for me, I'm driving. And it's opening night tonight.'

'It'll be great, hon,' Ruth said, squeezing her hand. 'You worry too much.'

Kas topped up his glass. 'Sorry I can't make it, Lots. Work is mad.'

'How about the matinee on Friday?'

He shook his head. 'I need to get stuff done before I make an early dart up to Keswick. I can get to yours at four thirty?'

'Perfect,' Lottie said. The play was starting at one, and the after-party wouldn't go on for more than a couple of hours.

She fished in her bag and pulled out her keyring, selecting a big silver-coloured key. 'Here, I'll give you the key for Fairview now, otherwise I'll forget.'

'I was just going to leave the paddleboard around the back?'

'It'd better go in the shed. Don't want anyone nicking it. And the key for the shed is in the cottage.'

Kas pocketed the key. 'Felix sorted the rat problem? Nick told me.'

Ruth's glass stopped halfway to her mouth. 'What rat problem? You know I can't stand anything like that. We're going to be there a week on Saturday.'

'They're only in the cellar.' Lottie patted her hand. 'You'll be fine. Claire can beat them off for you.' She winked at Kas.

Ruth took a swig of her drink before replying. 'I'm not sure she'll make it.'

'Oh?' Lottie and Kas exchanged a look.

'She's nearly finished the novel. Said she only needs one last push.'

'Oh, that would be a shame if she can't,' Lottie said, even though she didn't mean it.

Ruth shrugged.

Lottie widened her eyes at Kas. He got up and left the table.

'Everything okay, Ru?'

Ruth took a big slug of wine. 'I've decided to call it a day with Claire. I just haven't told her yet.' Ruth's bottom lip wobbled as Lottie rubbed at her arm.

'Have you met someone else? Good for you. Is it Tasha?'

'What?'

'Is it Tasha? I know you like her. You can tell me. I won't breathe a word.' Lottie looked around the table. 'Where is she?'

Ruth took a spring roll and bit off a huge chunk of it. 'What are you on about, Lottie?'

'Last time I was in the office you were going on about how lovely Tasha is? Your tongue was literally on the floor.'

'She is lovely. Was lovely.'

'Was?'

'She handed in her notice last week.'

Lottie nearly dropped her glass of water. 'What? Nick never said.'

'Well, he's pissed off about it, I imagine. Left him right in the lurch.' Ruth topped up her glass.

'I'm surprised he hasn't told me.' Lottie was surprised but in a way she was pleased she hadn't had to commiserate with him, to say it was awful Tasha had just upped and left like that – her face might have given her away.

After taking a gulp of her drink, Ruth put down her glass. 'Don't take it personally, Lots. Bil's got a lot on his plate. We all have.'

So, Nick had told Ruth about what was going on with the hotel complex. It made sense. They were close. Always had been.

'Why did Tasha hand in her notice?' Lottie asked in as disinterested a voice as she could muster.

Ruth frowned at her. 'I've just told you I'm splitting up with Claire and you're more interested in the career plans of some woman you've never met.'

'Sorry,' Lottie said. 'When will you tell Claire?'

'I thought I'd get Bil's birthday weekend out of the way. She's said she might not come, because of finishing her novel, but I doubt she means it. You know how she doesn't like to be on her own.'

Lottie topped up her glass. 'Good idea.'

'Yes. Anyway, I've got a few things I need to sort out first.'

'Does she have any inkling?'

Ruth nibbled at her thumbnail. 'She hasn't said anything, which makes me wonder if she does suspect something. And you know what she's like. Not much gets past her.' She took a slug of her wine.

Lottie pretended to study the menu. 'So, Tasha got a new job, then?'

Ruth shrugged. 'That's what she said. In London. But who knows? She was a bit non-committal on the phone.'

'I thought she loved it at Moore's? Wasn't she getting on really well?'

Ruth emptied her glass. 'Loyalty counts for nothing with some people. They just go for what they want and to hell with anyone else.'

Good for Tasha. As long as she didn't want her husband, Lottie wished her luck with getting whatever her heart desired.

Lottie glanced at the clock as she walked into her kitchen. An hour to have a quick cup of tea, a shower, and try Ginger again.

Her mobile buzzed as she was pouring milk into her mug.

'Hi, Lottie. Just wanted to check in with you. It's been a while since we last spoke. How are you doing?'

Emma's voice was warm and upbeat too. If Lottie believed that anybody could help her and Nick to achieve their dream, this woman was the one. 'Emma. It's nice of you to call.'

'How have you been?'

'Okay.' It was true. She had been okay. But, then again, a lot had been going on. She hadn't had much time over the past few months to dwell on their failed IVF attempt. Nor to ponder over whether she wanted to give it one last go.

'And physically? No problem with your periods? Some women can have a slight delay in getting their cycle back on track once they've had IVF.'

Lottie squinted at the National Trust calendar hanging

264

on the wall. 'Hmm, I had one period.' She remembered being in bed, the night she'd seen Tasha getting into Nick's car outside the office. That was nearly seven weeks ago. 'I think I'm late this cycle.'

'That can be normal.'

Lottie put her hand to her stomach. Her belly usually blew up like a balloon when she had her period. No, nothing yet. It had better not arrive over Nick's birthday weekend. Knowing her luck, it was bound to come then.

Emma wished Lottie well and told her to call if she ever needed anything. Lottie didn't for a second imagine the consultant was touting for business. They'd used a different clinic at the beginning and that had definitely been a money-making machine, but she could tell Emma only wanted to help the desperate couples who came to her.

Lottie headed up the stairs, hanging up her dress, before padding to the shower. She opened the bathroom cabinet to get out the posh shower gel Nick had given her last Christmas. Today was a celebration. The first night of the play. Her gaze lighted on a slim box, tucked away at the back of the shelf. It was probably empty. She'd lost count of how many pregnancy tests she'd taken over the years.

She lifted the box out of the cabinet and shook it. One in there. It wouldn't hurt to do a quick test. It wouldn't be positive, of course it wouldn't, but there was a slim finger of hope in her. She guessed there always would be. Emma had said sometimes couples fell pregnant naturally – once they stopped centring their lives around trying to get pregnant and relaxed, putting it out of their minds. It had been known to happen.

After ripping off the wrapper, Lottie held the wand in the stream of her wee, before placing it on the side of the bath. She stepped into the shower, shaking her head as she turned on the water. Why did she do it to herself? It was as if she wanted to make herself unhappy, as if she were addicted to that feeling of disappointment that every negative test gave her. Hannah often said that she catastrophised everything, looked at the glass as half empty, rather than half full. Was it a comfort to her to feel disappointed? Did she cling on to that familiar anxious feeling? Was that why she'd built up the story in her head of Nick falling for Tasha? Had she enjoyed the pain it brought her, the feeling that something bad was going to happen? She lifted her face to the jet of water. God, she needed to stop being a masochist.

She stepped out of the shower, reaching for a fluffy towel, staring at her reflection in the mirror as she dried herself. She really was an idiot. Her mad thoughts over the past couple of months had hurt her, and had hurt Nick. And they'd distracted her from what had really been going on with him – his troubles at work and with his father. She was a true prize idiot.

She took a calming breath. No more. She had the play and Nick's birthday weekend to look forward to. She just had one more thing to do – ring Ginger to tell her she wouldn't be accepting the part.

She lifted the pregnancy test, ready to fling it into the bin.

But her heart hammered in her chest as she peered at the little window on the wand. There were two lines. Two pink lines, forming a cross. She closed her eyes, counted slowly to ten and then opened them again. The two lines were still there.

She sat down on the edge of the bath. It couldn't be. She was reading it wrong. Maybe this test was the other way round than the previous ones she'd used? Two lines meant you weren't pregnant.

She read the instructions leaflet and then looked at the wand again, a gasp escaping from her lips. She was pregnant. She bloody was. When she'd given up hope, when she'd stopped thinking about it, it had happened.

Tears streamed down her face. How long? All those years of trying. The time spent in the clinics. The injections, the mood swings, excitement one minute, devastation the next. And all that hoping. And wishing. And praying. Finally, finally it had happened for them.

Nick. She couldn't wait to tell him. But should she wait? Make sure? She'd tell him next week. On their anniversary. Do another test before they went to the Lakes, just to be one hundred percent certain. She didn't know how she'd be able to keep the news to herself until then, but she would. This would be one anniversary present he'd never forget.

There was one person she needed to tell though. Ginger. Now she had the perfect excuse not to take the part. She was scrolling through, searching for the casting director's number, when her mobile started to buzz. Hannah.

Her finger hovered over the button to accept the call. Hannah could read her like a book. Even over the phone. But she was so excited. She needed to tell someone. And her best friend wouldn't breathe a word.

'Hannah,' Lottie said. 'You are not going to believe what's happened.'

CHAPTER 27

'This is gorgeous!'

Nick dumped my bag on the kitchen table, before shrugging. 'It's been in the family for years.'

Fancy having a cottage, somewhere lovely like this, just sitting empty most of the time, waiting for whenever one of the family wanted to use it. I'd known all along that Nick came from a bit of money, could tell by the designer clothes he wore, the Mercedes he drove. From the way he spoke. He was a northern lad but he'd softened his accent, mellowed it.

I hadn't been surprised when he'd called me. Even after last Wednesday night in the pub when he'd just upped and left. I'd thought he was going to faint when I told him I was up the duff. He'd gone a funny shade of white before his skin had taken on a grey tinge. And then he'd grabbed the glass of red wine I'd bought him and had knocked it back as if it were water.

'You're lying,' he'd said. But when I'd shown him the

wand with the two intersecting lines on it, he could see I wasn't.

It was shock. Shock that had made him snatch up his laptop bag and leave, ignoring my pleas for him to stay. Ignoring the amused sniggers of the drinkers around us.

Slowly, I'd sipped at my wine. I hadn't been worried. He needed time to let the news sink in – that was all.

So I hadn't been surprised when he'd called me a few days ago and told me to meet him outside the office at three on Friday afternoon. He was going to take me out for a late lunch, somewhere away from the city, away from prying eyes, so we could talk, properly talk about what we were going to do.

I hadn't expected him to bring me here. Even though the cottage was gorgeous, a pub somewhere in the Peaks would have done. Perhaps we were going to stay the night? Our first full night together. I wished he'd told me though. I hadn't packed anything, not a change of knickers, nor a toothbrush.

He switched on some lamps, making the room cosy. It was cold though. I shivered, wrapping my coat around me.

'I'll light the fire.' Someone, whoever had been here before us, had left kindling and newspaper in the grate, waiting to be lit. Nick struck at a match a couple of times, cursing as the paper smouldered but wouldn't take. Eventually, on his third attempt, the flame took hold, the kindling crackling away.

There was a wrought-iron wine rack standing near to the door, a set of hooks above it, a dog lead hanging from one of them. 'Do your parents have a dog? I love dogs.' I did too, even Kenny's pit bull that slobbered all over me.

He didn't answer so I picked out a bottle from the rack, the first one I laid my hand on. 'Fancy a glass?'

He narrowed his eyes at me.

'I'll just have the one. It'll be fine.'

I opened the cupboard doors, searching for some wine glasses. The cupboards were fully stocked with tins and packets. The freezer was jam-packed too.

'Is there a pizza in there?' Nick said.

'Are we not eating out?'

'We can talk better here.' He moved me out of the way, wrenching open one of the drawers and taking out a Hawaiian pizza. Not my favourite. Pineapple on a pizza?

'You hungry?'

'Starving.' I put his hand to my stomach. 'Eating for two, aren't I?'

His Adam's apple bobbed as he swallowed. He pulled two wine glasses out of the only cupboard I hadn't looked in and opened the wine, pouring himself a large glass, me a much smaller one. He handed mine to me.

'Cheers!' I said. 'To—'

'Have you told anyone?' He ignored my raised glass.

'What? Are you joking? Of course I haven't.' I would have done if I'd had anyone to tell. But all my close mates, the ones I'd grown up with, had long escaped from our scummy estate. And I was hardly going to tell my old man, was I? Or Kenny.

271

'Good.' He put down his glass and took the pizza out of its wrapping, throwing it onto a shelf in the oven, and slamming shut the door.

'Going to give me the tour while we wait?'

He took another swig of his drink. 'Later.'

'Are we staying the night?'

His glass was halfway to his lips. 'We've just come here to talk. That's all.'

'Seems a shame not to. We could make a weekend of it. You could do with a break. I know how busy you've been with the hotel—'

'We're not staying.' He shook his head and took a large slug of his drink.

I went over to him, taking the glass from him and putting my arms around his waist. 'It's going to be okay, you know. It's a shock, isn't it?'

He pushed my hands away and stepped back. 'Is it?'

'Well, it was for me.'

'So you didn't plan this?' His lips had turned thin.

'You reckon I tricked you?'

'You tell me,' he said as he ran his hand through his hair.

I took a deep breath before answering. 'I wouldn't do that. You think I'd do that?'

'You said you were on the pill.'

'I never said I was.' I hadn't lied. He'd asked me if things were *safe* – those were the words he'd used, and I'd said they were.

I took a sip of my drink. I had planned to get pregnant by him. To give him everything he'd ever wanted. Because that's all I wanted to do. Make him happy. I'd just never imagined things would happen quite so quickly.

Shaking his head, he turned away from me and busied himself laying the table, lining everything up just so. Nick would make a brilliant dad. A million times better than my old man. I wouldn't have got myself pregnant by him if I'd had any doubt about that.

I went up behind him, putting my arms around his waist, my head on his back. 'What do you want? A boy or a girl? Or could be one of both. Twins run in my family.' They did. My mum was a twin. And I was too. Only my twin, Danny, hadn't lived. He'd died in my mother's womb at twenty-eight weeks. I'd crushed him. I remember my mother saying that to me as she ran the brush hard through my hair again and again, so hard that I'd squealed like a pig. Or maybe she hadn't said it. Maybe it was something I'd made up. Maybe it was my old man who'd told me that.

Nick's body stiffened. He removed my hands from around his waist. 'We need to talk about things. Let's eat while we do that, shall we?'

I wanted to pinch myself. Could there be anything better than sitting in this gorgeous cottage with the man I loved more than life itself, discussing our future? Okay, it was only pizza. And bloody Hawaiian at that. Still, I could pick off the bits of pineapple. I wanted to laugh. To twirl around and around. To open that stable door and shout and tell everyone that no, things couldn't get any better.

* * *

273

My mouth watered as he set the pizza down on the table, the spicy smell of the ham hanging in the air.

'Dig in.'

I did as I was told. I was starving. It was only when I was halfway through my first slice that I noticed he hadn't touched the food.

'Aren't you hungry? It's delish. Apart from the pineapple.' I laughed and pointed at my plate, hoping he would laugh too.

'I'm fine.'

'You need to eat. You need to keep up your strength. I've got plans for you later.' I winked at him.

He frowned back.

'Don't worry. It won't hurt the baby.'

He winced and took a slug of his wine.

'I like the name Alfie for a boy. What do you think?' I'd always loved Shane in Westlife but guessed that name might be a bit too common for Nick. 'Have you got any favourites? I've got a feeling it's going to be a boy.' I hadn't, but I knew men longed for a son, someone they could take to the football, someone they could share a pint in the pub with as soon as the kid could stomach the taste of it.

'Excuse me,' he said, getting up from the table and heading up the stairs.

I could hear him being sick from where I sat. I put down the slice of pizza. 'You all right?' I shouted. Poor thing. All this was a bit too much for him.

His face was red when he came back into the kitchen, his eyes watery from the retching. He poured himself a glass of water and downed it in one go. 'You need to get rid of it.'

A piece of ham got lodged in the back of my throat. I coughed and spluttered. He filled a glass but only handed it to me once I held out my hand.

'Thanks for the slap on the back,' I said, after I'd had a few gulps of water. 'Were you just going to watch me choke?'

He didn't say anything in answer to that.

'You need to get rid of it,' he said again, sitting down next to me at the table and taking hold of my hand. 'We can't have a baby together. Can't you see that?'

'Of course we can. We are, Nick.' I put his hand on my stomach. 'We're having a baby. Our baby. It's what you've always wanted, isn't it? Isn't it?' I repeated when he didn't answer.

'Yes. But not . . . not with you.'

I flinched as if he'd slapped me. 'But we're meant to be together, Nick. I know it. You know it.'

He put his head in his hands. 'I love my wife.'

'Now we both know that's a lie or else why would you be here with me now?'

He ran his fingers through his hair, before taking a deep breath. 'I wanted to get away from Manchester. To explain to you that I can't have a baby with you. I'm really sorry, but I can't. It would kill my wife if—'

'I'll tell her.' I picked a piece of pineapple from the slice in front of me and dropped it onto my plate.

'No, you won't.' He grabbed my wrist, gripping it so tightly I thought I might faint.

'You're hurting me. Nick!'

He let go of me and stood up, resting his elbows on the edge of the sink, his head pushed forward as if he might be sick again.

My wrist tingled with pins and needles. 'If you can't tell her, I will.'

'You need to get rid of it.'

I got up and went over to him. 'It's not an "it", Nick. It's our baby. And I'm not going to get rid of our baby.' As I rubbed his back tears dripped from his face into the washing-up bowl. 'Shush, shush. It's going to be all right. I'll tell her.'

He wiped at his face and pushed me away so that I nearly stumbled. 'No, you won't. Do you hear me? You tell my wife and I'll fucking kill you.'

CHAPTER 28

'You were fabulous,' Lottie said to Daisy, kissing her on the cheek as the final curtain went down. 'You too,' she said to Dylan as he pouted at her. 'All of you, in fact.' The smaller ones came over to her, accepting a quick hug, while the others gave her high fives as they skidded past. 'Let the wrap party commence!'

'Trey and I will get the drinks set up,' Daisy said.

Lottie smiled at her goddaughter. 'That was supposed to be your mum's job.' Hannah had texted her earlier, saying she was so sorry she hadn't been able to make any of the performances, she'd been *otherwise engaged*. Lottie was surprised that her friend hadn't made it to any of the shows. It must be serious between her and Craig if Hannah had opted to spend time with him, rather than watching her daughter, the star of the show.

It was as if Daisy had read her mind. 'I'm happy for her,' she said, blushing. 'She's spending a lot of time at Craig's.'

Lottie grinned. 'Which means Trey is spending a lot of time at yours, I bet?'

277

Daisy went even redder.

'Don't be getting up to anything.'

'I am seventeen now, Lottie!' It had been Daisy's birthday last week.

'That's what I was on about. No drinking while your mum's not there.'

She laughed. 'Sure.'

'At least if you drink, clean the bathroom if you throw up.'

A look of horror swept across Daisy's face. 'Oh my God, I'm sorry. I was sick in your bathroom, wasn't I? I was a right mess.'

Lottie put her arm around Daisy's shoulders. 'Bet you won't drink that much ever again.'

Daisy shook her head. 'No way.'

'Yeah, that's what they all say.'

'I'm hopeless when I drink. I lost my bank card that night, and my house keys, and a lip gloss. You didn't find them, did you?'

'What sort of lip gloss?'

'I can't remember the make.'

'Strawberry-flavoured?'

'That's the one.'

Lottie wanted to laugh. The lip gloss she'd found under their bed belonged to Daisy. She felt a prickle of sweat on the back of her neck. Of course it did. What an idiot she was. All that worry she'd put herself through – for nothing.

As Daisy skittered off to find Trey, Lottie surveyed the room. Had Ginger been in the audience? She hadn't spotted her, but the hall was packed, and it was difficult to see from her view in the wings. Daisy had been fabulous – Lottie hadn't been lying when she'd told her goddaughter that. Wouldn't it be wonderful if Ginger thought so too? Surely Daisy would prefer an acting career to cutting up dead bodies?

Lottie wanted the casting director to be there for another reason too – even though she dreaded telling Ginger she wasn't going to take the role, it would be far better to tell her in person, than on the phone. She owed her that much at least. So she'd texted her, reminding her that she'd saved her a seat at the matinee performance.

People were pushing the chairs to the side when Lottie finally made it out from backstage and into the hall. There was a hubbub of conversation and squeals from some of the younger kids who seemed to be having a game of tag. 'Well done,' one of the mothers, who Lottie thought had been bitching about her, said.

'Brilliant,' said another.

Another person started clapping, and then Dylan's dad started a round of 'For She's a Jolly Good Fellow' while Connor, holding on to crutches – so he had broken his leg, after all – awkwardly gave her a thumbs up.

Lottie blushed and took a bow before making her way to the serving hatch, where Trey was handing out plastic cups filled with warm wine. 'Thanks,' she said, taking one, before putting it down again. For a second, just a second, she'd forgotten. Picking up a glass of orange juice she tried to catch Daisy's attention. 'Have you seen Nick?'

But Daisy was busy handing out cups of juice to a gang of flushed-faced kids.

Lottie looked around her. Where was he? A meeting about the Dolos project had been arranged at short notice in Liverpool that morning, the new owners flying in from Italy. But he had called her on his way to it, said he'd try to make it back in time for the matinee performance. She fished her phone out of her pocket. Nothing. *Where are you?* she quickly tapped out and pressed send.

'Have you seen Nick?' she said again to Daisy.

Trey grimaced. 'He's not coming here, is he?'

Daisy shot her boyfriend a look. Lottie frowned. What was all that about? Either Hannah had been bad-mouthing Nick to Daisy's boyfriend, or Nick had said something to upset Daisy at work. It wouldn't surprise her if he had; he'd been under a lot of pressure. This project was really stretching him to his limit. Or perhaps it was Craig who'd said something? Maybe he had Nick pegged as a bit la-di-da?

Lottie walked through the crowd, getting caught up in one or two groups' conversations, murmuring a *yes* or *no* here and there as she surveyed the room. Ginger hadn't turned up. Even with this number of people, Lottie was sure she'd be able to spot her. Maybe she'd returned to the States? Perhaps that's why she hadn't come back to her – perhaps she was tied up with another show.

Lottie glanced at her watch. Where was everyone? Gwen and Felix hadn't come and Ruth was nowhere to be seen either. Lottie sighed. Maybe it was for the best. She didn't want anyone to guess her secret. And if anyone would guess, it would be Ruth. It must be written all over her face, after all. Hannah had wished her luck in keeping it under wraps. But Lottie knew she would. And she'd sworn Hannah to secrecy too. Nick must be the next person to know. She really couldn't wait to tell him. How special that she was going to tell him on their anniversary. Only a week away. What was a week when they'd been waiting for over five years? She would buy a bottle of champagne – for him, not for her – so he could toast their happiness.

By four o'clock everyone had gone. Daisy and Trey had been brilliant – tidying everything up, making the community centre presentable again. She'd given them fifty quid and told them to treat themselves to a pizza.

She flicked off the lights, pulled the door shut, and turned the key in the lock, before picking up the bin bag of rubbish Trey had collected. She would drag Nick over tomorrow and get him to help her collect Felix's chair. She wouldn't want to be lifting – she'd feign a hurt wrist, something like that.

She sang along to the radio as she drove home. 'Walking on Sunshine'. God, she was so happy. She really did feel fit to burst. Life was strange, wasn't it? One minute you were down, thinking there was nothing to look forward to, only gloom ahead, and the next you were thinking – no, knowing – that life couldn't get any better.

She flicked the switch to the garage door and waited while it opened. Damn! Nick's paddleboard. She called Kas's number, waiting as it rang. 'Did you forget?'

'Oh, Lots, sorry! I can come back. It completely slipped my mind.'

'Don't worry, I forgot too. Where are you?'

'At junction thirty-five. I don't mind, honestly.'

Junction thirty-five? He was nearly there.

'I'll get off at thirty-six.'

'No, don't be daft. I'll nip up with it.'

'Are you sure?'

'I'm sure. Say hello to your parents. And see you next weekend.'

The digital clock on the dashboard said just after four thirty. It was a three-hour round trip to Fairview, three and a quarter at most. She'd be back before eight. Lottie tried Nick's mobile again. No answer.

Sod it. She'd go. She was buzzing with adrenaline after the party. The drive would calm her down.

After twenty minutes of sweating and swearing as she carefully secured the paddleboard to the roof rack of her BMW, she jumped back in the car and headed for the M6 and Fairview.

CHAPTER 29

'I'm sorry,' Nick said as he came back through the front door of the cottage. It was just before six. He'd been gone for nearly an hour. I'd been starting to think he might never come back. 'For getting angry. Sorry.' He ran his hand through his hair.

I shrugged. He called that angry? He ought to have been on the receiving end of my old man's fists over the years. Then he would really know what angry was all about. I'd been adept at hiding the bruises, wearing my threadbare cardigan even in summer, thick black tights too, skiving off games at school when my legs were too black and blue to show.

'Eat the pizza,' he said. 'Do you want me to warm it up?'

I shook my head. 'I live on cold pizza.' I held the plate out towards him.

He picked up a slice and then threw it down again. 'I can give you more money. To have it done privately. And more money after that.'

I chewed my slice of pizza slowly, savouring the spiciness of the tomato sauce, pulling with my teeth to break the stringy Mozzarella before I spoke. 'I thought you wanted a baby? You told me you hoped you'd be blessed with them.'

He slammed his hand on the table. 'With my wife,' he said, 'not with you.' He pronounced the words slowly, like one of my teachers at school used to do, as if I couldn't understand what he was saying. As if I was thick.

'But you want a baby,' I said again.

'For fuck's sake, with my *wife*!'

I covered my mouth with my hand to hide my smile. It turned me on, that such filthy words could come out of the mouth of someone who appeared to be so pure, so wholesome. So gorgeous.

'You think this is funny?'

He grabbed me by my jumper and pulled me out of the chair until I was standing, our faces an inch apart. 'This is all a game to you, isn't it?'

'No,' I whispered. 'I know it's a lot for you to get your head around but I love you, you love me and we're having a baby. Our baby.'

'You stupid bitch!' He slapped my face so hard that my head whipped to the side, the pain not coming for a second. I don't know who was more surprised he'd hit me – me or him.

My palm flew to my face. Let him hit me. I didn't care. I was used to it. Unlike my dad, who hit me out of spite for my mother leaving him, I knew Nick was

284

hitting me out of fear. Fear of what his wife would say. What his family would say. Fear of taking that jump into a new life with me. Fear of doing what he wanted to do.

He started to cry again. 'I'm sorry,' he said, his hands on the sink, his shoulders heaving in time with his sobs. 'I'm sorry.'

I went up to him and circled his waist with my arms, laying my head on his back, the soft cashmere of his jumper as soft as a baby's blanket against my hot, stinging cheek. 'It's okay. I forgive you.' He turned to me and I wiped his fringe back from his face. 'It's going to be okay.' And it would. We were going to have this baby. And we'd look after it, both of us, love it. I would never walk away like my mother had done.

'You'll do it?'

'Yes.'

'Thank you.' For the first time since we'd got here there was a genuine smile on his face. He lowered his forehead to mine. 'Thank you.'

'Shall I ring her and tell her, or would face to face be better?'

'What?' He stepped away from me.

'I'll tell her. You don't need to do anything. I'll tell your wife.'

'Not that! I was asking you if you'd get rid of it.'

'No.' I shook my head. 'I won't do that. And stop calling them "it". This is our baby. I know it's a shock. But once you get your head around it, you'll realise it's the best thing that could ever have happened.'

The front door creaked as it opened. We both turned towards it. Nick went so white I thought he was going to faint.

The door creaked again as it was pushed shut. 'What's the best thing that could ever have happened? Nick?'

'I'm having Nick's baby,' I wanted to say but the words got stuck in my throat as the chain of the dog's lead whipped through the air towards me.

NOW – ONE WEEK AFTER THE MATINEE PERFORMANCE OF *TIME-SLIP*

CHAPTER 30

Lottie stares at the dead woman on the floor. Is she dreaming? She must be. She's in Nick's parents' holiday cottage. Still asleep on the sofa upstairs. When she wakes up, all this – this nightmare she's conjured up in her head – will be gone.

She screws her eyes shut, is halfway through counting to ten, when there's the bang of a door. And then Nick's voice calling her name.

She opens her eyes.

She's still in the cellar.

The woman is still on the floor.

Lottie wants to reach out and touch that long red hair, tug it so Tasha's face comes into view, but she can't.

Instead, she throws the tarpaulin back over Tasha's body, and – with one hand clinging to the banister – heaves herself back up the cellar steps.

She's expecting Nick to be at the top of them, looming over her, blocking out the bright light from the kitchen, asking her where she found the key, asking her what

289

she's doing down there. The electricity tripped – that's what she'll say. It's not a lie, is it? But another lie is already forming in her mind, ready to spill out of her lips: she just went to the bottom of the steps, flicked the switch, came back up. Just to the bottom. She hasn't been in the cellar. She hasn't seen anything. She hasn't done anything.

But Nick's not there. The front door is wide open, the night, the storm rushing into the empty room.

She closes the cellar door behind her, locks it and puts the key in her pocket, all the while wondering why her first thought is to lie to her husband, why she won't scream and cry and tell him what she's seen. Is it because – and she can hardly admit it to herself – she believes he, the person she loves more than anyone else, has something to do with this? The moods, the edginess, the way he always clams up – or gets angry – when she mentions Tasha's name. And what he said earlier, when she told him about the baby – *I'll never let anyone or anything hurt you.*

Blinding headlights sweep through the windows. There's the crunch of tyres on gravel. And then car doors are slamming shut, people talking as they spill out into the night.

A drenched Nick barrels through the door. 'Darling! Look who I found in the village.' Hannah appears behind him, shrugs off her wet coat and comes hurtling towards Lottie, scooping her up in a hug.

'Bloody hell, you're freezing, Lots. You okay? Feeling all right?' She glances at the fire crackling away in the

290

grate. 'It's roasting in here.' Taking Lottie's left hand between her own hands, she rubs it back and forth, before swapping it with the right. Hannah peers at her. 'You're ever so pale. Are you sure you're okay? Nothing wrong is there?'

Hannah means with the baby. Lottie pulls her hand out of her friend's grip, pushing away her fringe that's plastered to her forehead with sweat. 'I'm fine. What are you doing here? I thought you were coming up tomorrow?' That was the plan – everyone was supposed to arrive at lunchtime tomorrow. Lottie was going to make Nick go for a walk with her while the surprise visitors arrived. When they got back, the house would be decorated, birthday banners and balloons strung everywhere. Gwen was bringing a cake.

'The weather forecast wasn't great so we all decided to come up tonight and stay at the B&B in the village. Good job we did – it's supposed to be even worse tomorrow. Storm Apate. The first of the year.'

Lottie peers through the open door. Worse than this? It's howling outside.

'There are trees down in the village, you know. One blocking the lane at the bottom too. We're lucky to make it up here.'

'I'm glad you did.' Lottie hugs her friend tight to her until Hannah pulls away.

'You told Nick then? I've never seen him so happy. He came into the pub, fit to burst, and bought drinks all round to celebrate.' Hannah makes a face. 'He should have waited until we got here, so you could tell us together.'

'It's fine.' Lottie tries a smile. 'I bet everyone was shocked, weren't they?'

'Too right!' Hannah leans towards her. 'Gwen had to have a brandy.'

Lottie blows out a long breath. 'I could do with one of those.'

'What's the matter, Lots? Everything's okay, isn't it?'

'Of course it is. I just wasn't expecting you until tomorrow – that's all.'

Craig sweeps through the door. He's wearing an AC/DC T-shirt and denim shorts. Both are wet through. 'Aye aye. I told you we'd be spoiling their fun by rocking up like this.' He dumps a rucksack and a crate full of booze on the floor.

Lottie attempts a smile, but nothing will come. What is she going to do? Hannah and Craig will think she's mad if she tells them there's a dead woman in the cellar. She'll take them down there . . . they won't think she's mad then. But what will happen if she does that? One of them will call the police. Just like she should be doing now. Let people in suits with questions and firm handshakes deal with this. And they will. They'll take the body away. They'll nod their heads and reassure her that Tasha lying dead in the cellar has nothing to do with her. With Nick. It's nothing to do with them. Nothing at all.

Bile shoots into the back of her throat. But, of course, it has everything to do with them. This isn't some random woman. This is Nick's PA. *Was,* she reminds herself – Ruth said she'd handed in her notice, had taken a job in London. But Nick has worked with her. Closely. A sudden thought makes Lottie start to shake. What if they think she's done this? What if Nick thinks she has? What if the police suspect her? Her hand moves to her stomach. What if she ends up in prison? What if they take the baby off her?

'Have you told Lottie?' Craig says to Hannah, before going over to the fridge and peering inside.

'Told me what?'

But they don't have to say anything as the headlights of another car light up the night sky. A Land Rover. Felix's. It stops just short of Hannah's old banger, causing a whoop from Craig who's staring out of the kitchen window. Lottie goes to the door. Out of the four-by-four spills Ruth, followed by Gwen and Felix, a glum-faced Claire bringing up the rear. Felix raises a hand. 'Sorry, Lottie.'

They're all here. All apart from Kas.

One after the other, Nick carries in holdalls, small suitcases, carrier bags, a crate full of beer. 'What happened to no surprises?' he whispers in Lottie's ear as he passes her.

Her eyes well with tears. This was supposed to be a perfect weekend. Just them tonight, celebrating their anniversary and the baby they've longed for, and then the family and friends tomorrow, to celebrate Nick's birthday and their news. Nothing will ever be perfect again. Why had she gone down into the cellar? She wants to turn back the clock, to have not seen what she's seen.

'Hey, Lots, I'm only joking.' Nick drops the bag he's holding. 'Thank you for organising all this,' he says as he pulls her towards him, kissing the top of her head.

She wants to let him hold her, soothe her, tell her all this will go away, but her body stiffens. He said he didn't know where the cellar key was, when it was on his keyring all along.

'We're going to have a brilliant weekend,' he murmurs into her hair. A brilliant weekend? His PA is lying stone-cold dead in the cellar. Lottie knows they're not going to have a brilliant weekend. Knows that, from that moment when she saw Tasha's body – was it only ten minutes ago, fifteen? – nothing is going to be brilliant ever again.

'Congratulations, darling,' Felix says, shrugging off his blouson jacket, and wiping the spatters of rain from his glasses before planting a wet kiss on her cheek. 'Wonderful news. Just wonderful.'

Lottie places her hand on her stomach. How is it possible to go from being so euphoric to feeling so scared in the space of an hour? She breathes in, holds the breath for a count of four, and then releases it slowly. She must try to remain calm. Stress is no good for the baby.

'Well, what a shock,' Gwen says. 'We were all there, having a drink after dinner and in walks my Nicky, proud as punch.' Gwen, removing the plastic scarf from her head, shoots Lottie a smile. One that doesn't reach all the way up to her eyes. 'You don't mind him telling us?'

Lottie shakes her head.

'My Nicky is going to make such a good daddy.' She holds a bottle of champagne in the air. 'This was to celebrate Nicky's birthday but I suppose we should open it now.'

Lottie ignores her and starts to get the champagne flutes out of the cupboard.

'Lots, let me.' Standing on tiptoes, Ruth reaches the glasses from the top shelf. She places them on the side and then puts her hands on Lottie's shoulders. 'Am I the last to know?' There's a deep etch in her forehead.

'No, don't be daft, Ru. I've only just told Nick. I wanted to tell him first.' She doesn't tell Ruth that she's lying, that she told Hannah first. Ruth would only be miffed that Lottie hadn't confided in her.

'Of course you did.' Ruth kisses her on the cheek. 'I'm thrilled for you. I'm going to be an auntie. Finally.'

'How are things?' Lottie glances in the direction of Claire, who's made herself comfy on the sofa, her Kindle in hand.

'She's nearly finished it. Just giving it one last read-through.'

'I wasn't talking about her novel.'

'Not tonight, Lots. Let's just have tonight, at least.'

Lottie rubs at Ru's arm. She couldn't have spoken truer words. Should she let them have tonight? Just tonight? A night of love and celebration before she asks Nick what the hell is going on, why his PA is lying dead on the floor of the cellar? One last night before she calls the police? She shakes her head. Has she gone mad? What is she thinking? Of course she won't. She needs to tell them what's in the cellar. She needs to tell them now. She takes a deep breath and opens her mouth.

'I'd like to raise a toast,' Felix says as he finishes filling everyone's glasses.

'No,' Nick says. '*I* would like to raise a toast.'

'Craig,' Hannah whispers to her boyfriend. 'Put that down.'

Craig reluctantly puts down the bottle of Stella he's clutching and grabs the champagne flute Hannah is holding out to him.

Ruth beckons Claire over. With a sigh, she switches off her Kindle and makes her way to the kitchen, accepting a glass from Felix. Her hand slides around Ruth's waist before dropping to her side when Ruth shifts ever so slightly away from her. Claire scowls and takes a big glug of her drink.

Lottie raises her glass of sparkling mineral water in the air. Her arm feels heavy, as if she's in a dream and, for the second time that night, she wonders if she is, if she really did fall asleep on the sofa when Nick went out and if she's still asleep. If she's dreamt everything since then.

But a blast of cold air, rushing in from the front door, tells her otherwise. They all turn to look as Kas fills the doorway, rain dripping from his hair, his coat, the tip of his nose. 'We had to park at the bottom of the lane,' he says. 'No room outside.'

'We?' Nick says, giving Kas a wink.

Kas wipes his hand across his face. Lottie isn't sure if it's to wipe away the rain or the blush spreading across his cheeks.

'You said it was okay to bring someone, Lottie?'

She tries to smile. Kas is here. Kas is practical. Kas will know what to do. 'Of course it is,' she says.

He steps back to allow his guest to enter. She has a coat on that probably belongs to Kas. It drapes her thin frame, nearly reaching the floor, the hood covering her face.

She lifts the hood, to reveal a mass of long red hair and ruby lips.

Lottie doesn't know if the gasp comes from her or from someone else in the room. She puts down her champagne flute before it slips from her fingers.

'For those of you that haven't met her,' Kas says, putting his arm around the woman's shoulders next to him. 'This is Tasha.'

Tasha? Lottie's hand flies to her mouth. That can't be Tasha. Tasha is in the cellar. Lying on the floor. Tasha is dead.

A frown is sketched on Nick's lips and his forehead.

'Your PA?' Lottie's voice comes out as a whisper. She coughs and tries again. 'Your PA?'

'Ex-PA,' Nick says, crossing the kitchen and pecking Tasha's cheek. 'Well, I didn't expect to see you again.'

'Neither did I.' Ruth frowns at Kas's companion.

Claire grimaces as if she has a bad taste in her mouth.

'Nice to meet you finally,' Tasha says to Lottie as she links her arm through Kas's.

'Good for you two.' Nick's mouth is set in a thin line. 'Champagne?'

As he picks up the glasses, Lottie sees the smile turn to a scowl. He's not pleased that Tasha, the PA who upped and left at the worst possible moment, is here. He's not pleased at all.

But Lottie is. Lottie is overjoyed. For if Tasha is here, living and breathing in front of her, then she can't be lying dead in the cellar, can she?

Lottie lets out a long sigh. She's had a funny turn – that's all. The excitement of the day, the stress of the past couple of months have got to her. Her hormones, shooting up and crashing down again and again, making her crazy. There is no dead woman in the cellar. Relief bubbles up inside her. The mind is amazing. She's conjured up a dead Tasha because, at times over the past few months, that's what she wanted to see.

She's imagined it all. Hasn't she?

CHAPTER 31

Sleep won't come. Lottie isn't surprised. The noise coming through the thin floorboards would be enough to wake the dead. The dead. Lottie shudders. It's not the noise keeping her awake, of course it's not, it's that thing itching away at her, the thought she can't shake from her head – that she needs to go down into the cellar. There isn't a dead woman in there. A dead Tasha. She knows that now. But it wouldn't hurt to check. Wouldn't hurt to look in the corner of the cellar, to find out just what was there. What her overactive imagination had conjured up. She turns over, plumps up the pillow. She can never tell anyone what she thought she'd seen – they'd think she'd lost it.

Nick had made her go to bed. He'd told her she looked tired, was very pale, needed to get some rest. She'd protested, saying she was fine, but it was as if they'd all turned against her, had all decided that an early night was what she needed.

So now she lies in the dark, listening to the rain battering the bedroom window, wondering if it's her pregnancy hormones that have made her go just a little bit funny. She's heard other women on the online pregnancy forums she's lurked on over the years say that being pregnant can addle your brain, make you forget things or invent things. Did she invent a dead Tasha in the cellar because, deep down, that's what she'd wanted to see these past months? Hadn't the fact that Ruth said Tasha had left the business, moved to London, been enough to satisfy the fear that Tasha might be trying to take Nick away from her? It mustn't have been.

She hears movement on the stairs, people saying 'goodnight', the clink of glasses and plates as the dishwasher is stacked and then the hum as it's switched on.

Her eyes are tightly shut when Nick comes into the room. He closes the door softly behind him, makes his way around to the other side of the bed, swearing quietly as he stubs his toe on the wooden bed leg.

He slips under the duvet and curls up behind her, his hands cold around her stomach. 'Okay?' he whispers.

'Mmm.' Should she tell him, should she tell him what she thinks she's seen so he can laugh at her? So he can go down to the cellar with her and tell her she's imagined the whole thing?

Within a few minutes, Nick is snoring softly behind her. She hears the wheeze of pipes as people use the bathroom, the screeching sound of the toilet in Gwen and Felix's en suite. Nick shifts away from her, turning to face the window.

Lottie's fingers find her mobile on the bedside cabinet. One bar, a faint signal. She taps in her password and

300

then googles 'pregnant women imagining things that aren't there'. There are over fifty-four million results. It can happen. There's a woman who imagined she'd seen a man in her house and there hadn't been one there at all. Another who swore a ghost had walked through the wall of her bedroom. Lottie shudders and snuggles further down into the bed. It can happen. She puts her hand to her tummy and rubs it gently. She doesn't care if she is going mad. It'll all be worth it when she cradles her child in her arms.

It's 2.45. She flicks through her phone. No messages from Ginger. Is it because the signal is in and out in the cottage, or is it because Ginger is busy? Lottie is probably the last thing on the casting director's mind. If she hasn't heard from her after the weekend, she'll tell Jasper. Let him sort it out. He'll have a fit. Will probably strike her from his books and tell her to find a new agent.

Now it's 3.12. She should sleep. She needs to be as fit as possible for this little one. She's a geriatric mother, after all. She'll be forty-six when she gives birth. Older than the grandmother of one of the kids in her theatre group. Will people mistake her for the little one's granny? Will she forever be having to explain who she is? She doesn't care. Let people think what they want to.

She closes her eyes, willing sleep to come; 3.47. The house is quiet. The groans and creaks as it cooled down have stopped. Through the walls she can hear someone snoring. Craig probably.

It's no use. She has to know. She won't sleep until she does.

She gets out of bed as quietly as she can. The cellar door key is in the pocket of her dressing gown. Holding her breath, she opens the bedroom door and peers along the corridor. All is quiet. If anyone gets up, sees her, questions what she's doing, she'll say she needs a drink.

Gripping the banister, she pads softly down the stairs. At the bottom, the slate floor is chilly under her feet. There's a draught too, from somewhere. Not wanting to switch on the bright overhead spotlights, she goes over to the cooker and turns on the light on the extractor hood. There's definitely a draught. And then she realises where it's coming from. The back door that leads from the kitchen to the garden – the one that's hardly used in the autumn and winter because the wood often swells and then jams in the doorframe – is open an inch. Her breath catches in her throat. Has someone been in here?

She's being stupid. They are out in the middle of nowhere. There's no one around. No one in their right mind, anyway. The wind is still whipping back and forth outside. And the rain is pelting down. She opens the back door fully and peers out into the blackness. Nothing but the dark shadow of the swaying trees and the drumming of the rain. At her feet is the crate Craig carried in earlier, now full of empty cans and bottles, resting next to the step. She lets out the breath she's been holding. Someone has put the empties out here and forgotten to close the door. That's all. What's wrong with her? It's as if someone has drugged her – her imagination is running wild.

She shuts the door, turning the key in the lock, pushing the bolts across.

She looks at the cellar door. She doesn't want to go down there again; she really doesn't. But she won't be able to sleep until she has, until she's proven to herself she's imagined what she saw earlier.

She takes the key out of her dressing gown pocket. It's stiff in the lock. Eventually the bolt slides back. With a quick glance towards the staircase to check no one is coming, her ears pricking for any movement from above, she opens the cellar door, flicks on the light switch and peers down the steps.

From where she's standing, she can't see anything, of course. There's just a solid white stone wall at the bottom, the cellar swinging away to the right, under the kitchen.

With her hand gripping the banister, she starts her descent. When she reaches the bottom, before she turns the corner, she takes a deep breath and closes her eyes for a second. 'There's nothing there. There's nothing there,' she says to herself before stepping into the room.

She blinks. Blinks again. The mound in the corner is still there, covered by the tarpaulin. Her hand flies to her tummy as a putrid stench fills her nostrils.

Just because there's a mound and a smell doesn't mean there's a dead body under the tarpaulin though. She's being silly. It's probably old boxes of stuff, wood for the fire maybe. She takes a deep breath and steps towards the corner of the cellar.

Another deep breath and she's reaching down, lifting the edge of the khaki fabric, hauling it away from what it's covering.

She clamps her hand over her mouth as a scream fills it. She didn't imagine it. She isn't going mad. The woman is still there, her long red hair curls down her back. Tasha.

But Tasha is upstairs. Tasha is in bed with Kas. Isn't she?

But, if she is, then who is this?

She catches hold of a shoulder, pulling until the woman is lying flat on her back. Her thick, red hair covers her face. Lottie sweeps the hair to the side until the woman's face is in full view.

Lottie screams this time. But it must be in her head because no one comes. No one comes haring down the stairs, demanding to know what's wrong, demanding to know why she's in the cellar.

Demanding to know why the woman she knows as Ginger – Nuala Rogers – is lying dead, a thick, gleaming silver dog chain, like a garrotte, around her neck.

CHAPTER 32

Lottie sits at the kitchen table, a glass of water in front of her. She doesn't want to admit it to herself but when she'd first seen the dead woman, the woman she believed was Tasha, she had suspected Nick, had thought he was capable of killing someone. How could she have thought that of her own husband? It had been bad enough to suspect he'd been having an affair – but to suspect him of murder?

It doesn't matter now, though. Nick hasn't murdered Tasha. Tasha is upstairs, in bed with Kas. The dead woman is Ginger. Nuala. Nuala Rogers. And Nick doesn't know her – he's only met her once.

The questions, the possibilities swirl around in her head. Who has done this? Lottie rubs at her wedding ring. Ginger has only been in her life for a couple of months. And now she's lying dead in the cellar. How can it be?

Lottie wipes her face with the sleeve of her dressing gown. And then it comes to her. Craig. Of course. Craig knows her. They went *way back* – that's what Ginger had said that night he'd picked her up in his taxi. Way back to when? And to what? Did something go on between them in the past? Something that has slipped over into the present?

Craig. Lottie takes a sip of her water. What do they really know about him? What does Hannah really know about him?

A shudder goes through her. Hannah. Her friend is upstairs lying next to him.

Lottie jumps up, knocking the tumbler as she does so, water spilling everywhere, as it rolls to the end of the table. Her hand stretches for the glass, but it's too late. It somersaults in the air before smashing onto the slate floor.

Someone must have heard that? Her head swivels to the stairs. She holds her breath and listens. Nothing. Apart from the rumble of snoring she's sure is coming from Craig.

She stares at the shattered splinters of glass on the floor and then looks back at the stairwell. She needs to warn Hannah. But how? What will Craig do if he realises Lottie knows what he's done? They're in danger. All of them. Nick. She needs to tell him. He'll know what to do. He can go down into the village. Find out if the phone lines are okay down there, see if he can get a signal on his mobile. And if not, he can find out where the nearest police station is.

They'll come, the police, in vans with flashing blue lights. They'll come and sort out this whole mess.

She looks at the glass on the floor. She can't leave it there. The dust pan and brush are under the sink. She's leaning down, reaching for it, when there's a shuffling noise behind her. She turns so quickly she loses balance, her ankle twisting under her.

'Aargh!' A white-cold pain blocks everything else out.

Felix rushes over to her. 'Lottie? Are you okay?'

'Watch the glass,' she manages to get out.

Skirting around it, he bends down to help her up.

'Just give me a minute,' she says, taking a few deep breaths. She's not sure a minute will do, though, her ankle is throbbing. As she tips her head forward, grey dots dance in front of her eyes and a rushing sound crowds her ears.

And then Felix is handing her a glass of water. 'Here. Take your time.'

Clutching the tumbler, she slowly lifts her head to take a sip.

'Better?'

'Yes.'

'Come on, then, let's get you up. You'll die of hypothermia on this floor.'

An image of Ginger's body swims in front of Lottie's eyes. Maybe it was an accident. Maybe Ginger tripped, fell. Maybe it was the cold that got her. But what was she doing here at Fairview? Lottie shakes her head. It makes no more sense than it did five minutes ago.

'My ankle,' Lottie says, 'I don't think I can.'

'Let's have a gander.' Felix pushes his glasses up onto his head and, with a hand on the kitchen counter, lowers himself to his knees. 'The number of sprained ankles, cuts and bruises I had to deal with when I was a teacher, you wouldn't believe,' he says, smiling at her. 'Can I?' He points at her sock.

Lottie nods.

Gently, he rolls back her fluffy pink sock and pulls it from her toes.

His hands are warm. He feels from her calf down to her toes, pressing lightly, asking her to move her foot this way and that. 'Hurts?' he asks when he gets her to point her toes.

'Hmmm.'

'It's just a sprain. Nothing broken. Let's get you moving.'

He heaves himself back up and then stands behind her, his hands under her armpits. 'On the count of three.'

With much huffing and puffing from both of them, she's finally on the sofa, her foot resting on top of a pile of cushions, a faux-fur throw covering her.

'A strong cup of tea is called for,' Felix says, 'with plenty of sugar.'

Lottie closes her eyes. She can hear him moving about the kitchen, filling the kettle, brushing up the broken glass. She should tell him. Tell him about what's in the cellar. Felix will know what to do.

'Here you go.' He hands her a mug and takes his to the chair nearest to the fire. It's still smouldering away. He jabs at the embers with the poker and throws on another couple of logs.

Lottie takes a sip of her tea, grimacing at its sweetness although she knows the sugar will do her good. She feels so tired, as if she could sleep for a week. She yawns. Sleep isn't the answer. She needs to stay awake.

'You'll not be going to America, I take it, to do that TV show?'

Lottie puts her hand on her stomach. 'God, no. This one comes first.'

'You've told her, that woman? That you're pulling out?'

'Not yet.' Lottie takes a deep breath. Now is the time to tell Felix. To tell him she won't be able to tell Ginger because she's lying dead in the cellar.

'I'm glad.' Felix stares into the fire.

'I thought you wanted me to take the part?'

'Oh, I did. But that was before . . .'

He leans forward as a log falls onto the hearth. Quickly grabbing it between thumb and forefinger, he flings it back onto the fire.

'Before?' Lottie prompts him.

He takes a mouthful of tea before answering. 'Before I knew you were pregnant.'

Lottie gives him a weak smile. Now. She should tell him now. 'Felix, I need to tell—'

'What on earth is going on?' Gwen is standing at the foot of the stairs.

Felix jumps up. 'I came to get a glass of water. I startled Lottie. She twisted her ankle.'

'Goodness,' Gwen says, shaking her head. 'I'm sure it's only a sprain. You'll be all right, won't you, dear? Come on, Felix, come back to bed. It's four thirty in the morning.'

She holds out her hand. Felix goes to her, ruffling Lottie's hair as he passes, which earns him another scowl from Gwen.

The moment has gone. She could tell Gwen, but she knows her mother-in-law – she'd be hysterical. She'd shout the house down. And then Craig would hear. Who knows what he might do if he was cornered?

She needs to get back upstairs to Nick. She'll just rest for a minute, just a minute, no longer, and then she'll try to make it up the stairs. Perhaps she could sit on her bottom and drag herself up backwards? The fire is crackling away. She yawns. Another minute, just one, and then she'll move.

CHAPTER 33

'What are you doing down here?'

Lottie opens her eyes. Hannah is standing over her. 'What time is it?'

'Six twenty. I was going to do my yoga before anyone else got up.' Hannah frowns. 'You and Nick had a row?'

'A row? No. Why?' Lottie says, pushing herself up so that she's sitting, rather than lying down.

'Er, you've slept on the sofa? And I take it His Lordship's upstairs in bed? Nice of him when his wife's pregnant. I warned him—'

'You warned him? Warned him what?'

Hannah unfurls her yoga mat. 'Just to take good care of you. Best friend advice and all that.'

'He is taking care of me. I came down to get myself a glass of water. I tripped and sprained my ankle.' Lottie yawns. She's tired. So tired. She must have only had a couple of hours' sleep. If that. She needs to rest for the baby. And then it all comes rushing back to her. Why

311

she couldn't sleep. Her stomach lurches and, for a second, she thinks she's going to be sick.

'You okay? You're ever so pale.' Lottie leans into the palm Hannah places on her forehead. 'You're burning hot. You should be in bed.'

'My ankle,' Lottie says pointing to where her foot lies, still aloft on the bed of cushions.

Hannah peels back the throw covering Lottie and peers at her foot. 'Wow, that is swollen.'

Lottie follows Hannah's gaze. Her friend is right. It's blown up like a big pink balloon.

'You need some ice on that.' Hannah goes to the freezer and comes back with a bag of peas.

'Ow!' Lottie squeals as Hannah places the bag on her ankle.

'Don't be a wuss.'

Lottie pouts. 'It hurts.'

'It's only a sprain.' Hannah tuts. 'You've always had weak ankles. Do you remember that time in Oz when you jumped off that table we were dancing on? You carried on like you'd broken your leg.'

'It felt like I had.'

'Your ankle was the same then.'

'We had some good times, didn't we?'

Hannah squeezes her knee. 'The best.'

Tears clog Lottie's throat. How on earth is she going to tell Hannah about what she thinks Craig has done?

'Mind if I do my practice?' Hannah says. 'There isn't room in our bedroom.'

'Be my guest.'

312

'Let me get you a cup of tea first,' Hannah says, her long legs reaching the kitchen in a couple of strides.

A few minutes later she's handing a mug to Lottie.

'I put some honey in it. Healing properties, you know.'

'Right.'

Hannah shifts the yoga mat so that it's not so near the fire. 'It's only a twenty-minute routine. You snooze on. I won't make any noise.'

Lottie sips at her tea as Hannah does a few stretches to warm up before she gets down onto her hands and knees.

Her lovely friend. The one constant in her life. The person she trusts more than anyone. Even more – and she hates to admit it to herself – than Nick. The one person she'd protect above all others. How to tell Hannah that there's a woman lying dead eight feet below them and that she, her best friend, fears that Hannah's boyfriend has something to do with that? It can't be a coincidence, can it, that Craig used to know Ginger and now she's dead in the cellar while he's upstairs in bed?

Lottie swallows, takes a sip of tea, swallows again. 'Did Craig tell you he knew my casting director? From the US TV show? Ginger?' Lottie says, leaning back on the cushion, pretending she's just making idle chitchat.

For a brief moment, Hannah stops moving her back up and down – in the position Lottie knows is called the cat-cow – before she continues. 'Ginger? Do you mean Nuala? Yeah, of course he did. They were old friends. They grew up on the same estate. Went to the same school. Not for long though. Craig was expelled

313

in his first year there.' Hannah rolls her eyes but smiles.

'Right. Yes. He picked her up from my house the night she came for dinner.'

Hannah stretches herself into another position, her weight supported on her hands. 'Yeah, he said.'

'Did he meet up with her again?'

Hannah lets out a long breath. 'No, I don't think so. Why?'

'Just wondering.'

Hannah pushes herself up into the sphinx, her head lifted, her body stretched behind her, the weight on her arms. She takes a deep breath in through her nose before letting it slowly out through pursed lips. 'Just wondering?' she says as she lowers herself onto her stomach. 'C'mon, Lots. You know I'm not the jealous type.'

'I just wanted to know if they'd caught up again, that's all. I've been trying to get hold of her and she's not answering her phone.'

'What? You've got a signal? Here? I could do with ringing Daisy, making sure she's okay.'

Lottie shakes her head. 'It's patchy. I got one last night.'

'And the landline isn't working?'

'Nor the Wi-Fi. You should have brought Daisy with you. And Trey.' She doesn't know why she's saying this – why drag a pair of innocent teenagers into this nightmare?

'She was adamant she wasn't coming. We had quite the row about it.'

'Probably just wanted the house to herself so she could have Trey round.'

'Hmm.' Hannah's nose wrinkles as she stretches her arms over her head.

'Anyway, has Craig spoken to Ginger? Or seen her?'

'Nuala? They might have messaged each other.' Hannah shrugs. 'But he definitely hasn't seen her. We were away in Cardiff all last weekend at a motorbike show.'

Hannah stands on one leg. One arm stretched out to the front. One to the back.

'He might have caught up with Ging . . . Nuala when you got back?'

Hannah's gaze doesn't falter but a huge grin spreads across her face. 'I doubt it. I've been wanting to tell you. I've moved in with him. Been there all week. We took the week off. We've been,' she says, her leg wobbling until she almost falls over, 'otherwise engaged.'

'Oh, right.' Lottie bites her lip. It doesn't sound like Hannah has been apart from Craig. But she can't have been with him twenty-four-seven, can she? All he would need would be four hours to get here and back. Maybe he killed Nuala elsewhere and dumped her here? Lottie's not an expert on dead bodies but it doesn't look like Nuala has been dead long. A week maybe? She remembers watching a documentary on some obscure channel about the stages of decomposition – she's sure that the skin turns from green to red at about eight days. Her stomach lurches as she remembers the green tinge of Nuala's skin. She takes a sip of tea, trying to calm herself. She doesn't know why Craig would bring her here to the cottage – it makes no sense – but it has to be him who has done this. No one else knows Nuala. 'What did he say about her – Nuala? Does he like her?'

Hannah stretches first one arm and then the other over her head. 'Congratulations, Hannah, I'm so pleased for you.'

'Sorry,' Lottie says, hiding behind her mug, 'it's just . . . It's a bit sudden, isn't it? You hardly know him.'

'I've known him for ages, Lots. He's Trey's dad remember? Trey and Daisy have been an item for nearly two years. I've bumped into him plenty of times when I've been dropping Trey off. And the tarot cards say it's a good match.'

Lottie rolls her eyes.

Hannah sinks down onto her knees. 'You don't like him.'

'I don't know him.'

Hannah gets into a pose Lottie knows that, even if she hadn't sprained her ankle, she could never get into. 'Is this something to do with Nuala? Has she said something about him?'

Lottie shakes her head even though Hannah, in the position she's in, can't see her. Nuala hadn't said anything. But her face, when Craig had turned up that night in his taxi to pick her up, had said it all. She wasn't happy to see her old school friend – that much had been clear to Lottie. And he wasn't happy to see her either. He'd been shocked. And more than that, he'd been angry.

Lottie grips her mug. She needs to tell Hannah what she suspects. 'Hannah, I need to tell you something,' she says as Craig suddenly appears at the foot of the stairs.

CHAPTER 34

'Wondered where you'd got to,' Craig says, yawning and stretching so that his AC/DC T-shirt rides up to show a pale pot belly.

Hannah blows him a kiss. 'What are you doing up?'

'I've got a mouth like the Sahara desert,' he says, before making his way to the kitchen and pouring himself a glass of water.

Lottie can hear him glugging it down.

'Ah, that's better.' He lets out a huge belch. 'Coming back to bed, angel?' He holds out his hand and winks at Hannah who giggles like a schoolgirl. 'Nothing else to do in weather like this,' Craig says, nodding towards the window, where the rain is lashing against the glass.

Panic rises in Lottie's chest, a tightness, like a band around her, so tight that she feels like she might pass out. She can't let her friend go back to bed with this man. She pats the sofa next to her. 'Stay and keep me company?'

Hannah comes over to her and plants a kiss on the top of her head. 'You need to get some sleep, Lots. Come on, me and Craig will get you upstairs. She's twisted her ankle,' Hannah says in answer to Craig's puzzled look.

'Fireman's lift or piggyback?' Craig belches again.

'I'm fine,' Lottie says. She can't stand the thought of Craig touching her. 'I'll snooze on here. Go on.' Hannah will be fine. Won't she? Craig isn't going to do anything to her while everyone else is in the house.

'You sure?'

Lottie does her best to give her friend a reassuring smile. 'Pass me my mobile before you go? It's on the kitchen table.'

Hannah finds her phone and throws it to her. 'Good luck,' she shouts as she grabs Craig's hand and follows him up the stairs.

Lottie stares after them. Hannah will be all right. She will.

Lottie waves her phone in the air. A bar suddenly appears on it. And then disappears again. She presses the browser button anyway and types in the address of the BBC news website. It opens up. She's connected. The top news story is about the storm sweeping the country. Power lines are down in the North West; five people have been killed. There's another storm on its way.

But she's not interested in the storm. *Nuala Rogers* are the words she types into the browser.

There are thousands of results. She scrolls down, opening a few of the web pages, reading about the productions Nuala has worked on. It's all work stuff, nothing that gives a hint of her personal life, nothing that gives a hint of why she's lying dead in the cellar. There's an

318

interview with her in an industry magazine. Lottie quickly scrolls through it. Boring, boring. Nothing of any interest. And then her finger stops. The interviewer is asking who she would like to work with, if she could work with anyone, dead or alive. Paul Newman is the answer.

Those blue eyes! And I always told the kids at school that he was my uncle as my maiden name was Newman.

Nuala Newman. That's who she was when she lived in the UK, in Manchester. That's who she was when Craig knew her.

She types in Nuala Newman, Manchester. There are hundreds of hits. She clicks on the first. It's the *Manchester Evening News* website. An article from seventeen years ago. She reads the headline – *Woman Sent to Prison for Attack on Husband's Lover*. There's a photo. A man walking away from court, a newspaper covering his face. She reads the caption. Dominic Atkinson leaves court. Dominic Atkinson. She doesn't know any Dominic Atkinson.

Her breath catches in her throat. Dominic? She does know a Dominic. Her Nick. Nick is short for Dominic. But no one ever calls him by his full name. He's Nick. Nick Moore. Gwen's son. Gwen Moore. Gwen and Felix Moore. She breathes a long sigh of relief. This isn't her Nick. Of course it isn't. She can't see the face of the man in the photo, but he looks bigger than her Nick anyway, a lot bigger, and he has on some sort of beige mac – her Nick wouldn't be seen dead wearing a mac.

She reads on. *Louise Atkinson was today convicted of GBH for an attack on her husband's lover, Nuala Newman.* Louise?

319

She swallows. That's the name of Nick's first wife.

Lottie jumps as she hears footsteps on the stairs.

Gwen appears. 'You still here?' she says with a sniff. 'Want a cup of tea? I'm making a pot for me and Felix.'

Lottie shakes her head. She watches Gwen as she moves about the kitchen. 'Gwen,' she says.

'Changed your mind?'

'No. I was just wondering. What was your name before you married Felix? Your surname?'

'Whatever makes you ask that?'

Lottie tries to come up with a plausible reason. 'A grandma of one of the kids at the theatre group thought she recognised you. Spotted you when you came to the rehearsal. Said she might have been at school with you. I said I thought it was Smith.' She cringes at her lack of imagination.

'Smith? Do I seem like a Smith? It was Cavendish. Some long-lost ancestors were landowners back in . . .'

Lottie tunes out from what Gwen is saying. Thank God. She peers at her phone. This article isn't about her Nick and his first wife. It's just a coincidence.

'Yes, I wasn't happy when I changed it to Atkinson.'

Lottie's head shoots up. 'Atkinson?'

Gwen puts the teapot, two cups, a milk jug and sugar bowl onto a tray.

'Atkinson?' Lottie says again.

'My first husband's surname. Nigel's. Nick's dad.' Gwen sniffs again before carefully balancing the tray in her hands and heading for the stairs.

320

Lottie swallows as bile shoots into the back of her throat. She picks up her phone again but the connection is lost and, while the page she'd opened is still there, she can't scroll down any further.

She stares at the photo again, scrunching up her eyes. Is this Nick? Her Nick? It can't be, can it?

For, if it is, it means that seventeen years ago, Nick – her husband – had an affair with Nuala – the woman who's now lying dead in the cellar.

CHAPTER 35

Sweat is dripping from her forehead, down her back, prickling under her armpits by the time Lottie reaches their bedroom. She tried hopping on her good foot at first but each jump had jarred her swollen ankle, making her wince with pain.

She throws herself onto the bed, wincing again as her foot knocks against the wooden bedframe.

'Hey,' Nick says, rubbing at his eyes as he opens them. 'What time is it? You okay?' The smile drops from his face. 'Hey, what is it?'

'I've hurt my ankle. I've been on the sofa for most of the night.'

'Oh, God, sorry, darling. Let me look.' He makes her lie down as he checks out her ankle. 'I didn't even realise you weren't in bed. I was dead to the world. Blame Craig. That man can drink.' Tenderly he kisses her ankle. 'Nasty. You should have shouted me. You need to be careful.'

'I'm fine.'

He scoots back up the bed towards her, smothering her face in kisses, putting his hand gently on her stomach. 'You two are the most precious things in my life – you know that, don't you? I won't let anything or anyone hurt you.'

Lottie shifts away from him.

'I bet you're done in, darling. Get some sleep. I'll go and grab a shower,' he says.

'No. Not yet.'

'Oh, all right, saucy madam.' He tries to kiss her again but she moves away from him.

'Nick, no. I need to ask you something.'

'It's a bit too late to ask me if I have protection.'

She lets the words spill out of her mouth before she has time to think what she's asking him. 'Had you met Nuala before she came to dinner that night?'

'Who?'

'Ginger. The casting director.'

He gets out of bed, opens the curtains. 'It's still hammering it down.'

'Nick? Had you met Nuala before?'

'No. What do you fancy doing today?'

'Don't lie to me.'

He starts to root through his overnight bag. 'I'm not.'

'Nick. Please.'

His shoulders lift as he takes a deep breath. 'She's told you, hasn't she?' he says, sitting down next to her and grabbing her left hand, rubbing his thumb over her wedding ring. 'I swear, Lots. I swear nothing has gone on. I thought I'd never hear from that woman again. Seventeen years. And then she turns up. Worse than a

323

bed penny. Like a fucking nightmare. I couldn't believe it. You do believe me?'

'Go on.'

'She wanted to start things up again. She's just got divorced. Said she'd never loved her husband. That I'd always been her one true love. Her first love.' A sneer flashes across his lips. 'I couldn't believe it. After what she did to me.' He shakes his head. 'To me and Louise.'

'You had an affair with Nuala. When you were married to Louise.' The words hang there in the air between them.

'No. Not an affair. No. It was one night. One stupid night. I was at an exhibition with Ruth.'

'An exhibition?'

'The one in Birmingham. The one you came down to a few weeks ago.'

Lottie's heart starts to pound. She'd gone to the very same exhibition, trying to catch her husband out, thinking he was having an affair. But she'd been seventeen years too late – the affair was in the past. 'Go on,' she says again.

'Nuala turned up. Out of the blue. Ruth and I hadn't asked her to go with us. She was just an office junior. But she turned up. Some excuse about visiting her grandmother in Birmingham and she thought she'd call in and see us. She'd been coming on to me for weeks, flirting with me, trying to catch me alone at the office, pretending she'd lost her purse, stuff like that. She even turned up at our house once when Louise was out. Pretended it was a coincidence she'd been cycling past. Said she'd got a puncture.'

'And you couldn't not help a damsel in distress.'

Nick rubs at his face. 'I was drunk, that night at the exhibition. Ruth and I had taken Nuala to an Italian restaurant. You know what Ruth's like. She ordered tequila shots. Nuala was supposed to be catching the last train home. She ended up staying at the hotel. In Ruth's room.'

'But somehow she made it into yours?'

'I was flattered, wasn't I? I was hardly a pin-up in those days. You've seen the photos – I was packing a bit of extra weight back then. But none of that mattered to Nuala. She wouldn't take no for an answer. She thought I was God's gift.'

Lottie wants to snatch her hand from his, but he's holding it too tightly. 'And Louise didn't?'

He takes a deep breath. 'You don't know how many times I wish I hadn't done it.'

'Louise found out.' It's not a question.

He nods.

'I read something. Online. Louise was sent to prison for attacking Nuala?'

He nods again. His Adam's apple bobs up and down as he swallows.

'I'd brought Nuala up to the cottage to talk to her. Louise came here the same afternoon. She'd had her suspicions, been following Nuala. She tailed my car up here and then . . .' He closes his eyes, before opening them. 'She went for Nuala, picked up a dog lead, tried to strangle her with it.'

So that was what the scar on Nuala's neck was. It was nothing to do with her ex-husband, Frankie. It had all been down to Louise. I didn't have to close my eyes to picture Louise's fury, to feel it even. Could see Louise lunging for Nuala, wailing like a banshee, whipping the chain of the dog lead at this woman who had seduced her husband.

'She cut her neck. Nearly killed her.'

'My God.' Lottie looks at her husband. 'You said it was one night though. If it was just a one-night stand, why did you bring Nuala up to the cottage?'

'I . . . I—'

'For God's sake, Nick. Just tell me!'

'She was pregnant.'

'Louise?'

He shakes his head. 'Louise and I had been trying. Not for long, not even a year, but it was getting to Louise. And when she found out—'

Lottie feels as if someone has punched her in the stomach. She puts her hand to it. 'Nuala? Nuala was pregnant with your baby?' Her hand flies to her mouth. 'No, I can't believe it.'

'Neither could I.'

'What happened to it? What happened to the baby?

Nick's face is ashen. 'I don't know. After the trial, Nuala went to the States with her mother.'

'You don't know what happened to your own child?'

'Please, Lots. Don't. I've regretted it ever since. There's not a single day I haven't thought of what could have been.'

'You wanted her? Nuala? You wanted to be a family with her?'

'No! God no. Of course not that. But the baby—' He puts his head in his hands. 'I'd lost Louise. And then I lost my child.'

Lottie takes a shuddering breath. 'All this is why Louise killed herself?'

Tears mist his eyes. 'She did it while she was in prison. She got it into her head that I was going to leave her for Nuala and the baby. I kept telling her that I loved her, that she would soon be out. But it was no use. She was very delicate, Louise . . .' Nick bites his bottom lip so hard that blood pools on his skin.

'And then Nuala turned up again? Just like that? After seventeen years?'

'She was waiting for me outside the office, a couple of months ago. You know that night when you saw me taking Tasha and Ruth out to the Dolos complex? I saw her. I saw her as I pulled out of the underground car park. She was in a four-by-four.'

Lottie remembers the woman in the four-by-four, the one who had blasted her horn at her. Was that Nuala?

'She's been pestering me. Texting me. She wanted to meet up.'

'And you met her?'

'But only to tell her to leave us alone. To leave me alone. She ruined my first marriage, Lots. There was no way I was going to let her do that again.'

'And what did she say,' Lottie says, putting her hand to her stomach, 'about your child?'

'She wouldn't tell me anything about them. Wouldn't even say if it was a boy or a girl. She's evil, Lots. She

327

said she'd tell me everything I wanted to know if I slept with her.'

Lottie thinks she's going to be sick. 'Tell me, tell me you didn't.'

'Of course I bloody didn't!' Nick starts pacing up and down.

'When?' Lottie asks. 'When did you meet her?'

'The night that Hannah and Craig came round for dinner. When I said I was out with Kas.'

'But you said you'd met up with your dad that night. That's what you told me. After Claire's writers' event. You said you'd met up with him, with Nigel.' She remembers the text message. *Thanks for tonight x*. 'You used his name as a cover for Nuala's? You haven't seen your dad? It was all a lie?'

'I have seen him. But it wasn't that night, the night of the dinner party. It was a few days later. I told him to get lost, not to contact me again. Nuala kept on texting me so I used my dad's name as a cover for her number.'

Lottie twists her wedding ring around her finger. 'I don't know what to believe anymore. So those text messages, threatening to tell me what was going on. That wasn't your dad, that was her – Nuala?'

Nick nods. Just once. But it's enough. Enough to tell her he's been feeding her a pack of lies. Just like he probably told Louise all those years ago. Once a liar, always a liar. Isn't that how the saying goes?

Nick cups her chin in his hand. 'Listen to me. I met her once. Once – that's it. Told her not to contact me again but she—'

'She wouldn't take no for an answer.'

Nick's face is aflame. 'I thought not. But I haven't heard from her for over a week. I reckon she's given up; she thinks, perhaps, I've told you. I'm hoping she's gone slinking back to America.'

'There was no part, was there? For me, anyway?' Lottie flushes at her own arrogance – to think that she would be offered a part in a US TV drama. 'That's why the contract never came. That's why Brad never came for dinner. She lied to me.'

'When I saw her in our house . . .' He runs his fingers through his hair. 'I couldn't believe it. Couldn't believe that twisted bitch would come into our home, into our lives, would—'

'You hate her.' Lottie stares at her husband.

'Wouldn't you?' His voice is so quiet she can hardly hear him. 'She ruined everything.'

'And you'd do anything to stop that from happening again, anything to keep me and the baby safe?'

'Lots, you know I would.'

She knows he would. But he didn't know she was pregnant until last night. Did he? She recalls his face when she'd told him. Overjoyed, certainly, but surprised? And then it suddenly comes to her, what Hannah had said to her this morning about warning Nick to take care of her. 'You knew I was pregnant. Before I told you last night. Hannah told you, didn't she?'

'You've got a good friend, there. But maybe not so discreet.'

Lottie glowers at him. Hannah, always looking out for her, always wary of Nick. 'What did she say?'

'She warned me not to let you down.' He stares at her. 'But I'd never let you down, Lots. I love you.' He puts his hand on her stomach. 'I love this baby.'

'And that's why you'd do anything to keep us safe?'

'Anything.'

'Would you kill Nuala?'

'Lots, come on. Let's not talk about her. She's sick. One twisted bitch. Let's forget about her. She's gone now. She's out of our lives. And I love you.'

'Would you kill her, Nick?' She puts her hand on top of his. 'Would you kill her to keep me and the baby safe?'

'Lots,' he says, his eyes flashing with anger. 'How can you ask me that? Of course I fucking would.'

CHAPTER 36

There's no one downstairs. The kitchen is tidy. It's only half seven. Gwen and Felix have probably gone out for a walk. They always go for their 'morning constitutional', as Felix calls it, no matter where they are, or what the weather is like. The storm seems to have passed. It's still raining, but it's more like a fine drizzle now.

Lottie takes the cellar key out of her dressing gown pocket and unlocks the door.

'You've had the key all along?' Nick rubs at the stubble on his chin.

She narrows her eyes at him. He surely knows the spare key was on his fob. She took it from there last night. *He's* the one who's had it all along.

'You should be resting.'

She ignores Nick, just as she's ignored him since she told him to follow her, limping down the stairs, each step an agony.

'If you insist on dragging me down there,' he says, peering into the darkness of the cellar, 'let me at least carry you.'

'Get off me.' Lottie pushes Nick away as he tries to put his arms around her waist. Will he harm her? Will he pick her up and throw her down the stairs? But she knows he won't. She believes he loves her. She believes he loves the baby growing inside her. Anything that he's done to Nuala is because of that.

'You're not going to lock me down there, are you?' He laughs but it's a nervous laugh.

How much longer is he going to pretend he doesn't have a clue why she's brought him here? Is he so horrified by what he's done that he can't believe it? Does he think it's all a dream, just like Lottie had thought it was when she'd first seen the dead woman lying there?

At the bottom of the stairs, Lottie stops. Nick is standing at the top of the steps.

'Shut the door behind you,' she says.

Nick sighs, but then does as he's told.

'Is it cuttings? From newspapers? It devastated Mum, what went on. She couldn't get over it. I don't think she ever has. Has she made a file of the newspaper articles? Is that what you've found?'

Lottie turns the corner into the main room of the cellar. The tarpaulin is still there.

'What's all this about, Lots?' Nick is so close behind her she can feel his hot breath on her neck.

'God, it stinks in here,' Nick says. 'Felix really needs to do something about the rats.' He's peering behind boxes. 'Where are the little buggers? We should have brought Belle with us.'

Lottie bends down and snatches at the end of the tarpaulin, before yanking it, as much as she can, away from the body.

Nick is at the other end of the cellar, his back facing her. 'That's where they're coming in,' he says, squatting down. 'Here.'

He turns when Lottie doesn't answer. 'What?' He stands up slowly. He blinks. He rubs at his face. He looks at Nuala, lying on the floor. He looks back at Lottie. He blinks again.

'Oh my God, Lots. What have you done?'

CHAPTER 37

'Me? *I* haven't done this,' Lottie hisses.

Nick runs his hand through his hair. His head is shaking back and forth; his eyes are wide. 'You think this was me? You think I could kill someone? Lots, you know me. You know me.'

She does. Or, at least, she thought she did. But she hadn't known anything about his life before they met, had she? Not what had really happened. He'd given her a sanitised version, sketching over his past. She'd thought she'd known why he was so reluctant to talk about the years before he met her. There was a dead wife, after all. One who had killed herself. Nick never mentioned her. And Lottie, for fear of hurting him all over again, didn't either. 'You said you'd do anything to stop anyone hurting us,' she says now.

Nick grabs her by the arms, his fingers pinching into the soft flesh. 'Not this, Lots. Not this.' He shakes her. 'You think I could do this?' His face is white, dark circles under his eyes.

'You're hurting me.'

He lets go and steps back from her. 'Did she tell you? Did Nuala tell you something had been going on between us?'

'No!' Lottie's mouth fills with bile. She retches into a corner, pushing Nick away as he comes towards her. Is he suggesting she would try to finish what Louise had attempted to do?

She wipes her mouth on the sleeve of her dressing gown, tears streaming from her eyes.

Nick searches the cellar, finds a spade. 'We'll have to bury her. Have you told anyone?'

'What? We can't do that. Are you mad? We have to ring the police.'

'No! They'll think it was you. Have you touched her? Have you touched the body?'

In the early hours of this morning, when everyone else was asleep, she'd felt for a pulse. On Nuala's wrist. On her neck. She'd put her hand on her blouse, trying to feel a heartbeat. Had put her ear to her nose and listened for the soft wheeze of a breath. 'They won't think it's me. It isn't me.' She sits down on a crate. 'Nick. They'll understand. You lost one wife. You thought you were going to lose another.'

'For fuck's sake, Lots! I didn't do this. I didn't.'

She stares at her husband. The shock when he'd seen Nuala lying there. He can't have faked that, can he?

'You do believe me, don't you?'

She believes him. He hasn't done this. And she thinks he believes that neither has she.

'Then who did?' they both say at the same time.

*　*　*

335

Lottie shivers. 'Craig knew her.'

'What?'

'That night Nuala came for dinner. I called her an Uber. He was driving the car. She said they went way back. Hannah says they were at school together. Grew up on the same estate.'

'And he could have got hold of a key for this place,' he says, pacing up and down. 'Maybe that night he was at our house.'

'Hannah's been with him for the past couple of weeks. She told me.'

'Maybe she's lying.'

She glares at her husband. 'Hannah wouldn't cover for him. *She's* not a liar.'

If he notices the rebuke, he doesn't acknowledge it. 'Here.' He takes off the fleece he pulled on when they left their bedroom, and offers it to her.

Reluctantly, she accepts it and slips it around her shoulders.

His eyes widen. 'Felix knew she was back as well.'

'Felix?'

'I mentioned it to him.'

'Felix?' she says again.

'Nuala went to St Joseph's Catholic School. The school where Felix worked.'

Lottie frowns. 'The school that Craig was probably at, too. Funny that Craig and Felix haven't said they know each other. Mind you, didn't you say Felix was only there for a year? Craig was expelled in his first year – that's what Hannah said. Maybe their paths didn't cross.'

'Nuala was the girl.'

Lottie feels her stomach flip – she knows what's coming. 'What do you mean?'

'The girl who accused Felix. I told him she was back again. Set on causing trouble.'

Lottie pushes her hands into the pockets of the fleece to stop them from trembling. 'He saw us. When we were at the Sydney Grill. I thought he'd seen me. I waved but he pretended he hadn't.' She looks up suddenly. 'Did you sleep with Nuala to get at Felix in some way?'

Nick shakes his head. 'For God's sake, Lots. What do you take me for? Mum and Felix never told me at the time the real reason why he'd left his teaching job. They said he'd just had enough of it and wanted to go back into academia. What did I care anyway? I was away at uni and glad to be away from them slobbering over each other. I only found out about Nuala's accusation against him after Louise had attacked Nuala. Felix couldn't believe it when he found out that the thirteen-year-old who'd accused him was the same girl who set out to seduce me.'

Lottie snorts. 'Set out to seduce you? It takes two to have an affair.'

'How many more times? It was a one-night stand. I was drunk. Nuala turned up at the exhibition. And, yes, to *seduce* me. She went all out to get me.'

'But why you? First she accuses Felix and then she sets out to seduce you? Why?'

Nick leans against the racking lining the wall. 'It all came out in the trial. She was expelled from St Joseph's.

337

She blamed Felix, thought he'd turned everyone against her. She started hanging around near our house, kept doing stupid things like letting the tyres down on Felix's car. And then one day she saw me. Just the once. On a visit home from uni. She said I'd smiled at her. And, apparently, from that moment on she was smitten. But then she got done for shoplifting, underage drinking. She was out of control so she got put into care. For three years. Foster homes throughout the north. And then when she was sixteen she was kicked out of the system. Had no option but to go back to live with her dad. A right bastard, from the sounds of it. Abusive towards her. She was searching for a father figure. And then she remembered me. And how I'd smiled at her.' He shakes his head. 'And when a job for a junior came up at our practice she applied for it and got it. I had no idea who she was.'

'What happened to her mother? She told me she went with her mother to America? Where was she?'

'She left when Nuala was young. Six or seven, I think. But she came back into her life later. It fucked Nuala up, her leaving. Made her warped. Turned her into a lying bitch. It's all in the court transcripts. You can read it for yourself.'

'I'm sure Louise's defence attorney would try to make Nuala look as bad as possible. How old was she, Nick, when you slept with her? Sixteen?'

'She was nearly seventeen.'

'And you were – what? – twenty-five?'

'You're making me sound like a paedophile. She was nearly seventeen.'

'She was a child.'

'A manipulative, cruel child who ruined my life.'

'Or a lonely child who was desperate for love?'

Nick comes over to Lottie and kneels down in front of her. There's a crease on his face from where he's been lying on the pillow.

'I love you, Lots. I didn't tell you about what happened with Louise and—' he nods over his shoulder '—her, because it was in the past. Done. Finished.'

'Until she turned up again.'

Nick sighs, long and slow. 'I thought Felix was going to explode when I told him Nuala was back.'

Is Lottie wrong or is there a hint of glee on his face?

'She ruined him. It wouldn't surprise me if he'd done this.'

'No! You want it to be him, don't you?' Lottie can't believe it of Felix. She won't. 'He'll have told your mother. About Nuala being back.'

'Are you suggesting my mother killed her? She's many things. But a murderer? No.' He wraps his arms around himself to keep himself warm. 'I told Ruth.'

Lottie's hand flies to her mouth. 'Oh my God, you don't think—'

Nick stares at Nuala's body. 'Ruth hates her, sure she does. She and Louise were very close. More like twins than sisters. But there was a time when Ruth was smitten with Nuala. I think if Nuala had been up for it, Ruth would have left Claire like that.' He clicks his fingers.

'Does Claire know that?'

Nick shrugs. 'Kas knew Nuala was back.'

Lottie snorts. 'Kas?'

'It nearly killed him when the business went under. He had a breakdown.'

'The business went under?'

Nick shrugs. 'No one wanted to work with me. Clients, contractors – everyone left. Apart from Kas. He's always stood by me. And me, him. He got better. It's taken a lot of hard work to get the business back to where it is.'

'And then Nuala turns up again.' Lottie shivers. 'I gave Kas a key. He was going to drop your present off last weekend.'

Nick shakes his head. 'Kas hasn't done this.'

They both stare at Nuala's body.

'Then who has?' Lottie says.

CHAPTER 38

Lottie and Nick are in the kitchen when the others eventually make their way downstairs. They've come up with a plan, or rather Lottie has. Nick is hesitant about telling the police, fearing he's the most obvious suspect in all this, and that, knowing Nuala, she'll somehow have left a trail that leads to him.

But Lottie's insistent – they have nothing to fear if they're innocent. And this mess is far too big to sort out themselves. The stress of having all this hanging over them is not good for the baby – that's what she's told him. And it's not a lie. How can she get through the next eight months, never mind the rest of her life, with this secret hanging over her?

So, the plan is in place. They'll act as normal. She's cooked a big fry-up. Nick will suggest they all go for a walk, the one they always do when they're here, a circular route that takes in the grounds of the once grand stately home that's now a posh hotel. They'll stop there for some lunch. Hopefully, over there, they'll have a signal. And

341

while the rest of them are scoffing thick-cut ham sandwiches and chunky chips in the lounge bar, Nick can call the police.

Lottie will wait in the cottage. She has the perfect excuse: with her sprained and swollen ankle, she's going nowhere.

There's chatter and laughter as Lottie passes the tureens of bacon, sausages, and fried eggs to outstretched hands.

Hannah takes the warmed plates out of the oven. 'You okay?' she says to Lottie. 'How's the foot?'

'Fine. Fine.' It isn't. It's painful as hell. But her ankle is the least of her worries at the moment. She's trying not to put any weight on it, trying not to show how much it's hurting her.

Hannah narrows her eyes. 'Get some rest while we're out. Try to sleep. You look knackered.'

Lottie shakes her head. 'I'll never sleep.'

'A nice relaxing bath, then,' Hannah says as she carries the plates to the table.

Lottie stands with her back to the sink, sipping on a mug of tea as everyone eats. Is someone here a murderer? She knows she should feel scared. But these people love her. They love her and they all perhaps – for one reason or another – hated Nuala. That's the difference.

She imagines Louise, sitting alone in her prison cell. Louise thinking her husband was going to have a baby with another woman, thinking he was going to leave her. A sob escapes Lottie's lips, but no one has noticed. She puts down her mug and places her hands on her stomach. She can imagine how Louise felt. She can imagine lunging for Nuala herself if she believed she'd seduced her husband, if she'd known Nuala was pregnant, when she was struggling to conceive. But to take her own life? What a state Louise must have been in.

Nick catches her eye, a question on his face.

She crosses her arms. She hasn't changed her mind.

Twenty minutes later and people are pushing back chairs, passing plates to each other. Tasha is stacking the dishwasher. She's a quiet girl. Nice. Not what Lottie expected at all. Not the vamp she suspected her to be. And she's clearly mad about Kas. Lottie swallows. How could she have got everything so wrong?

'Shame you can't come,' Kas says, giving Lottie a kiss on the cheek. 'Will you be okay on your own?'

'I'll stay with her,' Claire pipes up. 'I want to finish reading through my novel.'

'No.' Lottie shakes her head. 'I want a bit of peace and quiet. The exercise will do you good, Claire. You're as white as a sheet.'

Claire sighs. 'I might go for a run then.' She springs out of the armchair and disappears up the stairs.

'Do you want me to come with you?' Ruth shouts up after her.

'No. I can't be waiting for you,' Claire's voice booms down the stairs. 'I want to get back to my novel.'

'I'll stay with you, then,' Ruth says to Lottie as she takes over the stacking of the dishwasher from Tasha. 'And I won't take no for an answer. I don't like to think of you here on your own.'

343

Lottie grabs the plate from her she's just picked up. 'Don't be silly. I'll be fine. You're going.'

Ruth sighs and holds up her hands.

Finally, they're all muffled up in raincoats and hoods. Wellies for some, walking boots for others. Claire has a thin windcheater on over her running gear. 'I won't be long,' she says to Lottie.

'Be as long as you like.'

Nick is the last out of the door. 'Are you sure you'll be all right?'

'Get them all seated in the hotel bar before you try to ring the police. We don't want whoever it is to get wind of what you're doing. Don't mess this up, Nick.'

He goes to kiss her but she moves her head so he catches the tip of her ear instead of her mouth. 'Go.'

'Lock the door,' he says. 'Just in case.'

Lottie closes the door behind him and locks it. She can't help thinking this is all Nick's fault. That if he hadn't succumbed to temptation all those years ago, they wouldn't be where they are now, a murderer possibly among them. And Nuala wouldn't be dead in the cellar.

CHAPTER 39

Lottie tidies up as best she can. Her ankle is still swollen. She should be resting it, but she can't just sit and wait – it'll take them an hour to walk to the hotel and then how long for the police to come? Another hour? She needs to occupy her mind, not think about what's eight feet below her. She's contemplated making a list, laying it all out on paper, but she's tired of going over everything, exhausted by her brain moving things around in her head like pieces of a jigsaw that just won't fit.

The kitchen doesn't take much cleaning. The recycling sits in a bag on the side. She'll take it down to the bin. It's at the bottom of the garden, next to the well Felix boarded up years ago, in case any children or – as he'd said at the time – drunk adults fell it into it.

Her ankle hurts but she could do with the fresh air. And so could her baby. It's so hot in the house. Oppressive. She needs to take a big gulp of rain-sodden air. Nick's sliders are by the door. His feet are a size twelve, much bigger than hers, but they're the only thing she can get her swollen foot into.

After much tugging, she finally gets the back door open. The crate full of bottles is blocking her way. She'll have to make two journeys, three maybe, transferring the empties from the crate into the bag for life. She can do it.

She hobbles along the garden path. The fresh air is invigorating, even though the clouds are low, heavy dark anvils hanging over her head. At least she can breathe out here.

The bottles and cans smash and clink as they land in the recycling bin. Lottie rests against the well. Pieces of the wood that used to cover the hole are missing. She leans over and looks down. There's just blackness below. With a shudder she straightens up and makes her way back along the path. This place has always been special to her – the picture-perfect cosy cottage. She'll never be able to come back to it though. Wonders if Gwen and Felix will be able to, or if they'll sell it. Will a family buy it, a second home for summer holidays, weekends away? Or will it become infamous? Will no one want to live here? She shudders again. Who has done this? Who has ruined this perfect life she was a part of?

She's gone over and over everything in her head and can make no sense of it, so she shakes the thought away. There's a light on in one of the bedrooms. In the room Ruth and Claire have slept in. She stops on the path. Claire. What was it Nick had said? That Ruth had been smitten with Nuala? A breath catches in her throat.

Could all this be something to do with Claire? Claire with her moods and her jealousy? Again, she shakes the thought from her head. She's as bad as Claire for making things up.

Lottie blinks as she stares at the window. Is someone in there? The light flickers and something black passes in front of the glass. She blinks. Everyone has gone on the walk. Perhaps Claire is back from her run? No – a glance at her watch tells her it's only twenty minutes since they all left. She looks up at the window. She's imagining things, that's all. Is it any wonder?

She makes two more trips to the recycling bin, staring up at the window each time she comes back up the path. There's nothing there. No one. Of course there's not.

It suddenly starts to pour, fat raindrops drenching her. Moving as quickly as she can, she slips back through the door. She tries to close it, but the door is too big for the frame. No matter how hard she pushes, it won't shut.

She's soaking. *A bath,* she thinks, remembering Hannah's suggestion, as she peels off the coat she took from the rack hanging by the back door. That's what she needs. She can prop up her leg. The heat might help it. She'll put the radio on. Claudia Winkleman can keep her company. There's time. Time to try to relax before the police arrive. And time to wash away all traces of Nuala.

On the way to the bathroom, she stops and pops her head around the door of Ruth and Claire's room. It's empty. She has a sudden urge to look under the bed, check inside the huge oak wardrobe that sits near the window, but then tells herself not to be silly. She switches off the light and heads for the bathroom, one hand on the wall to support her throbbing ankle.

There's still plenty of hot water. After wiping the steam from the mirror, she stares at her reflection – and grimaces. Her mascara has bled under puffy eyes and a spot is starting to erupt on her chin. Her finger finds it, traces the bump. A spot at her age! Is it her hormones, kicking in after all these years now that she has this new life inside her?

She slips off her dressing gown and her pyjamas, peering down at her stomach once she's naked. There's nothing there yet, no bump. Of course there isn't. She's only four or five weeks gone. And yet she knows this baby, her baby, is inside her. It's a miracle. She must call the clinic when all this is over, let Emma know that they've managed to make a baby all on their own.

She's adding some of Gwen's Molton Brown bubble bath to the water when she hears a noise. A thud, as if something has fallen over. She listens but all she can hear are the creaking pipes and the rain lashing against the window. It was probably the postman. Yes, that will have been it. Probably dropping a wedge of flyers through the letterbox. The tree blocking the lane must have been moved.

Her wrist flips upwards as she realises she's poured nearly half the bottle of bubble bath into the tub. Gwen will go nuts. She's very particular about people not using her things when they're in the cottage. Nick calls it particular, anyway. Lottie calls it mean.

She turns off the tap. She hasn't thought this through. The bath is a freestanding cast-iron affair, tall, hard to get into at the best of times. How's she going to get in there with her foot? She's just deciding how to tackle it when she hears another thud.

'Hello,' she calls, aware her voice is no louder than a whisper.

Perhaps one of them has come back? Perhaps all of them have, driven to return by this awful weather? Perhaps Nick has sent them back while he continues on to the hotel to get help? Or maybe it's Claire. Maybe the rain has cut short her run.

Pushing her arms into her dressing gown, and pulling the belt tight around her, she opens the bathroom door, turning her head in the direction of the stairs. 'Hello?' she shouts. 'I'm just having a bath. Who is it?'

There's no answer. She cranes her neck, listening. Perhaps some of the books in the bookcase have fallen over. People are always pulling them out and then not putting them back straight. They often tip and knock off the heavy bookend that holds them up.

She'll just go to the top of the stairs. If there is someone there, they might be shrugging off wet coats and boots. They might not have heard her.

But suddenly, there's a noise behind her and before she can turn or scream or do anything, a hand is clamped around her mouth.

'Shush,' the voice says. A man's. Deep. 'Shush now. I'm not going to hurt you. Just don't scream. All right?'

She nods and the hand moves slowly from her mouth.

Turning quickly she finds a bear of a man – a man she's never seen before – standing in front of her.

'Take what you want,' she says. Her voice comes out croaky.

The man snorts.

'My husband is downstairs.'

'Now, Lottie, we both know that isn't true.'

How does he know her name? She should run, fly down the stairs, but how can she on her ankle? And this man is strong. Despite his age. She can tell he works out, can see it in the bulge of his biceps through the lumberjack shirt he has on, the jagged veins that stand out on a thick neck.

'I'm not going to hurt you. Thought everyone was out, didn't I? Just come to pick up some stuff I left here.' He pushes a hand through his greying hair, a gesture she recognises.

'You're Nigel,' she says. 'Nick's dad.'

'That's right.' He holds up a carrier bag. 'Come to fetch my passport and some things I needed.'

Lottie edges away from him. 'Your passport? What's it doing here?'

'I've been staying here, haven't I? On and off. Over the years.'

'You have no right to.'

He glowers at her. 'Are you joking? I have every right to. Fairview belonged to my father and his father before him. This was mine before Gwen got it in the divorce.'

'You've been living in Spain. That's what Nick said.'

He hangs his head. 'Not permanently. I go over there for the summer season. I wanted Nick to think I was doing all right. To think that bitch—' he spits out the last word '—didn't ruin my life.'

'Gwen?'

He gives her a puzzled look. 'Nuala.'

'Nuala?'

He runs his hand through his hair again. 'Nick hasn't told you.'

Lottie pulls her dressing gown around her. Surely Nick has told her everything? Surely there can't be any more to this mess than she already knows?

'I don't know what you're on about.'

'Then you'll have to ask Nick.'

'Nick's not here. As you know.'

Nigel runs his hand through his hair again. 'I punched him, didn't I? Just one punch. But that was enough. He fell and banged his head.'

Lottie's hand flies to her mouth as she remembers what Nick had told her – that his dad had killed someone and he'd shopped him to the police. 'Who?' And yet, even as she asks the question, she knows what the answer is. 'Nuala's father?'

'He came round to Nick's house, kicking off about Nick getting Nuala pregnant, saying he wanted money. I saw red. It wasn't my fault though. Protecting my son, wasn't I?'

Lottie nods. She doesn't want to anger Nigel any more. Nick had called his dad a hothead, said he'd had a temper. And then it comes to her – who Nuala's murderer is. It's not anyone she knows. It's not her friends and family who have done this, who have brought this nightmare into her life – it's this man in front of her.

'You've got what you've come for,' she says, crossing her arms. 'You should go.'

'You won't say anything?'

She shakes her head. She's lying, of course. When the police arrive, she'll tell them everything. Does he have a car? Even if he does, he won't get far. They'll put out an alert for him at the ports and airports, this beast of a man who believes he can get away with what he's done.

'I won't tell anyone.' She lifts her chin, meeting his gaze.

'You're lying,' he says.

'I won't. I promise.'

He snorts. 'I know more than anyone that a woman's promise stands for nothing. Look at Gwen. Promised to stand by me when I went to prison that first time. To wait for me to get out. And what did I find? She was fucking the bloody next-door neighbour while I was away. And long before that as well. I should have bloody punched Felix too.' He clenches his fist and then smacks the wall, so hard that bits of plaster fly off into the air.

Lottie takes another step back away from him, wincing as her foot throbs.

'You'll have to come with me,' he says.

'No. What does it matter if I tell them anyway?'

He narrows his eyes at Lottie. 'Gwen'll call the police, won't she? Have me for breaking and entering. With my record? I'll be back inside before my feet can touch the ground.' He shoves her towards her bedroom door. 'Get dressed. You can come to the airport with me. Once I land in Spain, I'll tell people where you are.'

'No,' Lottie says again.

'Are you thick, woman?' He gives her a push. 'Get bloody dressed or you can come in your dressing gown.'

There's suddenly a noise from downstairs. Someone banging on the door. A voice shouting through the letterbox. 'Lots, let me in.'

Thank God! It must be Claire, back from her run. Lottie's never been happier to hear Claire's voice.

'Have you locked the door, Lots? Let me in.'

Lottie screams as Nigel lunges towards her. 'Claire!'

For a second, Lottie thinks he's going to pick her up and carry her, but he flies down the stairs, nearly hitting his head on the doorframe at the bottom. And then there's the screech of the back door, like fingernails down a chalkboard, as he tugs it open.

Lottie moves as quickly as she can down the stairs, ignoring the searing pain in her ankle. Reaching the front door, she turns the key in the lock. Ruth is standing there, dripping wet. 'I thought you were Claire,' Lottie says, before collapsing into Ruth's outstretched arms.

'What on earth?' Ruth ushers Lottie back into the cottage, kicking the front door shut, before helping her to the sofa. 'What the hell's going on?'

Lottie gulps as the tears refuse to stop. 'Nigel. He was here.'

'Nigel?' Ruth says, squatting down in front of her. She's wet through, her grey-tinged curls plastered to her head, lines of mascara streaking her cheeks. 'Nick's dad? He was here?'

Lottie can't get the words to form in her mouth.

'Where is he? Did he hurt you? Lots? Speak to me?'
Lottie shakes her head.

'God, you're freezing. Come here.'

Lottie lets herself be held by Ruth. She breathes her in, the overpowering scent of her *Poison* perfume, tells herself it'll be all right. Nigel has gone and Ruth is here. But she can't stop shaking. She's shaking so hard her teeth chatter in her head.

Eventually Ruth pulls away. 'What was he doing here? Has he hurt you?'

Lottie shakes her head. She finds a soggy tissue in her dressing gown pocket and blows her nose on it.

'Lots? What is it?' Ruth grabs hold of her hands again. 'What is it? Tell me.'

'He killed her,' Lottie says. 'He killed Nuala.'

CHAPTER 40

Ruth rears back, away from Lottie, as if Lottie has just slapped her. 'What do you mean?'

'Nigel. He killed Nuala.'

'Don't be silly, hon. Is it your hormones? I think they can make you a bit giddy.'

'It's not my hormones. And I'm not being silly. She's in the cellar. I found her last night. Only I thought it was Tasha. I thought Nick had killed her. And then Tasha turned up with Kas, and I thought I'd imagined it. But I hadn't. I went back down in the night. And there she was. And then I suspected Craig. He knew her, you see. Back then, when they were young. But it wasn't him. He's been with Hannah all week, so you see, he can't have done it, can he? And then Nick told me about Felix. Felix. How could I think that of him? Lovely Felix. But Nuala accused him of touching her. Did you know that? He lost his job – he was a teacher – and I don't think he's ever got over that so I thought—'

'Okay, okay. Cool it, sister. Take a breath.' Ruth grabs her hands and rubs them between her own. 'Have you hit your head? You're gabbling. You're not making any sense.'

'No. No.' Lottie's aware how mad she sounds. She is gabbling – Ruth's right – but she needs to let it all out. She's sick of having all these thoughts whirling around her head. And she wants Ruth to understand.

'Lock the back door,' Lottie says. 'And the front.'

Ruth doesn't move.

'Ruth! Please. Nigel might come back. Don't you see, he killed Nuala!'

With a long sigh and a shake of the head, Ruth levers herself up. Lottie hears her lock the front door. And then the screech of the back door as Ruth manages to close it.

'I think we both need a cup of tea,' Ruth says.

'Why are you back? Where are the others?'

'Do you want a tot of brandy in it? To calm you down.' Ruth fills the kettle and switches it on.

'No. The baby,' Lottie says as Ruth pops her head over the back of the sofa, making Lottie jump.

'I forgot.' Ruth slaps her forehead. 'How could I forget? It's wonderful news. I'm going to be an auntie.'

She disappears and comes back a couple of minutes later, a mug of steaming tea in each hand.

Lottie winces as she takes a mug from her, its heat burning her fingers before she sets it quickly down on the coffee table. 'Why did you come back? Have the others carried on? Nick is going to see if he can get through to the police from the hotel.'

'The police?' Ruth, her mug halfway to her mouth, frowns at Lottie. 'The police?'

'I told you.' Lottie takes a breath, speaking slowly as if Ruth is a child. 'Nigel was here. He murdered Nuala. She's in the cellar.'

A burst of laughter escapes from Ruth's mouth. 'Don't be ridiculous, Lots. Could it be your ankle? It's knocked you about, hasn't it? Did you cut it on the glass? Maybe it's infected? Or maybe you hit your head when you fell? No?' she says, when Lottie shakes her head. 'Well, I bet you didn't get much sleep, did you, down here on the sofa all night? Lack of sleep can do funny things to you. Especially when your hormones are all to cock.'

'I didn't sleep well but I'm not—'

'There you go then. You've had a nasty fall. You haven't slept. We left you here on your own. And don't forget, you're pregnant. It must be stress. Everything catching up with you. You're bound to be anxious. You're just imagining things.'

'I'm not imagining things. Nigel was here. And Nuala is dead in the cellar.'

The grandfather clock in the corner of the room booms eleven. Lottie picks up her mug. She gives up. It doesn't matter if Ruth believes her or not. 'The police will be here soon,' she says. 'Then we'll see. Nick's gone to call them.'

'Bil's gone to call a doctor.' Ruth eyes Lottie over the rim of her mug. 'He's worried about you. Says you've been imagining things for months. Thinking he's been having an affair.'

357

'He has been!' For a moment, Lottie is confused. 'I mean, he did have one.' She doesn't want to say it, doesn't want to upset Ruth but she needs to make her understand what is going on. 'I'm sorry about Louise. Nick told me. About Nuala. What she did. I didn't know.'

Ruth's expression is blank. 'It was a long time ago. Best leave the past to the past.'

'I know. But Louise was your sister. God, you must have hated her – Nuala. For what she did.'

Ruth bangs down her cup so hard onto the coffee table that Lottie is surprised the glass top doesn't crack. 'I did hate her. She came into my life and destroyed it.'

'Nick told you she was back.'

She gives a quick nod. 'I told him to tell her to do one. To tell her that if I ever saw her . . .' Ruth suddenly bursts into huge, racking sobs.

'Oh, Ru.' Lottie puts down her mug and hobbles over to her. 'It's okay. She can't do anyone any harm anymore. Nigel's put paid to that.'

Ruth sniffs. 'I did see her. A week or so ago. She apologised. Can you believe it? As if the word *sorry* was enough. What she did to my sister. What she did to me. And to think I was sweet on her. What a bloody idiot, eh? I lost my head over her. Bil too. She did that to people. Drew them in. And she didn't care one bit. She was nasty, out to cause havoc, out to get what she wanted. She told Claire I'd tried to kiss her when we were at the exhibition in Birmingham. Claire said she could never trust me again. It ruined what we had. I guess Claire hated me then. Probably still does. She certainly hated

Nuala. But all that . . . that's nothing compared to what Nuala did to Louise.' Ruth wipes her eyes on the sleeve of her jumper and takes a deep breath. 'I told Nuala to go back to the States, to leave us all be.'

'She isn't in the States, Ruth. She's in the cellar. Nick has gone to call the police.'

'Lots, what's got into you? You really need to get some sleep.'

Lottie heaves herself up. 'Come on. I'll show you. Come on.' She holds out her hand. She doesn't want to go down to the cellar. But she wants to prove to Ruth she isn't going mad, she isn't imagining things. And she wants Ruth to see what's down there with her own eyes. Out of all of them, Ruth deserves to know Nuala won't hurt any of them ever again.

It's cold in the cellar. Much colder than it was before. The putrid smell still hangs in the air, cloying, making Lottie want to gag.

'There.' Lottie nods towards the corner where the tarpaulin lies.

Ruth strides over to it. 'A body. Really?' she says as she tugs at the tarpaulin.

Lottie can't bear to look. She doesn't want to see Nuala again.

The tarpaulin doesn't come away. Ruth sighs and grabs hold of a different part of it, yanking it with a force that Lottie didn't realise she had. There's a ripping sound and then a gasp as Nuala's body comes into view.

'I told you,' Lottie says. 'I told you.'

359

Ruth shakes her head back and forth. 'Such a waste,' she says. 'Such a bloody waste.'

Lottie shudders. What an odd thing to say. Ruth is clearly in shock, just like she herself was when she first saw the body. Like she still is. She places her hands on her stomach, protecting her baby.

Ruth sniffs. 'We need to get rid of her. Before the police come.'

'No,' Lottie says, catching hold of Ruth's arm. 'We mustn't touch her. There'll be forensic evidence.' She doesn't mention she's already touched Nuala, that bits of her own skin, probably a hair or two, will be on Nuala's body. 'Come on. Let's go back upstairs. Wait for them to arrive.'

Ruth rubs her arm. 'Lots, don't you understand? I need to get rid of her. She was never here.'

Lottie shakes her head. No, she doesn't understand.

Ruth lowers her face, so close to Lottie's that Lottie can smell the earthy tang of tea on her breath, can make out the spidery veins on her nose. 'I think you do, Lottie. You haven't seen her, have you? You've hit your head. You're imagining things. And you're pregnant. Being pregnant, especially after everything you've been through, can be a shock to the system, can't it?'

Lottie starts to shake. What is this? Why is Ruth saying this? 'Nick is calling the police, Ruth. They'll be here soon.'

'But if the police come here, Lottie, they'll think you've done it, won't they?'

'Me? No!' Lottie starts to shake. She hasn't done this.

Why would she kill Nuala? 'It wasn't me, Ruth. How could it be? I didn't know who she was!'

Ruth's expression softens before she laughs. 'Of course it wasn't you.'

'No, it wasn't. The police will be here shortly. They'll sort this out.'

Ruth lets out a long sigh. 'Bil isn't calling the police, hon. I told Bil I'd sort Nuala and I have. Bil owes me. Has owed me since he slept with this slut, since my sister tied that bed sheet around her neck and hanged herself in that prison cell. Bil won't call the police.'

'You—' Lottie starts to back away.

'Don't you see, Lots, I did this for you? This bitch,' she says, kicking at Nuala's leg as if she's a bin bag full of rubbish, 'wanted to fuck up our lives again, didn't she? Do you think I'd let her do that? Again? After everything she did before?'

'You . . .' Lottie darts towards the stairs as Ruth lunges for her, grabbing her arm and forcing her back onto some boxes. 'Ruth! What are you doing?'

But Ruth doesn't answer. She whips the belt off Lottie's dressing gown, tying it tight around Lottie's wrists and fastening it with some fancy knot to the racking lining the wall. 'Now don't be silly. Just be a good girl while I get rid of her. Calm yourself down. And then we'll say no more about it. We can get on with our celebrations. You're going to have a baby, hon. Think of the baby.'

'Ru, come on. What are you doing? We can sort this out. Let me go.'

'For fuck's sake, Lots. Shut up! I can't think straight.'

Lottie swallows and closes her eyes. When she opens them, Ruth is dragging Nuala by the feet along the cellar floor towards the stairs. Nuala is – was – a tall woman, but Ruth has no trouble moving her.

'Let me go, Ruth. I'll help you.'

Ruth ignores her.

'I'll freeze down here.'

'Don't be daft. I won't be long.'

Long? How long does it take to dispose of a dead body? Is she going to bury her? But then Lottie remembers the well in the garden. The perfect place to put a body. A body that no one's looking for. Will anyone search for Nuala? Her father is dead. Is she still in touch with her mother? There's her ex-husband but she doubts he'll give her a second thought. And then she remembers the child. The child that Nuala had seventeen years ago. Maybe one day that child will try to find its mother.

'Ru, please. Don't do this. We can sort it out.'

'There's nothing to sort out, is there? I've sorted it.'

'Ru!'

'Have a little think while I'm gone, Lottie. About what's best for you and Nick and the baby. What's best for the family. You and Nick, Gwen and Felix – you're all I've got. Claire and I are finished. Were finished a long time ago. I've done a bad thing, I know, but I can live with it, because you know what? I put my family first this time. I didn't put Louise first before.' Ru wipes at the tears that are slowly starting to work their way down her cheeks. 'I should have seen what Nuala was up to all those years ago. She was lying, lying to us all. And I believed her. Claire didn't. She could see her for what she was. She caught them together, Nick and Nuala. She went to the office one night to find me and there they were, sharing a bottle of whiskey in his office. But I didn't believe Claire. I believed Nuala.' Ruth shakes her head. 'I should have dealt with the bitch then. And then—' Ruth gulps for air, her whole body shuddering as she starts to sob. 'My sister, my lovely, lovely sister would still be here. And my mother too. She had a heart attack. The night of Louise's funeral. Dropped down dead. It was too much for her. Too much.'

'Ruth.' Lottie wipes at her own tears that have started to fall. 'I didn't know. Why didn't you tell me all this? Why has no one told me what went on?'

'What could you have done, Lots? I was made up you and Hannah decided to settle in Manchester when you got back from abroad. My old uni buddy. I thought about telling you, but the past was the past. And you fell for Nick so quickly. He deserved a bit of happiness, after . . . after losing Louise.'

'But he slept with Nuala. If he hadn't, then Louise—'

'Nuala seduced him. From the moment she met Nick, she wanted him. Just like you did. And nothing would stop her. She lied, lied to us all, turned and twisted things, made us believe she was sweet, innocent, wonderful. But she wasn't. She was a lying, manipulative cow. She ruined my life once, Lots. She took Louise and my mother away from me. I wasn't going to let her ruin our lives again.

363

I wasn't going to let her take you away from us. Especially not with the little one.'

'You knew?'

'Nick told me. He was so excited. He thought he'd been punished. All those failed IVF attempts. Thought the big man was punishing him for what happened to Louise. A baby. He can't believe it, Lots.' Ruth rubs at her face with her hand. 'Now let me do what I need to do.'

'Ru!'

But she's gone.

Lottie hears the slam of the cellar door. The key turning in the lock. She waits. Her breath is coming fast, grey dots dancing in front of her eyes. She puts her head between her legs, tries to calm herself, to concentrate on her breathing. That's what Hannah would tell her to do. She doesn't know how many minutes have gone by. She lifts her head. The buzz of the strip light blinds her. She closes her eyes, starts to count backwards from a hundred. Ruth is mad. Mad. Nick will have called the police. Won't he?

CHAPTER 41

Lottie doesn't know how long has passed when she hears the rattle of the key in the lock and Ruth's footsteps coming back down into the cellar.

'So, Lots. Do you see I'm right?' Ruth crouches down in front of her. 'You've imagined the whole thing, haven't you?'

'No,' Lottie says. 'The police will be here soon, Ru. You have to tell them what you've done.'

Ruth's hand moves so quickly Lottie doesn't have time to move. The slap knocks her from the crate she's sitting on.

'For fuck's sake, Lots. Look what you've made me do! Can't you understand that Nuala was a bitch?' Ruth says.

Lottie shivers, from the shock, from the pain in her side where she's knocked against the crate. If she's lost this baby—

'Say it.' Ruth's breath is hot on Lottie's cheek. 'Say it.'

'She was a bitch,' Lottie intones.

'For God's sake, say it like you mean it, Lots. She was a bitch. Don't you get it? I've done all this for you. Just bloody say it. For fuck's sake, our Louise could be stubborn but you, you're—'

'She was a bitch.'

'I'm not sure I believe you. I might have to leave you here. Get Bil to have a word with you when he gets back. What do you think? He's up to his neck in this too, Lots. He knew what I was going to do. He asked me to do it. He wanted me to get rid of—'

'I'm bleeding,' Lottie says.

'What?'

Lottie starts to cry. 'I can feel it, between my legs.'

'No, Lottie, no.'

Lottie moans as Ruth pulls back her dressing gown to reveal a small puddle of blood on the grey concrete floor.

'Oh my God, Lots, I'm so sorry,' Ruth cries as Lottie lunges forward, grabbing the bottle of champagne from the shelf next to her and slamming it down onto the back of Ruth's head.

EIGHT MONTHS LATER

CHAPTER 42

Lottie is lying on her side. As she opens her eyes, panic hits her. The plastic hospital cot next to the bed is empty.

Her head whips to the left and then she sees that it's okay. Nick is here. He is holding their daughter. He's rocking her back and forth, cooing to her, tears dripping off his face, landing on the multicoloured shawl Hannah crocheted for her.

'Hey, sleepyhead,' Nick says, when Lottie sits up and holds out her arms.

'Just one more minute,' Nick says. 'Just one.'

She can't deny him that. She'll never deny him time with his daughter. No matter what happens between them in the future.

She lies back on the pillows. She doesn't know what's going to happen. Nick is living with Gwen and Felix at the moment, begs Lottie every day to let him move back in, says he loves her, that he wants them to be a family with the baby, that they can put what happened behind them.

She's not sure she can though. He didn't cheat on her. That's what he keeps telling her – he would never do that. Never. But she knows he has the propensity to cheat. That one day he might be in a bar, drunk, and some young, pretty girl might come on to him. She's not sure she can live with the fear of him doing that. She's not sure she wants to.

Is she being paranoid? After all, doesn't she have a tendency towards that? But no, she doesn't think she is – what Hannah told her has made Lottie think she might never take him back. Daisy had confided in her mum, said Nick was always making suggestive – very suggestive – comments to her. Lottie hadn't wanted to believe her friend at first, had questioned her – was Daisy talking about Kas, rather than Nick? But, no, it turns out she wasn't. Daisy, only recently turned seventeen, just a few months older than Nuala was when Nick slept with her. Lottie can't think about it. She can't, or else she'll be sick.

Nick plants a gentle kiss on the baby's forehead and passes her back to Lottie. He is so close to her she can smell him – the soap he uses, the gel on his hair. Home. She wants to cry for what she's lost. And for herself. And her baby. And for what he's done.

There's a knock at the door. Hannah's head appears around it. 'Not disturbing you, are we?'

Lottie shakes her head. She hasn't quite forgiven Hannah yet. Hannah knew all about what had gone on in the past, with Nick and Nuala, had found out by accident, long after Lottie had married Nick. That's why her friend has always been so off with him. Lottie feels the tears stinging the back of her throat again. Why didn't she insist Hannah told her why she didn't like Nick? But she knows why – Lottie had ignored her best friend's digs because she was mad about Nick. Just like Louise was. Just like Nuala was. She glances at her husband, who's picking up his jacket. Now she's just mad *at* him.

Hannah shoots Nick a look as she bundles into the room, as do Craig, Daisy and Trey.

Craig leans forward and kisses Lottie, ignoring Nick's outstretched hand. He blames Nick for all this, of course. And blames himself too. Lottie smiles at him, a smile she hopes tells him it's all right, none of this mess is his fault. When he came to dinner with Hannah that night, he didn't recognise the forty-something Nick, the slimmed-down company director, didn't associate him with chubby Dominic Atkinson and all that went on in the past with Nuala.

Would things have been different if Craig had realised who Nick was? He's told Lottie that he couldn't believe it the night he arrived at the house and saw that the person he'd come to pick up was Nuala. After all those years. He couldn't believe it. He'd been angry with her, especially when she'd refused to give him her number. He hadn't told Hannah why he thought Nuala was back, had needed time to get things straight in his own head. Would Craig's first girlfriend still be dead if he'd pieced everything together? Lottie snuggles her baby to her. They'll never know. All she knows is that Craig Dalglish,

Kenny to his old friends, is never going to be able to forgive Nick. She kisses her baby's head. For her little girl's sake, maybe she has to find a way to forgive her husband. Forgive him but not forget what he did.

He's been questioned, of course. But Ruth confessed to everything, saying Nick knew nothing about what she did, that he didn't have any part in it. But he did, didn't he? He had the biggest part of all. If he hadn't slept with Nuala all those years ago, none of this would have happened.

And none of it needed to happen. Not seventeen years ago. Not eight months ago. Louise killed herself for nothing.

Trey smiles shyly at Lottie.

Out of all of them, he'll be the one who can never forgive Nick. For now Trey will never be able to get to know his mother, the mother who disappeared to America seventeen years ago and left him with his real father – Craig, not Nick. He'll never be able to get to know Nuala. Nuala Newman. Nuala Rogers. Ginger, to her friends.

ACKNOWLEDGEMENTS

First of all, a big thank you if you bought, read, reviewed or sold my debut novel, *Just Another Liar*. It made me very happy to hear the lovely things you said about it. And thank you for reading *The Younger Woman* – hope you've enjoyed this one too!

A big thank you also to Bill Goodall, my wonderful agent – yes, I am still pinching myself, Bill!

I'd also like to thank Lucy Frederick, my editor, for helping me to make this novel the best it can be, and Thorne Ryan for stepping in when Lucy left for pastures new. It's a great pleasure to work with the lovely and talented team at Avon – thank you to everyone who's helped me to get this book out into the world.

My friends (both writers and non-writers) have been so supportive over the years. A big shout out to Katie Armitt, Sharon Bale, Katherine Black, Emily Barr, Fran Benson, Julie Brazier, Libby Brookes, Hannah Brown, Rachel Cooper, Jacqueline Dale, Alan Jackson, Isabelle Killicoat, Denise Kuehl, Simon Margrave, Lynne McEwan,

Daniel Minchin, Amy Molden, Pat Page, Luisa Plaja, Kevin Ryan, Ruby Speechley, Sue Thomas, Gigi Vernon, Karen Wright and Rachel Wright. I'd also like to mention two much-missed friends who always cheered me on – Jeff Killicoat and John Nicholls.

I'm very grateful to Katherine Black and Rich Parkinson for reading this novel and pointing out when things weren't quite working (and when they were!).

A big hello to the wonderful Parkinson family – Bob, Anne, Tom, Sharon, Ben, Katie and Charlotte.

Emma, Sam and Beth – thank you for letting me (and Trevor) be part of your family. It's an honour and a pleasure to watch you grow and blossom.

Paul – thanks for being a great brother-in-law. Keep spreading the message about compassion.

Mum, Dad and Nic (and Trevor) – thank you for everything. I love you all very much.

Rich – thank you for always being there for me. You're still my favourite and always will be. Love you xx

He says he loves you. He says you're the only one.
He's just another liar . . .

A gripping, suspenseful debut thriller
with a killer twist, perfect for fans
of Adele Parks and Liane Moriarty.

Out now!